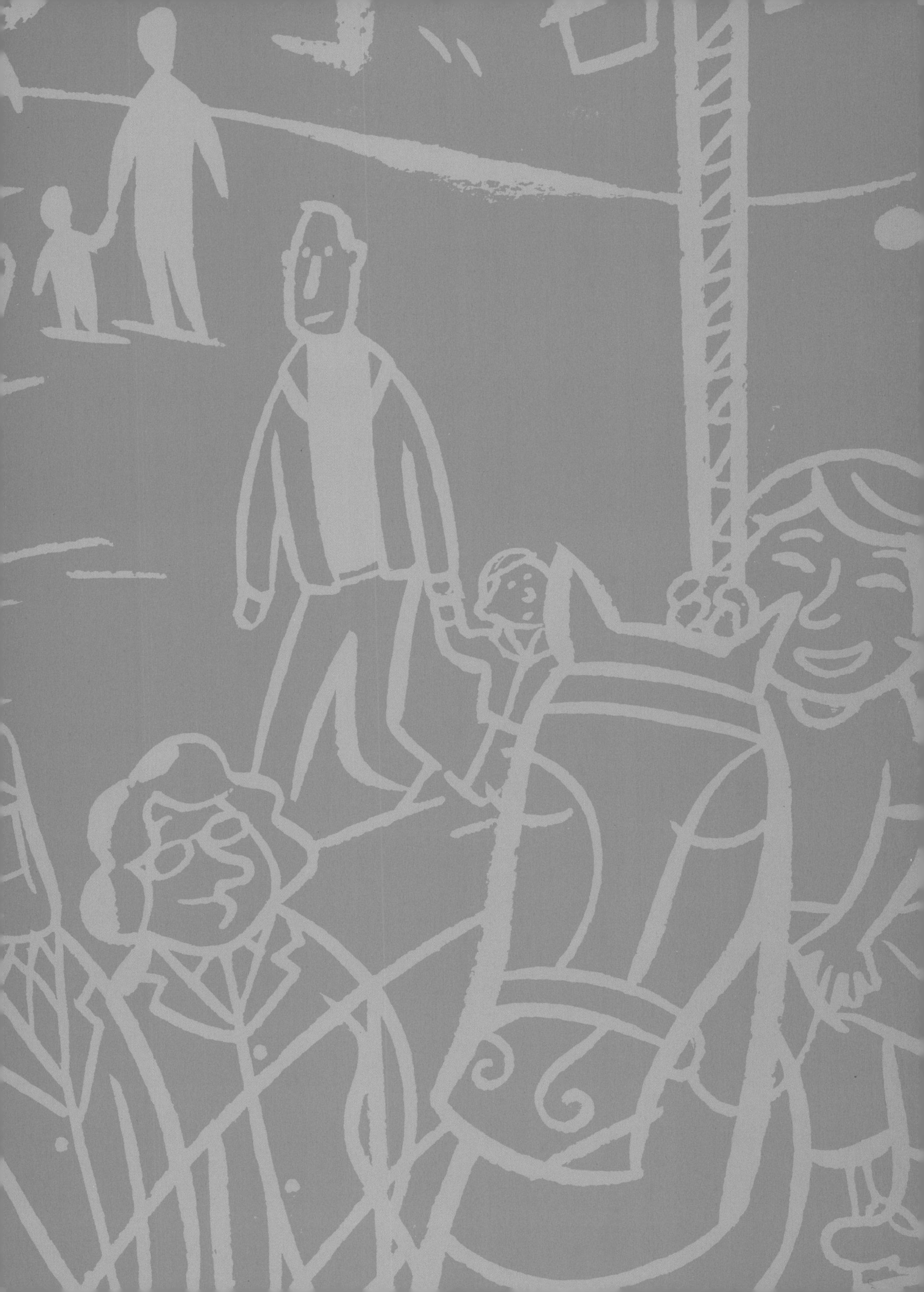

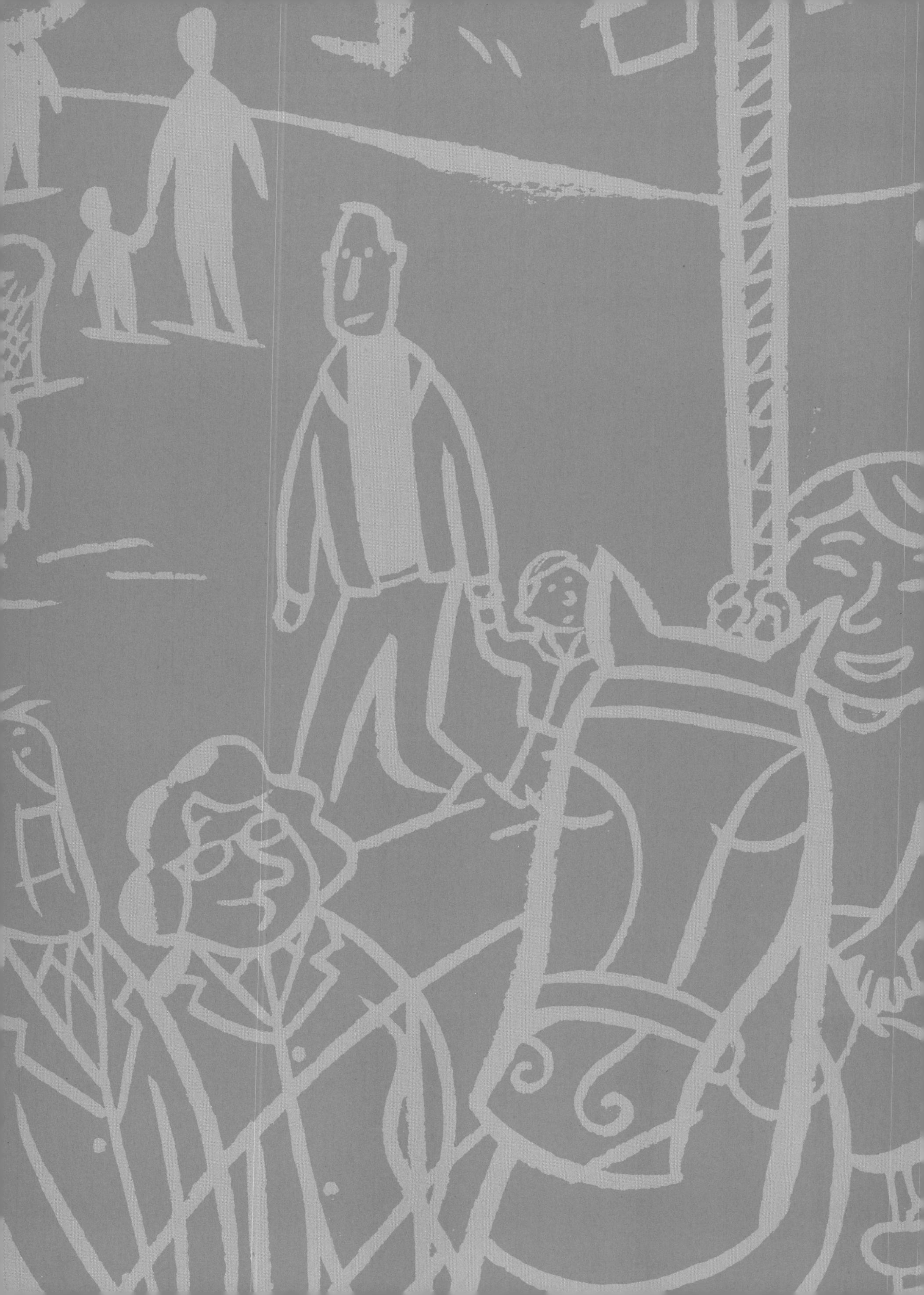

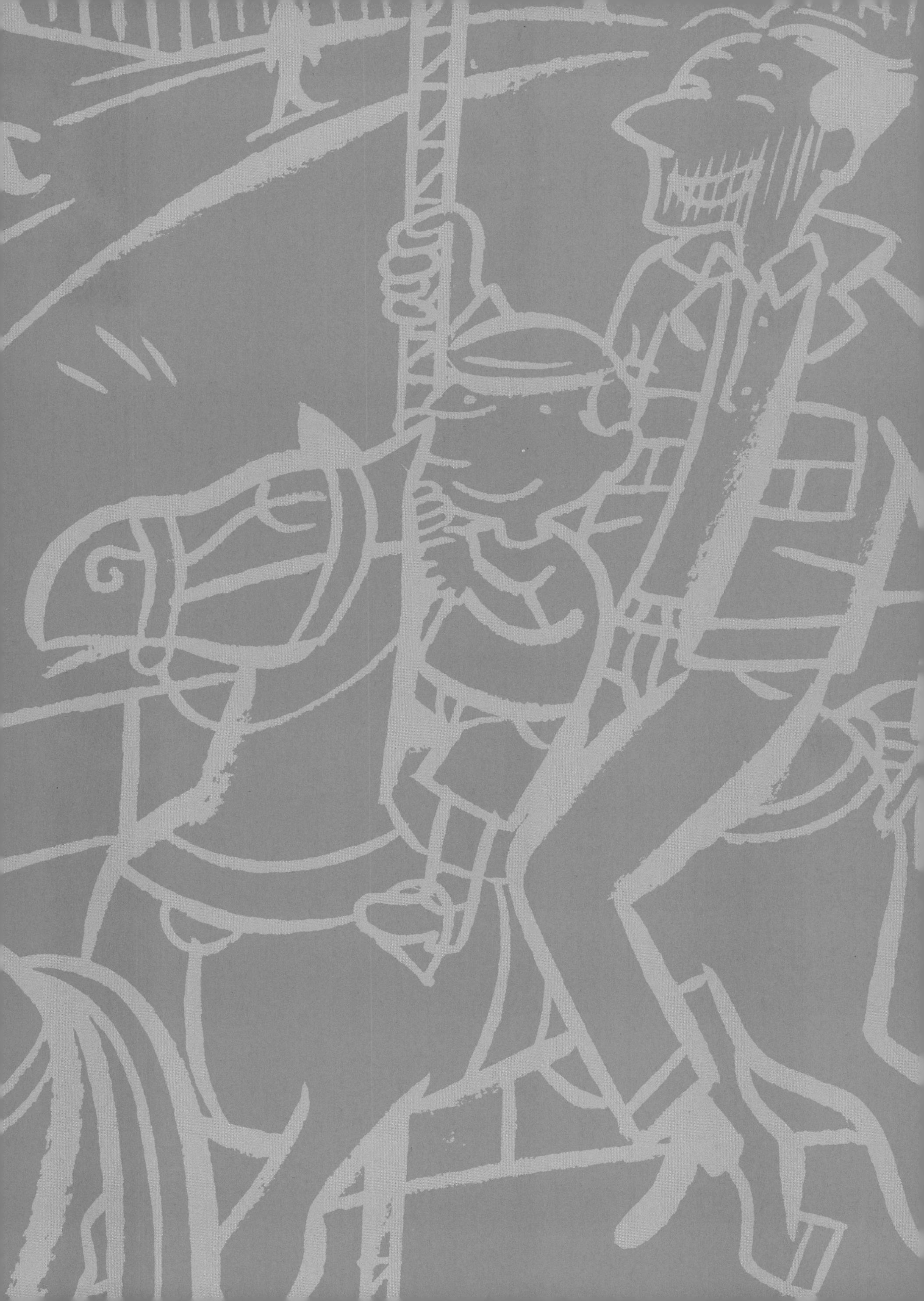

Monsie

Dupuy & Berberian

ur Jean

The Singles Theory

Philippe Dupuy & Charles Berberian
Text and Art

Natacha Ruck & Ken Grobe
Translators

Alex Donoghue
U.S. Edition Editor

Jerry Frissen
Book Designer

HUMANOIDS:
Fabrice Giger, Publisher
Alex Donoghue, Director & Editor
Jerry Frissen, Senior Art Director
Edmond Lee, Rights & Licensing - licensing@humano.com

MONSIEUR JEAN – THE SINGLES THEORY. This title is a publication of Humanoids, Inc. 8033 Sunset Blvd. #628, Los Angeles, CA 90046.

Monsieur Jean

Dupuy & Berberian

The Singles Theory

HUMANOIDS

"YOU MAY HAVE NOTICED THIS: MEMORIES ARE LIKE DEAD BODIES. WHEN DROWNED IN ALCOHOL, THEY BOB TO THE SURFACE IN THE MOST UNPREDICTABLE WAYS."

BENOÎT DELÉPINE

IN THE SEQUENCE OF THE MONSIEUR JEAN ALBUMS, THE SERIES OF STORIES YOU ARE ABOUT TO READ TAKES PLACE BETWEEN THE THIRD VOLUME (WOMEN AND CHILDREN FIRST) AND THE BEGINNING OF THE FOURTH (LET'S LIVE HAPPILY WITHOUT LOOKING LIKE IT). FELIX, THROWN OUT ON THE STREET, MOVES IN WITH JEAN, TEMPORARILY...

D&B

JEAN GETS SOME FRESH AIR: INSPIRED BY A JEAN LOUIS CAPRON NIGHTMARE.

Off to a Bad Start

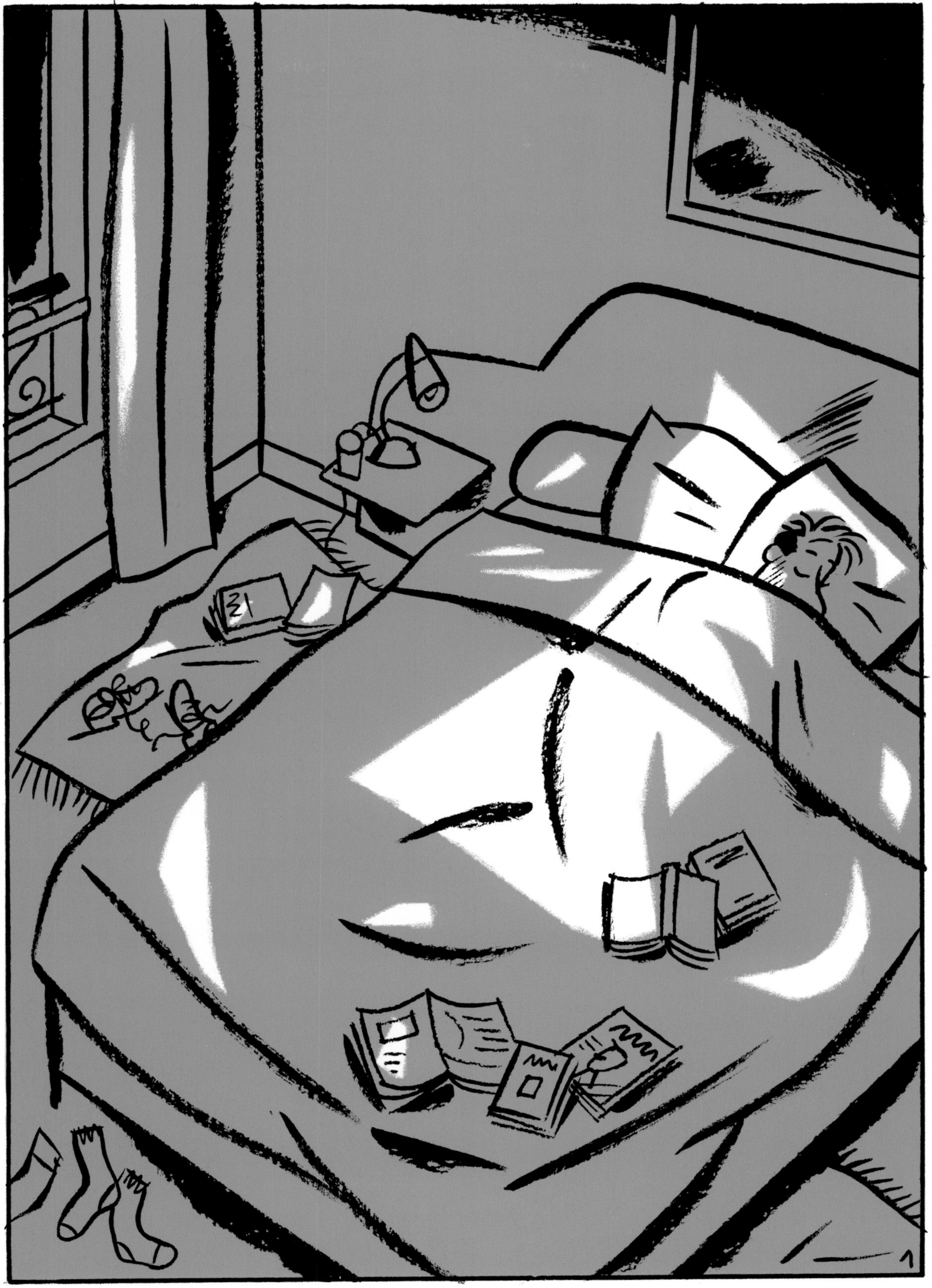

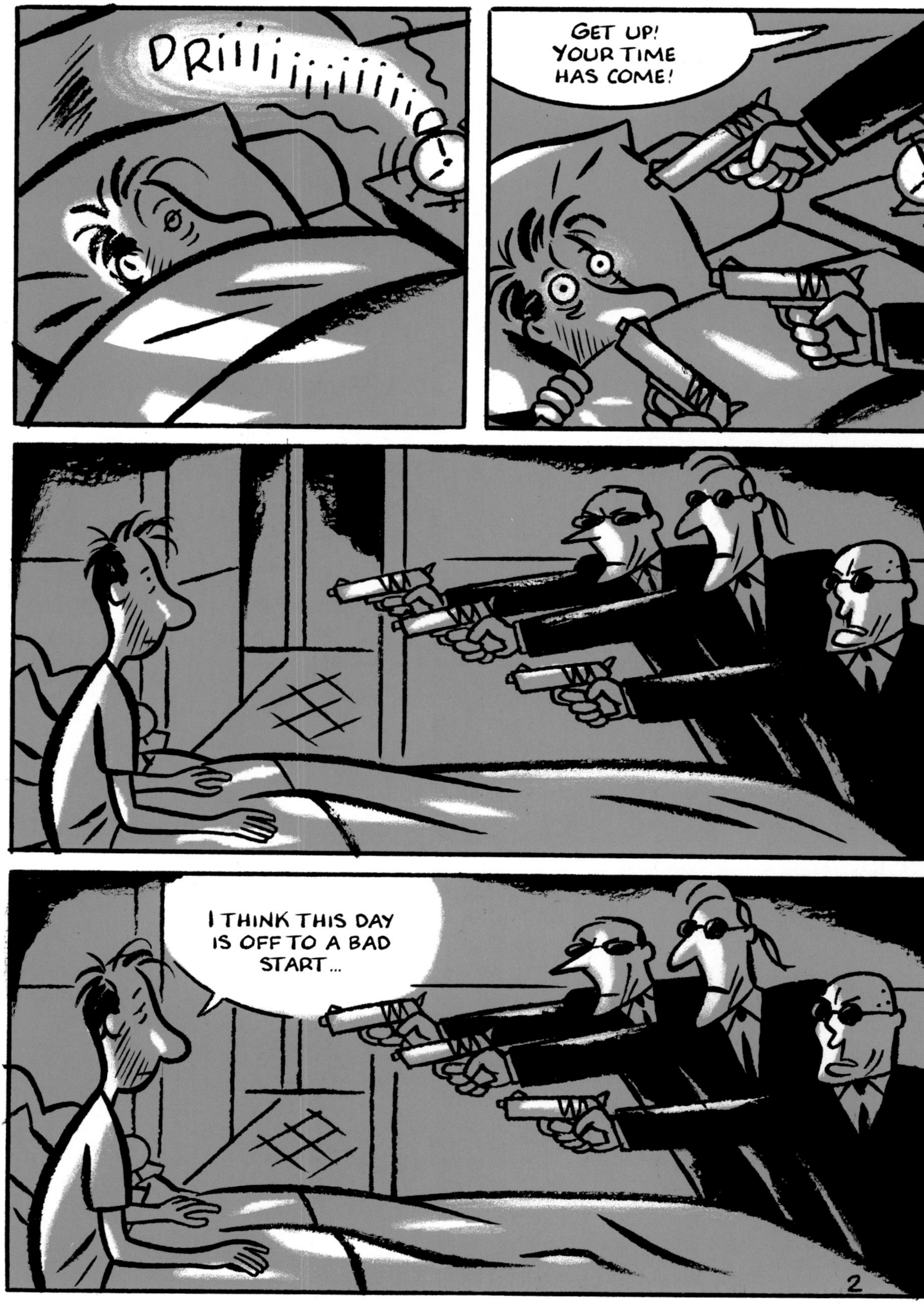
DRiiiiiiiiiiii
GET UP! YOUR TIME HAS COME!
I THINK THIS DAY IS OFF TO A BAD START...
2

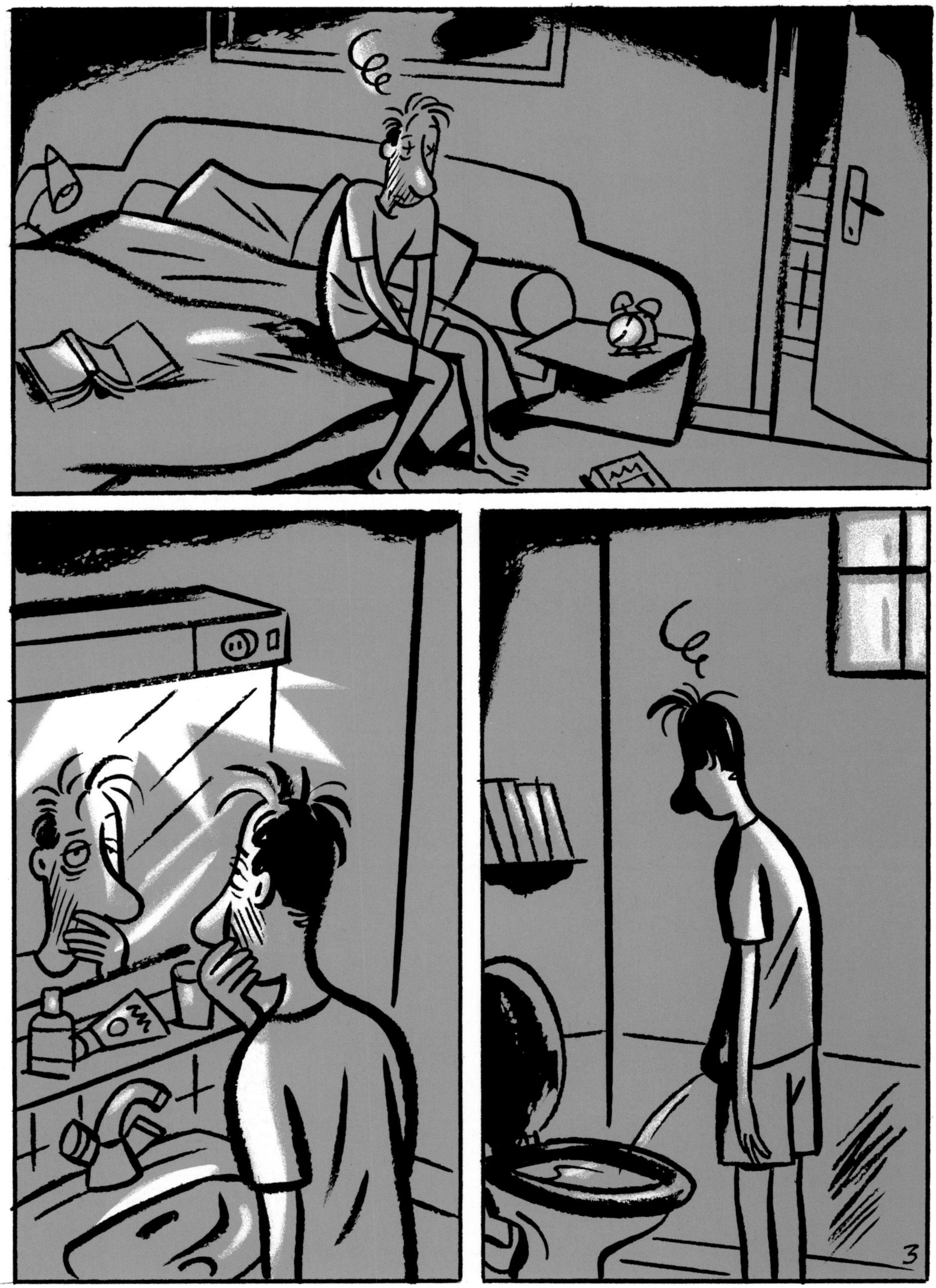
3

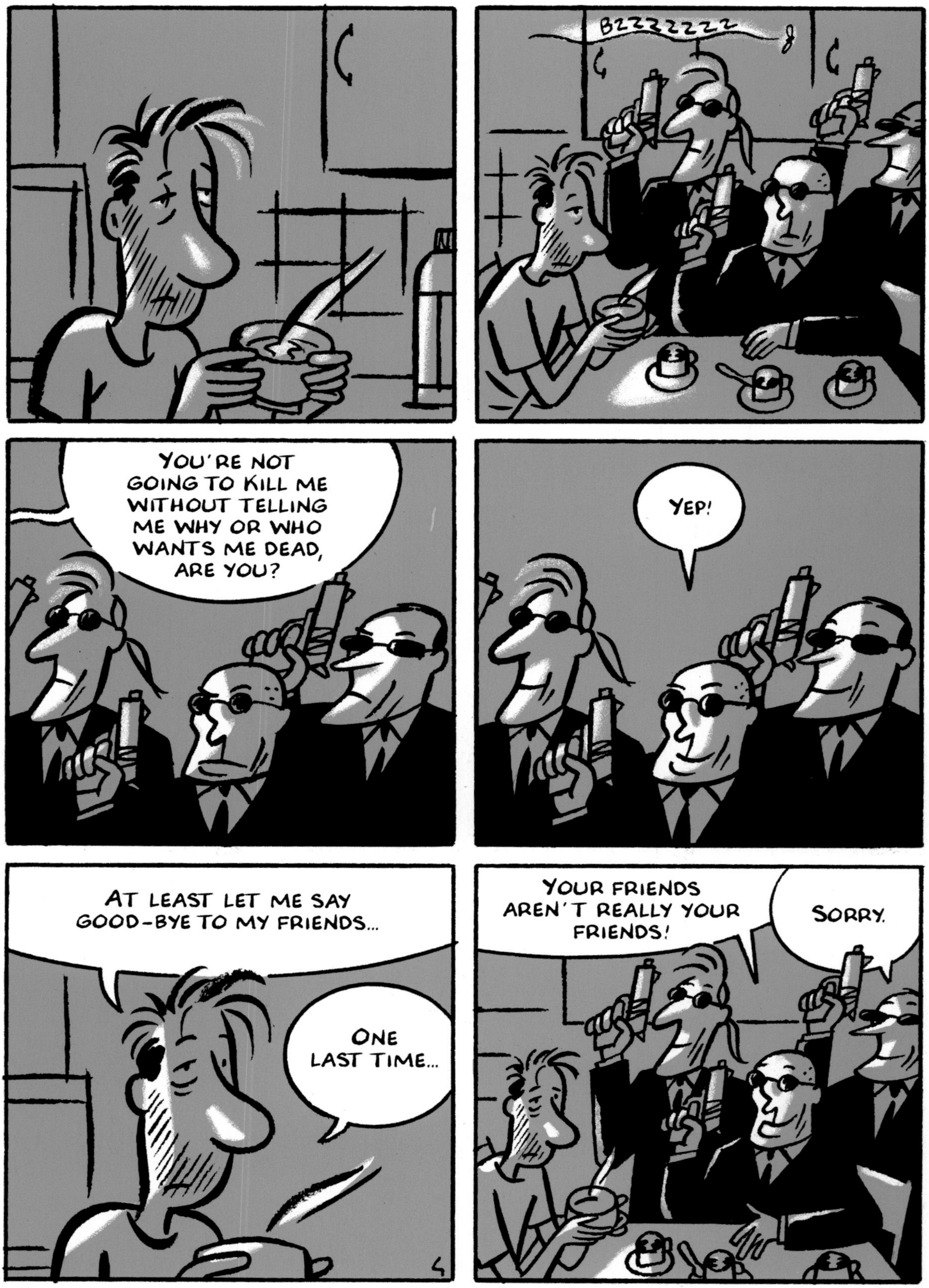
BZZZZZZZZ
YOU'RE NOT GOING TO KILL ME WITHOUT TELLING ME WHY OR WHO WANTS ME DEAD, ARE YOU?
YEP!
AT LEAST LET ME SAY GOOD-BYE TO MY FRIENDS...
ONE LAST TIME...
YOUR FRIENDS AREN'T REALLY YOUR FRIENDS!
SORRY.

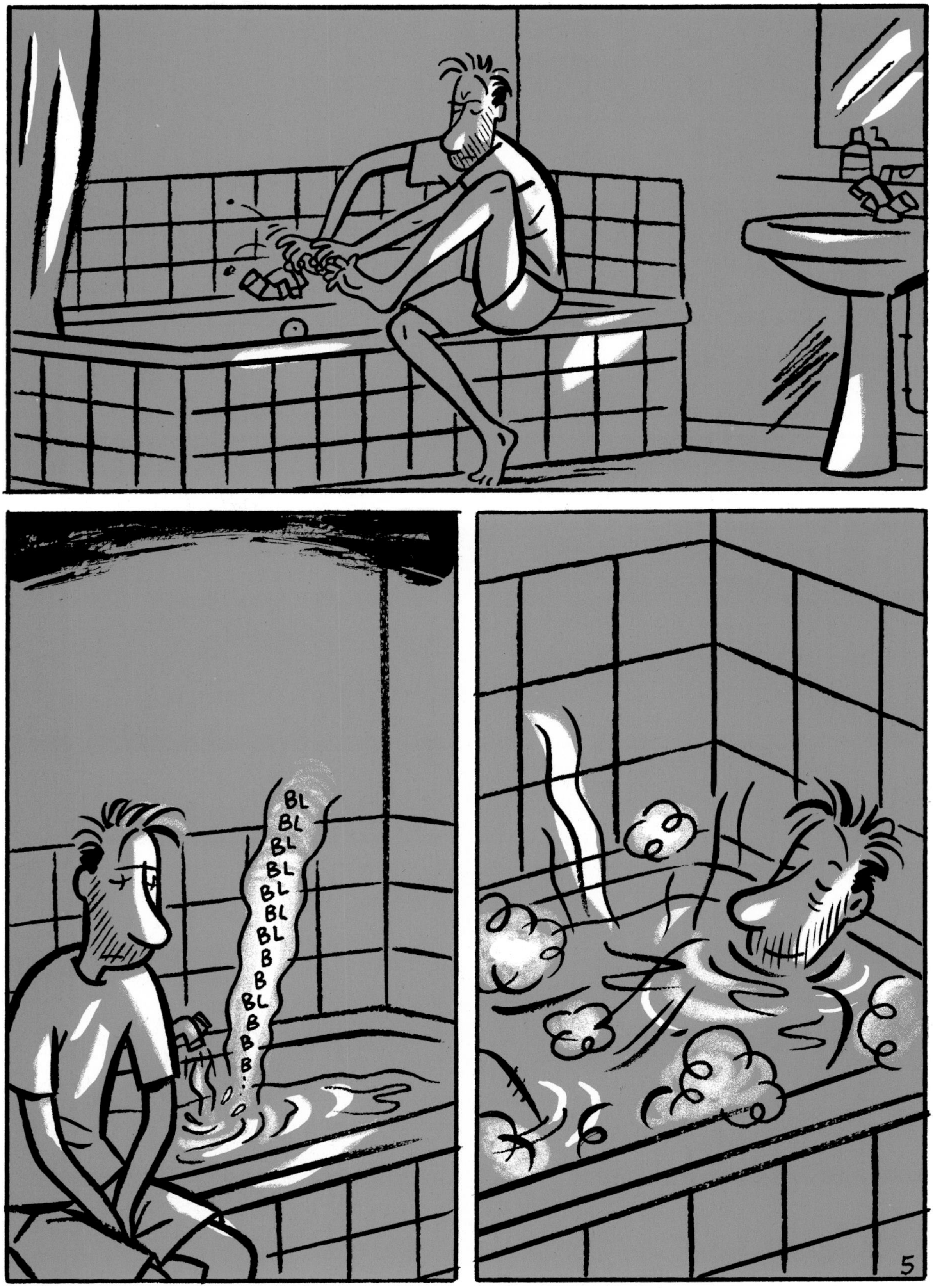
BL BL BL BL BL BL BL B B BL B B B...
5

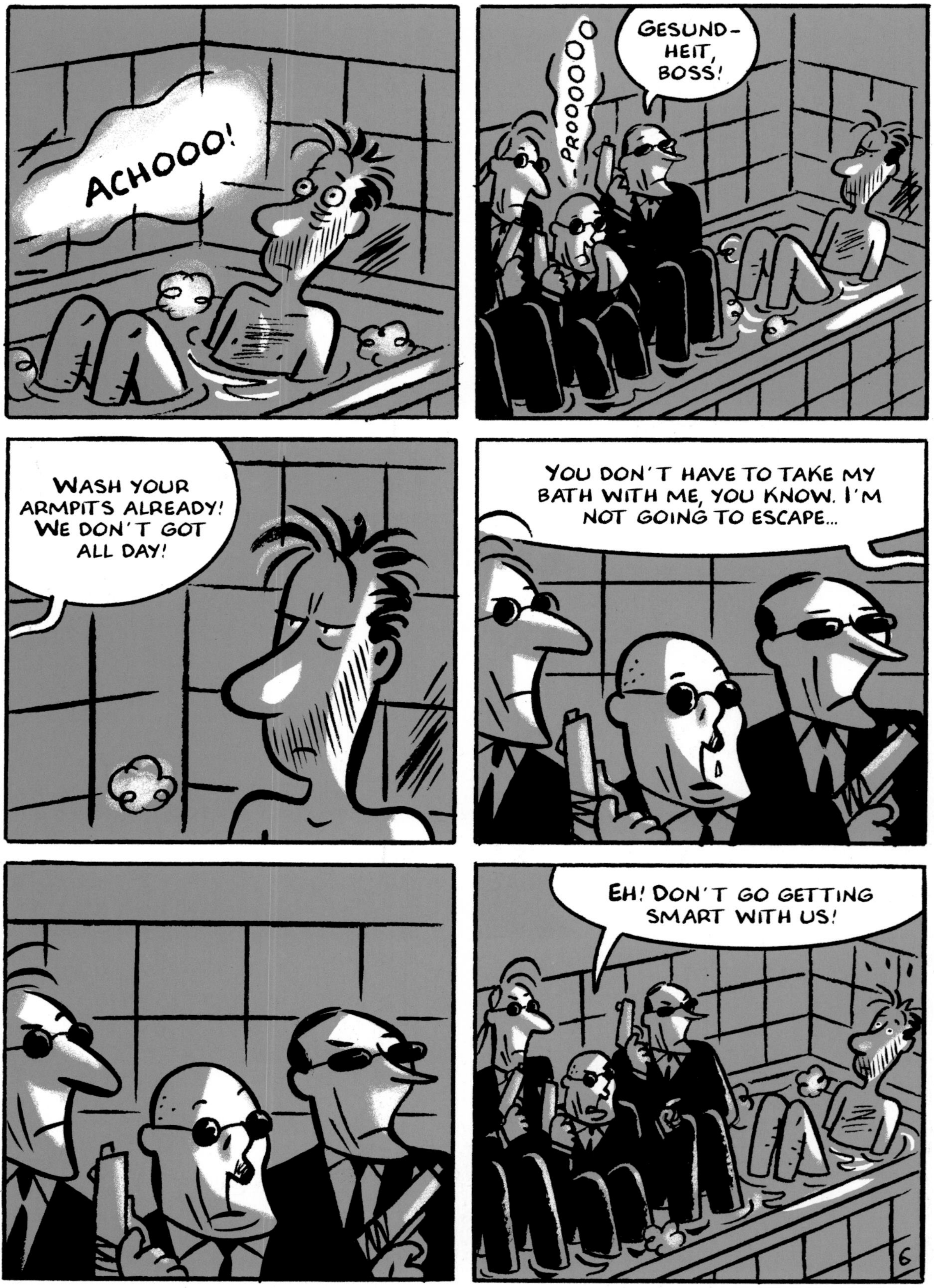
ACHOOO!
PROOOOOO
GESUND-HEIT, BOSS!
WASH YOUR ARMPITS ALREADY! WE DON'T GOT ALL DAY!
YOU DON'T HAVE TO TAKE MY BATH WITH ME, YOU KNOW. I'M NOT GOING TO ESCAPE...
EH! DON'T GO GETTING SMART WITH US!
6

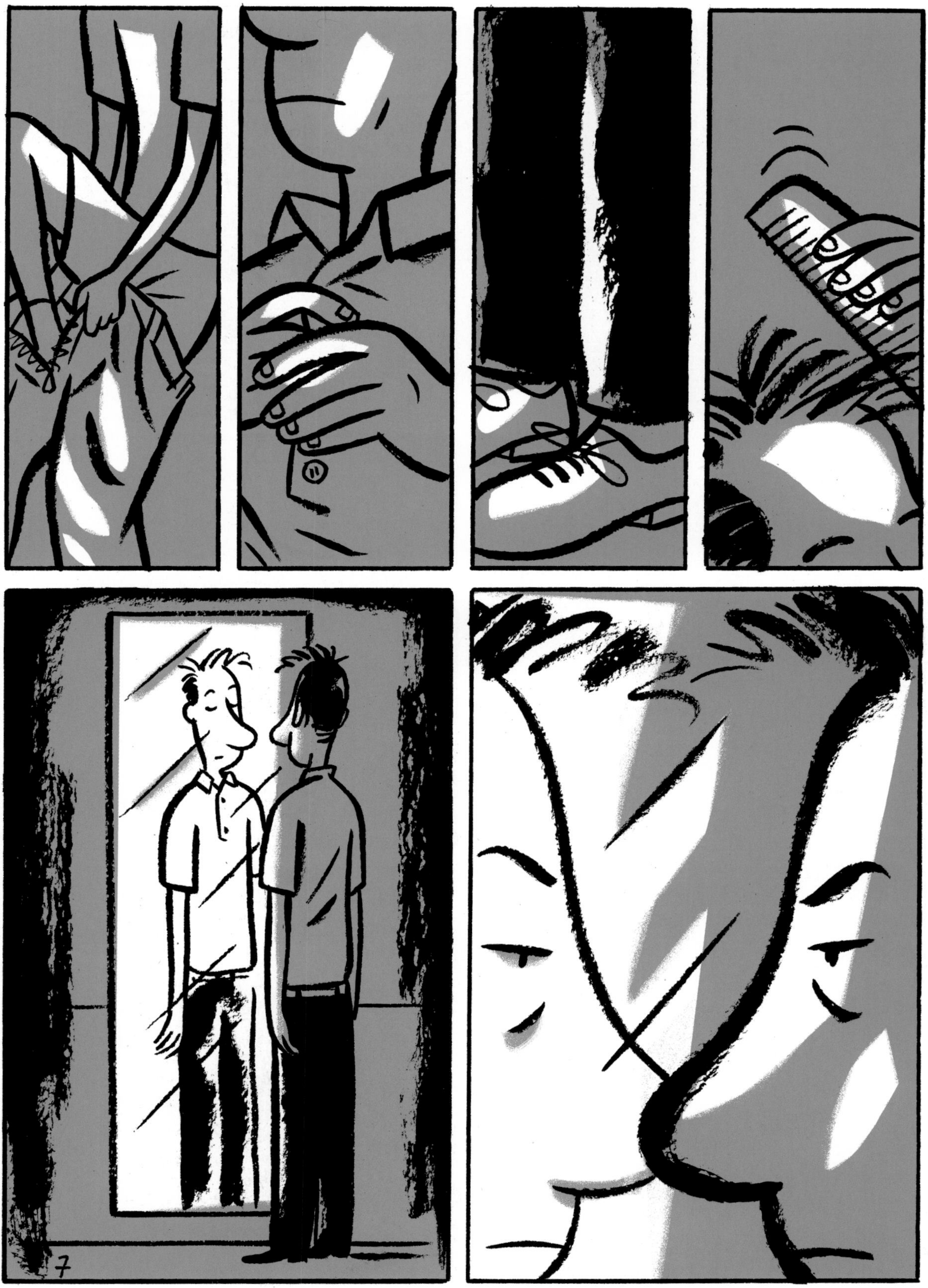
7

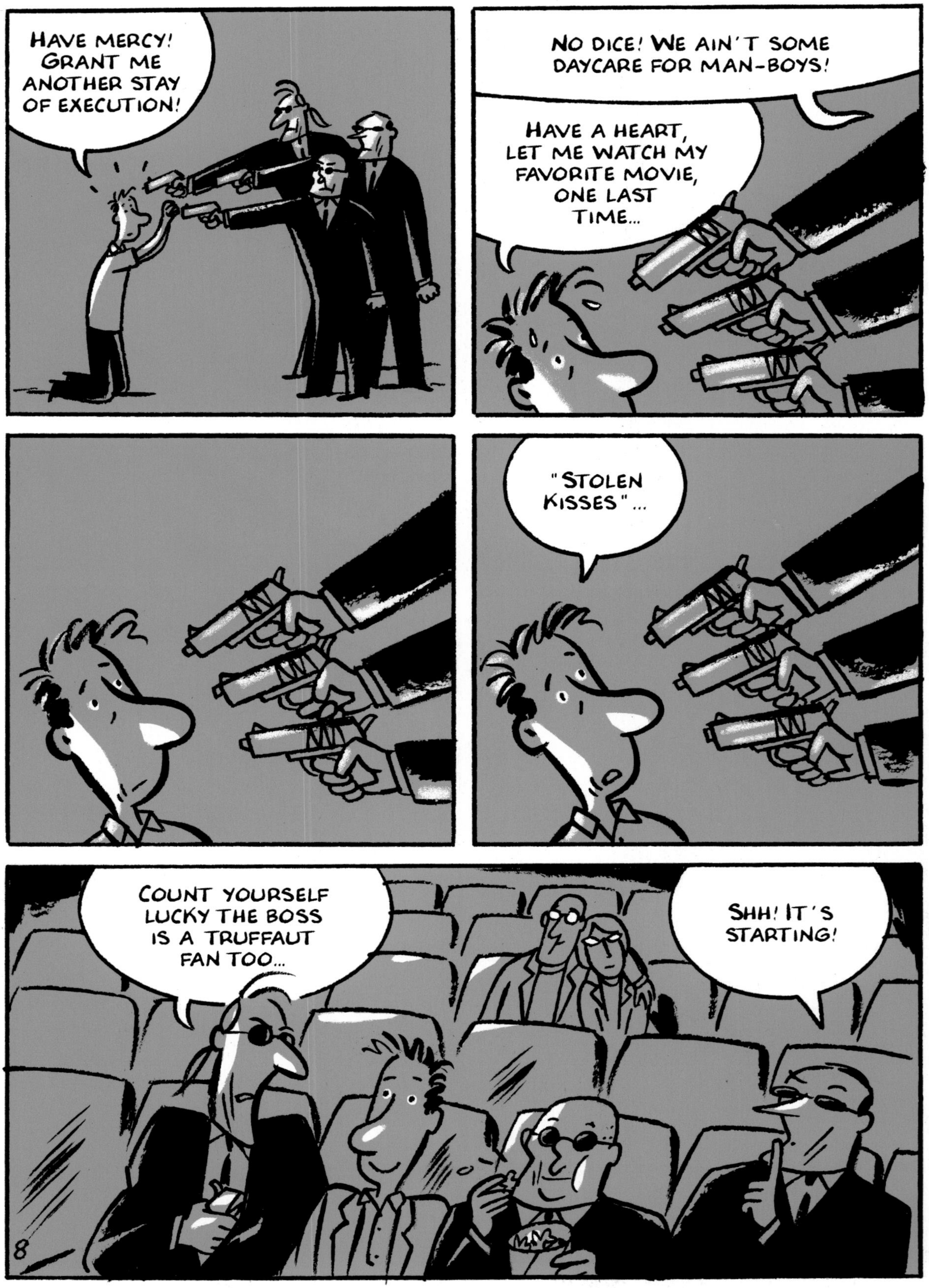
HAVE MERCY! GRANT ME ANOTHER STAY OF EXECUTION!
NO DICE! WE AIN'T SOME DAYCARE FOR MAN-BOYS!
HAVE A HEART, LET ME WATCH MY FAVORITE MOVIE, ONE LAST TIME...
"STOLEN KISSES"...
COUNT YOURSELF LUCKY THE BOSS IS A TRUFFAUT FAN TOO...
SHH! IT'S STARTING!
8

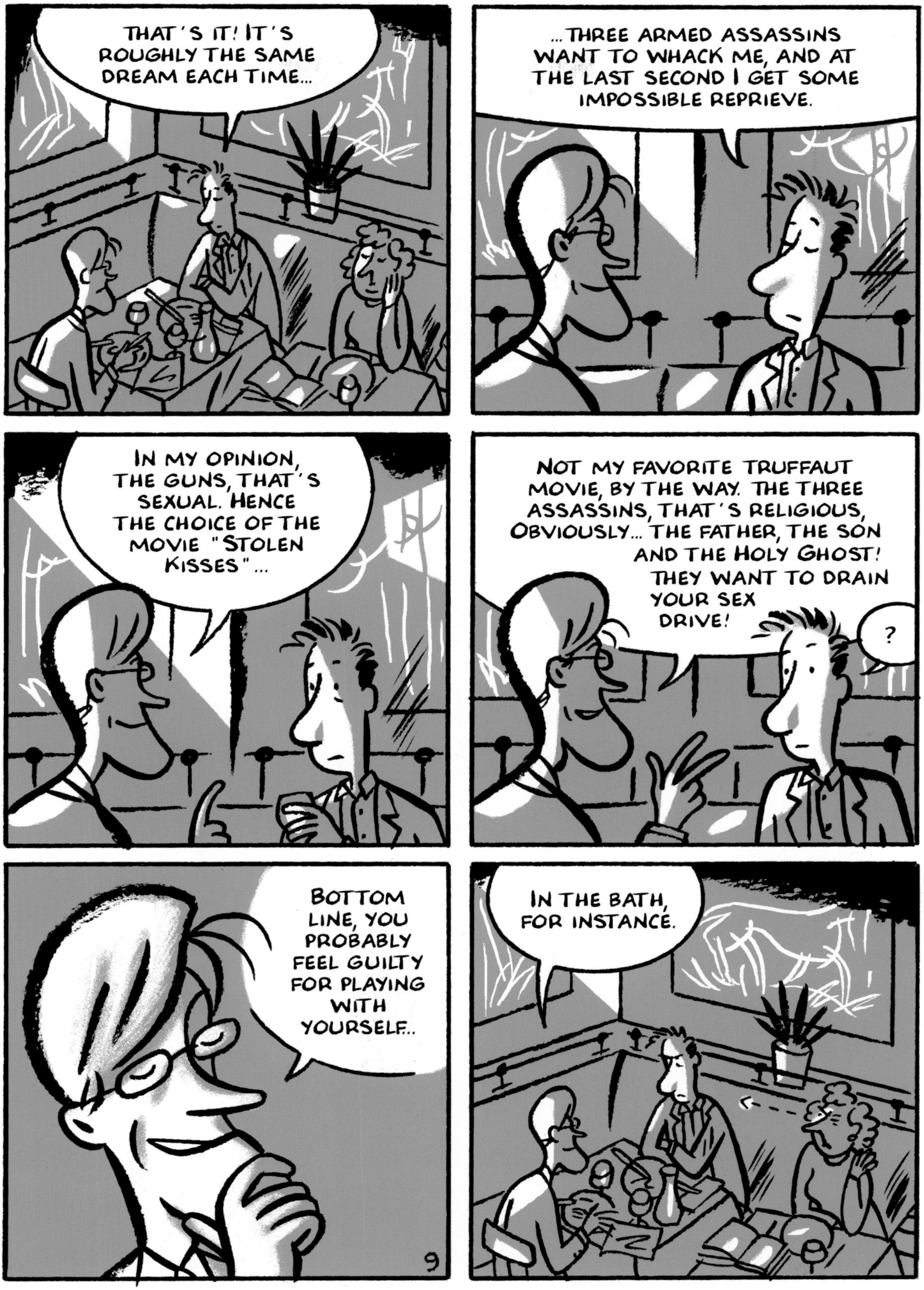
THAT'S IT! IT'S ROUGHLY THE SAME DREAM EACH TIME...
...THREE ARMED ASSASSINS WANT TO WHACK ME, AND AT THE LAST SECOND I GET SOME IMPOSSIBLE REPRIEVE.
IN MY OPINION, THE GUNS, THAT'S SEXUAL. HENCE THE CHOICE OF THE MOVIE "STOLEN KISSES"...
NOT MY FAVORITE TRUFFAUT MOVIE, BY THE WAY. THE THREE ASSASSINS, THAT'S RELIGIOUS, OBVIOUSLY... THE FATHER, THE SON AND THE HOLY GHOST! THEY WANT TO DRAIN YOUR SEX DRIVE!
?
BOTTOM LINE, YOU PROBABLY FEEL GUILTY FOR PLAYING WITH YOURSELF...
9
IN THE BATH, FOR INSTANCE.

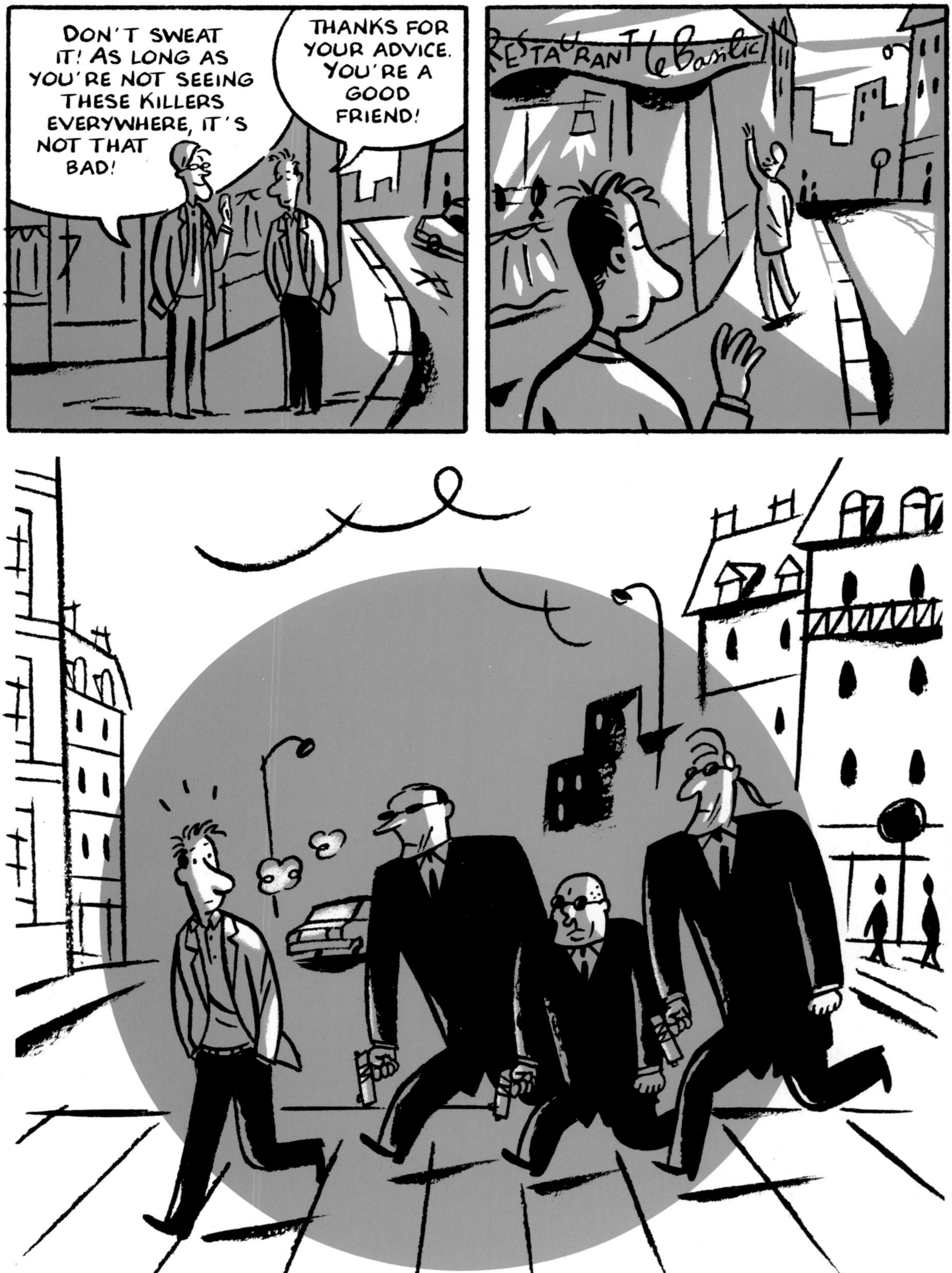
DON'T SWEAT IT! AS LONG AS YOU'RE NOT SEEING THESE KILLERS EVERYWHERE, IT'S NOT THAT BAD!
THANKS FOR YOUR ADVICE. YOU'RE A GOOD FRIEND!
RESTAURANT le Basilic

FELIX ON THE BUS

Science et vie
*SCIENCE AND LIFE MAGAZINE
WE'RE NOT DONE YET, YOU AND ME!

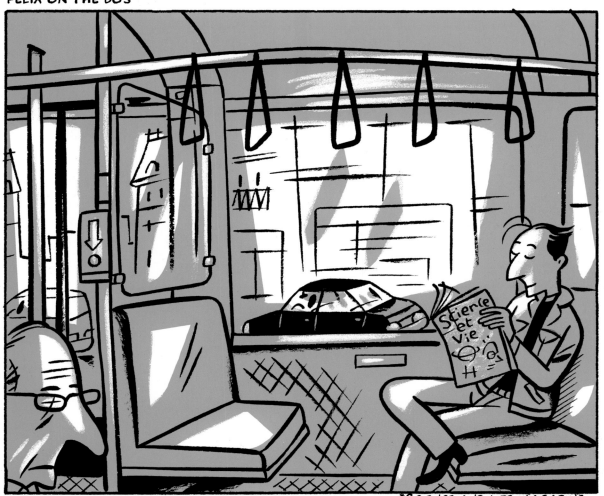

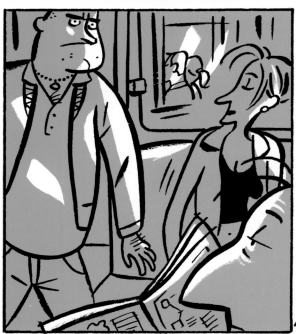

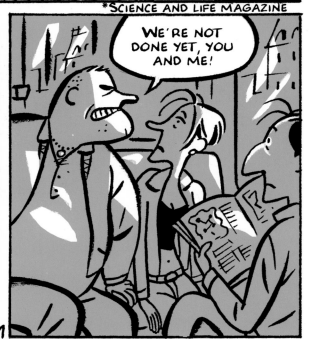

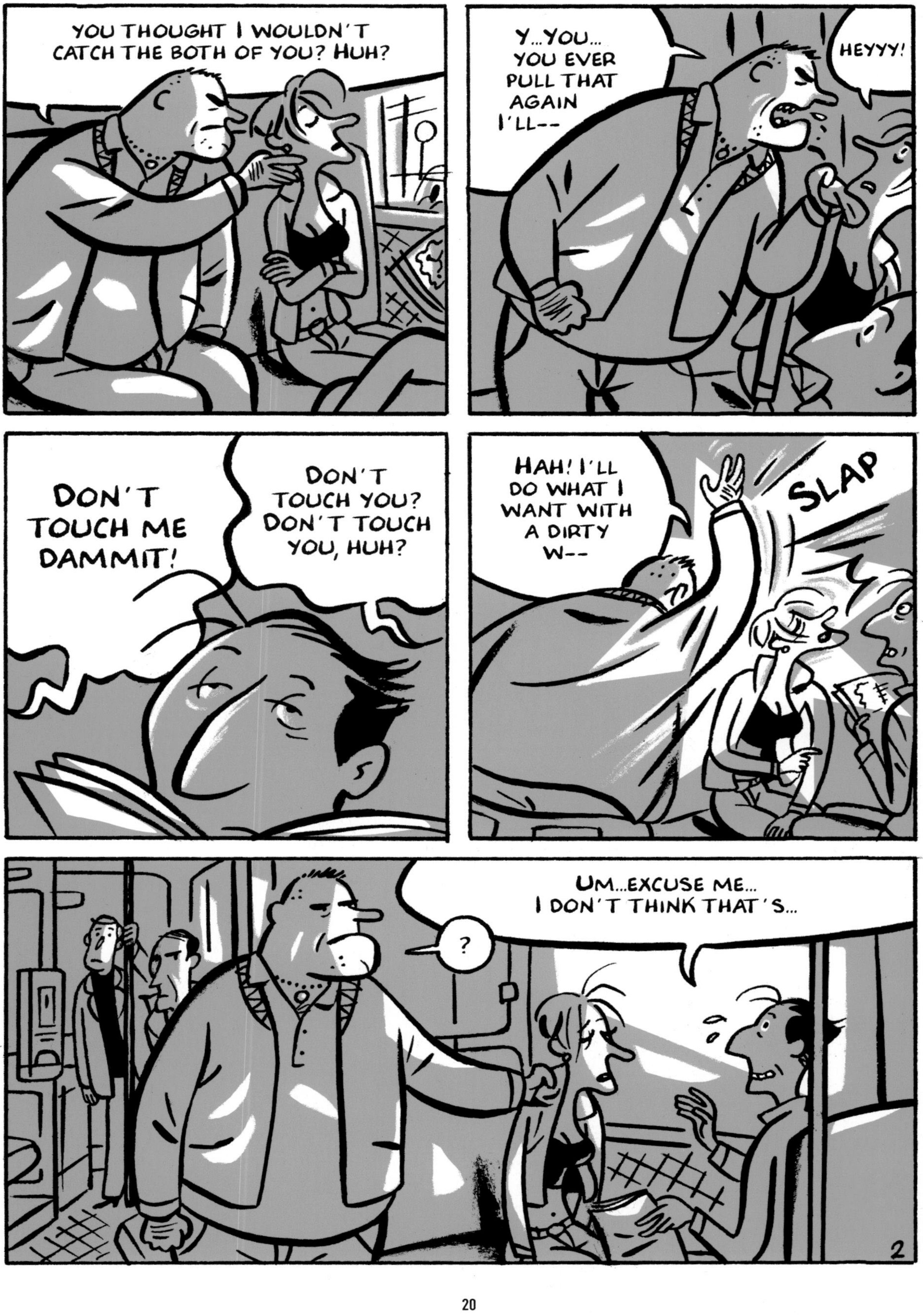
YOU THOUGHT I WOULDN'T CATCH THE BOTH OF YOU? HUH?
Y...YOU... YOU EVER PULL THAT AGAIN I'LL--
HEYYY!
DON'T TOUCH ME DAMMIT!
DON'T TOUCH YOU? DON'T TOUCH YOU, HUH?
HAH! I'LL DO WHAT I WANT WITH A DIRTY W--
SLAP
UM...EXCUSE ME... I DON'T THINK THAT'S...
?
2

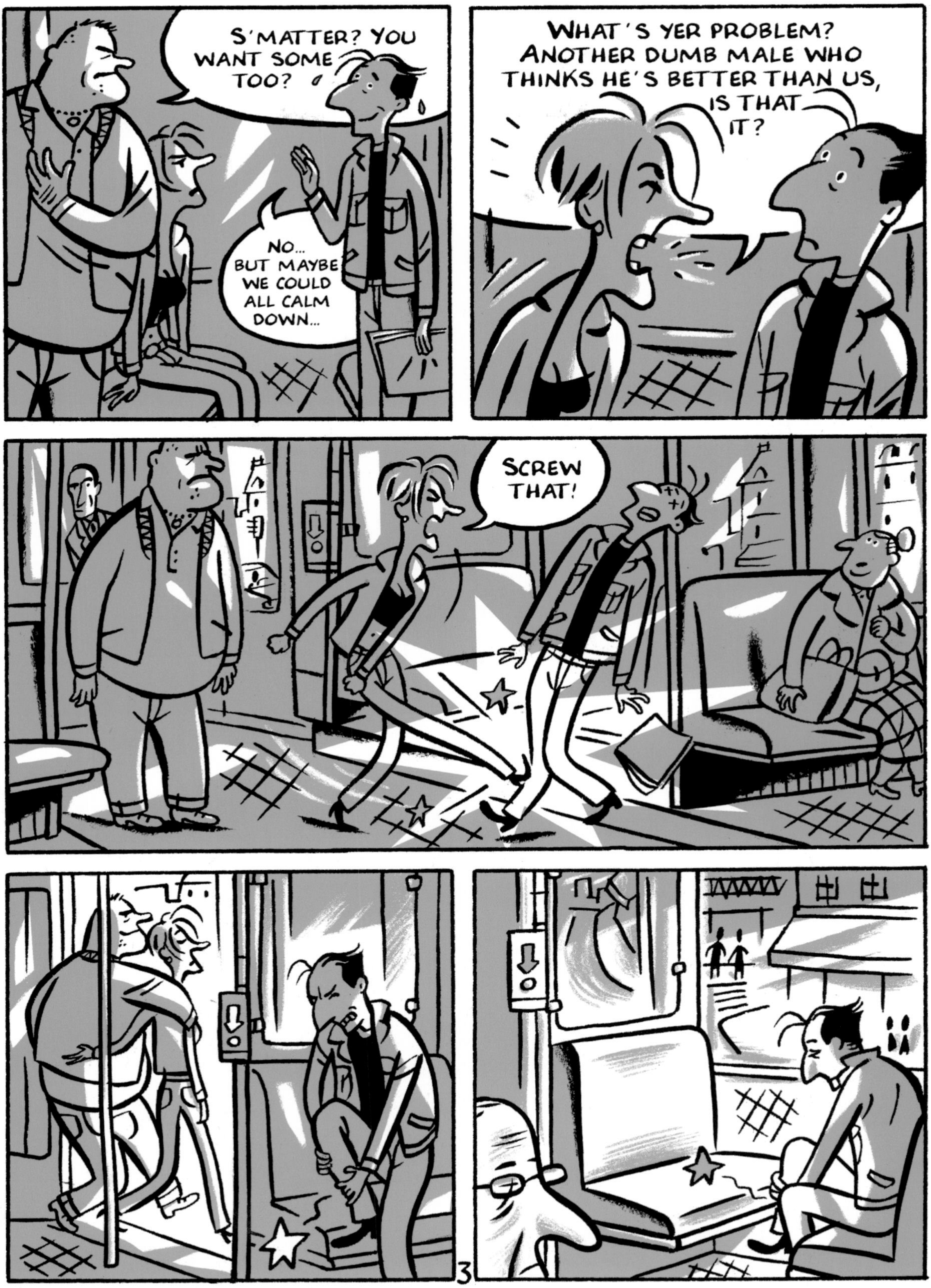
S'MATTER? YOU WANT SOME TOO?
NO... BUT MAYBE WE COULD ALL CALM DOWN...
WHAT'S YER PROBLEM? ANOTHER DUMB MALE WHO THINKS HE'S BETTER THAN US, IS THAT IT?
SCREW THAT!
3

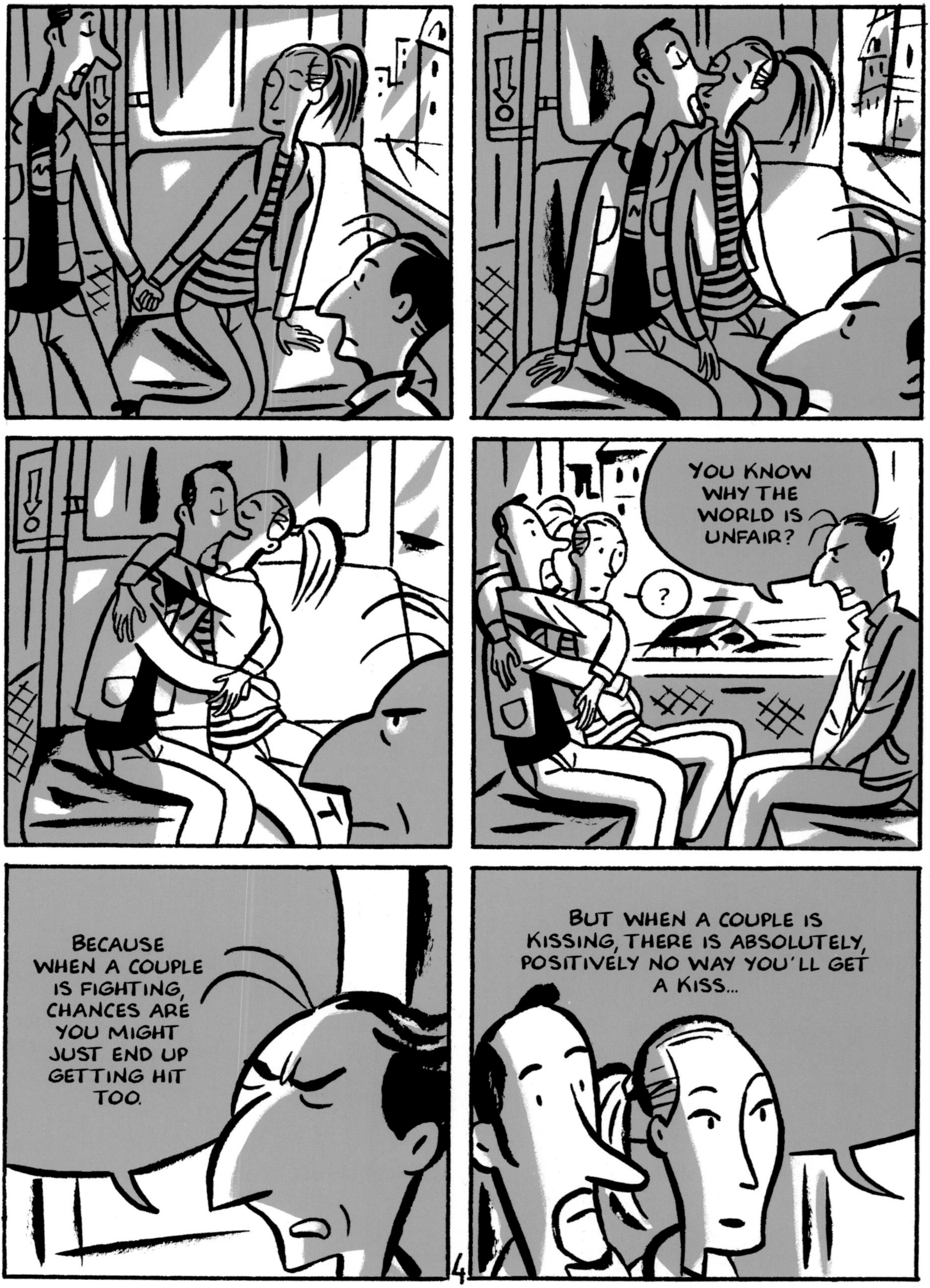
YOU KNOW WHY THE WORLD IS UNFAIR?
?
BECAUSE WHEN A COUPLE IS FIGHTING, CHANCES ARE YOU MIGHT JUST END UP GETTING HIT TOO.
BUT WHEN A COUPLE IS KISSING, THERE IS ABSOLUTELY, POSITIVELY NO WAY YOU'LL GET A KISS...

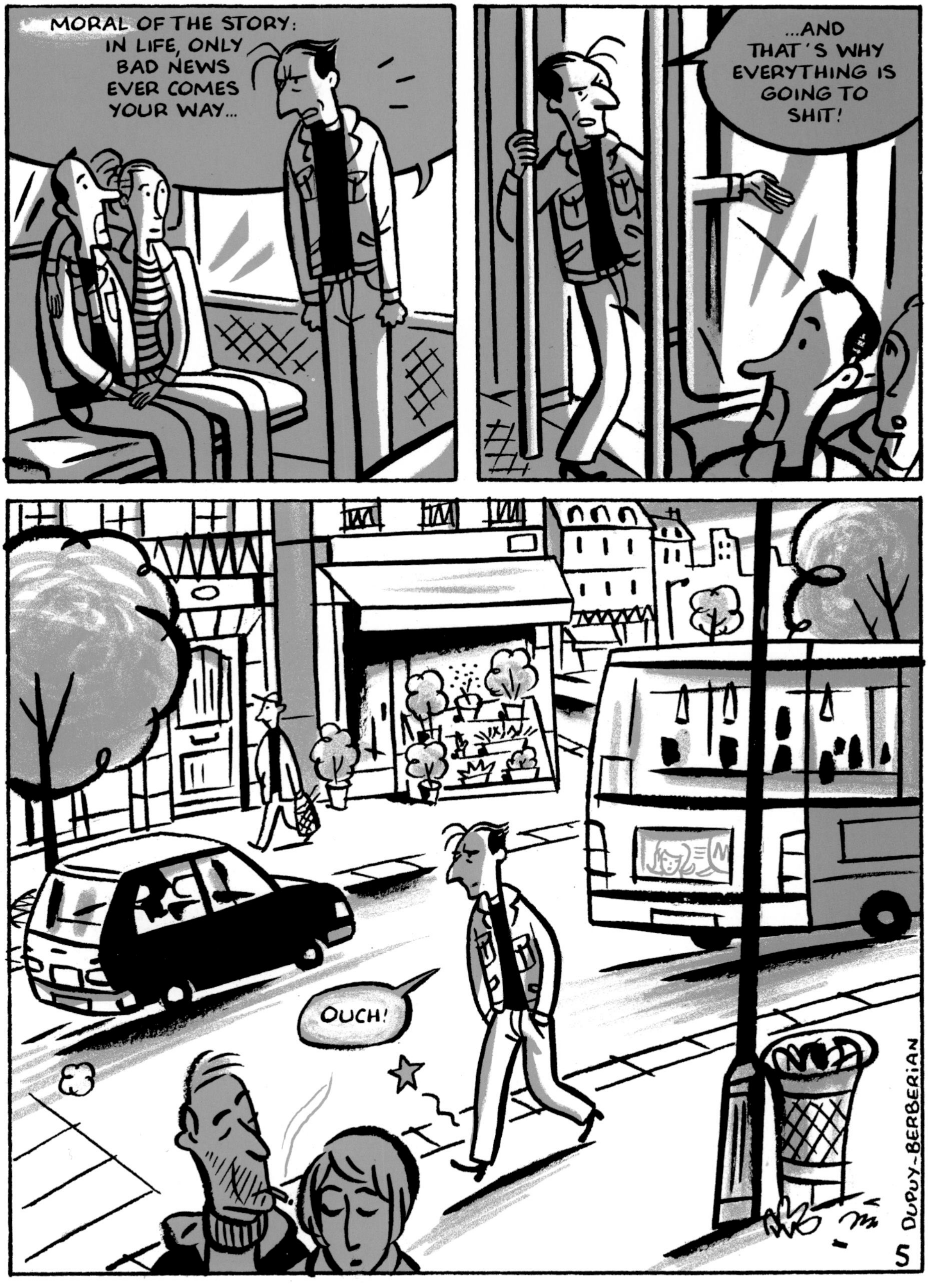
MORAL OF THE STORY: IN LIFE, ONLY BAD NEWS EVER COMES YOUR WAY...
...AND THAT'S WHY EVERYTHING IS GOING TO SHIT!
OUCH!
DUPUY-BERBERIAN
5

THE SINGLES THEORY

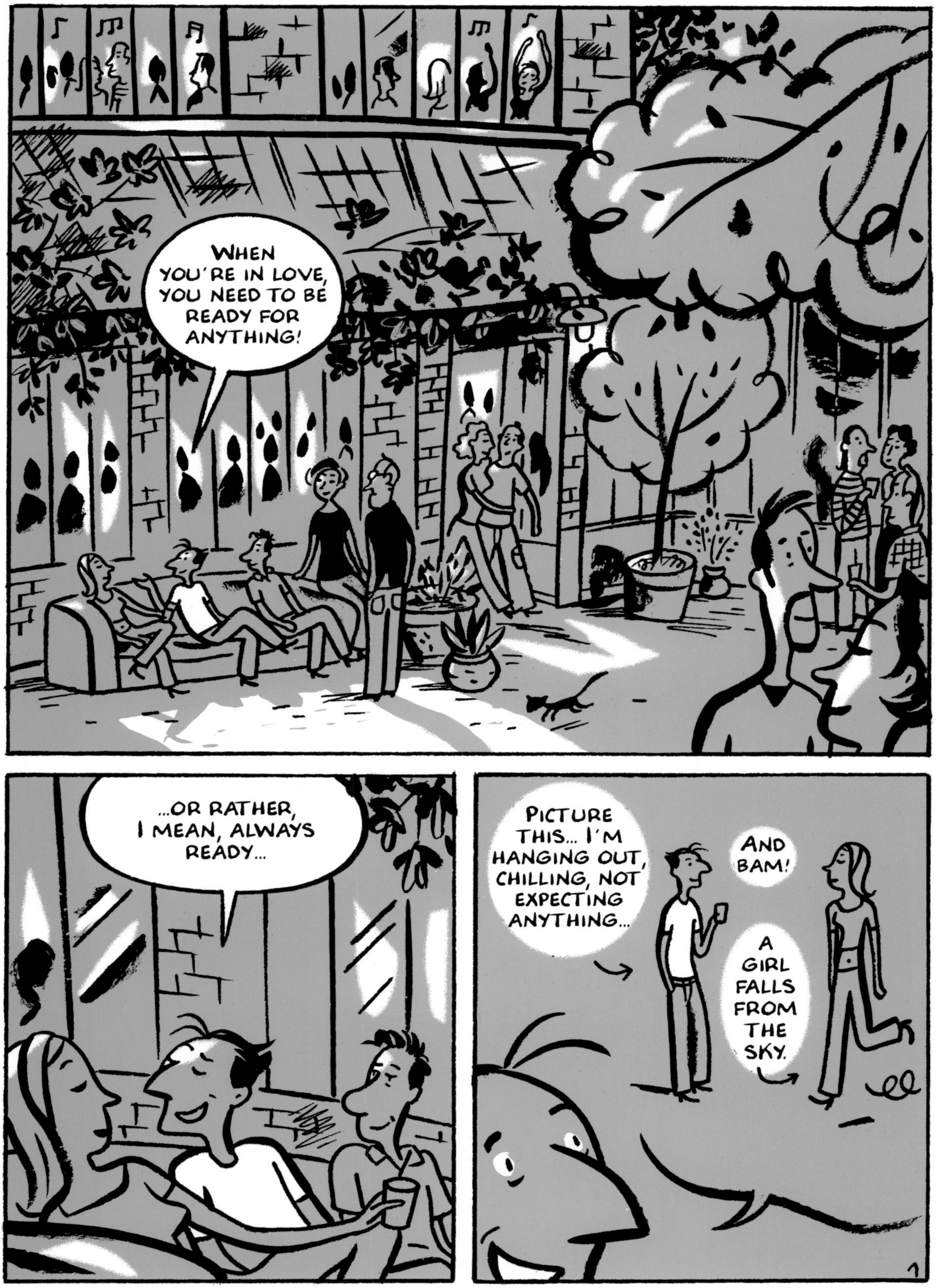
WHEN YOU'RE IN LOVE, YOU NEED TO BE READY FOR ANYTHING!
...OR RATHER, I MEAN, ALWAYS READY...
PICTURE THIS... I'M HANGING OUT, CHILLING, NOT EXPECTING ANYTHING...
AND BAM!
A GIRL FALLS FROM THE SKY.

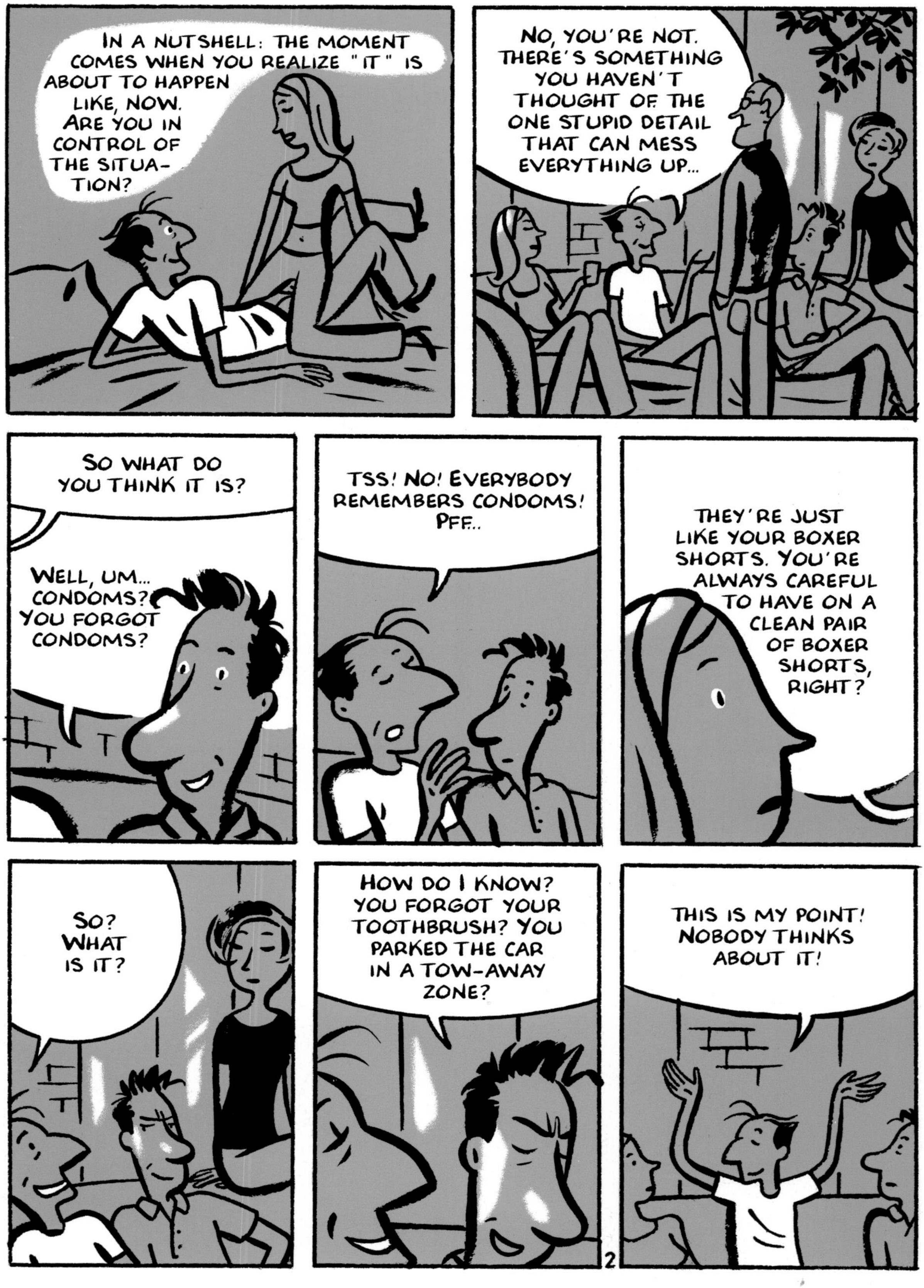
IN A NUTSHELL: THE MOMENT COMES WHEN YOU REALIZE "IT" IS ABOUT TO HAPPEN LIKE, NOW. ARE YOU IN CONTROL OF THE SITUA-TION?
NO, YOU'RE NOT. THERE'S SOMETHING YOU HAVEN'T THOUGHT OF. THE ONE STUPID DETAIL THAT CAN MESS EVERYTHING UP...
SO WHAT DO YOU THINK IT IS?
WELL, UM... CONDOMS? YOU FORGOT CONDOMS?
TSS! NO! EVERYBODY REMEMBERS CONDOMS! PFF...
THEY'RE JUST LIKE YOUR BOXER SHORTS. YOU'RE ALWAYS CAREFUL TO HAVE ON A CLEAN PAIR OF BOXER SHORTS, RIGHT?
SO? WHAT IS IT?
HOW DO I KNOW? YOU FORGOT YOUR TOOTHBRUSH? YOU PARKED THE CAR IN A TOW-AWAY ZONE?
2
THIS IS MY POINT! NOBODY THINKS ABOUT IT!

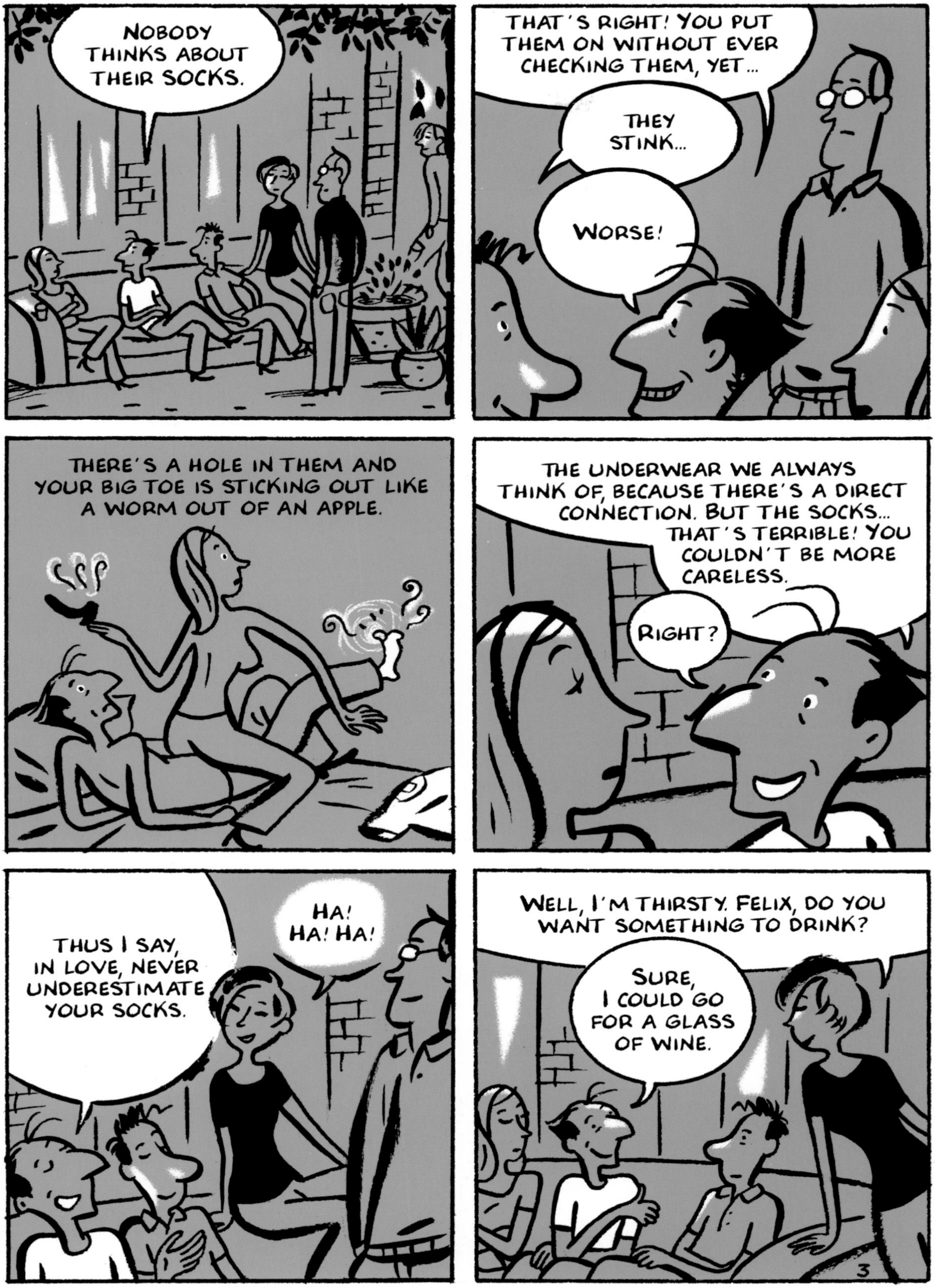
NOBODY THINKS ABOUT THEIR SOCKS.
THAT'S RIGHT! YOU PUT THEM ON WITHOUT EVER CHECKING THEM, YET...
THEY STINK...
WORSE!
THERE'S A HOLE IN THEM AND YOUR BIG TOE IS STICKING OUT LIKE A WORM OUT OF AN APPLE.
THE UNDERWEAR WE ALWAYS THINK OF, BECAUSE THERE'S A DIRECT CONNECTION. BUT THE SOCKS... THAT'S TERRIBLE! YOU COULDN'T BE MORE CARELESS.
RIGHT?
THUS I SAY, IN LOVE, NEVER UNDERESTIMATE YOUR SOCKS.
HA! HA! HA!
WELL, I'M THIRSTY. FELIX, DO YOU WANT SOMETHING TO DRINK?
SURE, I COULD GO FOR A GLASS OF WINE.
3

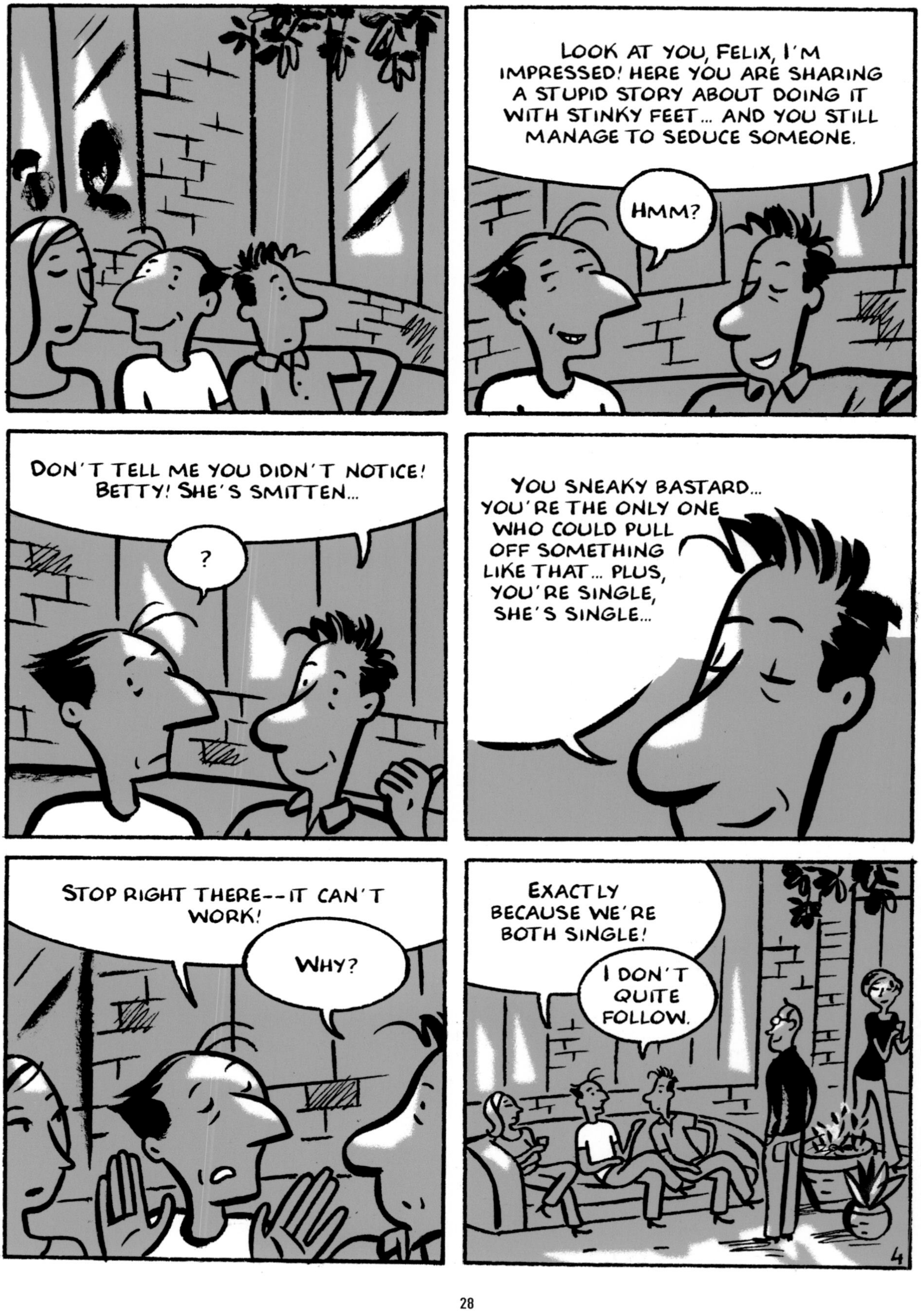
LOOK AT YOU, FELIX, I'M IMPRESSED! HERE YOU ARE SHARING A STUPID STORY ABOUT DOING IT WITH STINKY FEET... AND YOU STILL MANAGE TO SEDUCE SOMEONE.
HMM?
DON'T TELL ME YOU DIDN'T NOTICE! BETTY! SHE'S SMITTEN...
?
YOU SNEAKY BASTARD... YOU'RE THE ONLY ONE WHO COULD PULL OFF SOMETHING LIKE THAT... PLUS, YOU'RE SINGLE, SHE'S SINGLE...
STOP RIGHT THERE--IT CAN'T WORK!
WHY?
EXACTLY BECAUSE WE'RE BOTH SINGLE!
I DON'T QUITE FOLLOW.
4

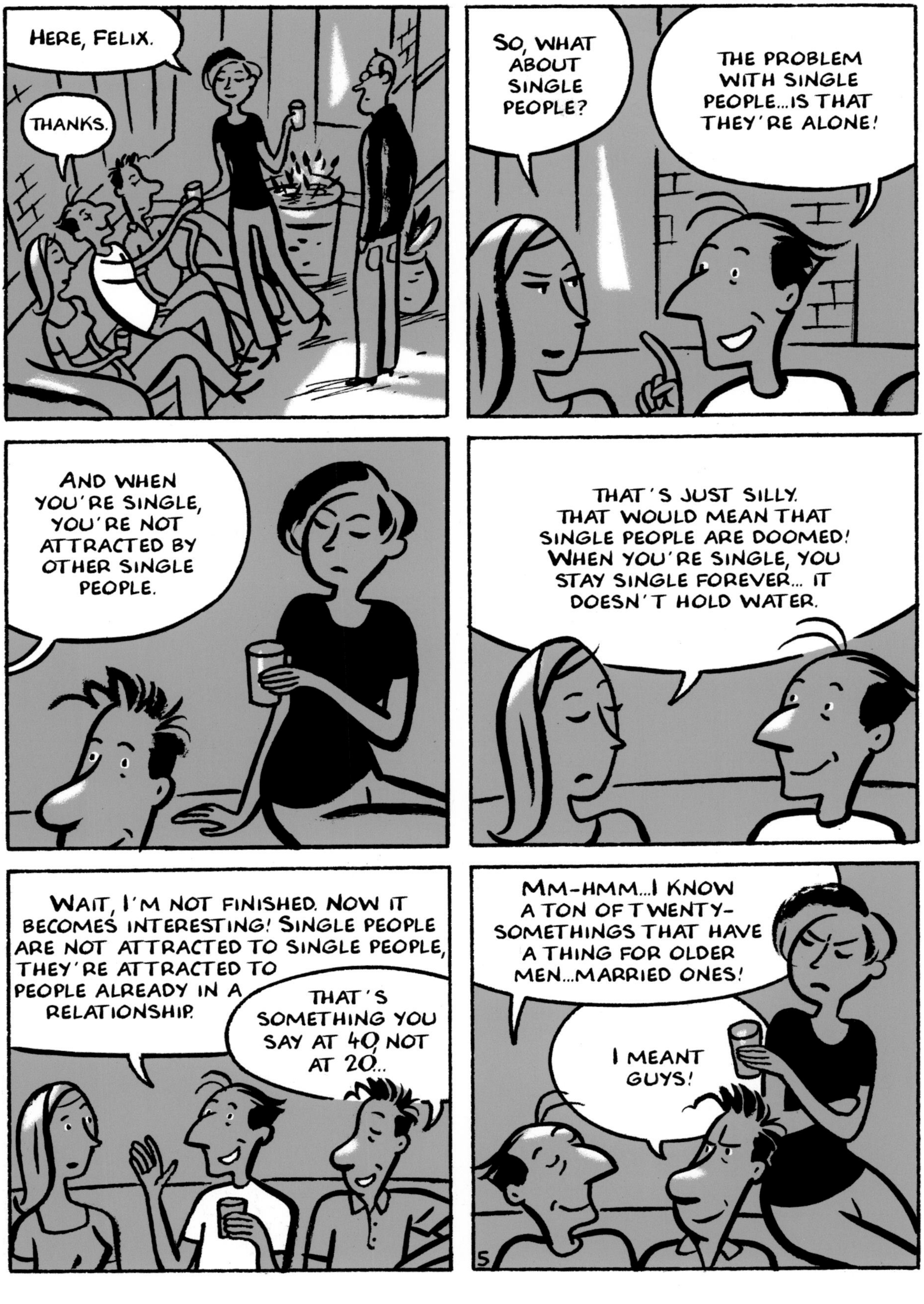
HERE, FELIX.
THANKS.
SO, WHAT ABOUT SINGLE PEOPLE?
THE PROBLEM WITH SINGLE PEOPLE...IS THAT THEY'RE ALONE!
AND WHEN YOU'RE SINGLE, YOU'RE NOT ATTRACTED BY OTHER SINGLE PEOPLE.
THAT'S JUST SILLY. THAT WOULD MEAN THAT SINGLE PEOPLE ARE DOOMED! WHEN YOU'RE SINGLE, YOU STAY SINGLE FOREVER... IT DOESN'T HOLD WATER.
WAIT, I'M NOT FINISHED. NOW IT BECOMES INTERESTING! SINGLE PEOPLE ARE NOT ATTRACTED TO SINGLE PEOPLE, THEY'RE ATTRACTED TO PEOPLE ALREADY IN A RELATIONSHIP.
THAT'S SOMETHING YOU SAY AT 40, NOT AT 20...
MM-HMM...I KNOW A TON OF TWENTY-SOMETHINGS THAT HAVE A THING FOR OLDER MEN...MARRIED ONES!
I MEANT GUYS!
5

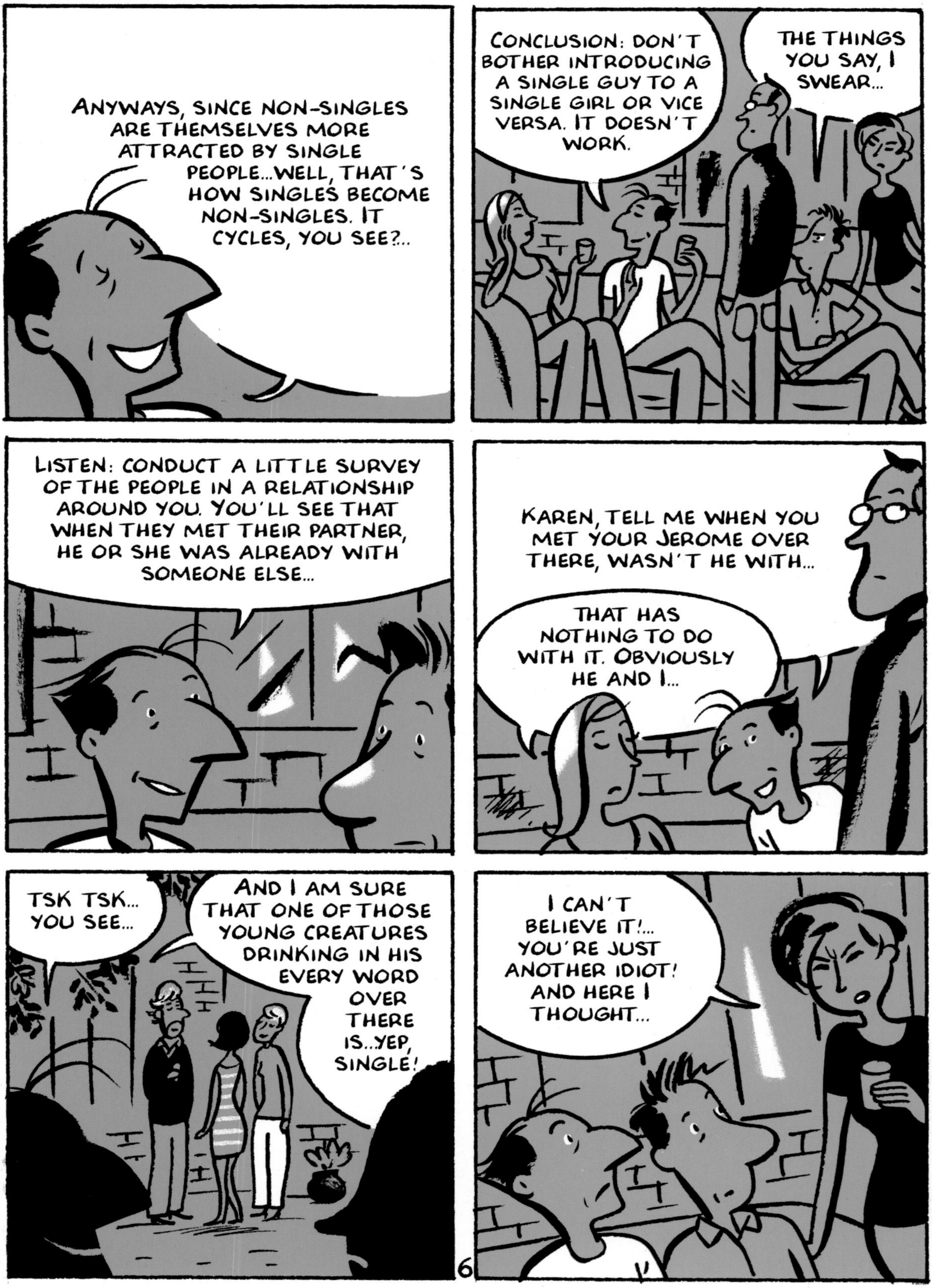
ANYWAYS, SINCE NON-SINGLES ARE THEMSELVES MORE ATTRACTED BY SINGLE PEOPLE...WELL, THAT'S HOW SINGLES BECOME NON-SINGLES. IT CYCLES, YOU SEE?...
CONCLUSION: DON'T BOTHER INTRODUCING A SINGLE GUY TO A SINGLE GIRL OR VICE VERSA. IT DOESN'T WORK.
THE THINGS YOU SAY, I SWEAR...
LISTEN: CONDUCT A LITTLE SURVEY OF THE PEOPLE IN A RELATIONSHIP AROUND YOU. YOU'LL SEE THAT WHEN THEY MET THEIR PARTNER, HE OR SHE WAS ALREADY WITH SOMEONE ELSE...
KAREN, TELL ME WHEN YOU MET YOUR JEROME OVER THERE, WASN'T HE WITH...
THAT HAS NOTHING TO DO WITH IT. OBVIOUSLY HE AND I...
TSK TSK... YOU SEE...
AND I AM SURE THAT ONE OF THOSE YOUNG CREATURES DRINKING IN HIS EVERY WORD OVER THERE IS...YEP, SINGLE!
I CAN'T BELIEVE IT!... YOU'RE JUST ANOTHER IDIOT! AND HERE I THOUGHT...
6

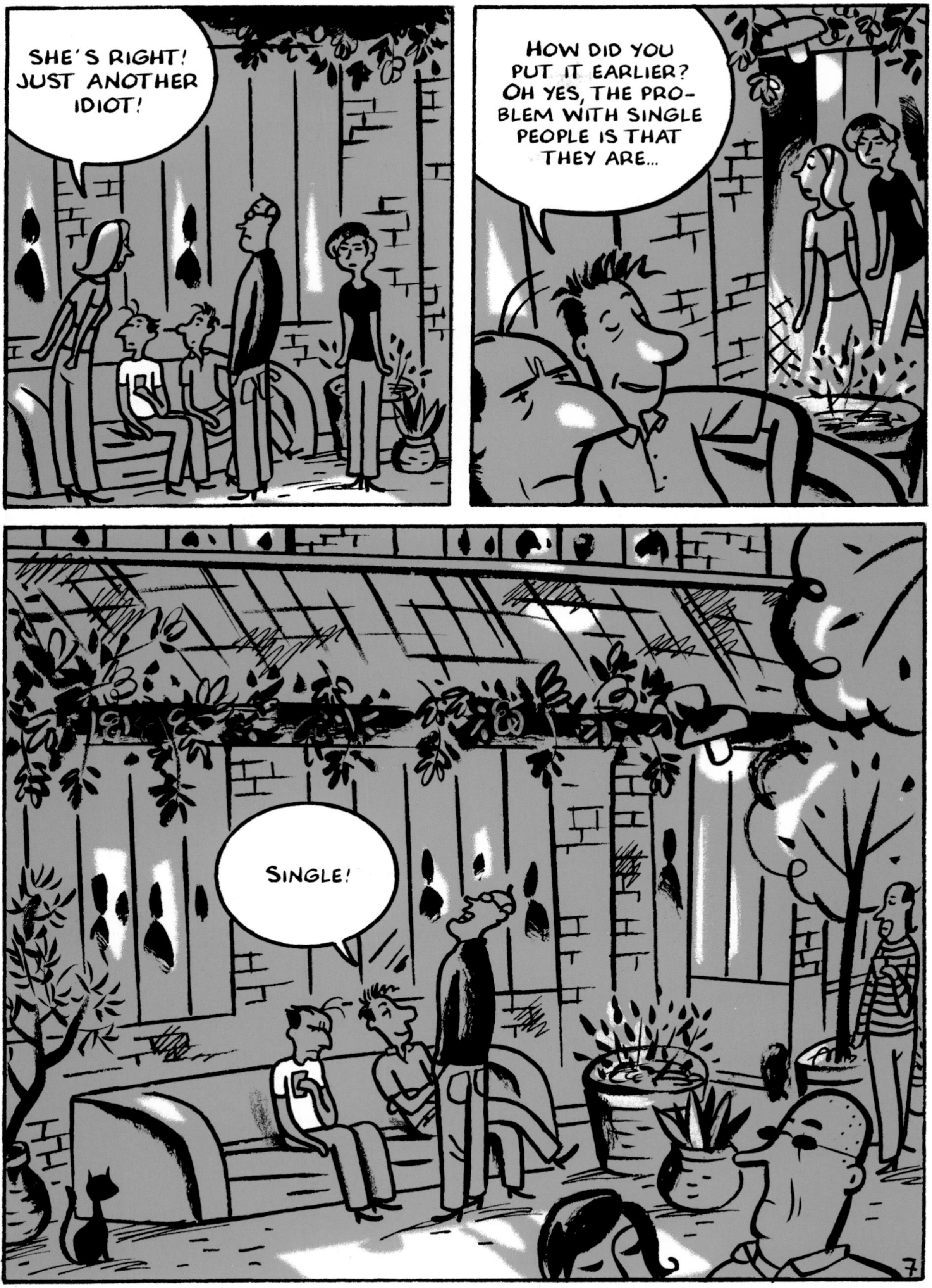
SHE'S RIGHT! JUST ANOTHER IDIOT!
HOW DID YOU PUT IT EARLIER? OH YES, THE PROBLEM WITH SINGLE PEOPLE IS THAT THEY ARE...
SINGLE!

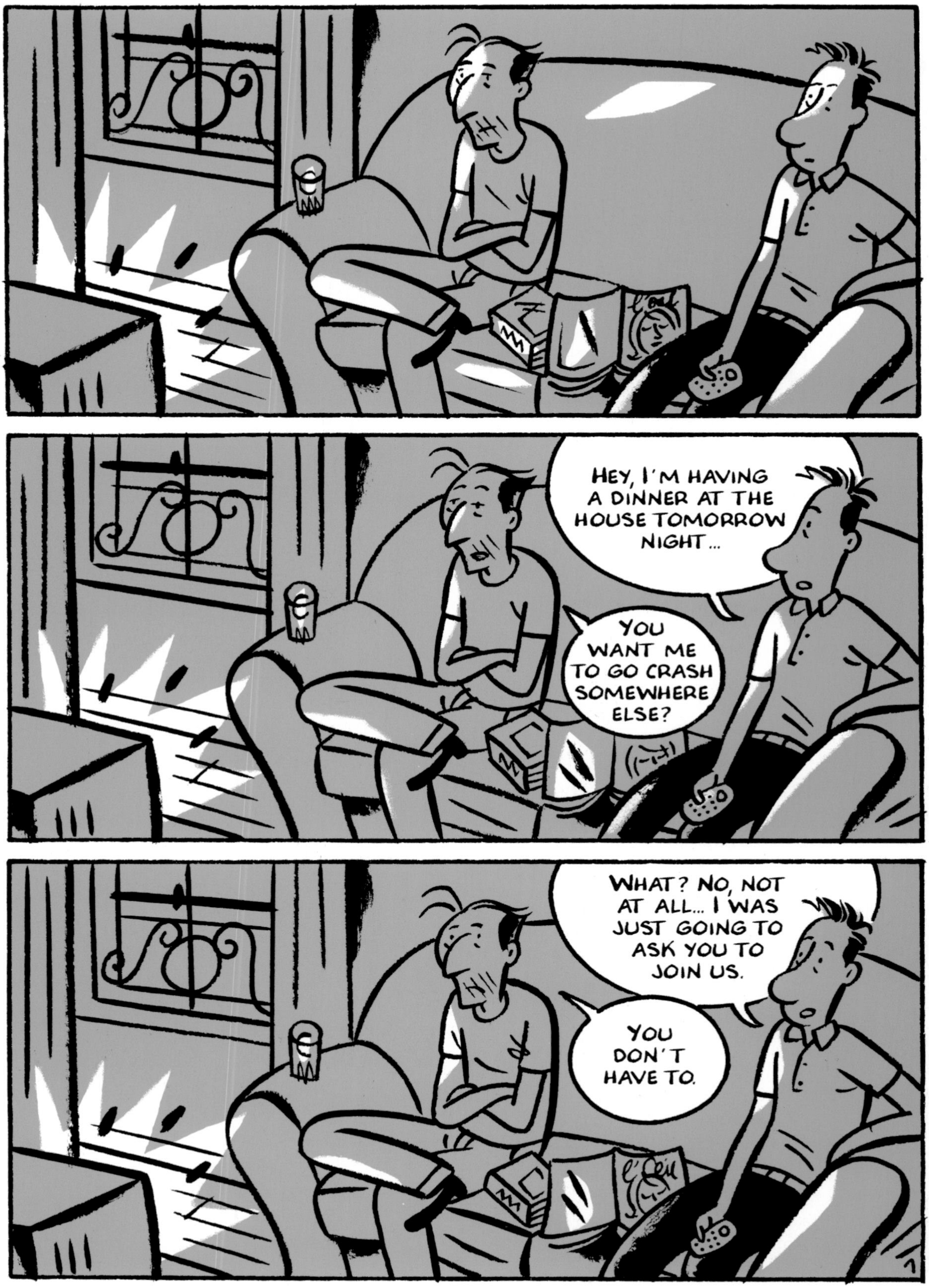
HEY, I'M HAVING A DINNER AT THE HOUSE TOMORROW NIGHT...
YOU WANT ME TO GO CRASH SOMEWHERE ELSE?
WHAT? NO, NOT AT ALL... I WAS JUST GOING TO ASK YOU TO JOIN US.
YOU DON'T HAVE TO.

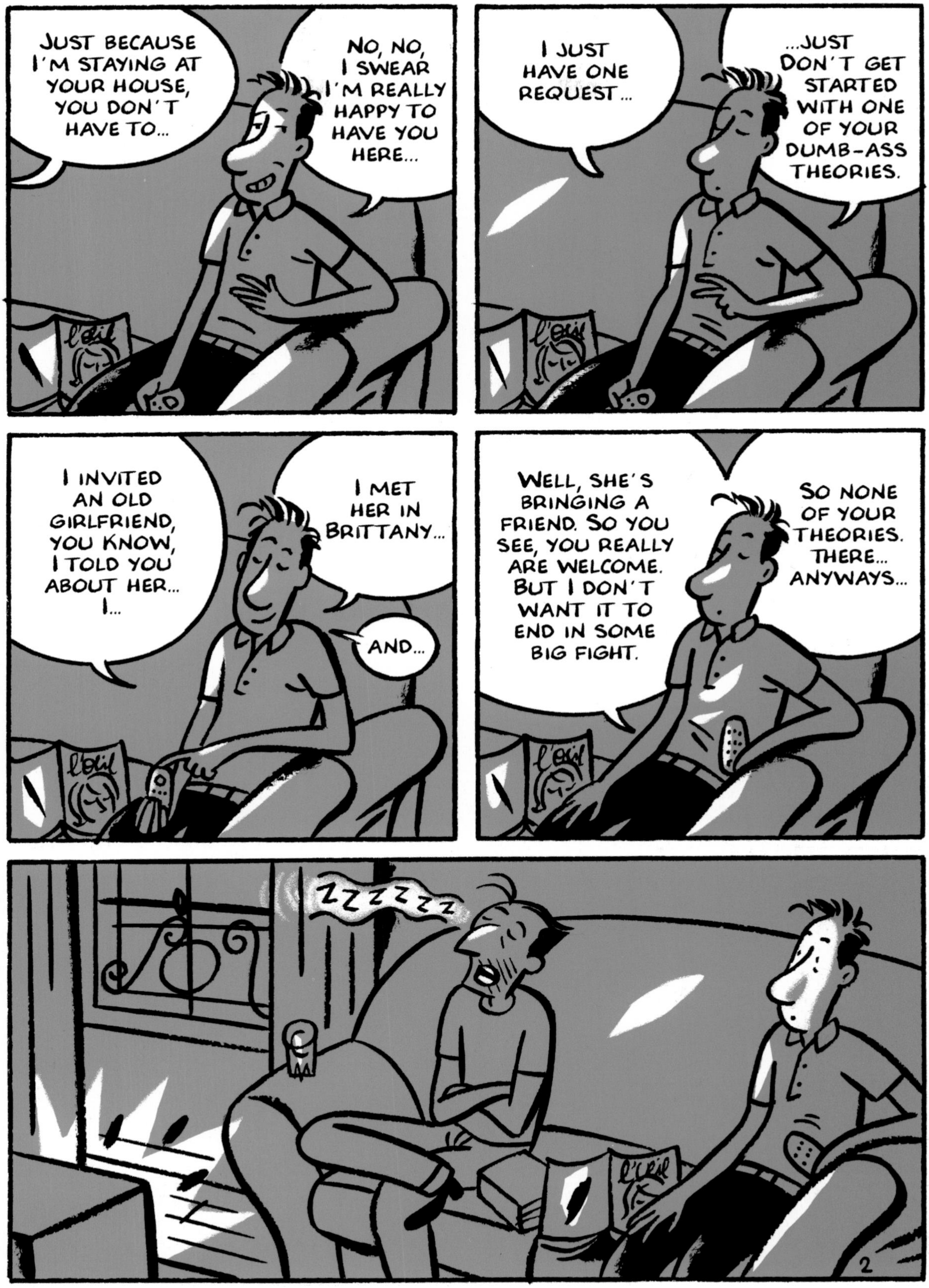
JUST BECAUSE I'M STAYING AT YOUR HOUSE, YOU DON'T HAVE TO...
NO, NO, I SWEAR I'M REALLY HAPPY TO HAVE YOU HERE...
I JUST HAVE ONE REQUEST...
...JUST DON'T GET STARTED WITH ONE OF YOUR DUMB-ASS THEORIES.
l'œil
I INVITED AN OLD GIRLFRIEND, YOU KNOW, I TOLD YOU ABOUT HER... I...
I MET HER IN BRITTANY...
AND...
WELL, SHE'S BRINGING A FRIEND. SO YOU SEE, YOU REALLY ARE WELCOME. BUT I DON'T WANT IT TO END IN SOME BIG FIGHT.
SO NONE OF YOUR THEORIES. THERE... ANYWAYS...
ZZZZZZZ
2

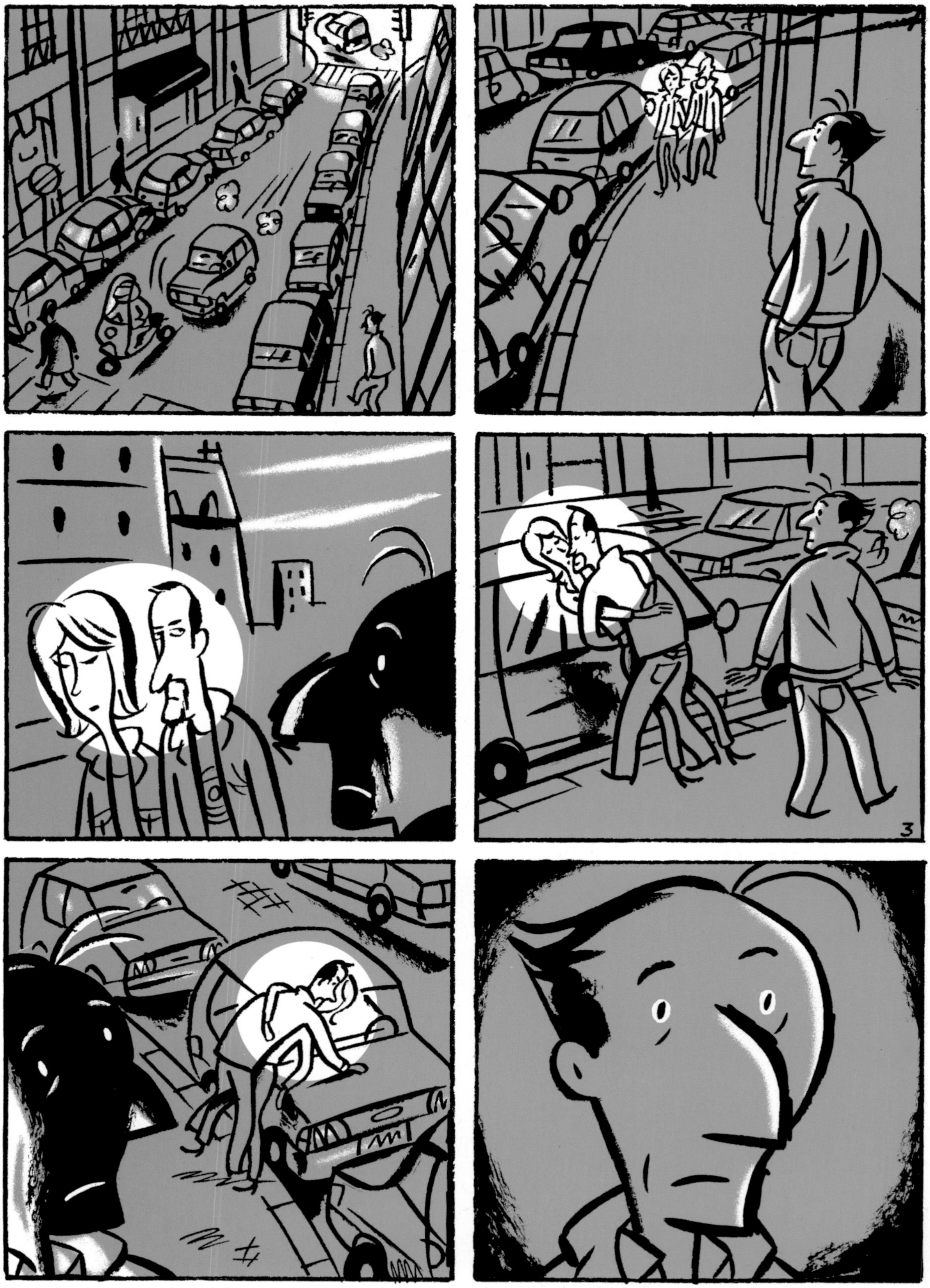
3

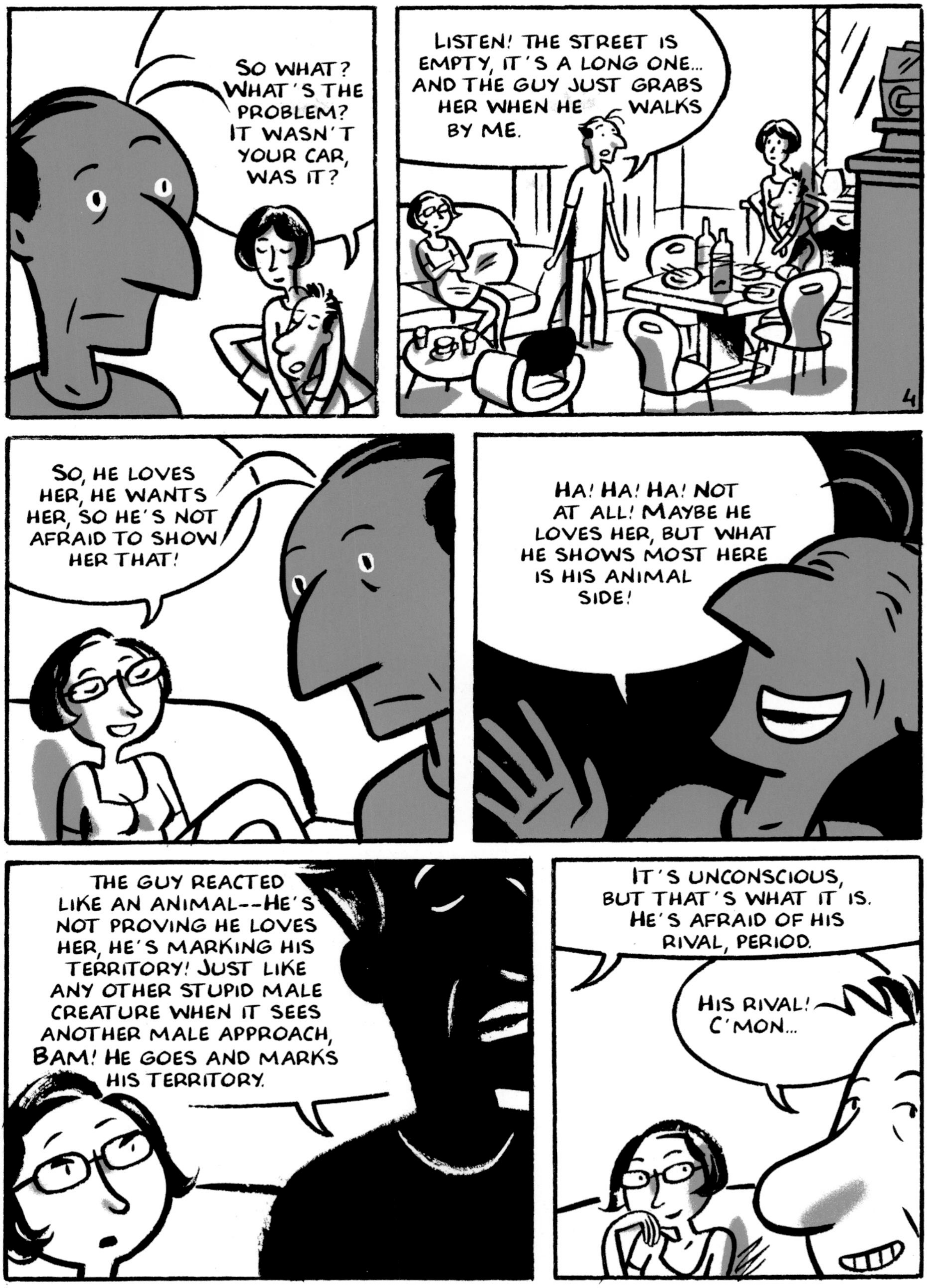
SO WHAT? WHAT'S THE PROBLEM? IT WASN'T YOUR CAR, WAS IT?
LISTEN! THE STREET IS EMPTY, IT'S A LONG ONE... AND THE GUY JUST GRABS HER WHEN HE WALKS BY ME.
SO, HE LOVES HER, HE WANTS HER, SO HE'S NOT AFRAID TO SHOW HER THAT!
HA! HA! HA! NOT AT ALL! MAYBE HE LOVES HER, BUT WHAT HE SHOWS MOST HERE IS HIS ANIMAL SIDE!
THE GUY REACTED LIKE AN ANIMAL--HE'S NOT PROVING HE LOVES HER, HE'S MARKING HIS TERRITORY! JUST LIKE ANY OTHER STUPID MALE CREATURE WHEN IT SEES ANOTHER MALE APPROACH, BAM! HE GOES AND MARKS HIS TERRITORY.
IT'S UNCONSCIOUS, BUT THAT'S WHAT IT IS. HE'S AFRAID OF HIS RIVAL, PERIOD.
HIS RIVAL! C'MON...

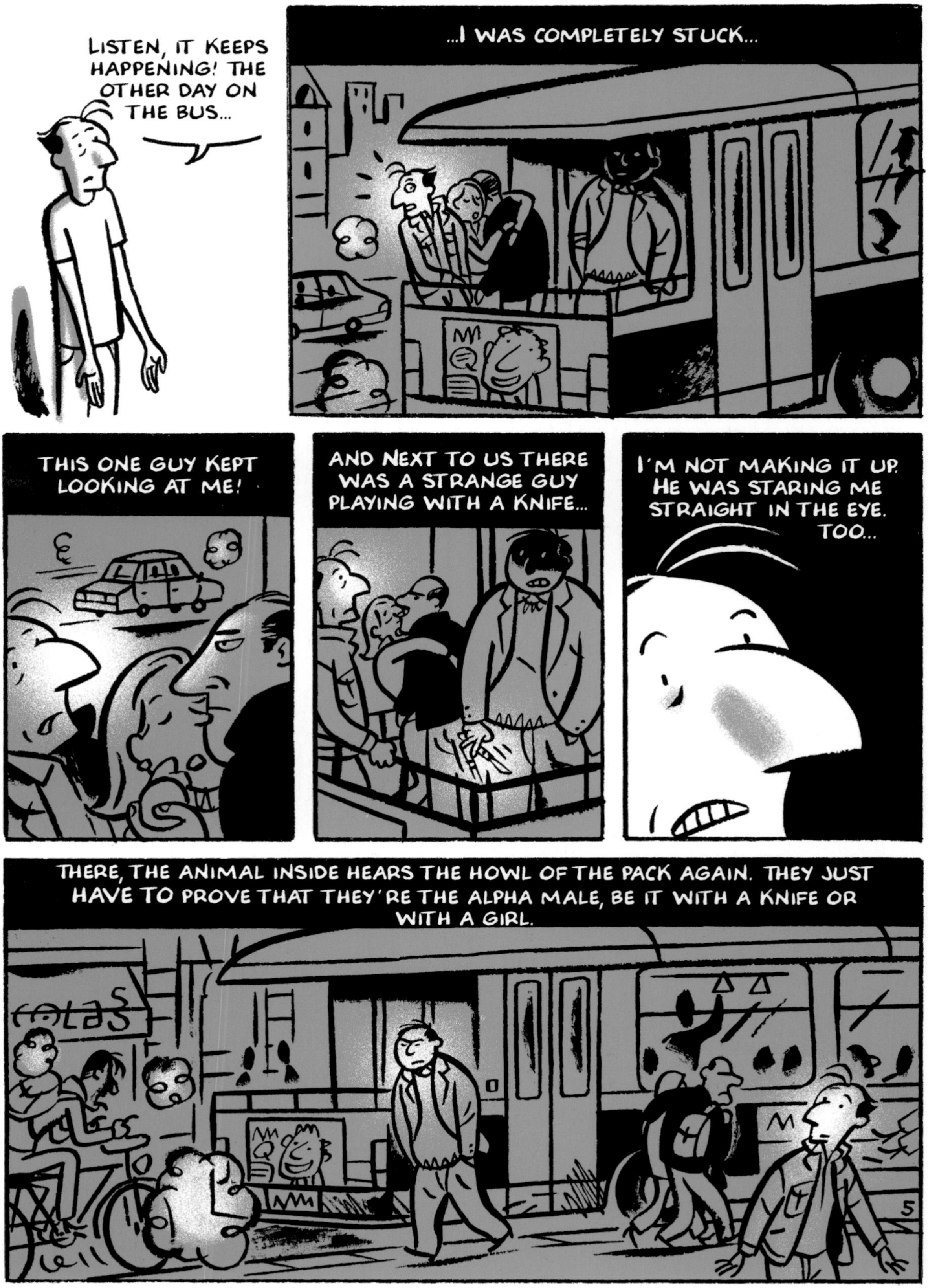
LISTEN, IT KEEPS HAPPENING! THE OTHER DAY ON THE BUS...
...I WAS COMPLETELY STUCK...
THIS ONE GUY KEPT LOOKING AT ME!
AND NEXT TO US THERE WAS A STRANGE GUY PLAYING WITH A KNIFE...
I'M NOT MAKING IT UP. HE WAS STARING ME STRAIGHT IN THE EYE. TOO...
THERE, THE ANIMAL INSIDE HEARS THE HOWL OF THE PACK AGAIN. THEY JUST HAVE TO PROVE THAT THEY'RE THE ALPHA MALE, BE IT WITH A KNIFE OR WITH A GIRL.

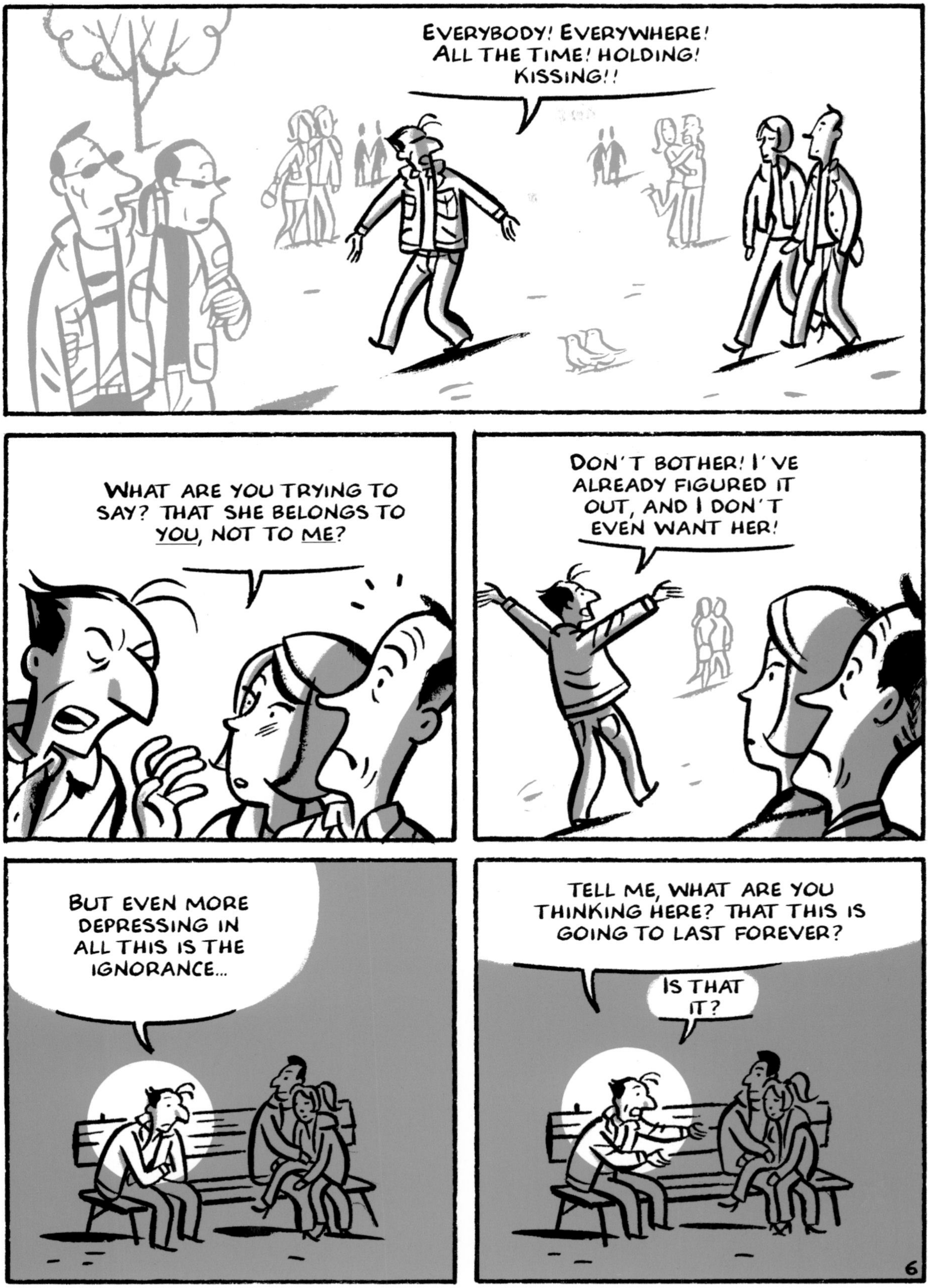
EVERYBODY! EVERYWHERE! ALL THE TIME! HOLDING! KISSING!!
WHAT ARE YOU TRYING TO SAY? THAT SHE BELONGS TO YOU, NOT TO ME?
DON'T BOTHER! I'VE ALREADY FIGURED IT OUT, AND I DON'T EVEN WANT HER!
BUT EVEN MORE DEPRESSING IN ALL THIS IS THE IGNORANCE...
TELL ME, WHAT ARE YOU THINKING HERE? THAT THIS IS GOING TO LAST FOREVER?
IS THAT IT?
6

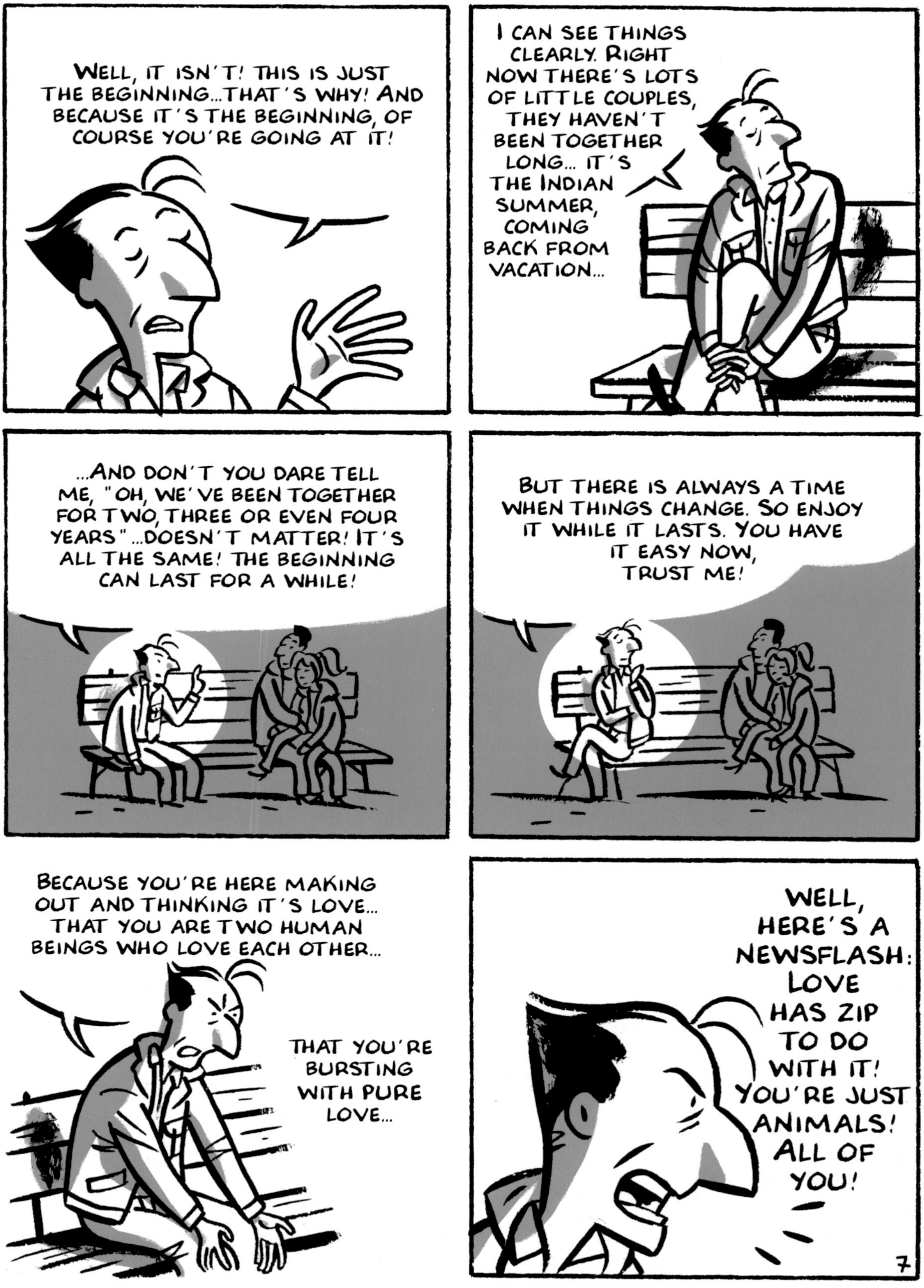
WELL, IT ISN'T! THIS IS JUST THE BEGINNING...THAT'S WHY! AND BECAUSE IT'S THE BEGINNING, OF COURSE YOU'RE GOING AT IT!
I CAN SEE THINGS CLEARLY. RIGHT NOW THERE'S LOTS OF LITTLE COUPLES, THEY HAVEN'T BEEN TOGETHER LONG... IT'S THE INDIAN SUMMER, COMING BACK FROM VACATION...
...AND DON'T YOU DARE TELL ME, "OH, WE'VE BEEN TOGETHER FOR TWO, THREE OR EVEN FOUR YEARS"...DOESN'T MATTER! IT'S ALL THE SAME! THE BEGINNING CAN LAST FOR A WHILE!
BUT THERE IS ALWAYS A TIME WHEN THINGS CHANGE. SO ENJOY IT WHILE IT LASTS. YOU HAVE IT EASY NOW, TRUST ME!
BECAUSE YOU'RE HERE MAKING OUT AND THINKING IT'S LOVE... THAT YOU ARE TWO HUMAN BEINGS WHO LOVE EACH OTHER...
THAT YOU'RE BURSTING WITH PURE LOVE...
WELL, HERE'S A NEWSFLASH: LOVE HAS ZIP TO DO WITH IT! YOU'RE JUST ANIMALS! ALL OF YOU!
7

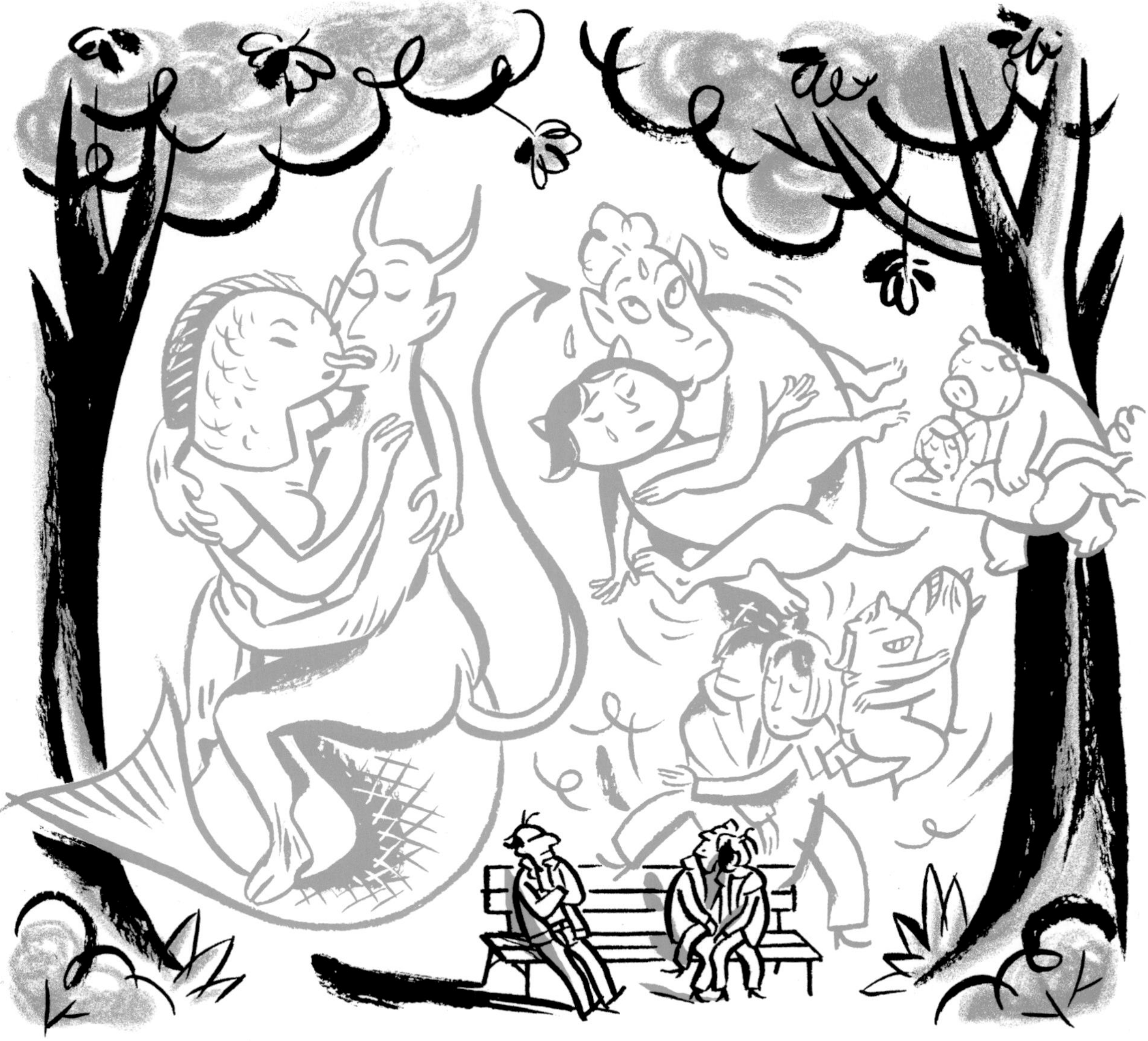

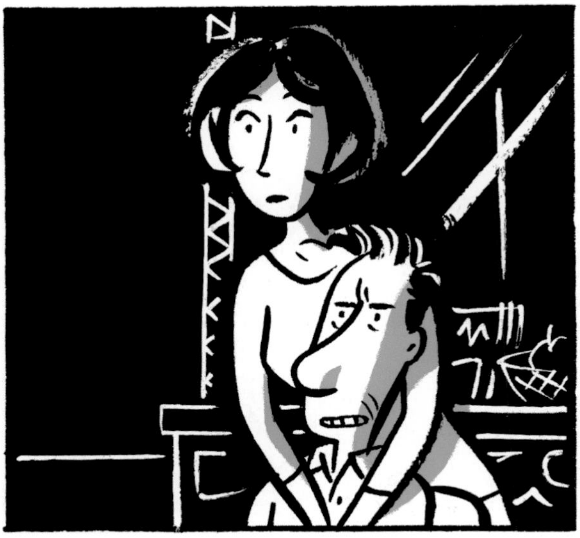

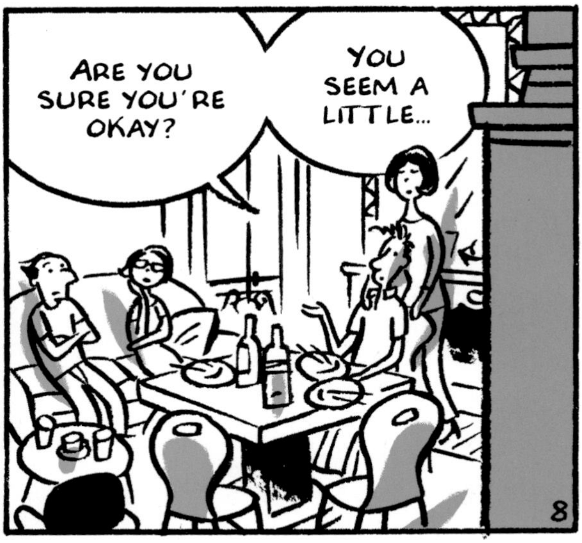
ARE YOU SURE YOU'RE OKAY?
YOU SEEM A LITTLE...
8

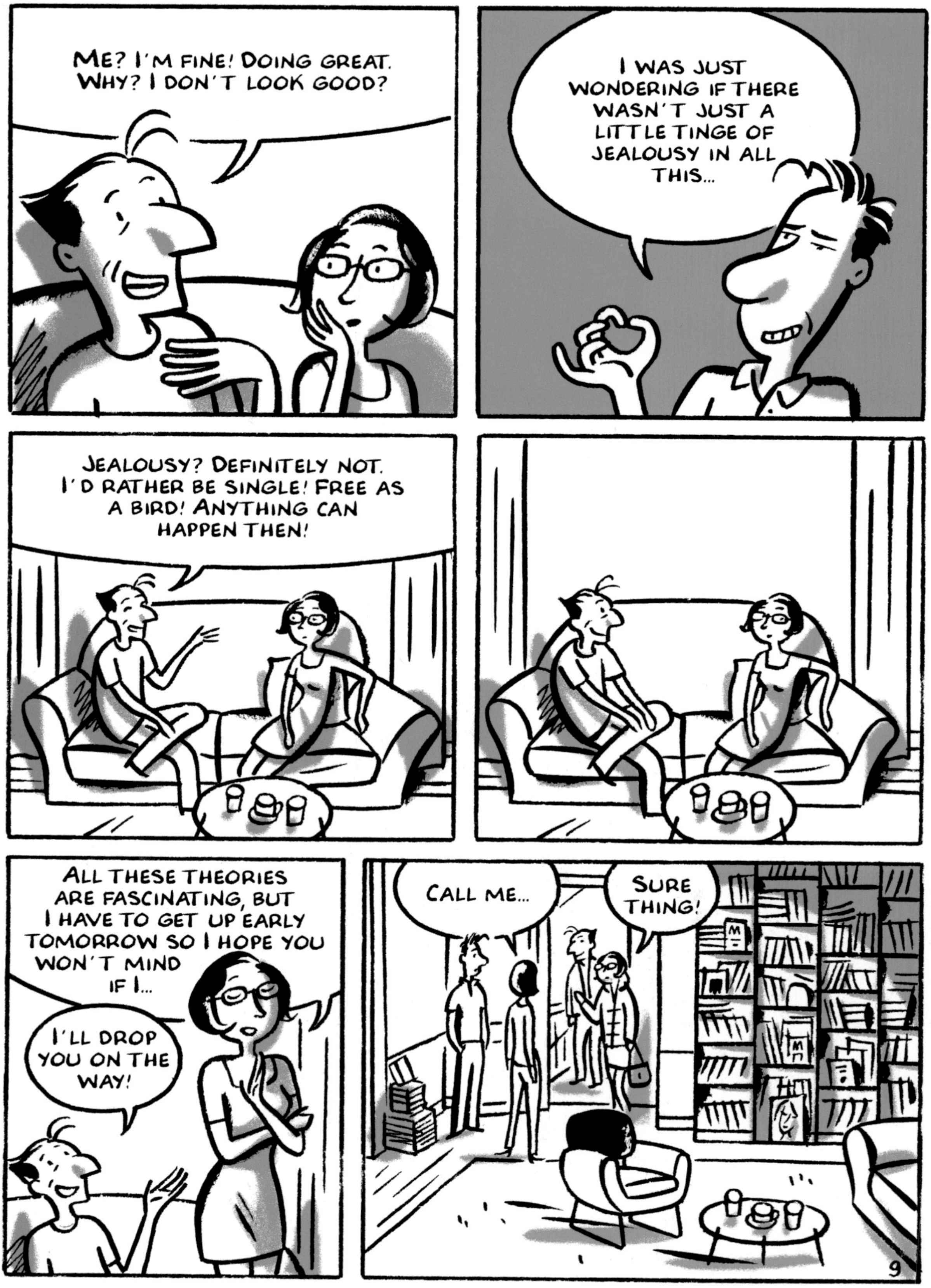
ME? I'M FINE! DOING GREAT. WHY? I DON'T LOOK GOOD?
I WAS JUST WONDERING IF THERE WASN'T JUST A LITTLE TINGE OF JEALOUSY IN ALL THIS...
JEALOUSY? DEFINITELY NOT. I'D RATHER BE SINGLE! FREE AS A BIRD! ANYTHING CAN HAPPEN THEN!
ALL THESE THEORIES ARE FASCINATING, BUT I HAVE TO GET UP EARLY TOMORROW SO I HOPE YOU WON'T MIND IF I...
I'LL DROP YOU ON THE WAY!
CALL ME...
SURE THING!
9

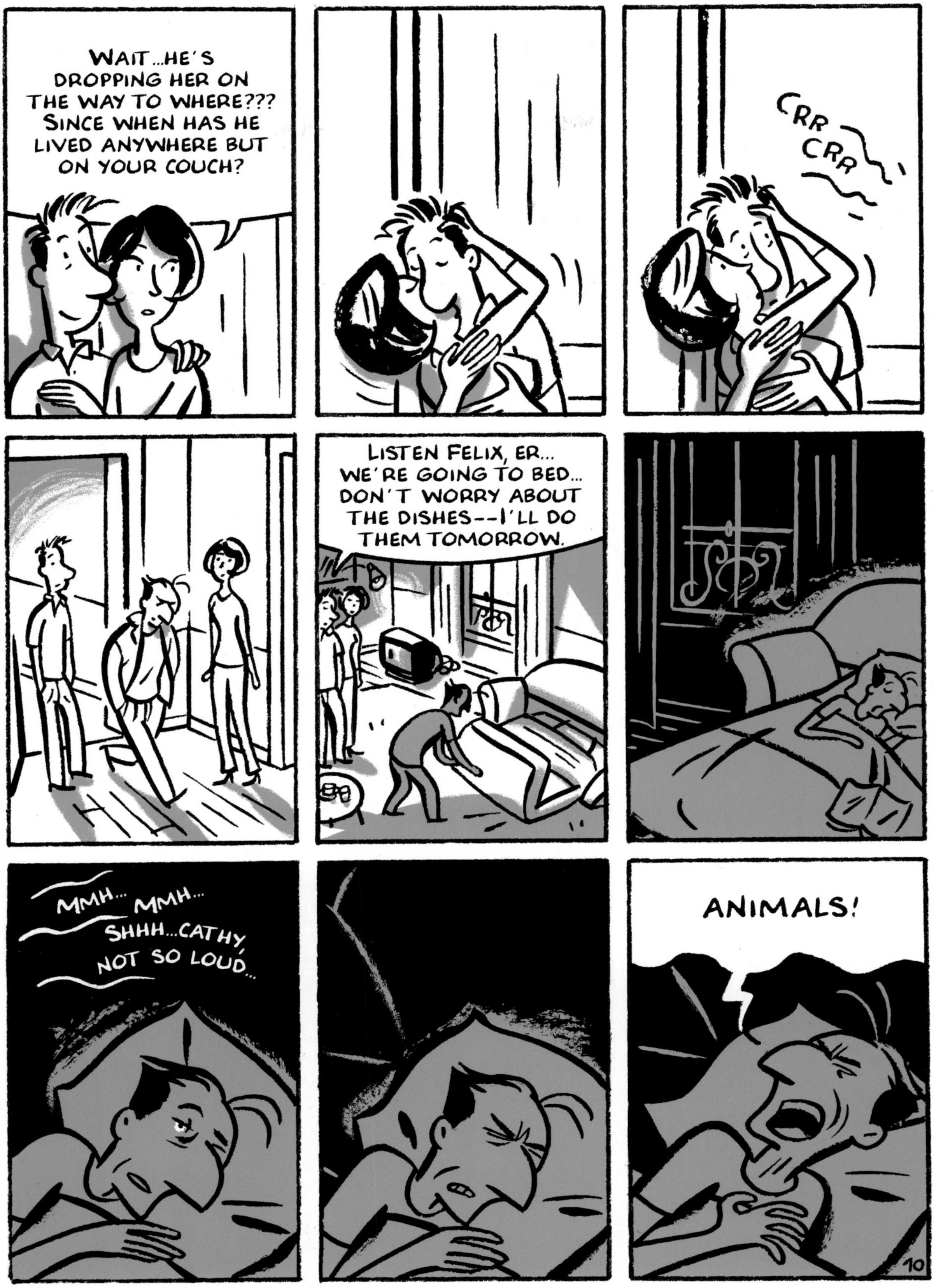
WAIT...HE'S DROPPING HER ON THE WAY TO WHERE??? SINCE WHEN HAS HE LIVED ANYWHERE BUT ON YOUR COUCH?
CRR CRR
LISTEN FELIX, ER... WE'RE GOING TO BED... DON'T WORRY ABOUT THE DISHES--I'LL DO THEM TOMORROW.
MMH... MMH...
SHHH...CATHY, NOT SO LOUD...
ANIMALS!
10

A BIRTHDAY PARTY IN THE COUNTRYSIDE

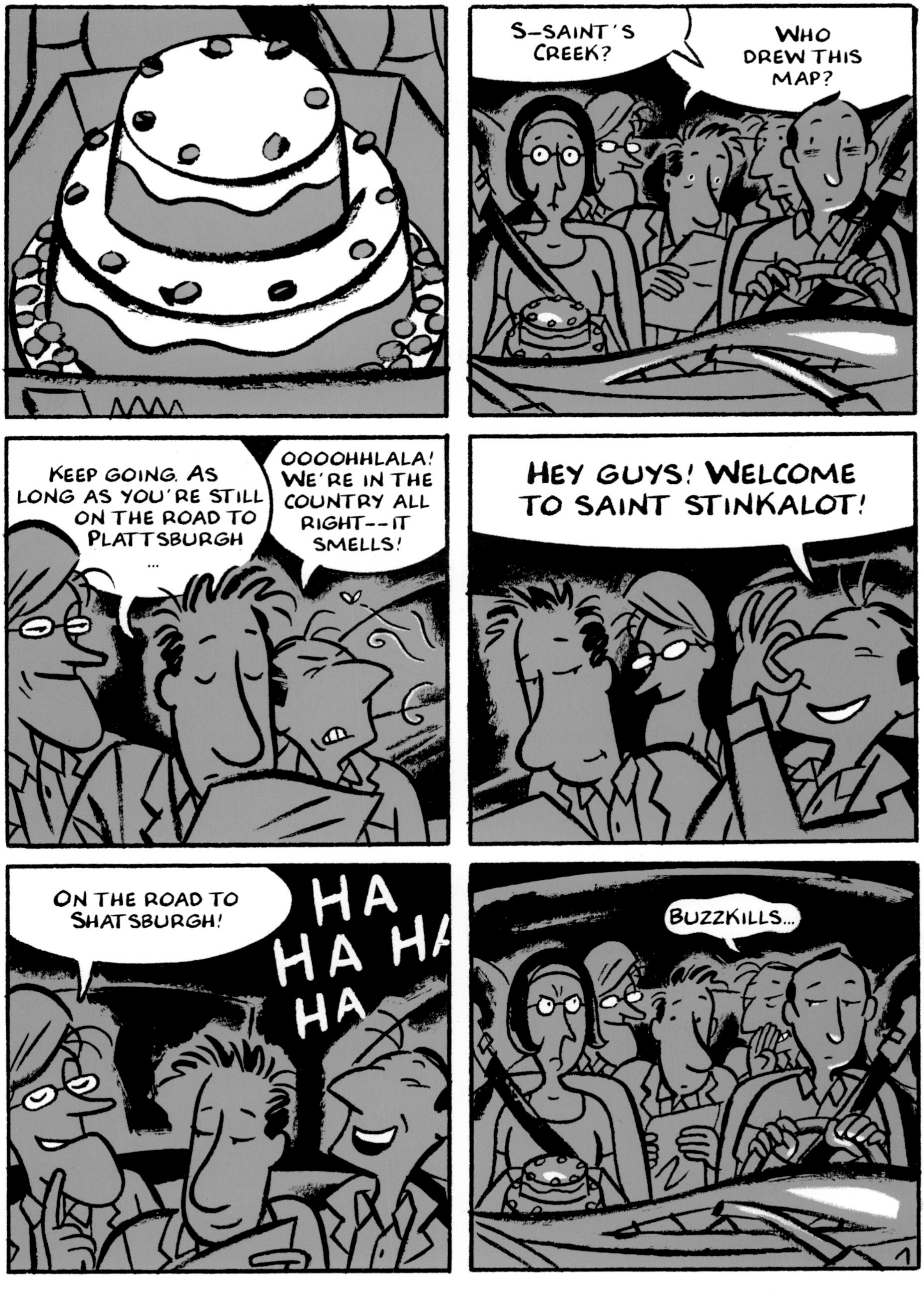
S-SAINT'S CREEK?
WHO DREW THIS MAP?
KEEP GOING. AS LONG AS YOU'RE STILL ON THE ROAD TO PLATTSBURGH ...
OOOOHHLALA! WE'RE IN THE COUNTRY ALL RIGHT--IT SMELLS!
HEY GUYS! WELCOME TO SAINT STINKALOT!
ON THE ROAD TO SHATSBURGH!
HA HA HA HA
BUZZKILLS...

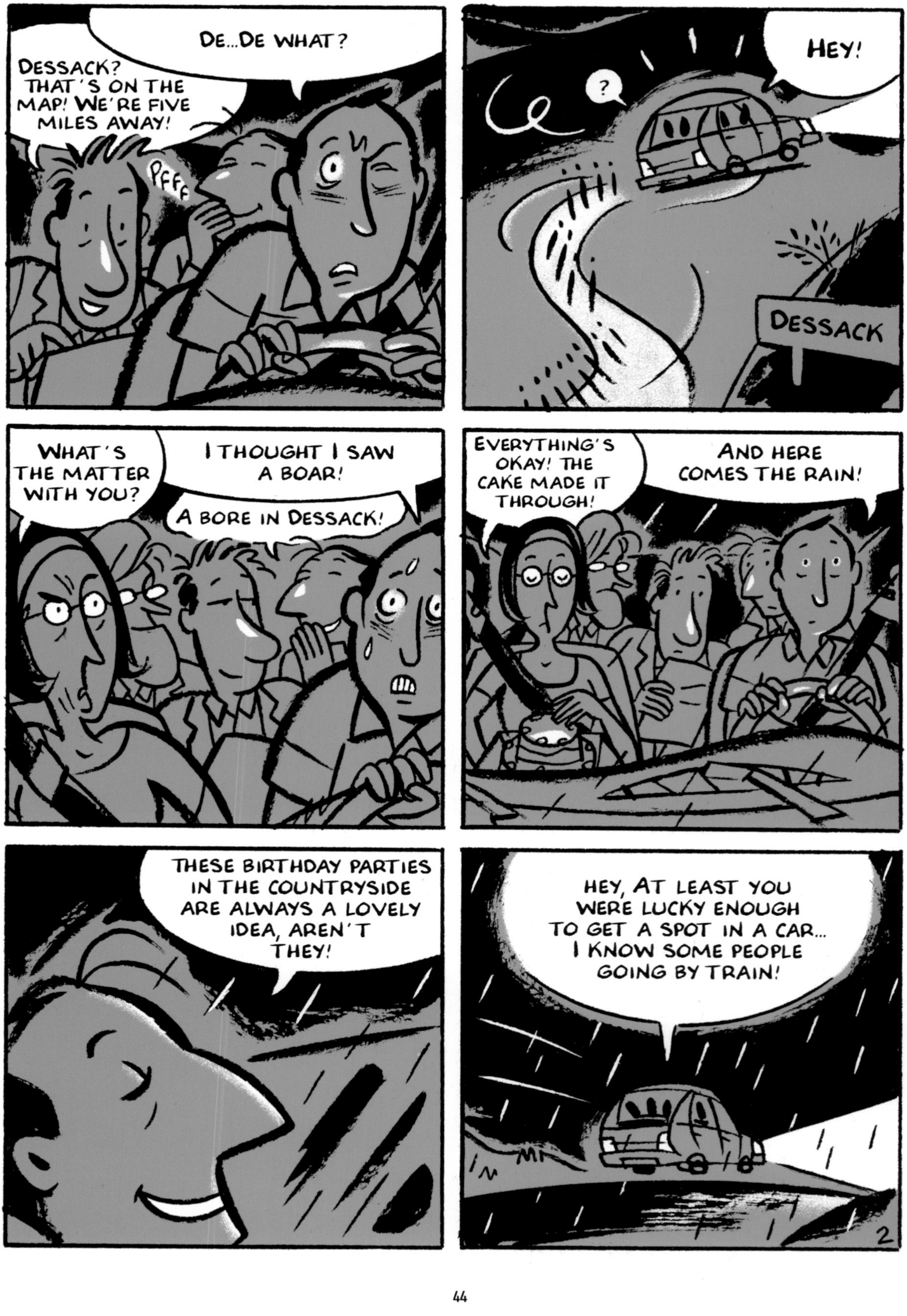
DE...DE WHAT?
DESSACK? THAT'S ON THE MAP! WE'RE FIVE MILES AWAY!
PFFF
HEY!
?
DESSACK
WHAT'S THE MATTER WITH YOU?
I THOUGHT I SAW A BOAR!
A BORE IN DESSACK!
EVERYTHING'S OKAY! THE CAKE MADE IT THROUGH!
AND HERE COMES THE RAIN!
THESE BIRTHDAY PARTIES IN THE COUNTRYSIDE ARE ALWAYS A LOVELY IDEA, AREN'T THEY!
HEY, AT LEAST YOU WERE LUCKY ENOUGH TO GET A SPOT IN A CAR... I KNOW SOME PEOPLE GOING BY TRAIN!
2

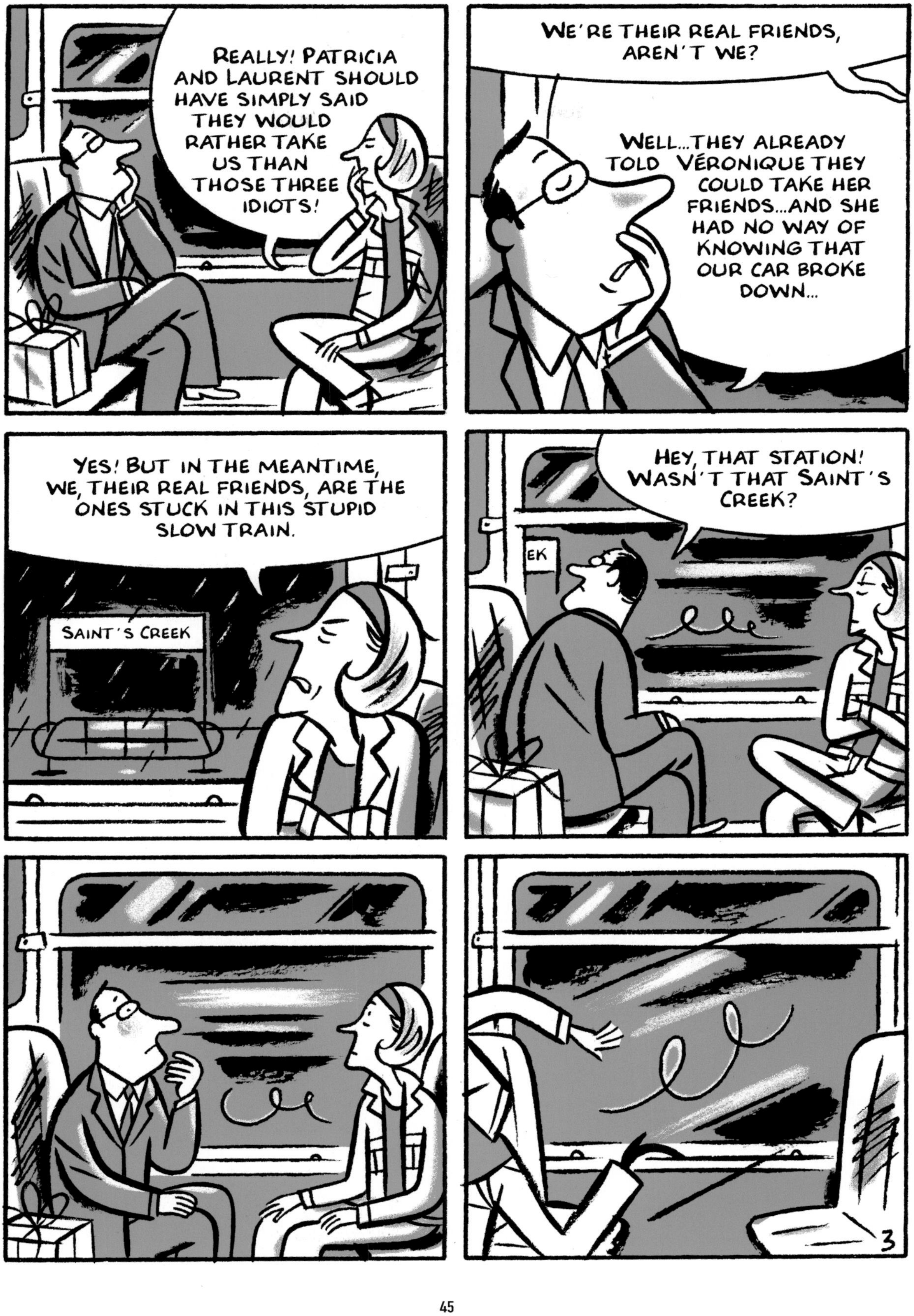
REALLY! PATRICIA AND LAURENT SHOULD HAVE SIMPLY SAID THEY WOULD RATHER TAKE US THAN THOSE THREE IDIOTS!
WE'RE THEIR REAL FRIENDS, AREN'T WE?
WELL... THEY ALREADY TOLD VÉRONIQUE THEY COULD TAKE HER FRIENDS... AND SHE HAD NO WAY OF KNOWING THAT OUR CAR BROKE DOWN...
YES! BUT IN THE MEANTIME, WE, THEIR REAL FRIENDS, ARE THE ONES STUCK IN THIS STUPID SLOW TRAIN.
SAINT'S CREEK
HEY, THAT STATION! WASN'T THAT SAINT'S CREEK?
EK
3

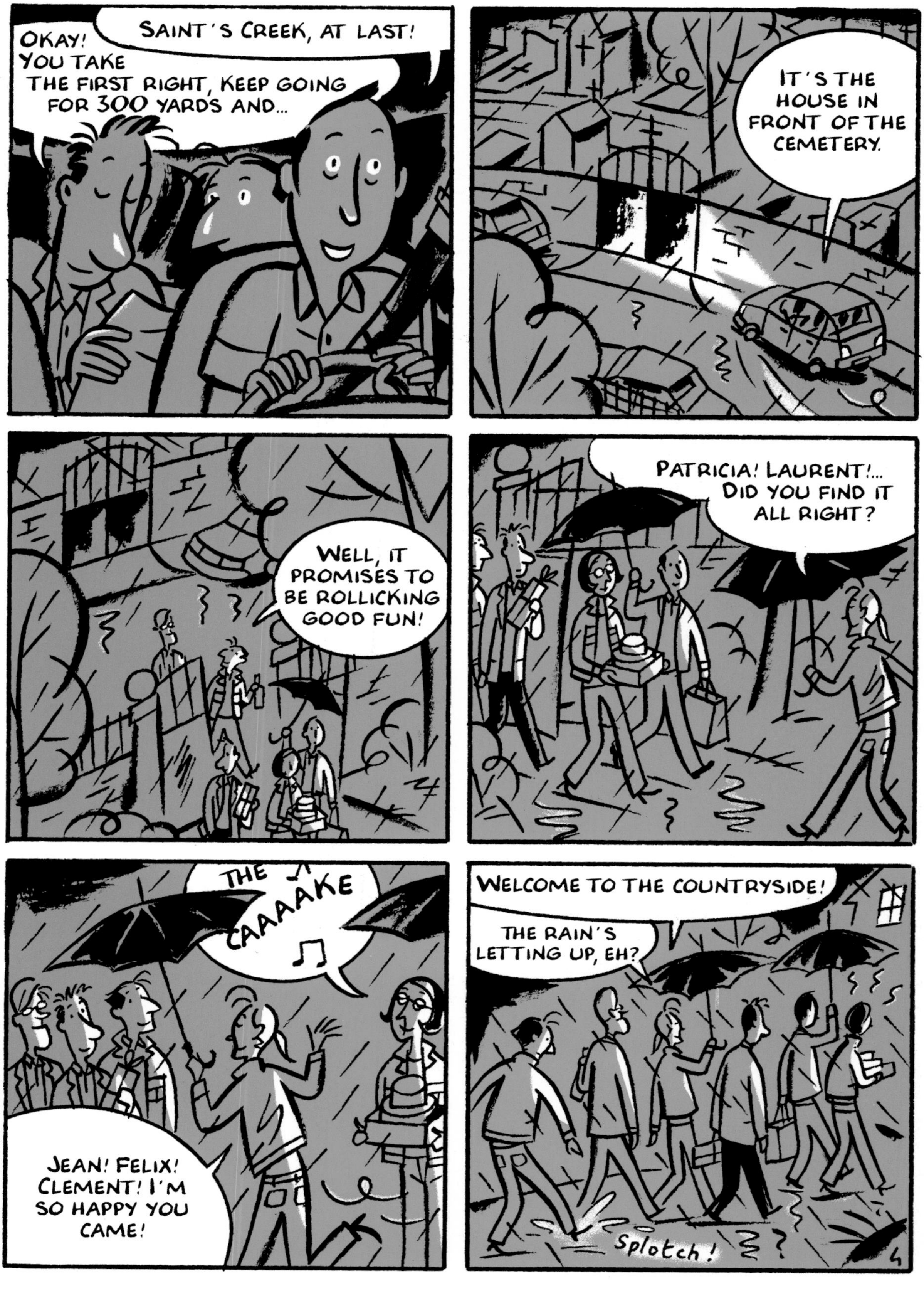
SAINT'S CREEK, AT LAST!
OKAY! YOU TAKE THE FIRST RIGHT, KEEP GOING FOR 300 YARDS AND...
IT'S THE HOUSE IN FRONT OF THE CEMETERY.
WELL, IT PROMISES TO BE ROLLICKING GOOD FUN!
PATRICIA! LAURENT!... DID YOU FIND IT ALL RIGHT?
THE CAAAAKE
JEAN! FELIX! CLEMENT! I'M SO HAPPY YOU CAME!
WELCOME TO THE COUNTRYSIDE!
THE RAIN'S LETTING UP, EH?
Splotch!

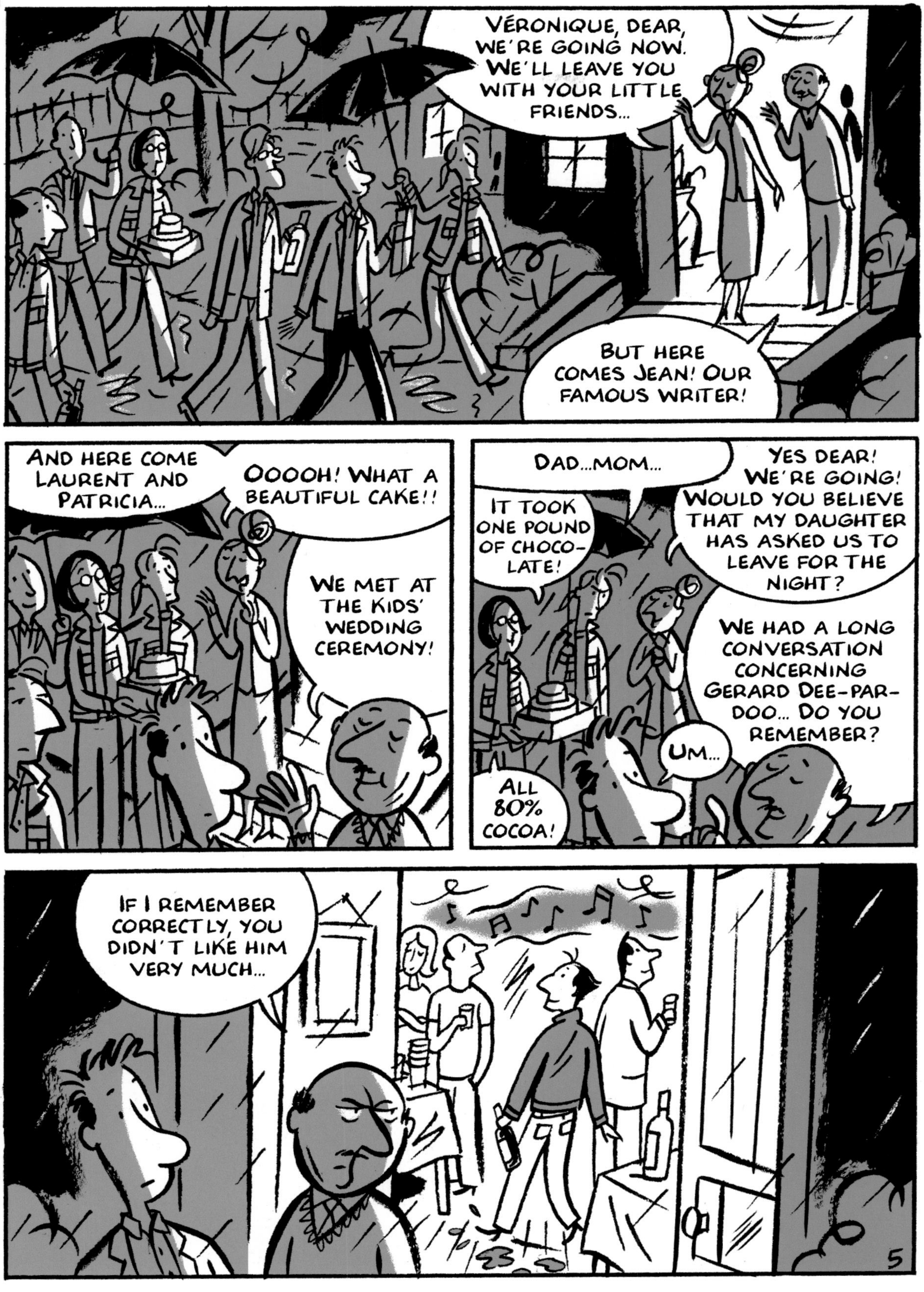
VÉRONIQUE, DEAR, WE'RE GOING NOW. WE'LL LEAVE YOU WITH YOUR LITTLE FRIENDS...
BUT HERE COMES JEAN! OUR FAMOUS WRITER!
AND HERE COME LAURENT AND PATRICIA...
OOOOH! WHAT A BEAUTIFUL CAKE!!
WE MET AT THE KIDS' WEDDING CEREMONY!
DAD...MOM...
IT TOOK ONE POUND OF CHOCO-LATE!
ALL 80% COCOA!
YES DEAR! WE'RE GOING! WOULD YOU BELIEVE THAT MY DAUGHTER HAS ASKED US TO LEAVE FOR THE NIGHT?
WE HAD A LONG CONVERSATION CONCERNING GERARD DEE-PAR-DOO... DO YOU REMEMBER?
UM...
IF I REMEMBER CORRECTLY, YOU DIDN'T LIKE HIM VERY MUCH...
5

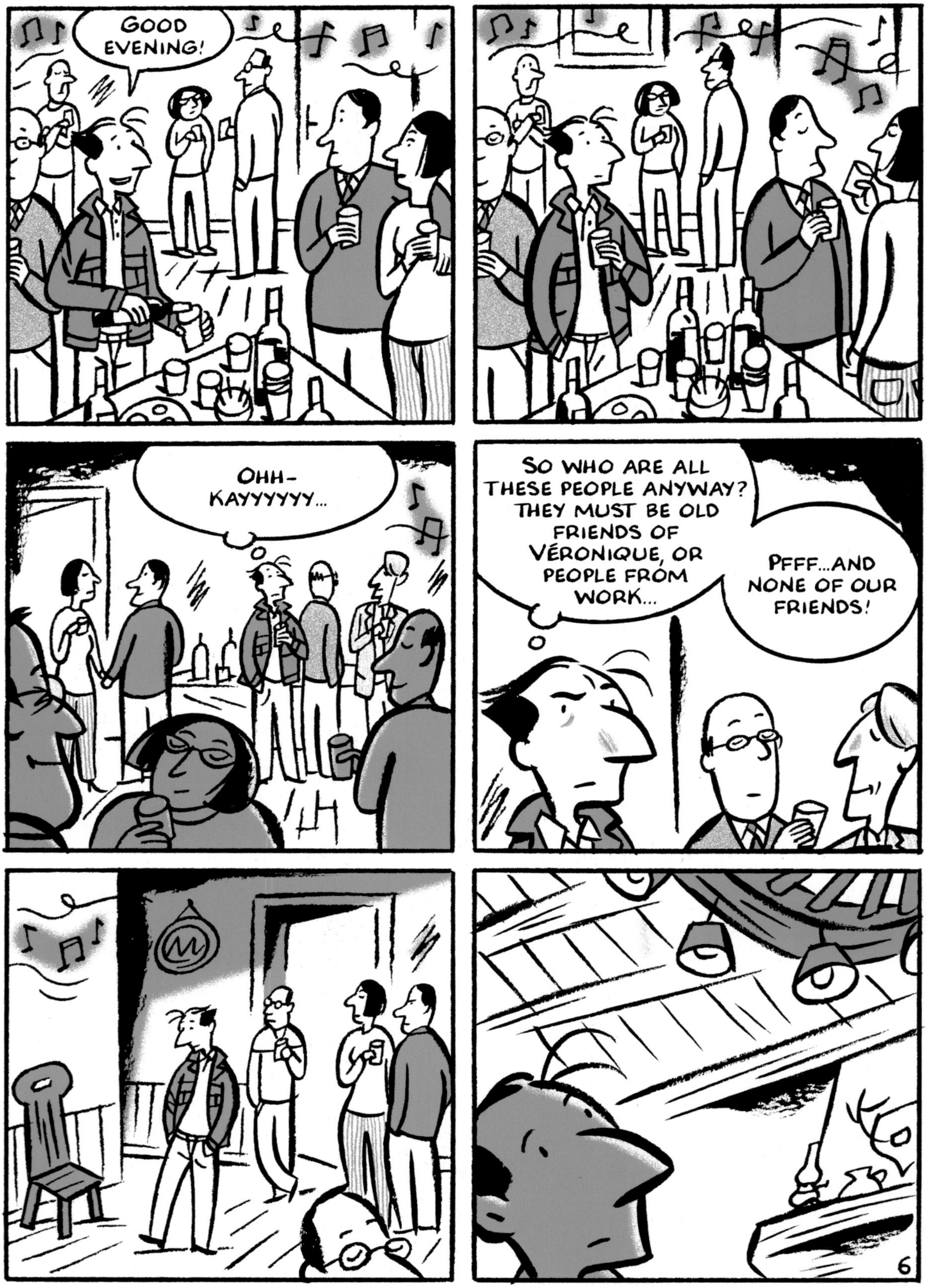
GOOD EVENING!
OHH-KAYYYYYY...
SO WHO ARE ALL THESE PEOPLE ANYWAY? THEY MUST BE OLD FRIENDS OF VÉRONIQUE, OR PEOPLE FROM WORK...
PFFF...AND NONE OF OUR FRIENDS!
6

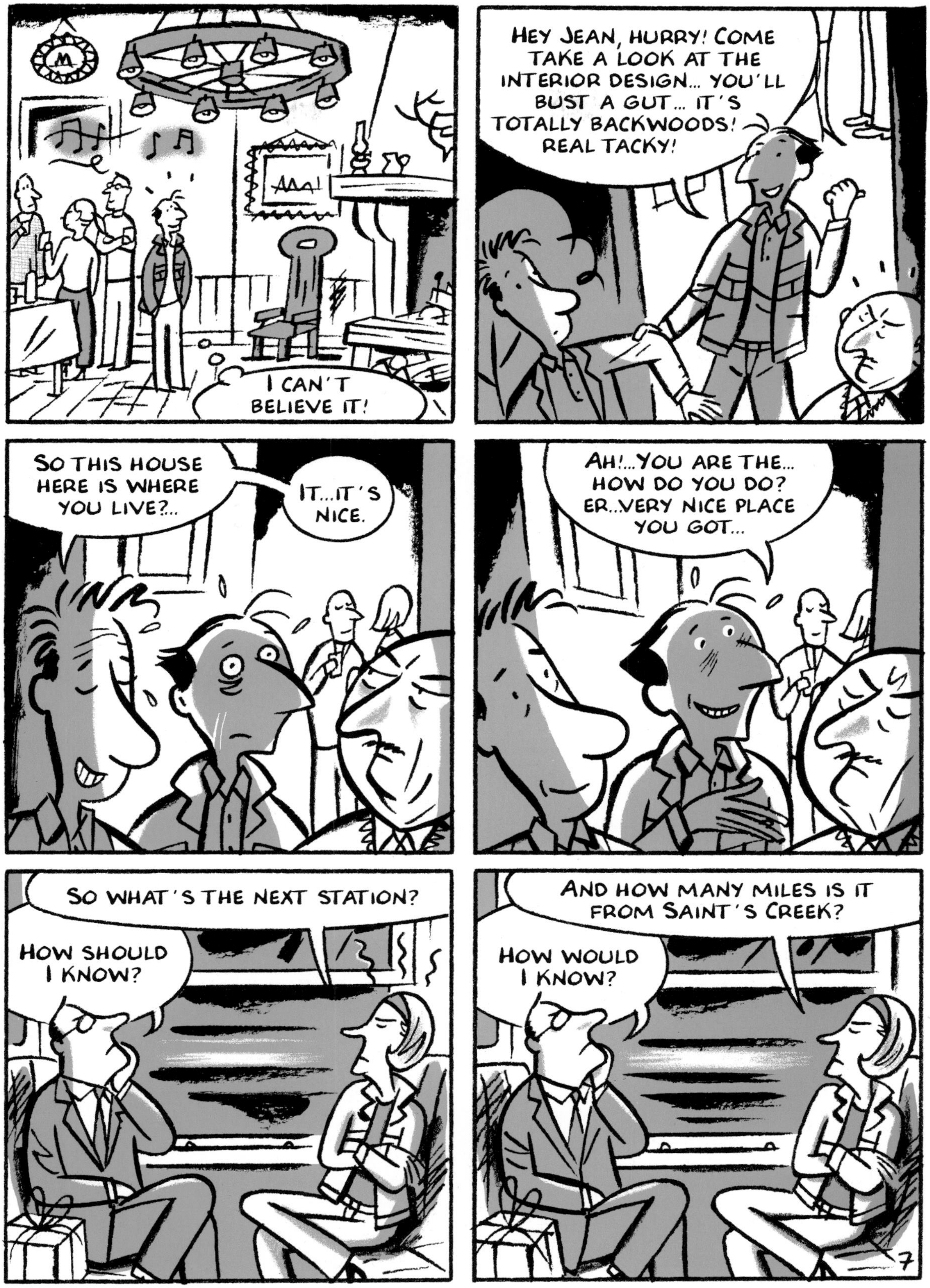
I CAN'T BELIEVE IT!
HEY JEAN, HURRY! COME TAKE A LOOK AT THE INTERIOR DESIGN... YOU'LL BUST A GUT... IT'S TOTALLY BACKWOODS! REAL TACKY!
SO THIS HOUSE HERE IS WHERE YOU LIVE?...
IT...IT'S NICE.
AH!...YOU ARE THE... HOW DO YOU DO? ER...VERY NICE PLACE YOU GOT...
SO WHAT'S THE NEXT STATION?
HOW SHOULD I KNOW?
AND HOW MANY MILES IS IT FROM SAINT'S CREEK?
HOW WOULD I KNOW?
7

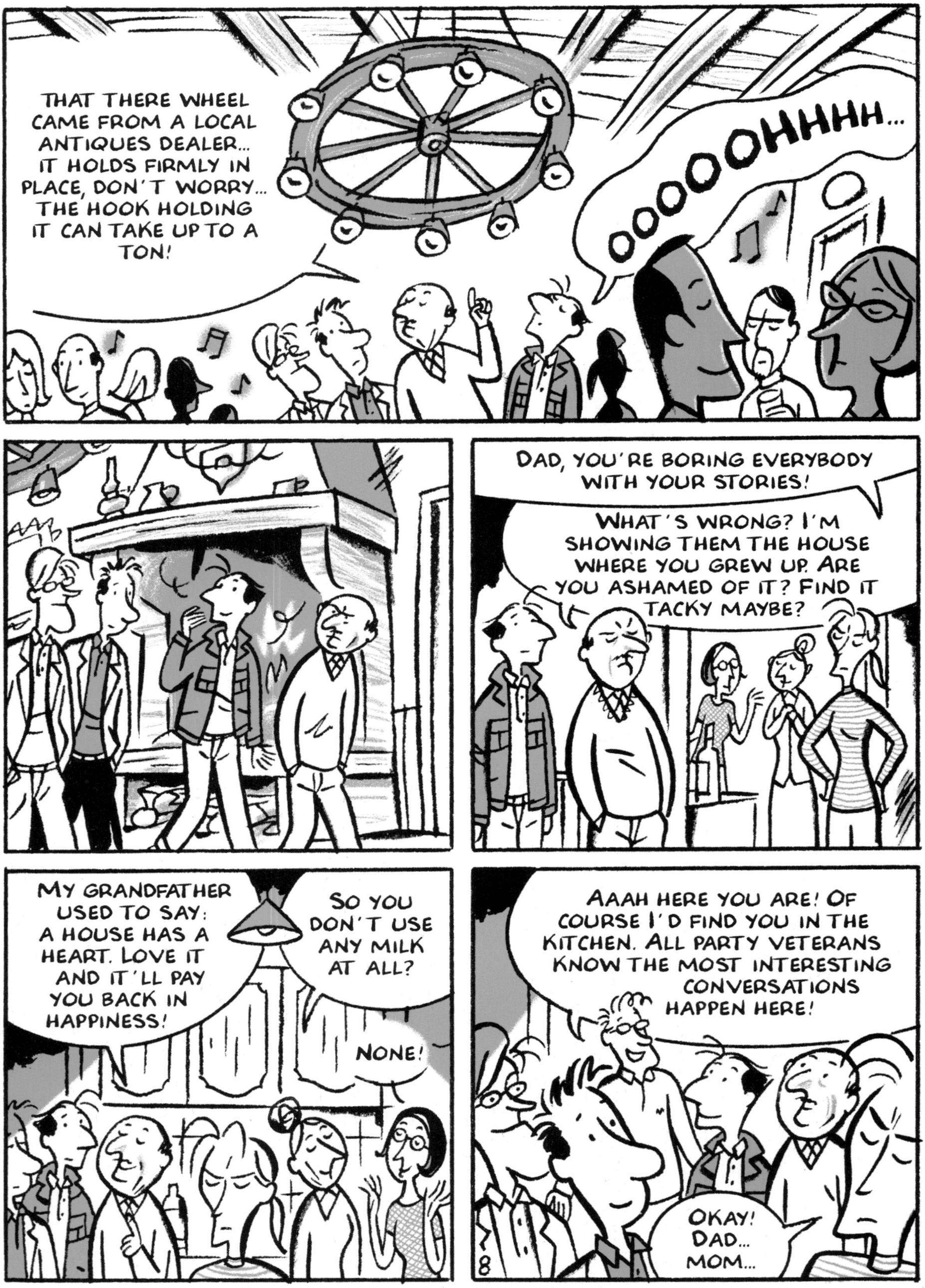

THAT THERE WHEEL CAME FROM A LOCAL ANTIQUES DEALER... IT HOLDS FIRMLY IN PLACE, DON'T WORRY... THE HOOK HOLDING IT CAN TAKE UP TO A TON!
OOOOOOHHHH...
DAD, YOU'RE BORING EVERYBODY WITH YOUR STORIES!
WHAT'S WRONG? I'M SHOWING THEM THE HOUSE WHERE YOU GREW UP. ARE YOU ASHAMED OF IT? FIND IT TACKY MAYBE?
MY GRANDFATHER USED TO SAY: A HOUSE HAS A HEART. LOVE IT AND IT'LL PAY YOU BACK IN HAPPINESS!
SO YOU DON'T USE ANY MILK AT ALL?
NONE!
AAAH HERE YOU ARE! OF COURSE I'D FIND YOU IN THE KITCHEN. ALL PARTY VETERANS KNOW THE MOST INTERESTING CONVERSATIONS HAPPEN HERE!
OKAY! DAD... MOM...

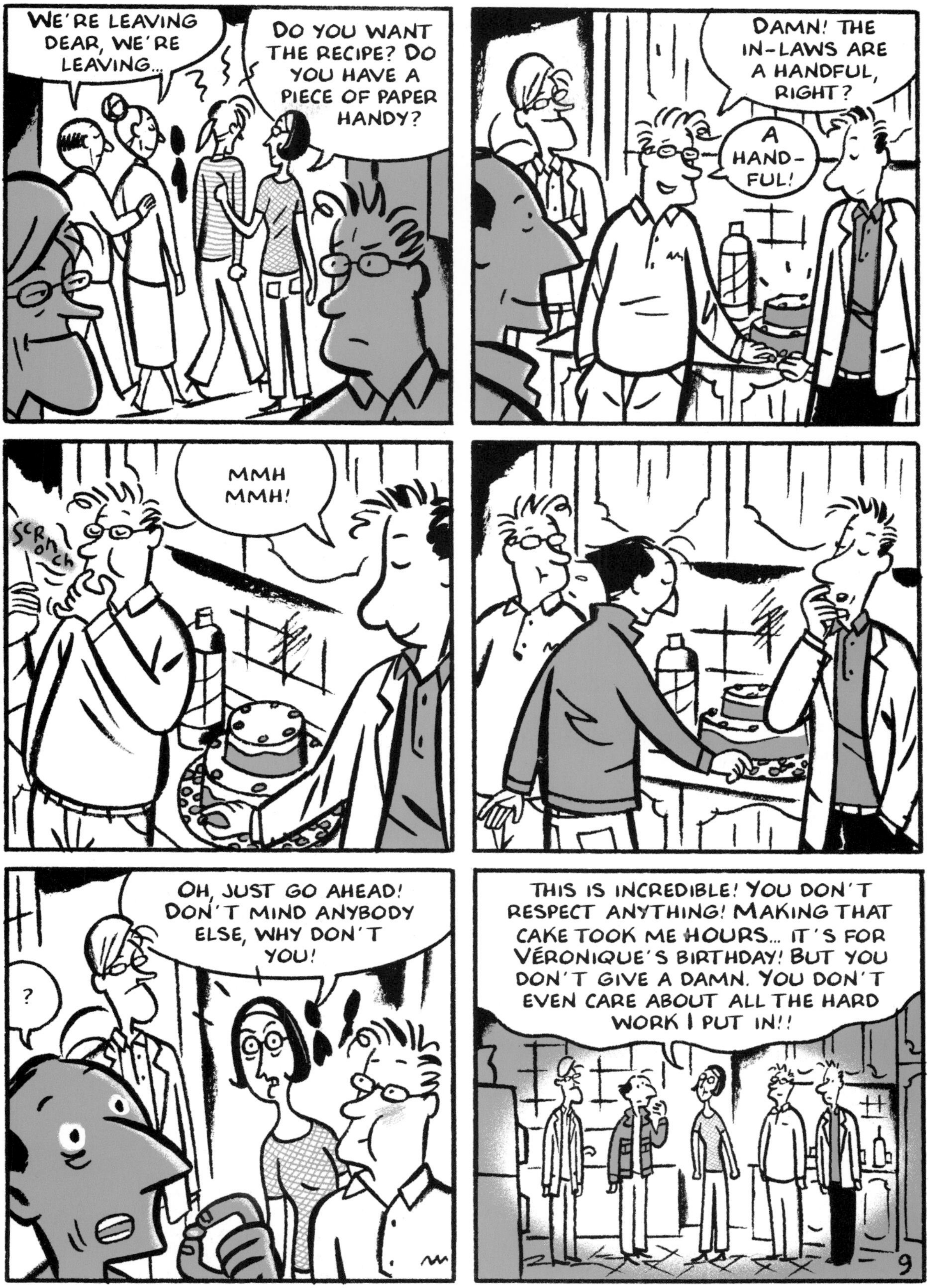

WE'RE LEAVING DEAR, WE'RE LEAVING...
DO YOU WANT THE RECIPE? DO YOU HAVE A PIECE OF PAPER HANDY?
DAMN! THE IN-LAWS ARE A HANDFUL, RIGHT?
A HANDFUL!
SCRONCH
MMH MMH!
OH, JUST GO AHEAD! DON'T MIND ANYBODY ELSE, WHY DON'T YOU!
?
THIS IS INCREDIBLE! YOU DON'T RESPECT ANYTHING! MAKING THAT CAKE TOOK ME HOURS... IT'S FOR VÉRONIQUE'S BIRTHDAY! BUT YOU DON'T GIVE A DAMN. YOU DON'T EVEN CARE ABOUT ALL THE HARD WORK I PUT IN!!
9

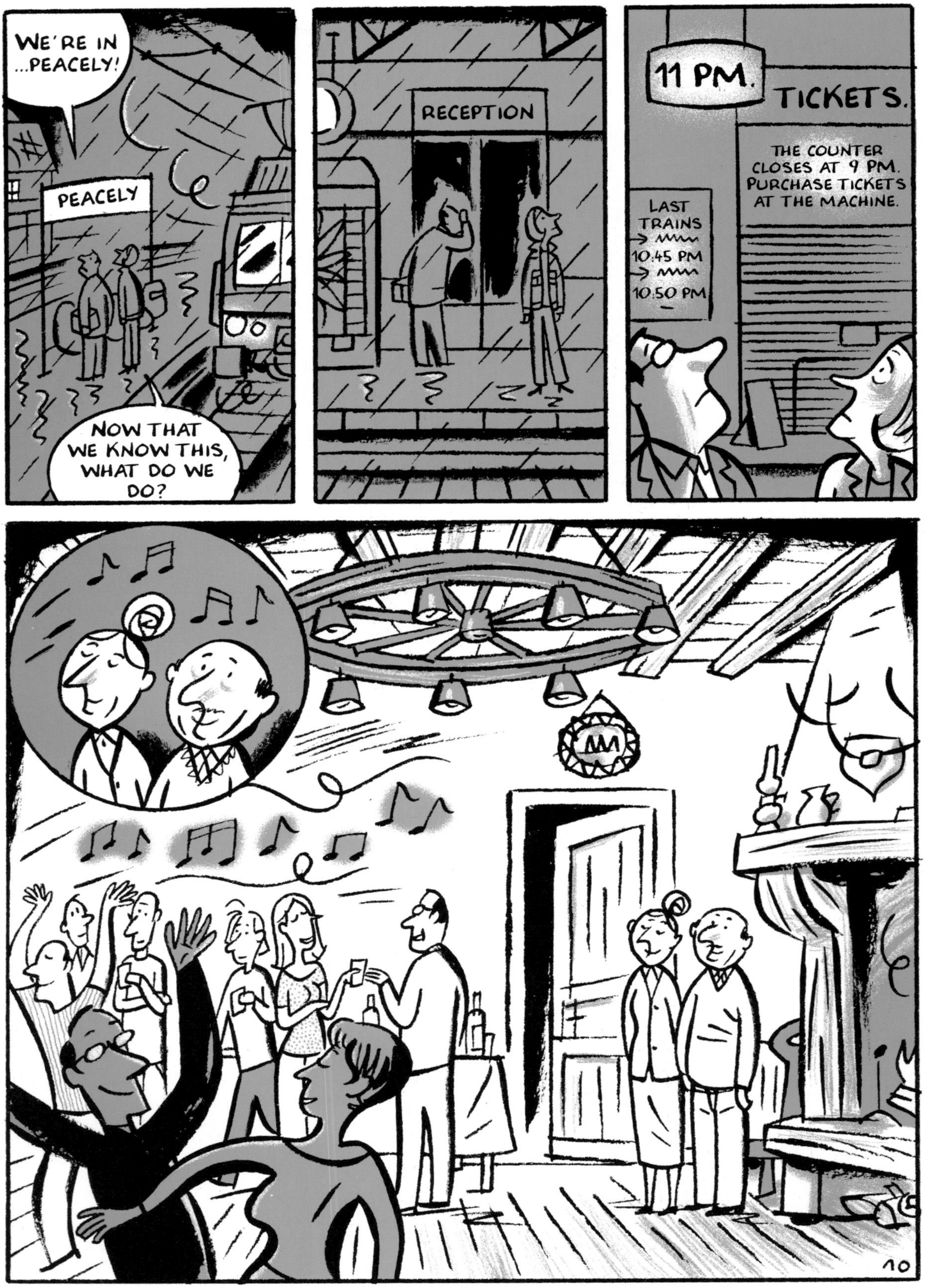
WE'RE IN ...PEACELY!
PEACELY
NOW THAT WE KNOW THIS, WHAT DO WE DO?
RECEPTION
11 PM.
TICKETS.
THE COUNTER CLOSES AT 9 PM. PURCHASE TICKETS AT THE MACHINE.
LAST TRAINS
10:45 PM
10:50 PM
10

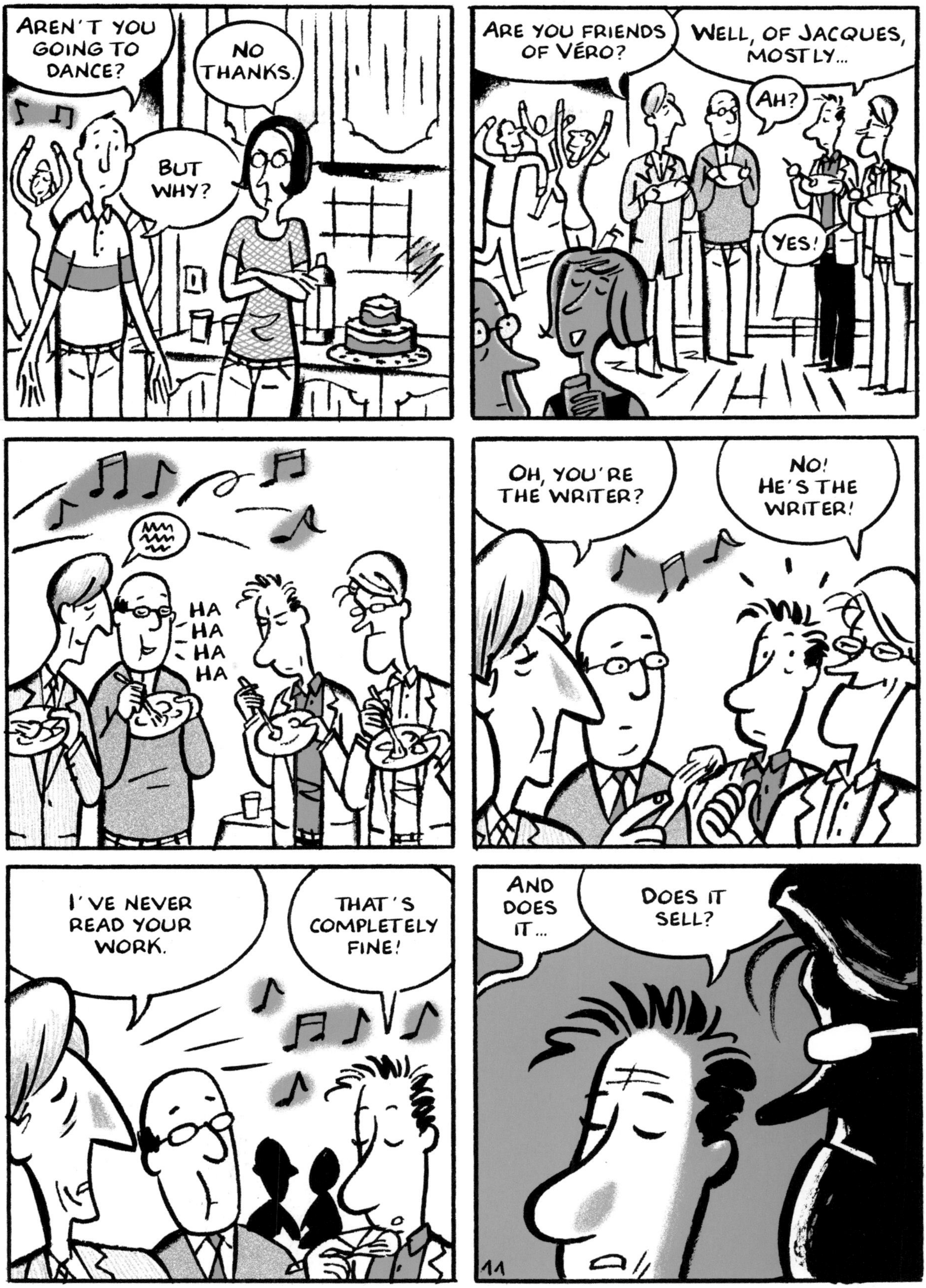
AREN'T YOU GOING TO DANCE?
NO THANKS.
BUT WHY?
ARE YOU FRIENDS OF VÉRO?
WELL, OF JACQUES, MOSTLY...
AH?
YES!
HA HA HA HA
OH, YOU'RE THE WRITER?
NO! HE'S THE WRITER!
I'VE NEVER READ YOUR WORK.
THAT'S COMPLETELY FINE!
AND DOES IT...
DOES IT SELL?
11

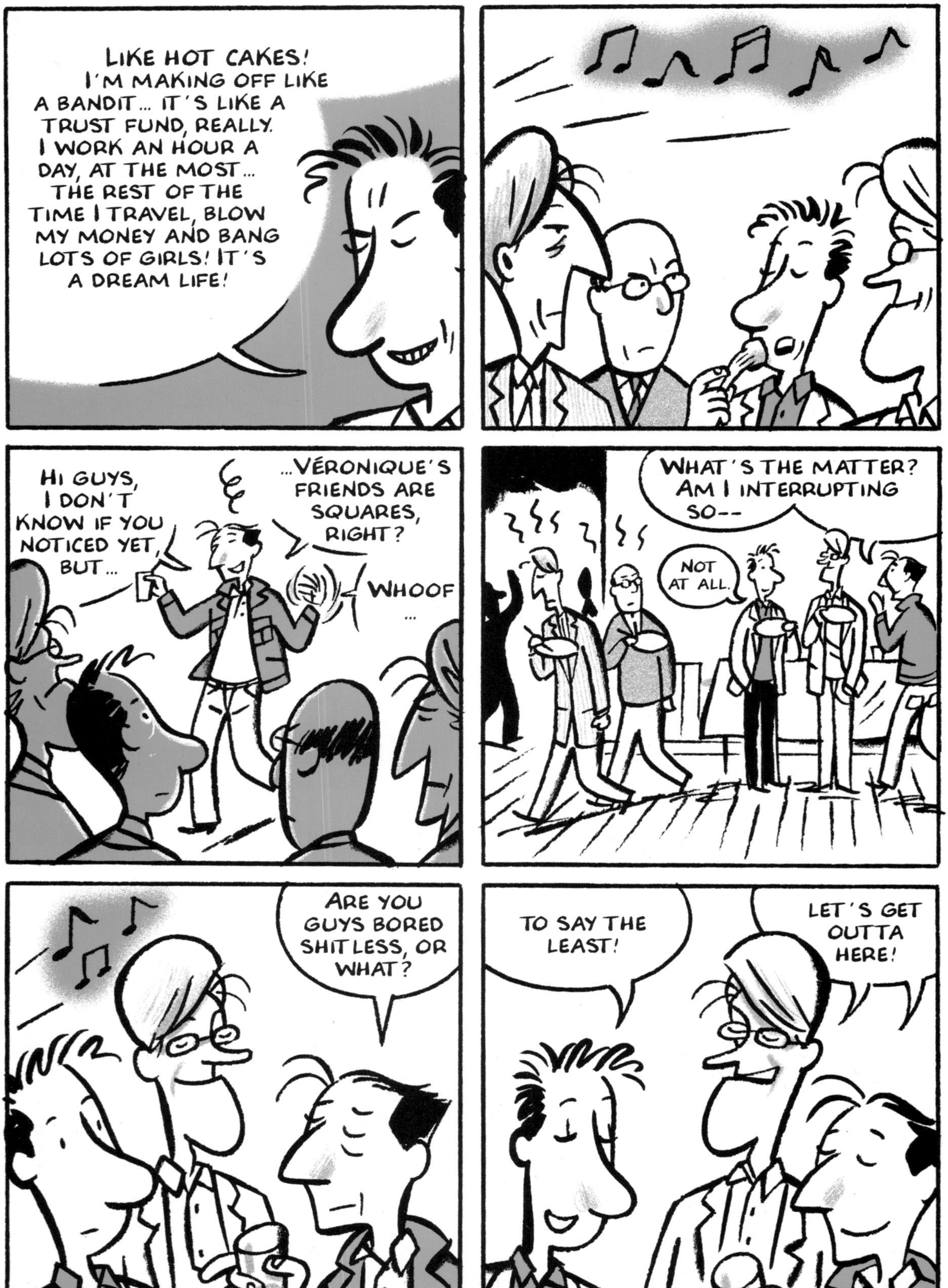
LIKE HOT CAKES! I'M MAKING OFF LIKE A BANDIT... IT'S LIKE A TRUST FUND, REALLY. I WORK AN HOUR A DAY, AT THE MOST... THE REST OF THE TIME I TRAVEL, BLOW MY MONEY AND BANG LOTS OF GIRLS! IT'S A DREAM LIFE!
HI GUYS, I DON'T KNOW IF YOU NOTICED YET, BUT...
...VÉRONIQUE'S FRIENDS ARE SQUARES, RIGHT?
WHOOF ...
WHAT'S THE MATTER? AM I INTERRUPTING SO--
NOT AT ALL.
ARE YOU GUYS BORED SHITLESS, OR WHAT?
TO SAY THE LEAST!
LET'S GET OUTTA HERE!

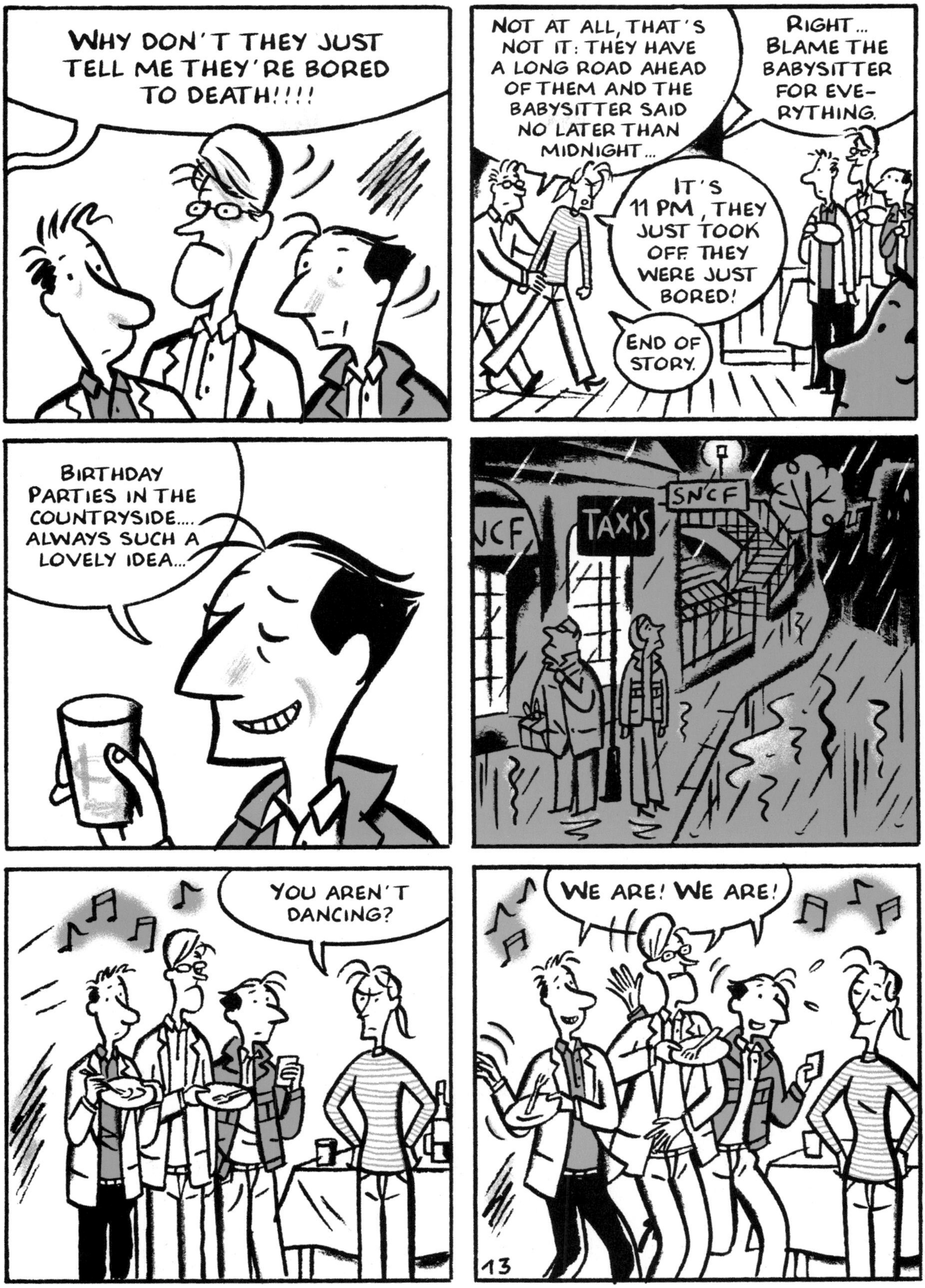
WHY DON'T THEY JUST TELL ME THEY'RE BORED TO DEATH!!!!
NOT AT ALL, THAT'S NOT IT: THEY HAVE A LONG ROAD AHEAD OF THEM AND THE BABYSITTER SAID NO LATER THAN MIDNIGHT...
RIGHT... BLAME THE BABYSITTER FOR EVE-RYTHING.
IT'S 11 PM, THEY JUST TOOK OFF. THEY WERE JUST BORED!
END OF STORY.
BIRTHDAY PARTIES IN THE COUNTRYSIDE.... ALWAYS SUCH A LOVELY IDEA...
SNCF
TAXIS
NCF
YOU AREN'T DANCING?
WE ARE! WE ARE!
13

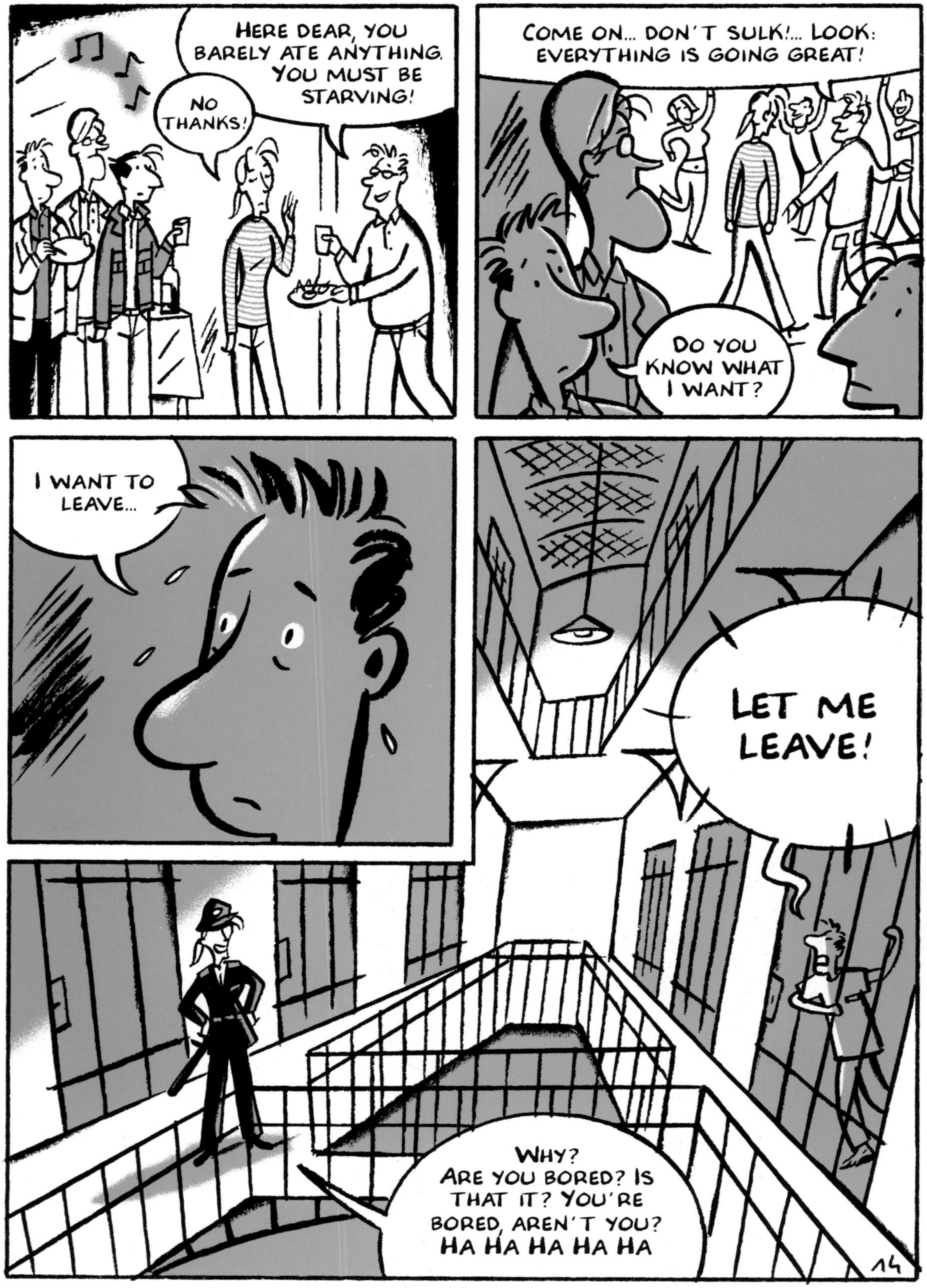
HERE DEAR, YOU BARELY ATE ANYTHING. YOU MUST BE STARVING!
NO THANKS!
COME ON... DON'T SULK!... LOOK: EVERYTHING IS GOING GREAT!
DO YOU KNOW WHAT I WANT?
I WANT TO LEAVE...
LET ME LEAVE!
WHY? ARE YOU BORED? IS THAT IT? YOU'RE BORED, AREN'T YOU? HA HA HA HA HA
14

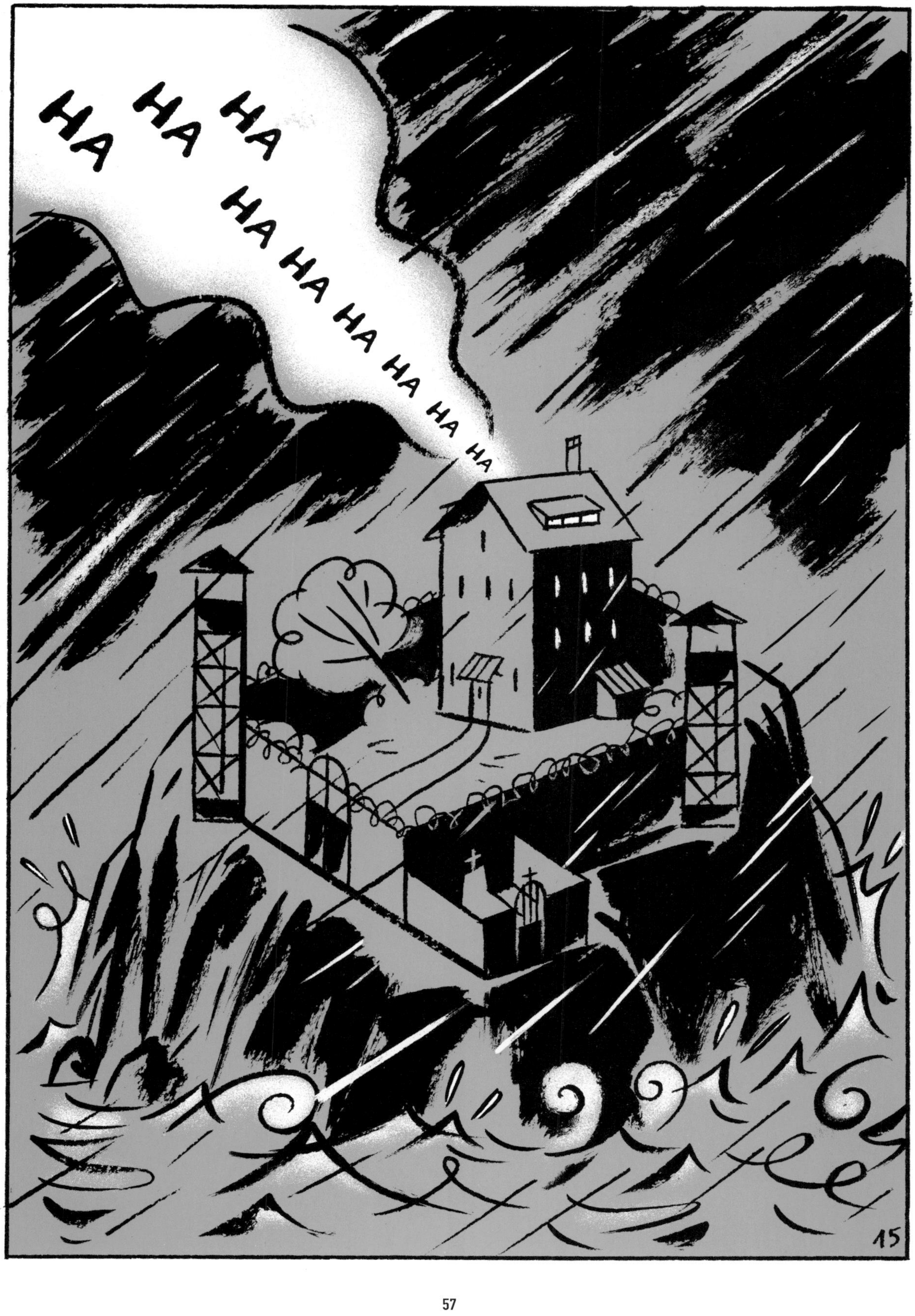
HA HA HA
HA HA HA HA HA HA
15

...BUT I DON'T THINK IT'S GOING TO BE AN EASY FEAT!

WAIT, I'M GOING TO ASK LAURENT AND PATRICIA, I SAW THEM EARLIER IN THE KITCHEN. THEY LOOK SERIOUSLY BORED TOO...

UM, FELIX, WAIT...

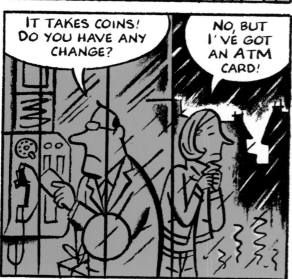

IT TAKES COINS! DO YOU HAVE ANY CHANGE?

NO, BUT I'VE GOT AN ATM CARD!

LET'S GET SOME CASH AND MAKE SOME CHANGE THEN...

WHERE?

SO, I FOUND PATRICIA, STILL IN THE KITCHEN, AND SHE TOLD ME SHE WAS HAVING A BALL AND THAT IT WAS RUDE TO LEAVE BEFORE THE BIRTHDAY CAKE...

BUT REALLY, SHE LOOKED LIKE SHE WAS BORED OUT OF HER MIND TOO...

GOOD GOD! THE CAKE, THAT'S IT!!

16

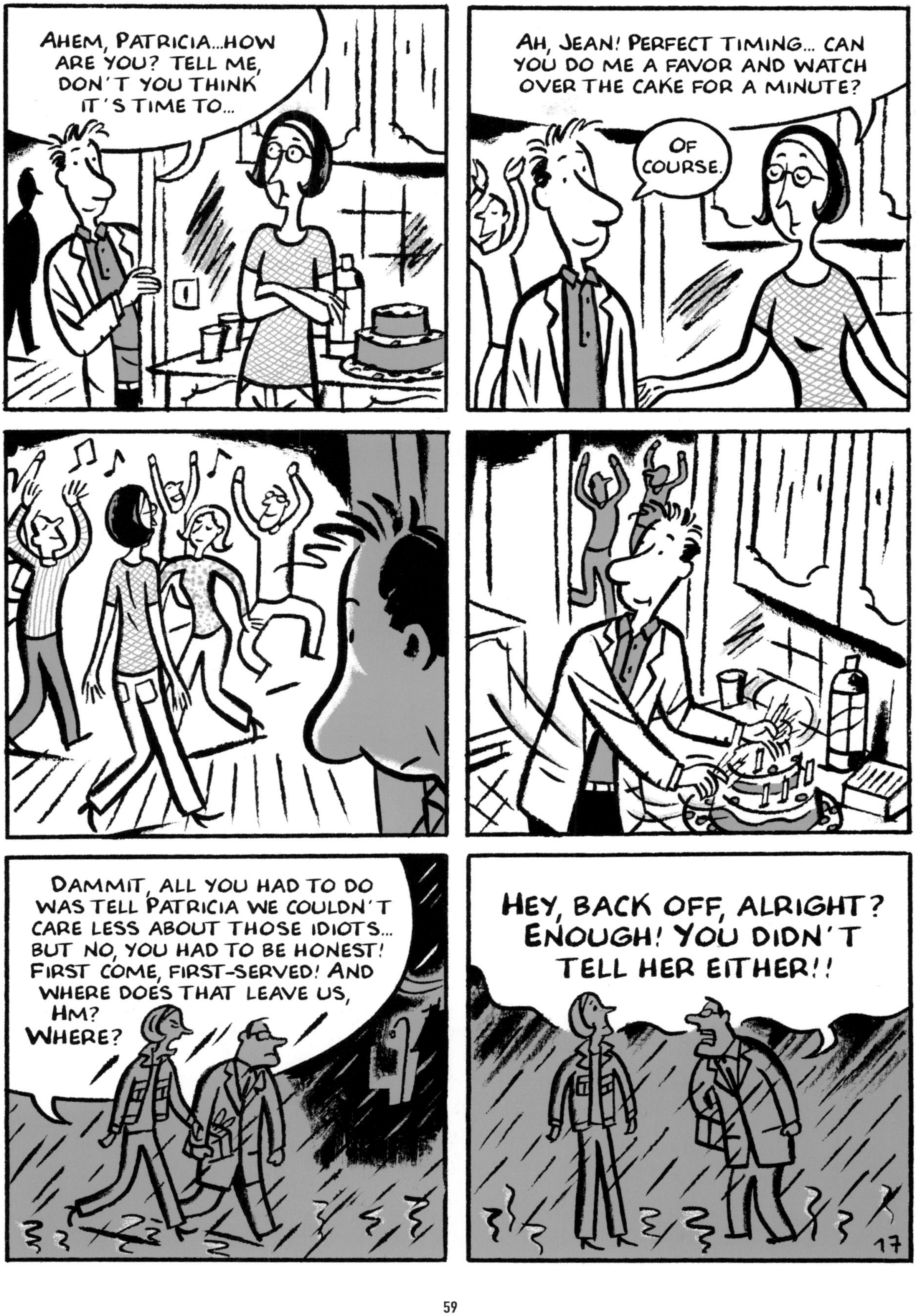
AHEM, PATRICIA...HOW ARE YOU? TELL ME, DON'T YOU THINK IT'S TIME TO...
AH, JEAN! PERFECT TIMING... CAN YOU DO ME A FAVOR AND WATCH OVER THE CAKE FOR A MINUTE?
OF COURSE.
DAMMIT, ALL YOU HAD TO DO WAS TELL PATRICIA WE COULDN'T CARE LESS ABOUT THOSE IDIOTS... BUT NO, YOU HAD TO BE HONEST! FIRST COME, FIRST-SERVED! AND WHERE DOES THAT LEAVE US, HM? WHERE?
HEY, BACK OFF, ALRIGHT? ENOUGH! YOU DIDN'T TELL HER EITHER!!
17

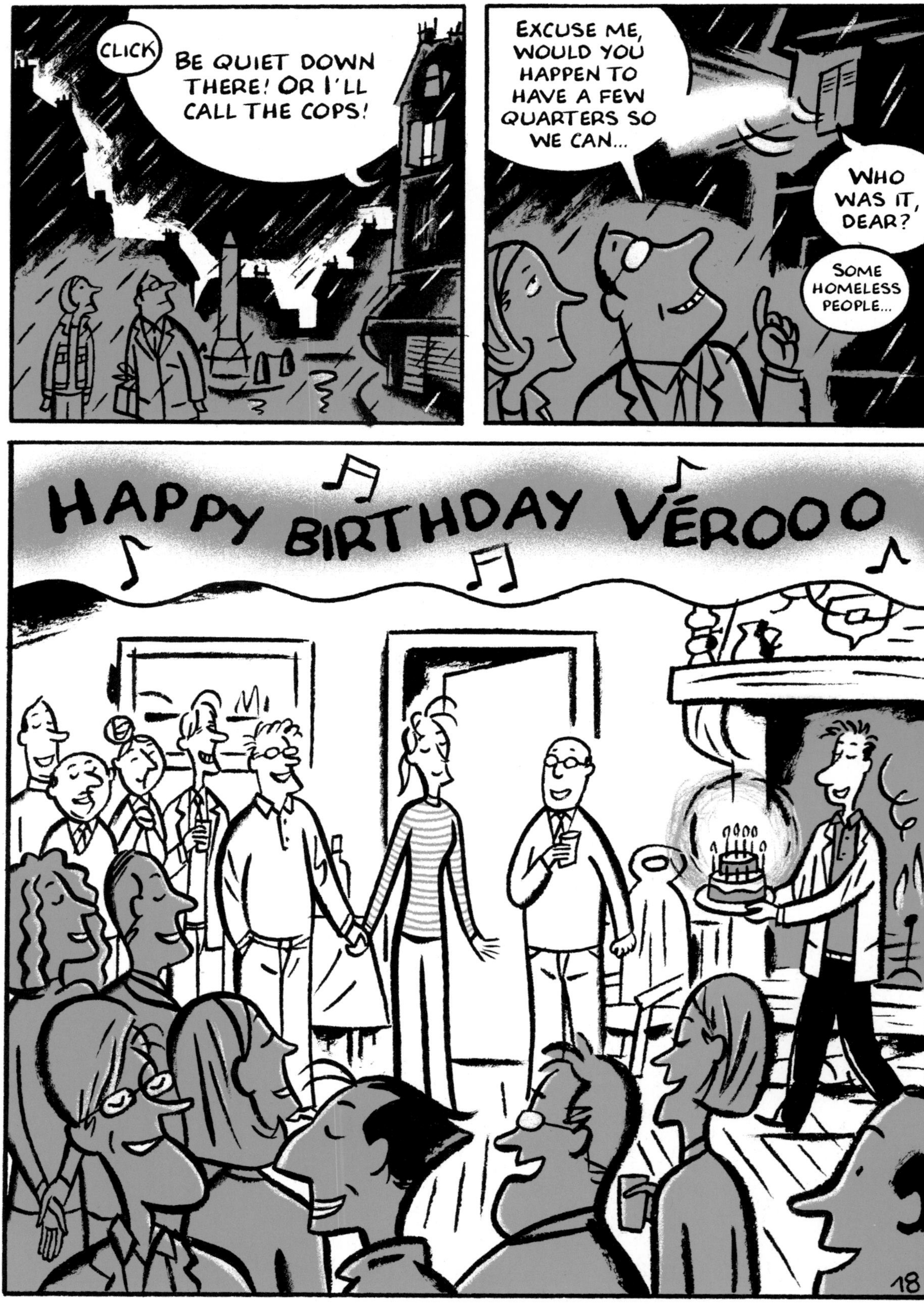
CLICK
BE QUIET DOWN THERE! OR I'LL CALL THE COPS!
EXCUSE ME, WOULD YOU HAPPEN TO HAVE A FEW QUARTERS SO WE CAN...
WHO WAS IT, DEAR?
SOME HOMELESS PEOPLE...
HAPPY BIRTHDAY VÉROOO
18

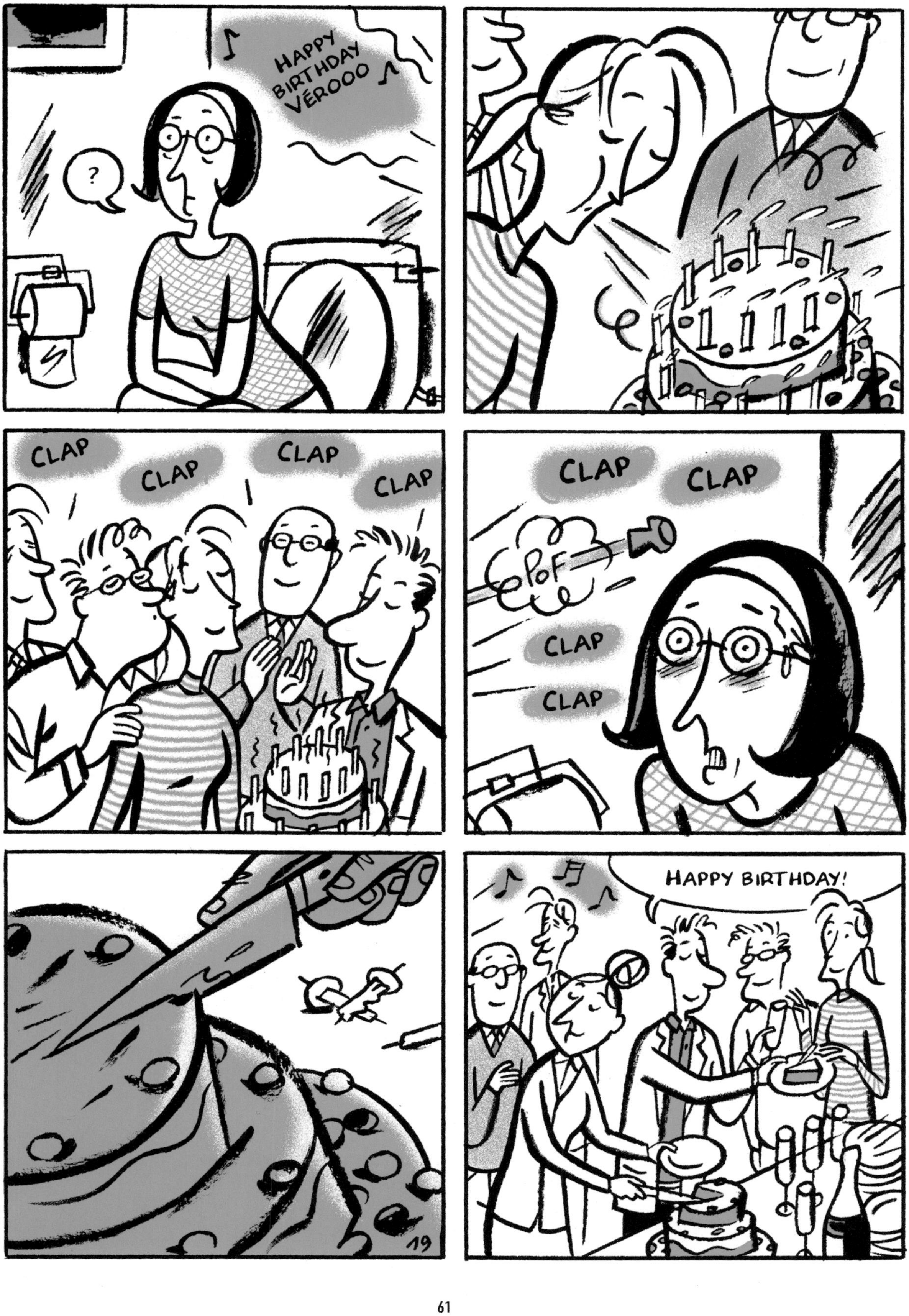
HAPPY BIRTHDAY VÉROOO
?
CLAP
CLAP
CLAP
CLAP
CLAP
CLAP
POF
CLAP
CLAP
HAPPY BIRTHDAY!

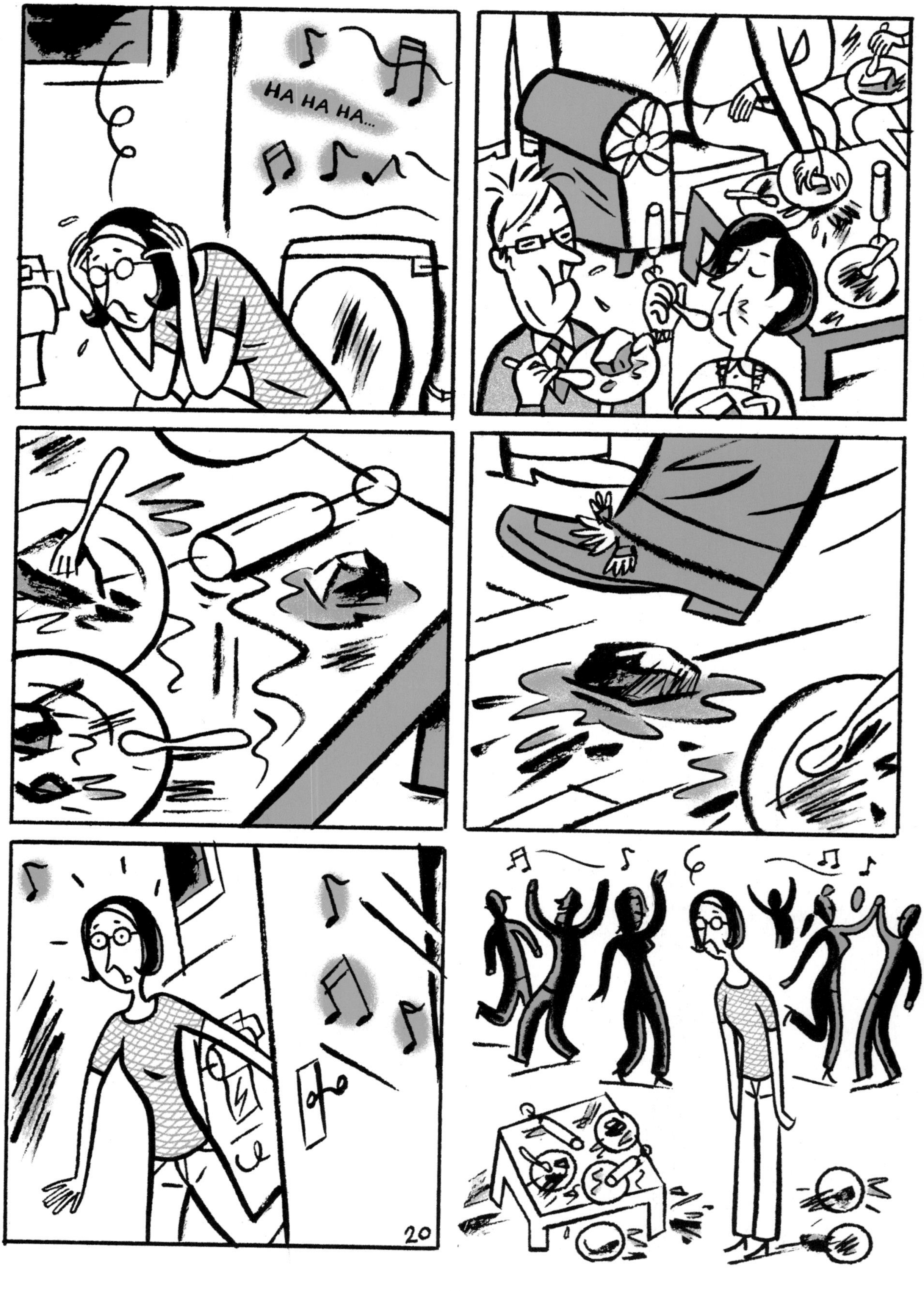
HA HA HA...
20

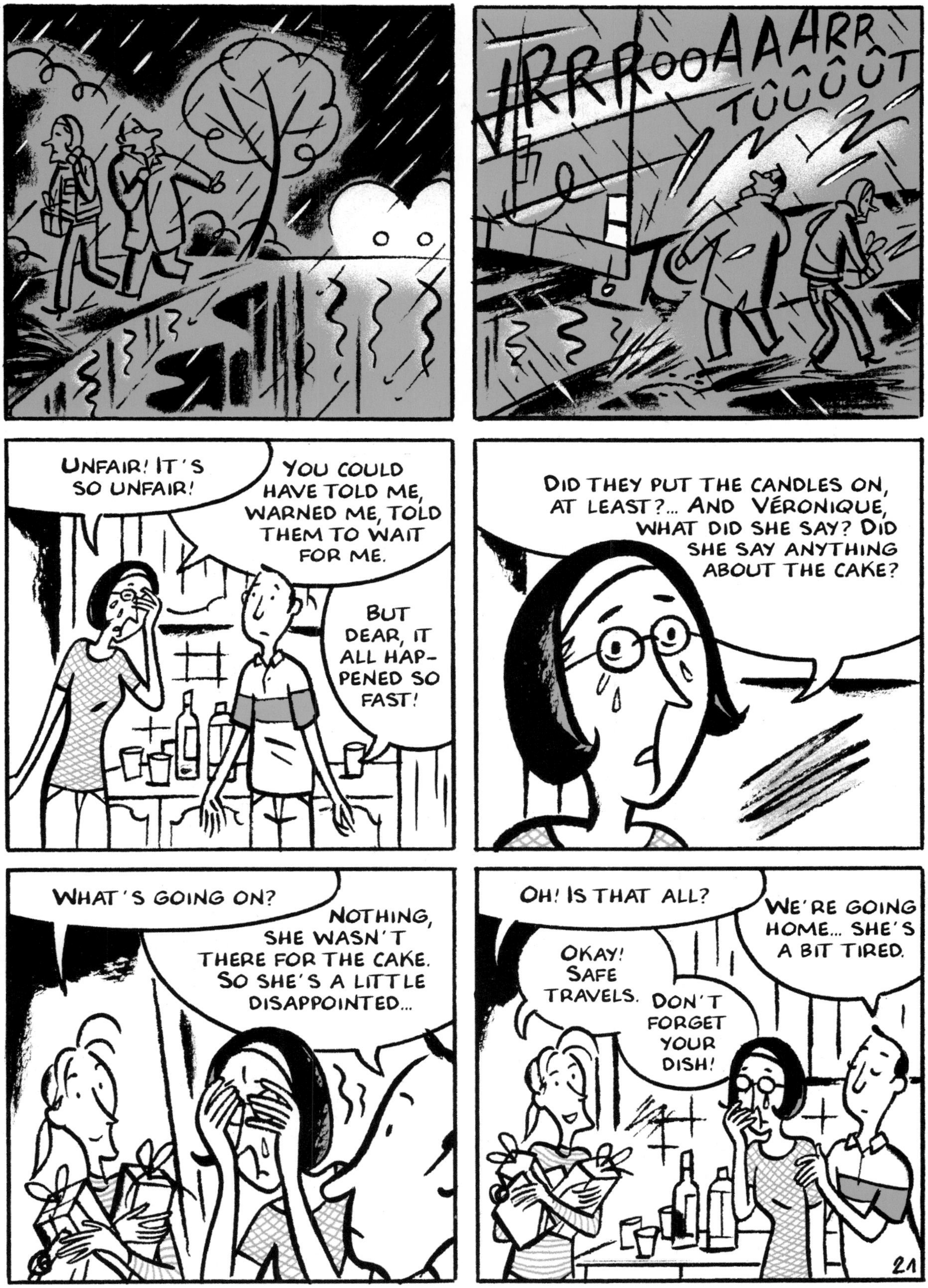

VRRRooAAARR
TÔÛÛÛÛT
UNFAIR! IT'S SO UNFAIR!
YOU COULD HAVE TOLD ME, WARNED ME, TOLD THEM TO WAIT FOR ME.
BUT DEAR, IT ALL HAP-PENED SO FAST!
DID THEY PUT THE CANDLES ON, AT LEAST?... AND VÉRONIQUE, WHAT DID SHE SAY? DID SHE SAY ANYTHING ABOUT THE CAKE?
WHAT'S GOING ON?
NOTHING, SHE WASN'T THERE FOR THE CAKE. SO SHE'S A LITTLE DISAPPOINTED...
OH! IS THAT ALL?
WE'RE GOING HOME... SHE'S A BIT TIRED.
OKAY! SAFE TRAVELS.
DON'T FORGET YOUR DISH!
21

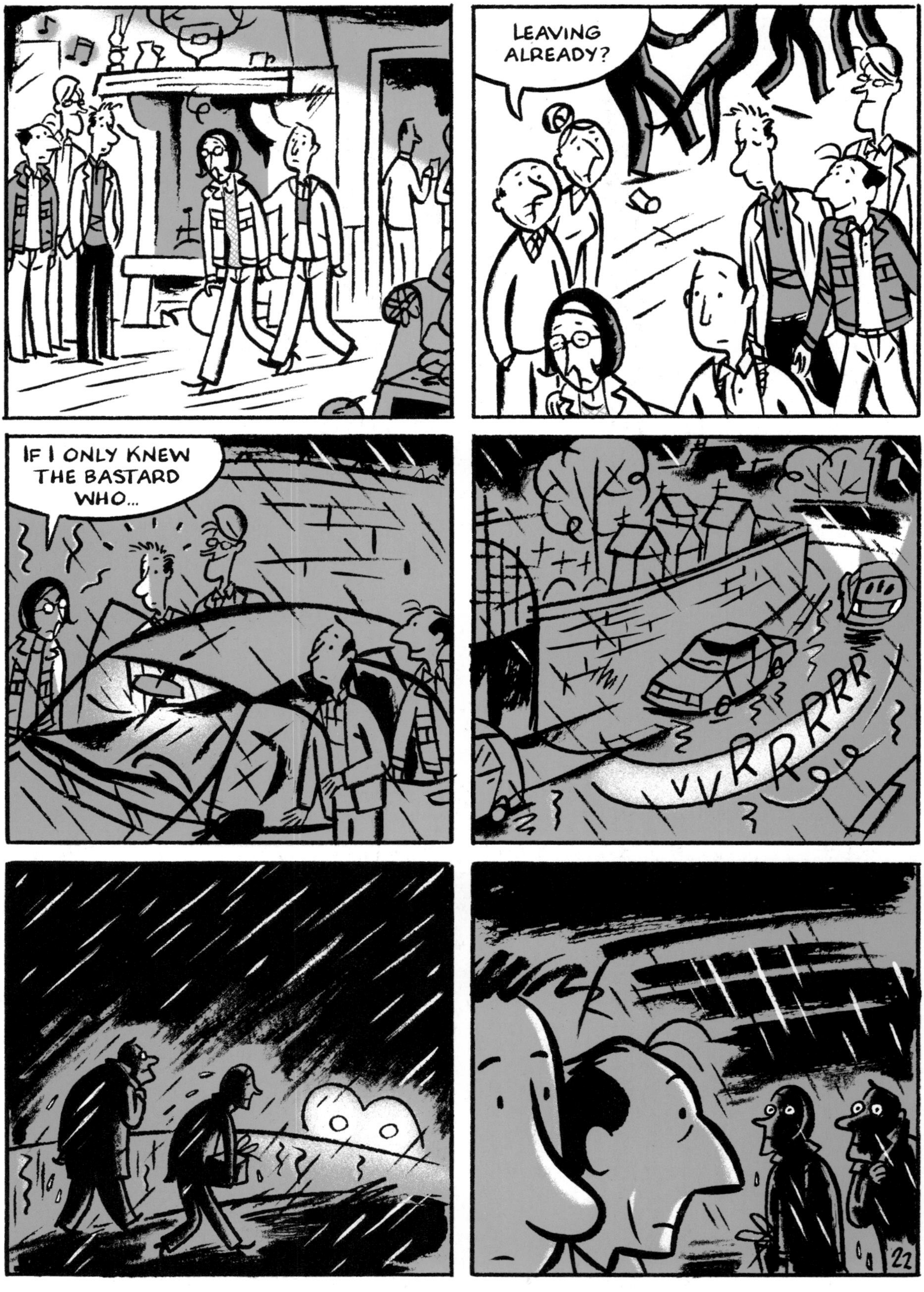
LEAVING ALREADY?
IF I ONLY KNEW THE BASTARD WHO...
VVRRRRRR
22

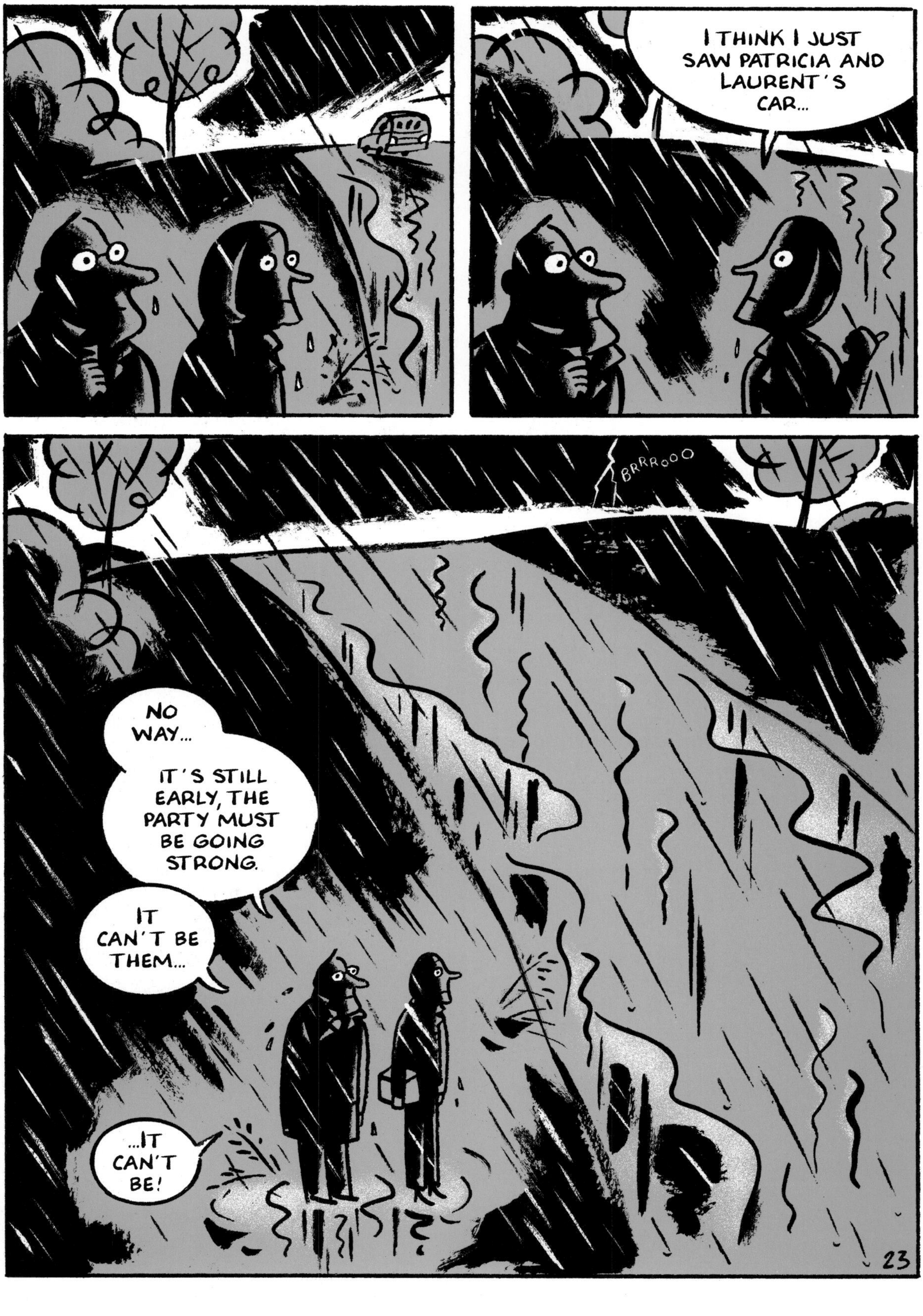
I THINK I JUST SAW PATRICIA AND LAURENT'S CAR...
BRRROOO
NO WAY...
IT'S STILL EARLY, THE PARTY MUST BE GOING STRONG.
IT CAN'T BE THEM...
...IT CAN'T BE!
23

The Upstairs Neighbor

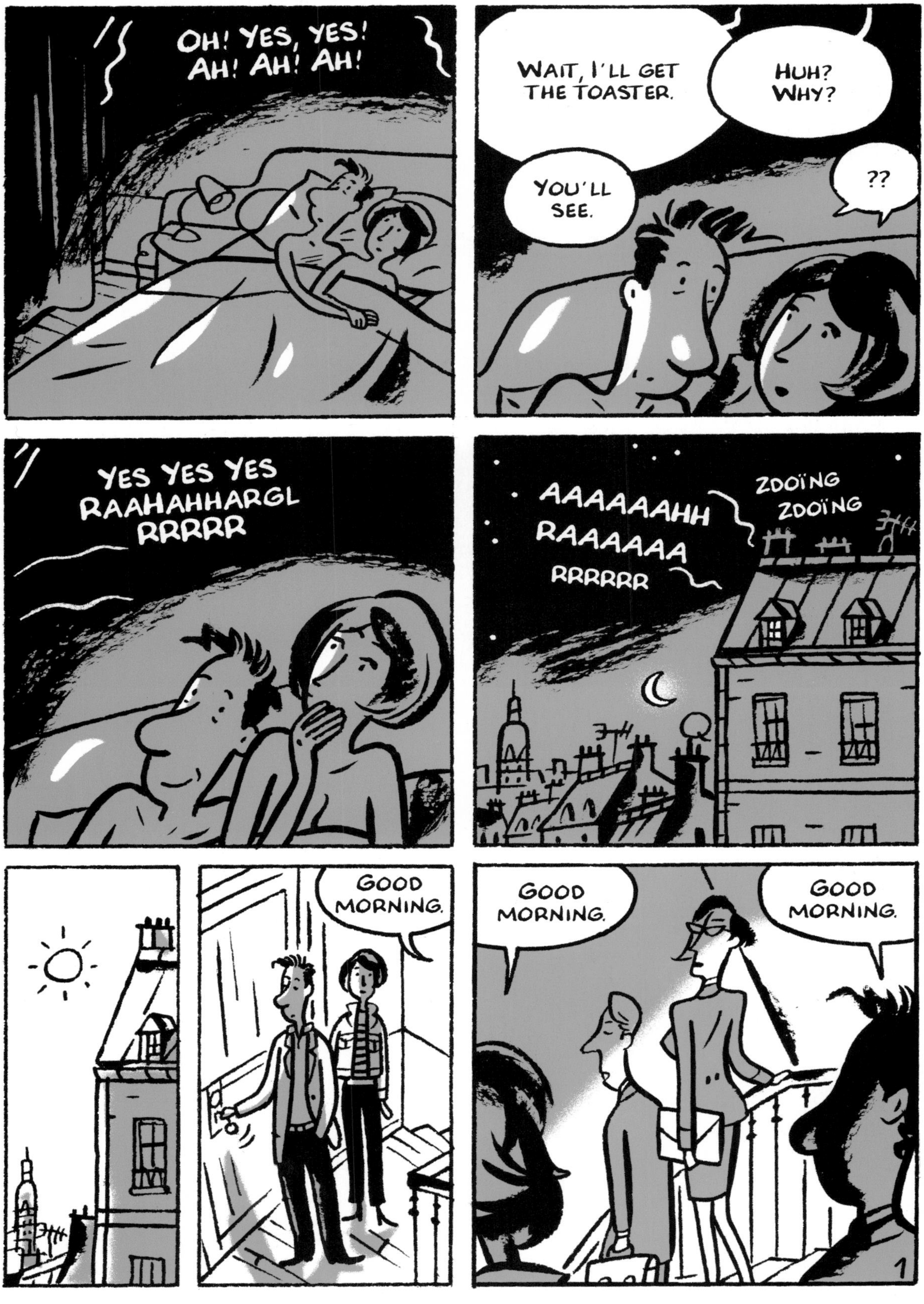
Oh! Yes, yes!
Ah! Ah! Ah!
Wait, I'll get the toaster.
Huh? Why?
You'll see.
??
Yes yes yes
RaaHahhargl
RRRRR
AAAAAAHH
RAAAAAA
RRRRRR
Zdoïng
zdoïng
Good morning.
Good morning.
Good morning.

AAAAAHHH
OOH
YES OOOOH YES
YES
RRAAHRAAAH
HEY, WHAT ARE YOU DOING WITH THIS TOASTER?
LET ME SHOW YOU...
CLIC
AHAHAHAHAHAHAHAHAH
RRRRRRRRRRRRRRRR YEEEEESSSS
YESYESOAAHAHAHAHAHAH
GOOOOD MORNIIING!
GOOD MORNING.
2

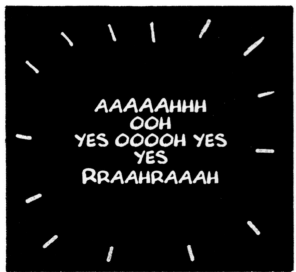

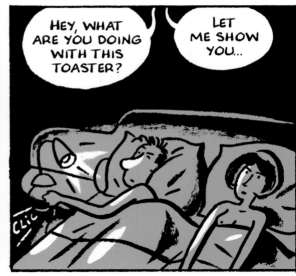

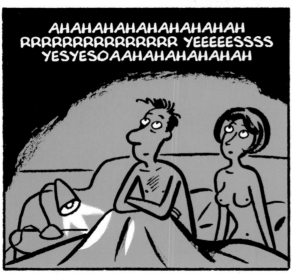

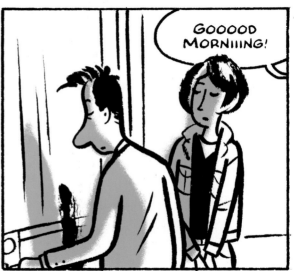

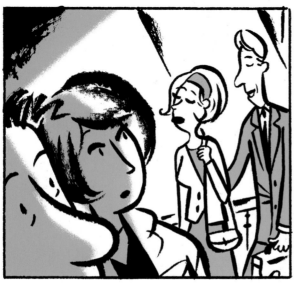

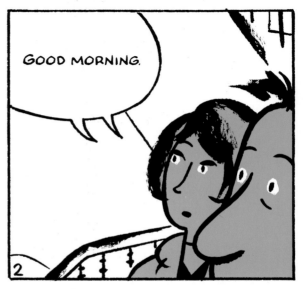

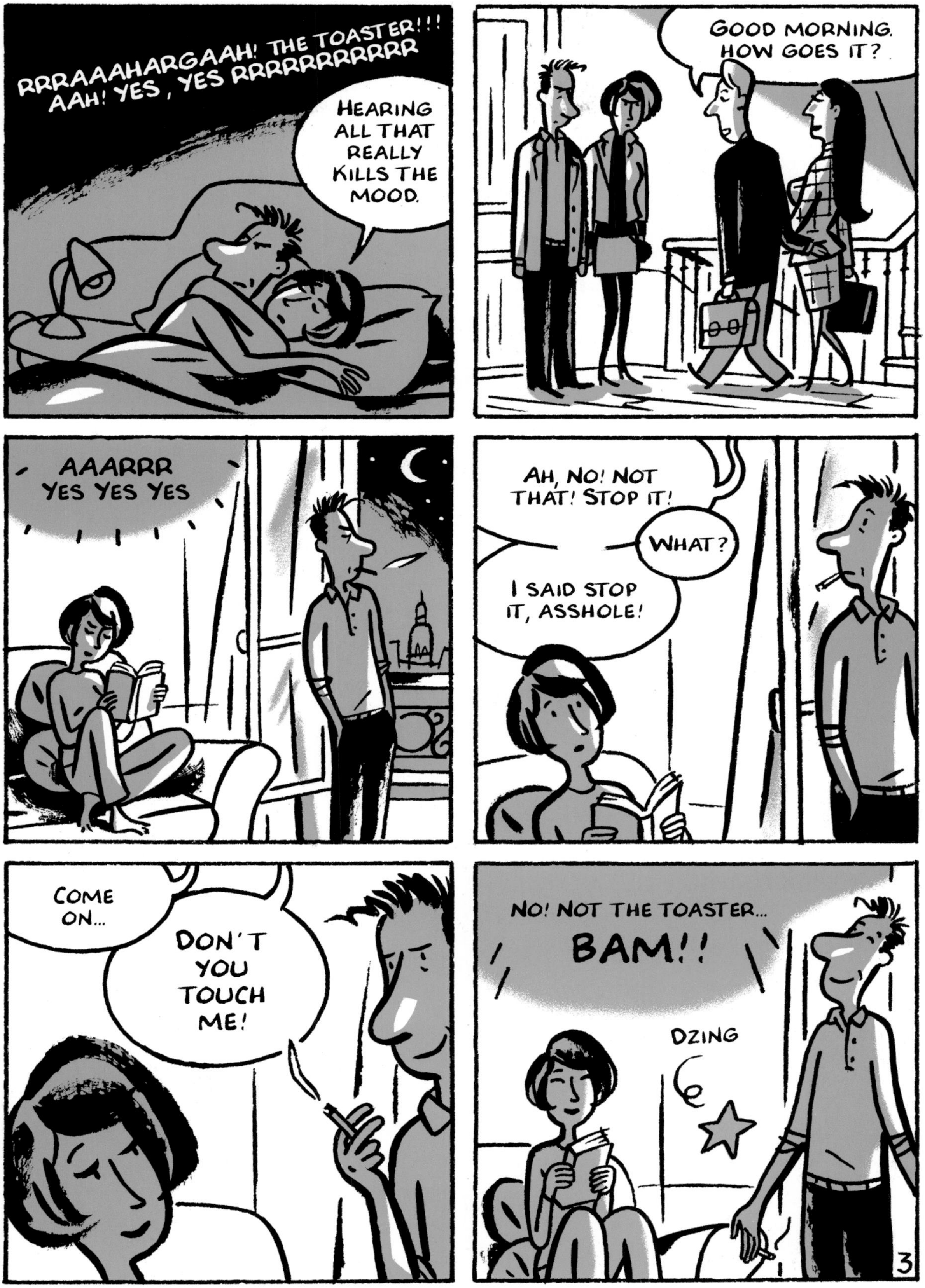
RRRAAAHARGAAH! THE TOASTER!!! AAH! YES, YES RRRRRRRRRRR
HEARING ALL THAT REALLY KILLS THE MOOD.
GOOD MORNING. HOW GOES IT?
AAARRR YES YES YES
AH, NO! NOT THAT! STOP IT!
WHAT?
I SAID STOP IT, ASSHOLE!
COME ON...
DON'T YOU TOUCH ME!
NO! NOT THE TOASTER...
BAM!!
DZING
3

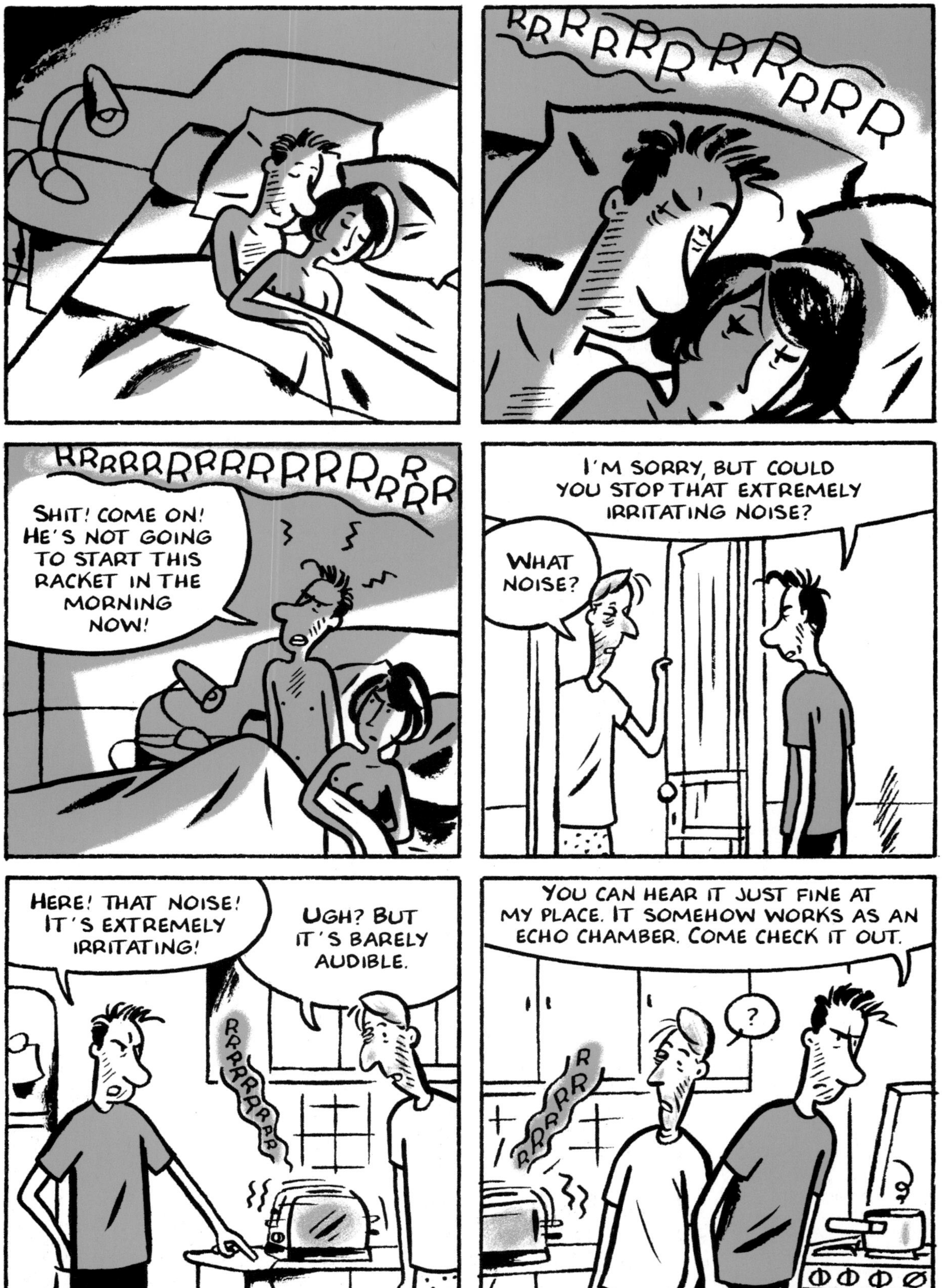
RRRRRRRRRRRRRRR
RRRRRRRRRRRRRRRR
SHIT! COME ON! HE'S NOT GOING TO START THIS RACKET IN THE MORNING NOW!
I'M SORRY, BUT COULD YOU STOP THAT EXTREMELY IRRITATING NOISE?
WHAT NOISE?
HERE! THAT NOISE! IT'S EXTREMELY IRRITATING!
UGH? BUT IT'S BARELY AUDIBLE.
RRRRRRRRRR
YOU CAN HEAR IT JUST FINE AT MY PLACE. IT SOMEHOW WORKS AS AN ECHO CHAMBER. COME CHECK IT OUT.
?
RRRRRR

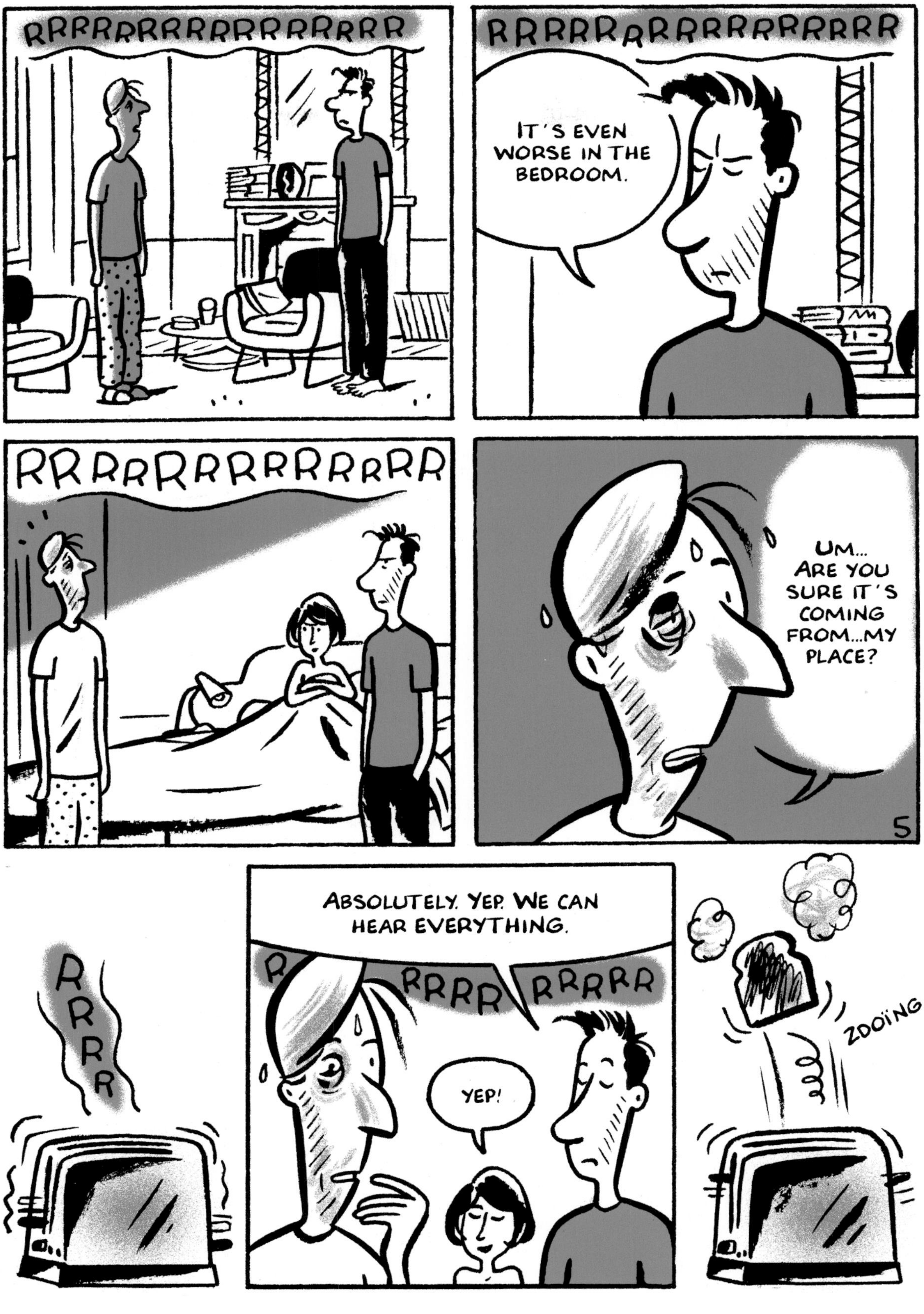
RRRRRRRRRRRRRRRRRR
RRRRRRRRRRRRRRRR
IT'S EVEN WORSE IN THE BEDROOM.
RRRRRRRRRRRRRR
UM... ARE YOU SURE IT'S COMING FROM... MY PLACE?
ABSOLUTELY. YEP. WE CAN HEAR EVERYTHING.
RRRRR
YEP!
RRRRR
RRRRR
ZDOÏNG

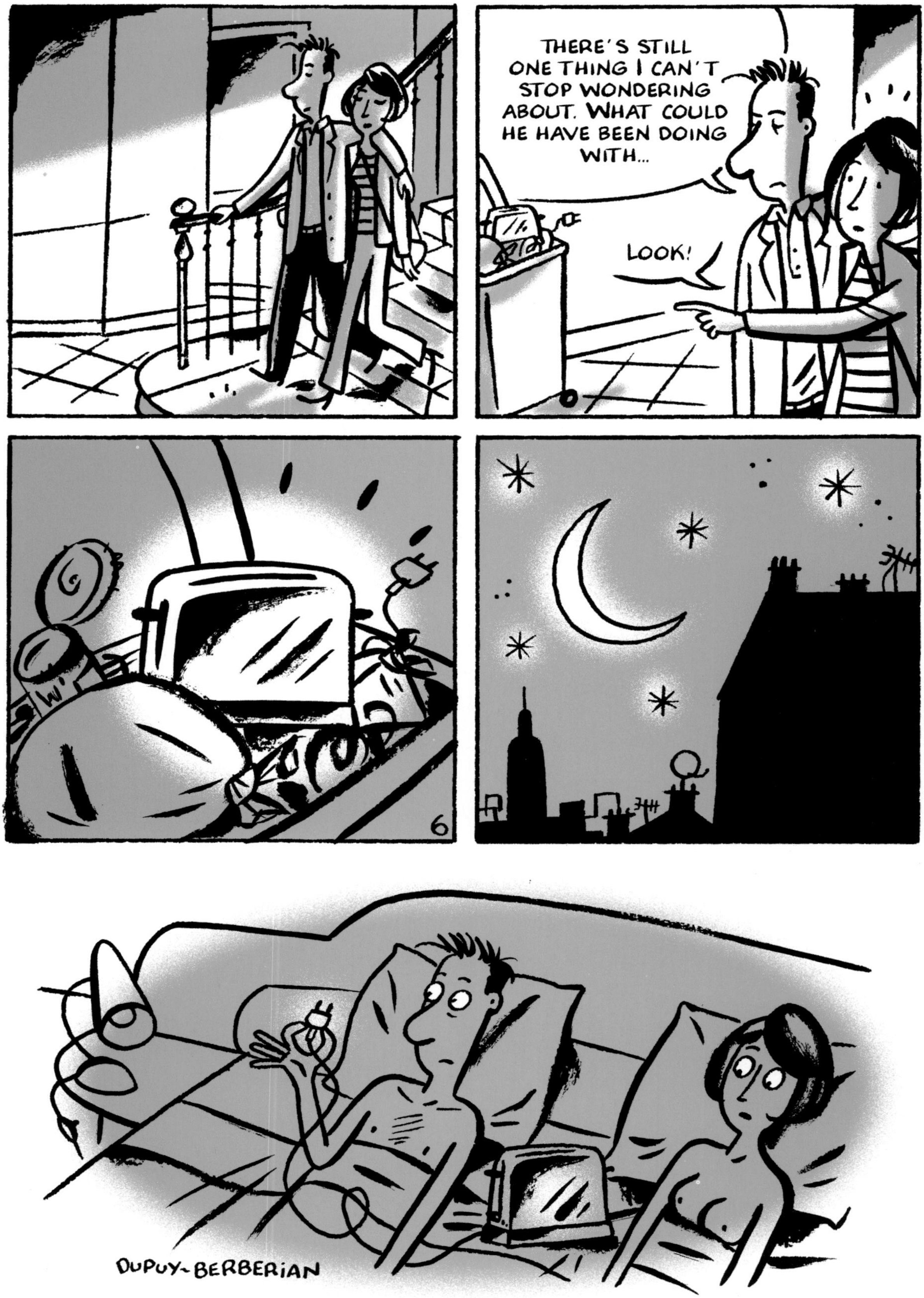
THERE'S STILL ONE THING I CAN'T STOP WONDERING ABOUT. WHAT COULD HE HAVE BEEN DOING WITH...
LOOK!
6
DUPUY-BERBERIAN

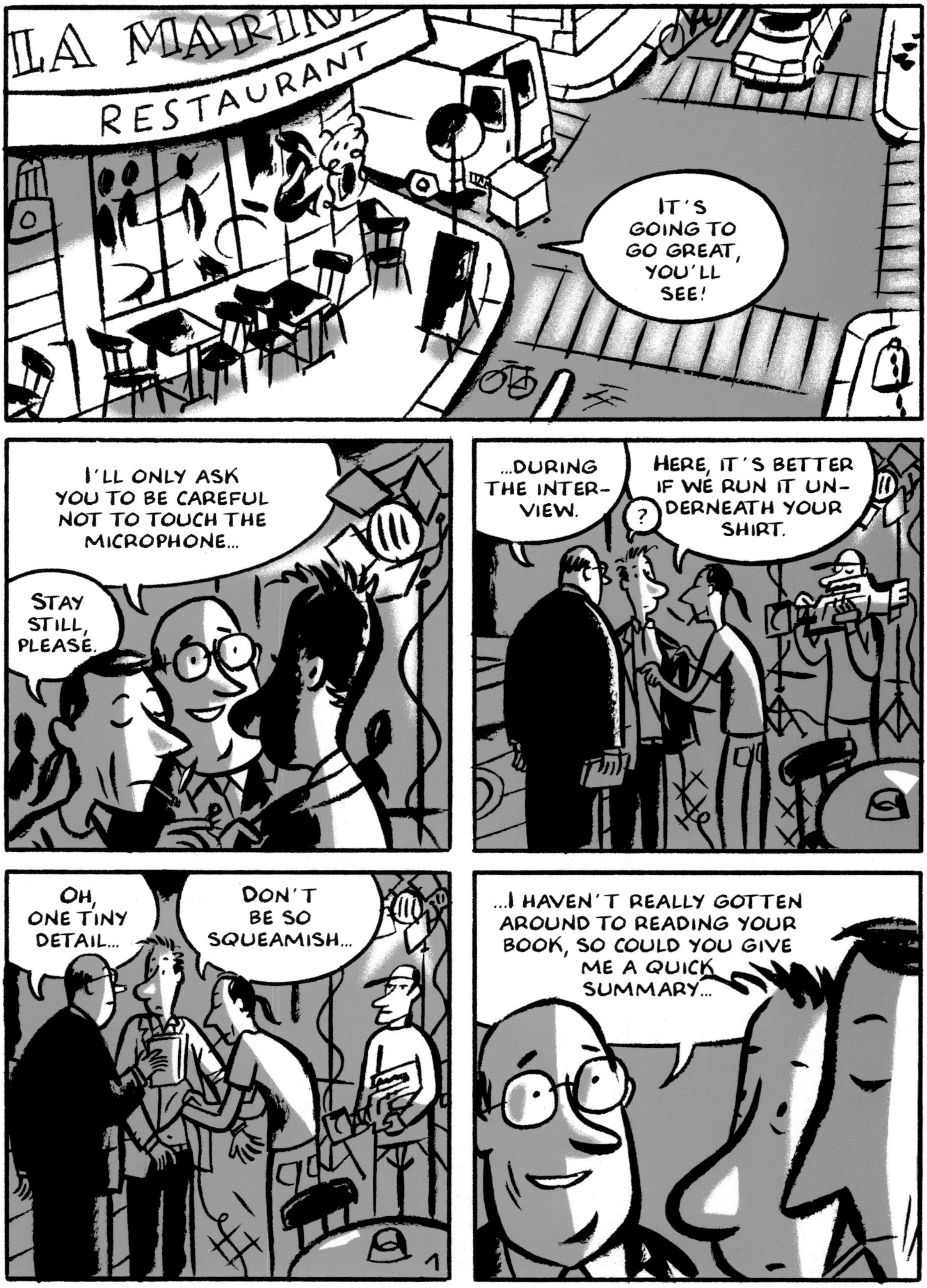
LA MARIN
RESTAURANT
IT'S GOING TO GO GREAT, YOU'LL SEE!
I'LL ONLY ASK YOU TO BE CAREFUL NOT TO TOUCH THE MICROPHONE...
STAY STILL, PLEASE.
...DURING THE INTER-VIEW.
?
HERE, IT'S BETTER IF WE RUN IT UN-DERNEATH YOUR SHIRT.
OH, ONE TINY DETAIL...
DON'T BE SO SQUEAMISH...
...I HAVEN'T REALLY GOTTEN AROUND TO READING YOUR BOOK, SO COULD YOU GIVE ME A QUICK SUMMARY...

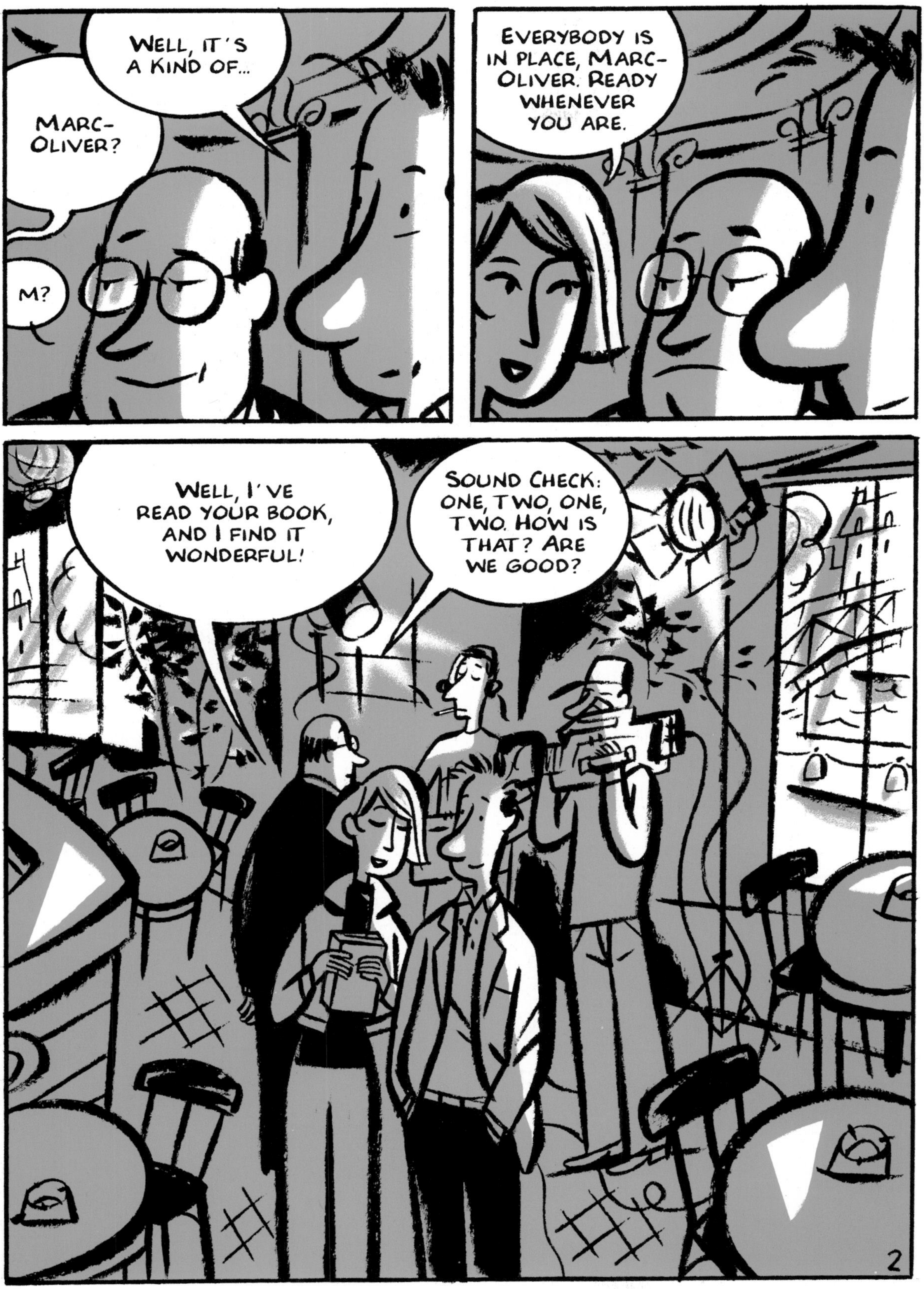
WELL, IT'S A KIND OF...
MARC-OLIVER?
M?
EVERYBODY IS IN PLACE, MARC-OLIVER. READY WHENEVER YOU ARE.
WELL, I'VE READ YOUR BOOK, AND I FIND IT WONDERFUL!
SOUND CHECK: ONE, TWO, ONE, TWO. HOW IS THAT? ARE WE GOOD?
2

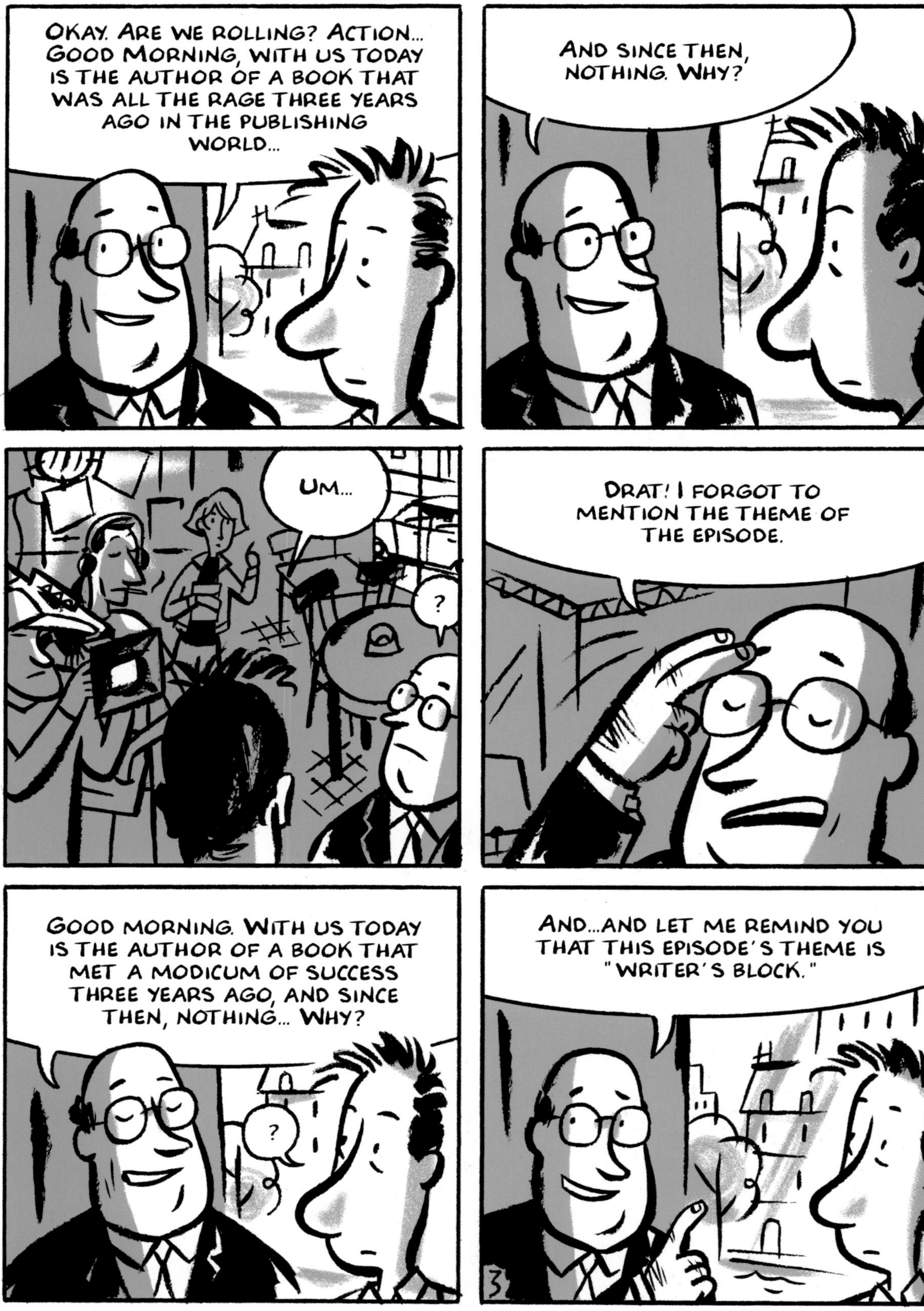
OKAY. ARE WE ROLLING? ACTION... GOOD MORNING, WITH US TODAY IS THE AUTHOR OF A BOOK THAT WAS ALL THE RAGE THREE YEARS AGO IN THE PUBLISHING WORLD...
AND SINCE THEN, NOTHING. WHY?
UM...
?
DRAT! I FORGOT TO MENTION THE THEME OF THE EPISODE.
GOOD MORNING. WITH US TODAY IS THE AUTHOR OF A BOOK THAT MET A MODICUM OF SUCCESS THREE YEARS AGO, AND SINCE THEN, NOTHING... WHY?
?
AND...AND LET ME REMIND YOU THAT THIS EPISODE'S THEME IS "WRITER'S BLOCK."
3

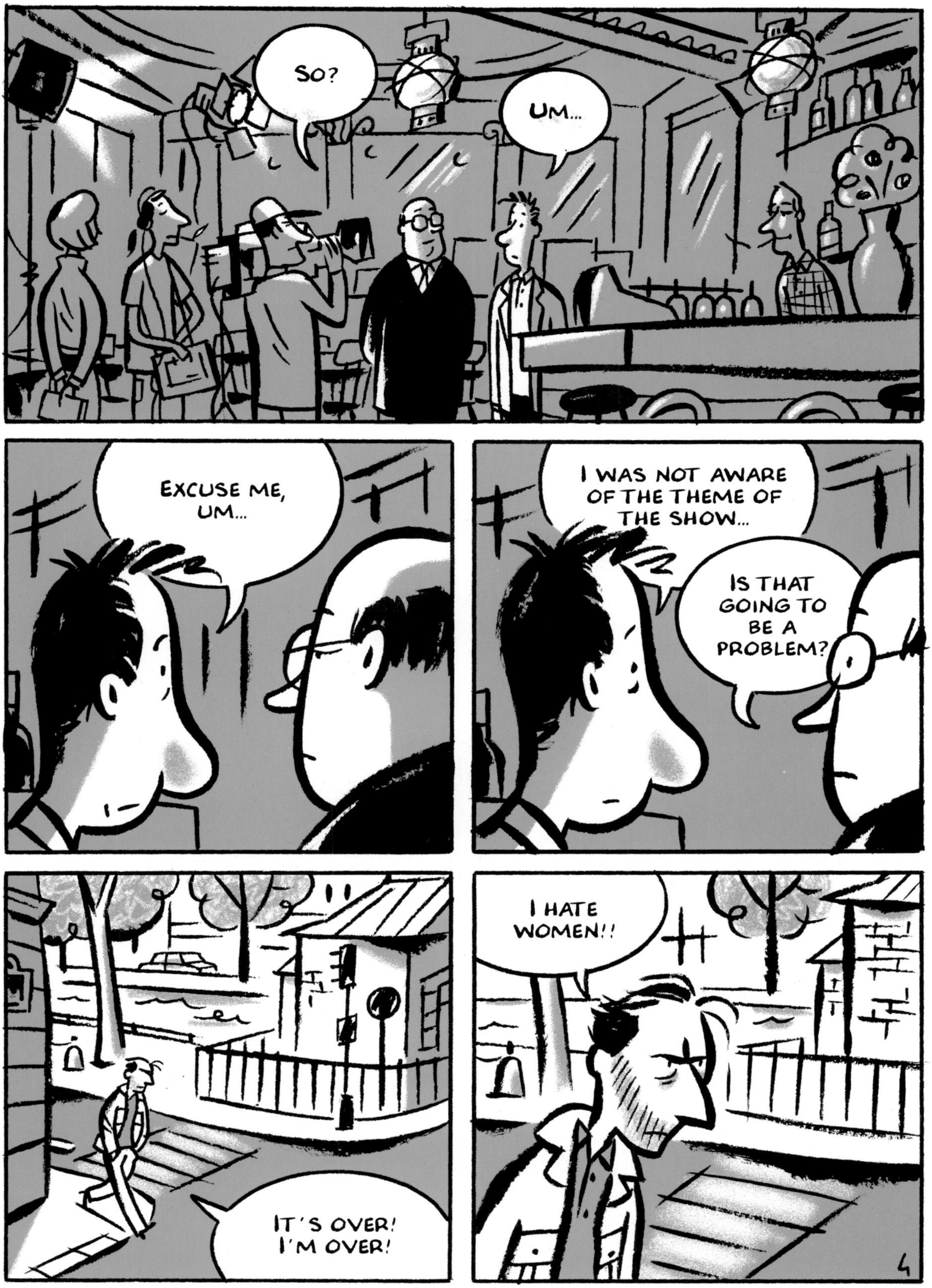
SO?
UM...
EXCUSE ME, UM...
I WAS NOT AWARE OF THE THEME OF THE SHOW...
IS THAT GOING TO BE A PROBLEM?
IT'S OVER! I'M OVER!
I HATE WOMEN!!

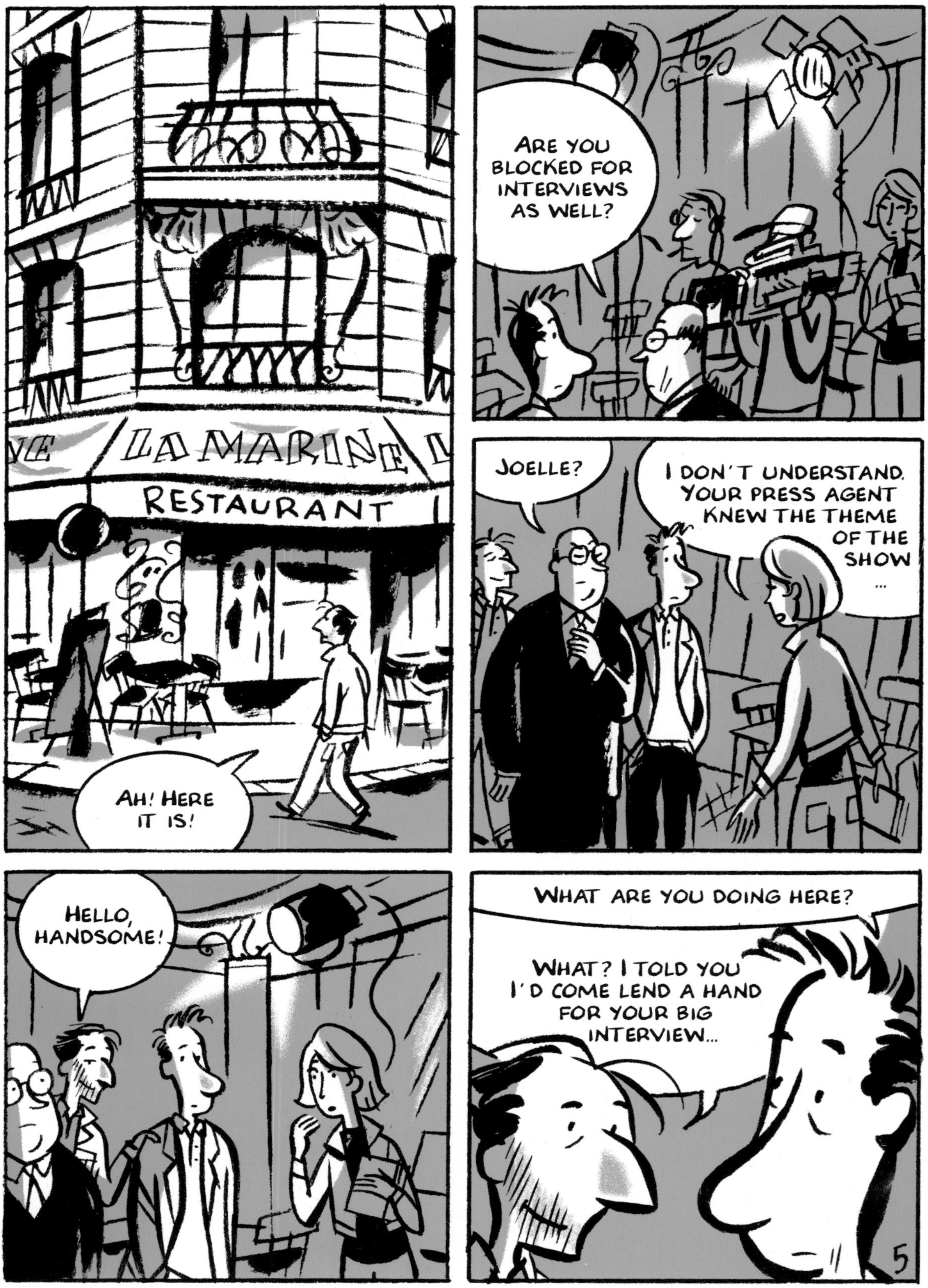

LA MARINE
RESTAURANT
AH! HERE IT IS!
ARE YOU BLOCKED FOR INTERVIEWS AS WELL?
JOELLE?
I DON'T UNDERSTAND. YOUR PRESS AGENT KNEW THE THEME OF THE SHOW ...
HELLO, HANDSOME!
WHAT ARE YOU DOING HERE?
WHAT? I TOLD YOU I'D COME LEND A HAND FOR YOUR BIG INTERVIEW...
5

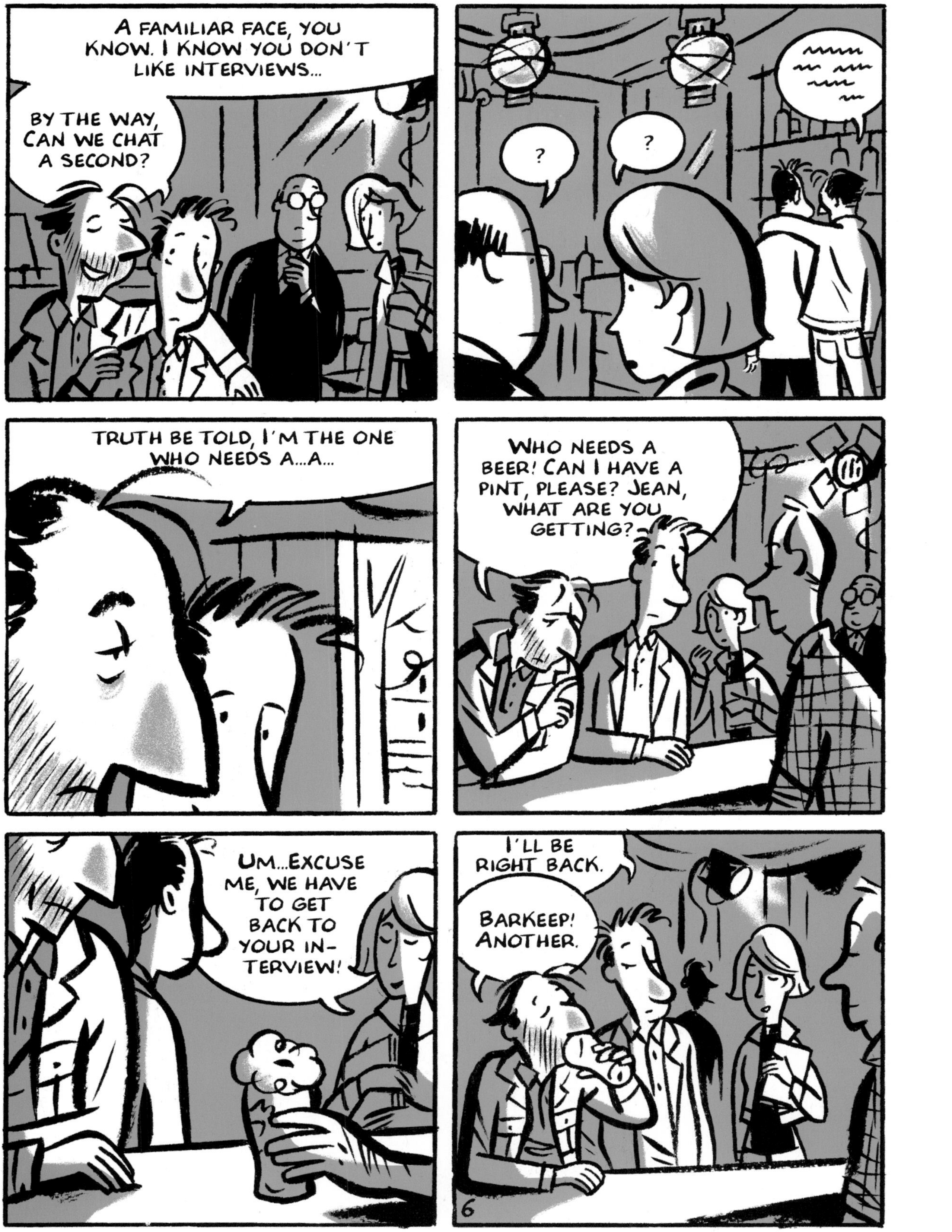
A FAMILIAR FACE, YOU KNOW. I KNOW YOU DON'T LIKE INTERVIEWS...
BY THE WAY, CAN WE CHAT A SECOND?
?
?
TRUTH BE TOLD, I'M THE ONE WHO NEEDS A...A...
WHO NEEDS A BEER! CAN I HAVE A PINT, PLEASE? JEAN, WHAT ARE YOU GETTING?
UM...EXCUSE ME, WE HAVE TO GET BACK TO YOUR INTERVIEW!
I'LL BE RIGHT BACK.
BARKEEP! ANOTHER.
6

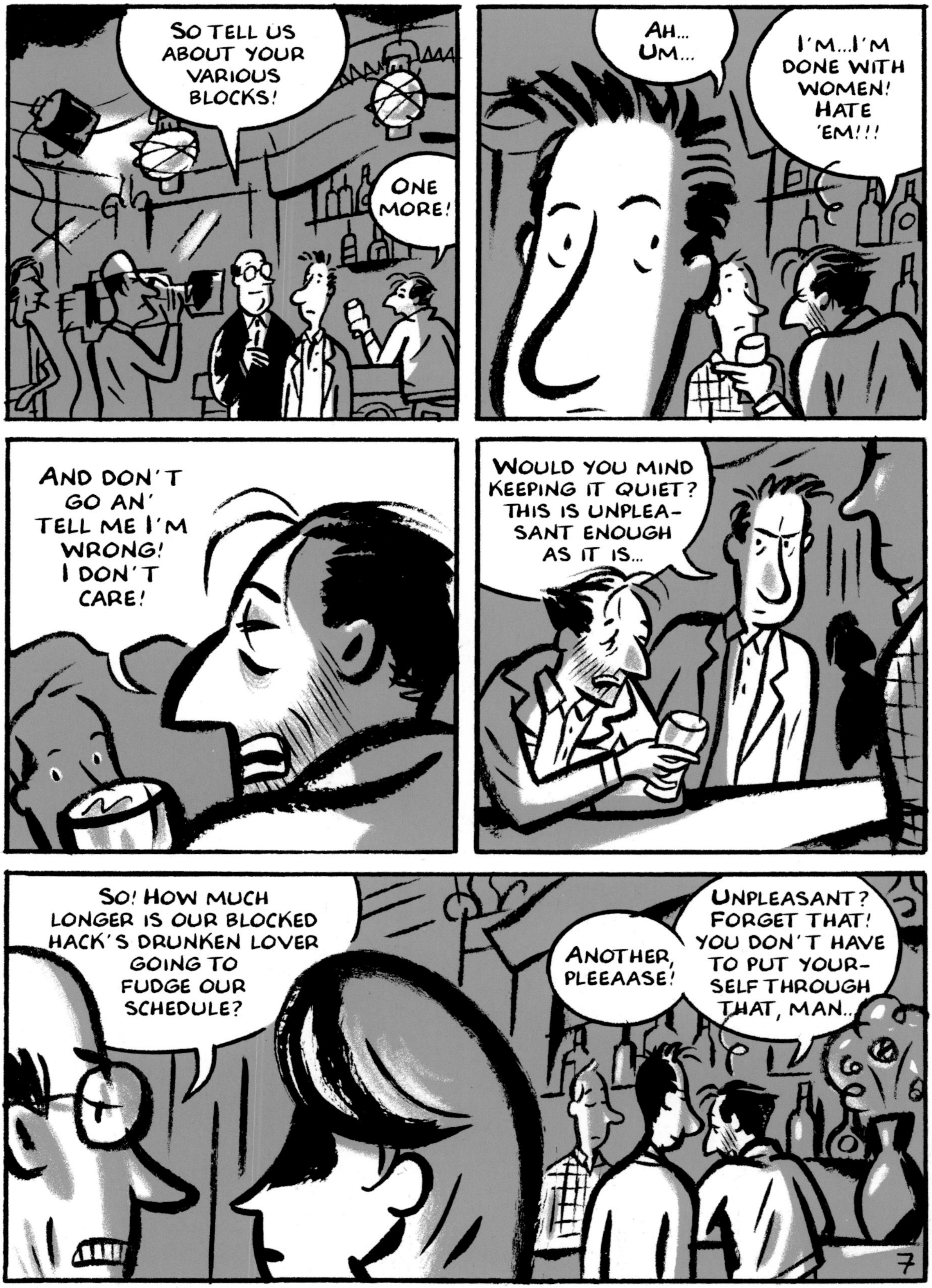
SO TELL US ABOUT YOUR VARIOUS BLOCKS!
ONE MORE!
AH... UM...
I'M...I'M DONE WITH WOMEN! HATE 'EM!!!
AND DON'T GO AN' TELL ME I'M WRONG! I DON'T CARE!
WOULD YOU MIND KEEPING IT QUIET? THIS IS UNPLEA-SANT ENOUGH AS IT IS...
SO! HOW MUCH LONGER IS OUR BLOCKED HACK'S DRUNKEN LOVER GOING TO FUDGE OUR SCHEDULE?
ANOTHER, PLEEAASE!
UNPLEASANT? FORGET THAT! YOU DON'T HAVE TO PUT YOUR-SELF THROUGH THAT, MAN...
7

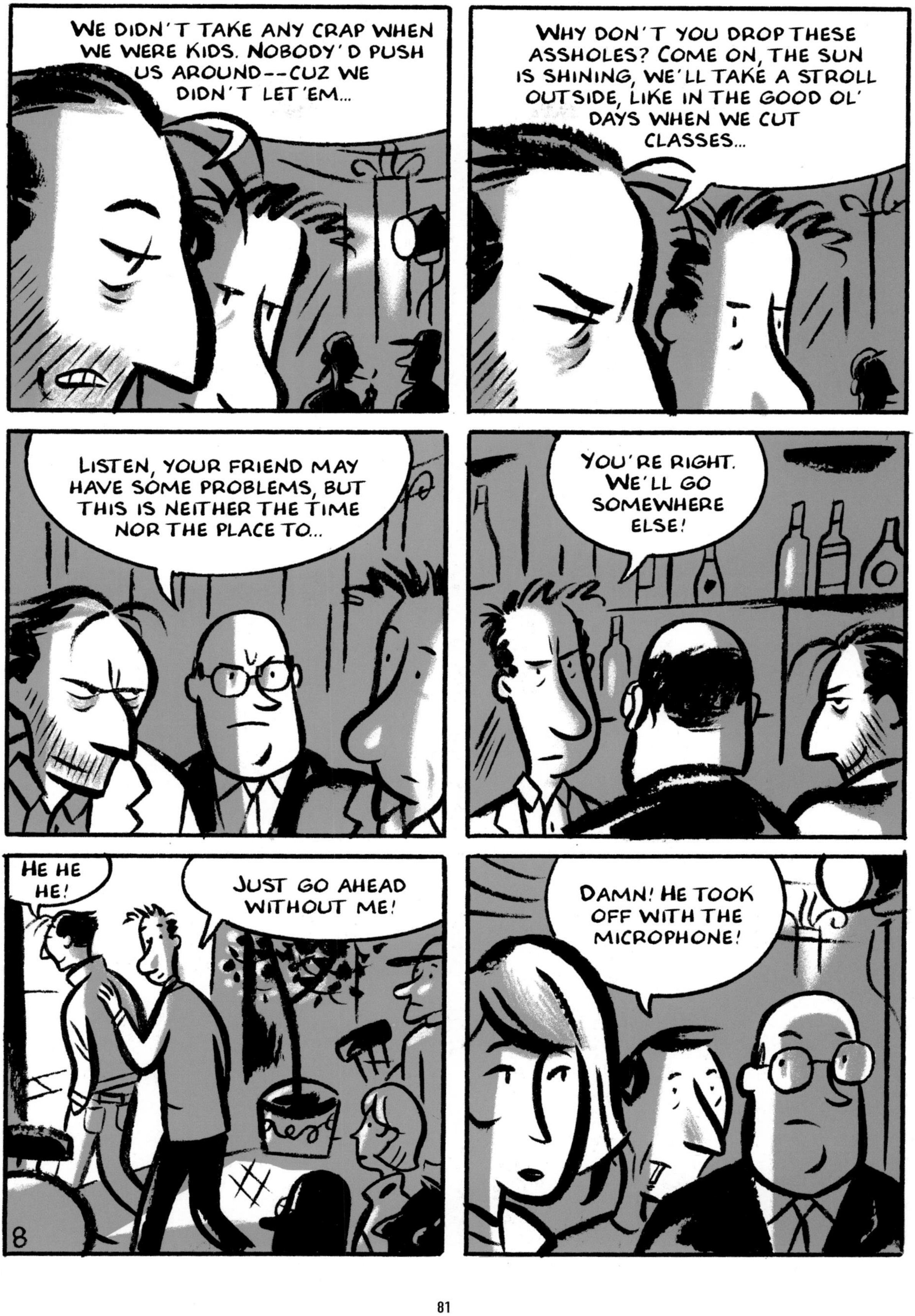
WE DIDN'T TAKE ANY CRAP WHEN WE WERE KIDS. NOBODY'D PUSH US AROUND--CUZ WE DIDN'T LET 'EM...
WHY DON'T YOU DROP THESE ASSHOLES? COME ON, THE SUN IS SHINING, WE'LL TAKE A STROLL OUTSIDE, LIKE IN THE GOOD OL' DAYS WHEN WE CUT CLASSES...
LISTEN, YOUR FRIEND MAY HAVE SOME PROBLEMS, BUT THIS IS NEITHER THE TIME NOR THE PLACE TO...
YOU'RE RIGHT. WE'LL GO SOMEWHERE ELSE!
HE HE HE!
JUST GO AHEAD WITHOUT ME!
8
DAMN! HE TOOK OFF WITH THE MICROPHONE!

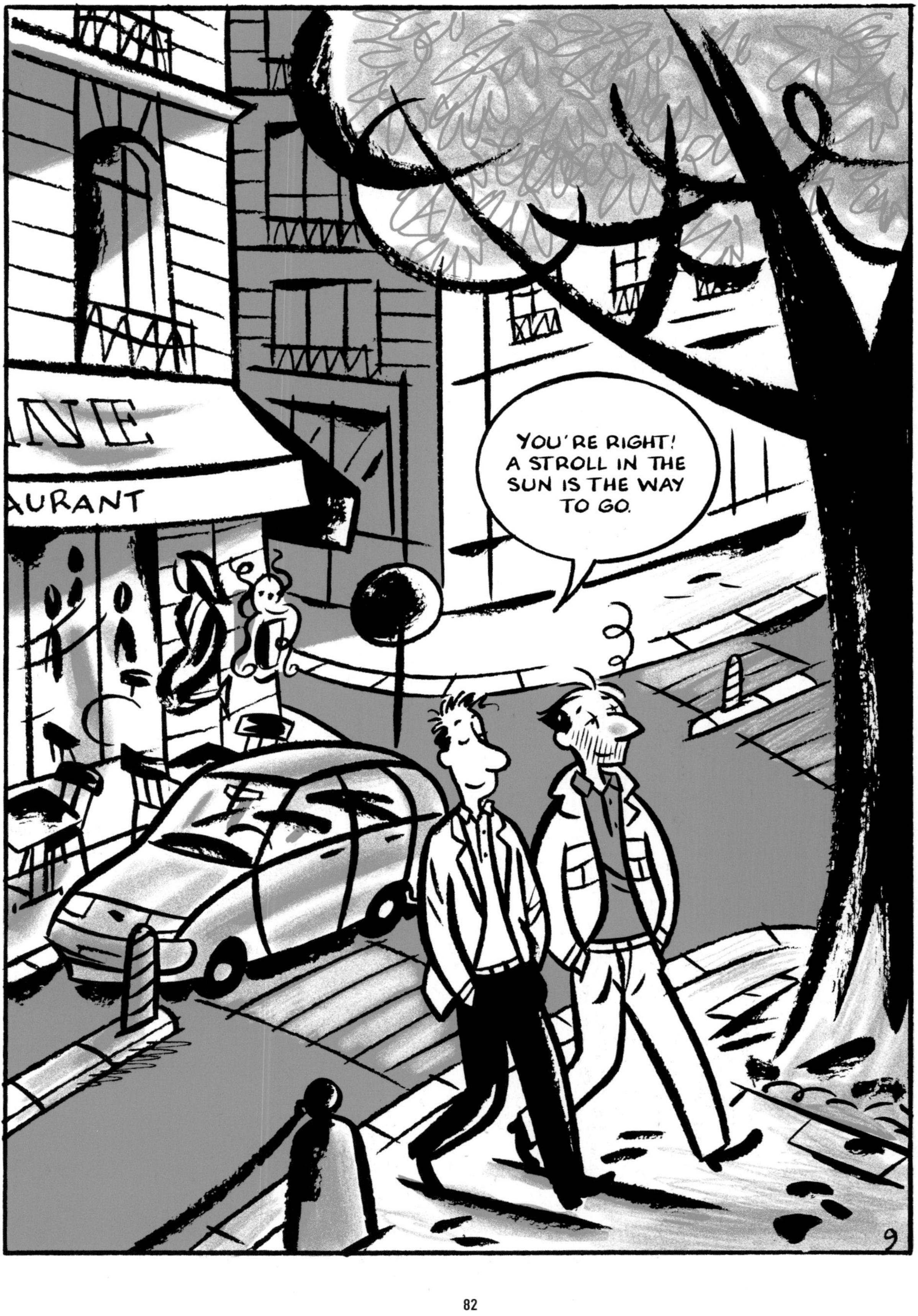
YOU'RE RIGHT! A STROLL IN THE SUN IS THE WAY TO GO.

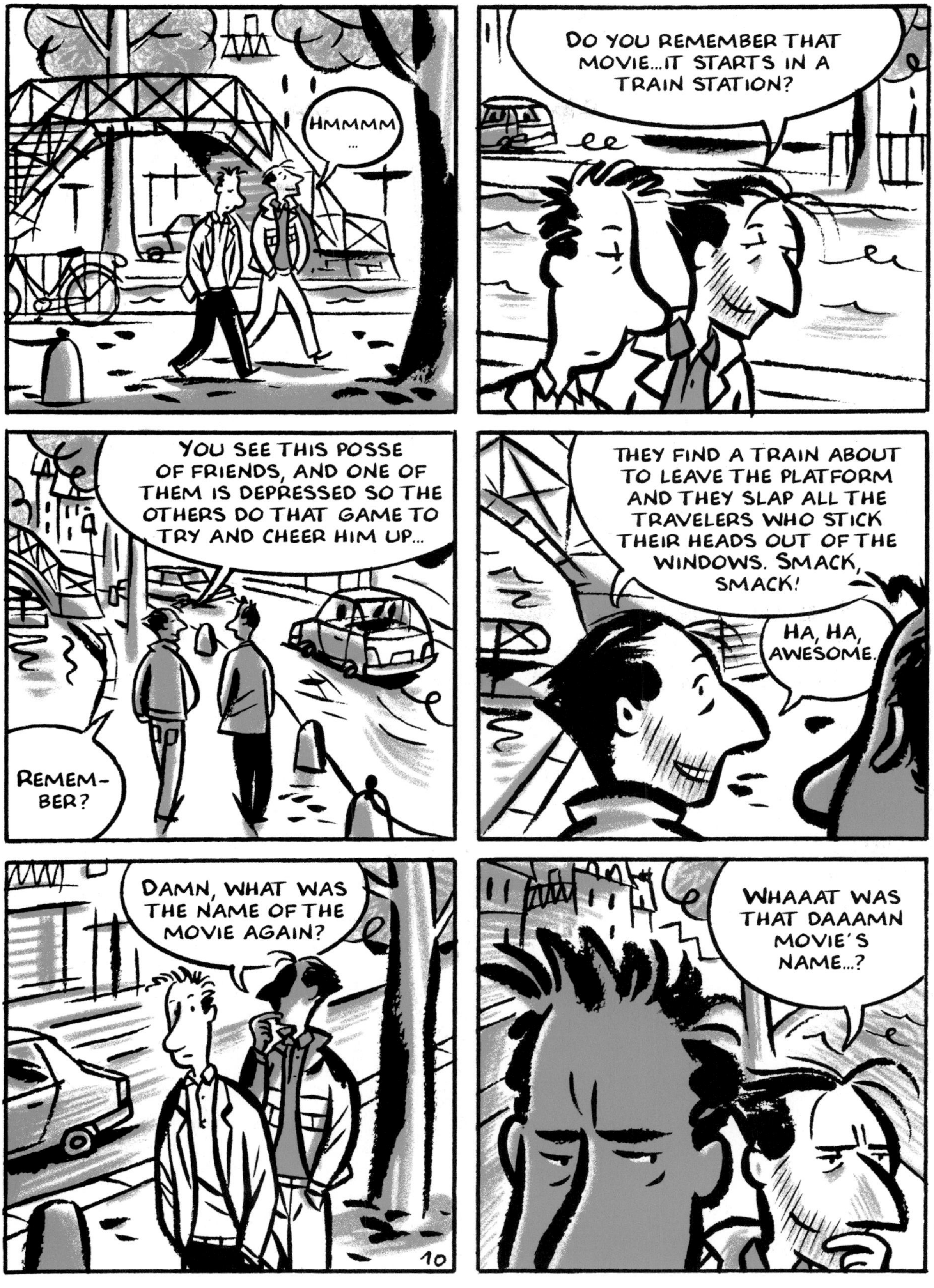
HMMMM
...
DO YOU REMEMBER THAT MOVIE... IT STARTS IN A TRAIN STATION?
YOU SEE THIS POSSE OF FRIENDS, AND ONE OF THEM IS DEPRESSED SO THE OTHERS DO THAT GAME TO TRY AND CHEER HIM UP...
REMEM-BER?
THEY FIND A TRAIN ABOUT TO LEAVE THE PLATFORM AND THEY SLAP ALL THE TRAVELERS WHO STICK THEIR HEADS OUT OF THE WINDOWS. SMACK, SMACK!
HA, HA, AWESOME.
DAMN, WHAT WAS THE NAME OF THE MOVIE AGAIN?
10
WHAAAT WAS THAT DAAAMN MOVIE'S NAME...?

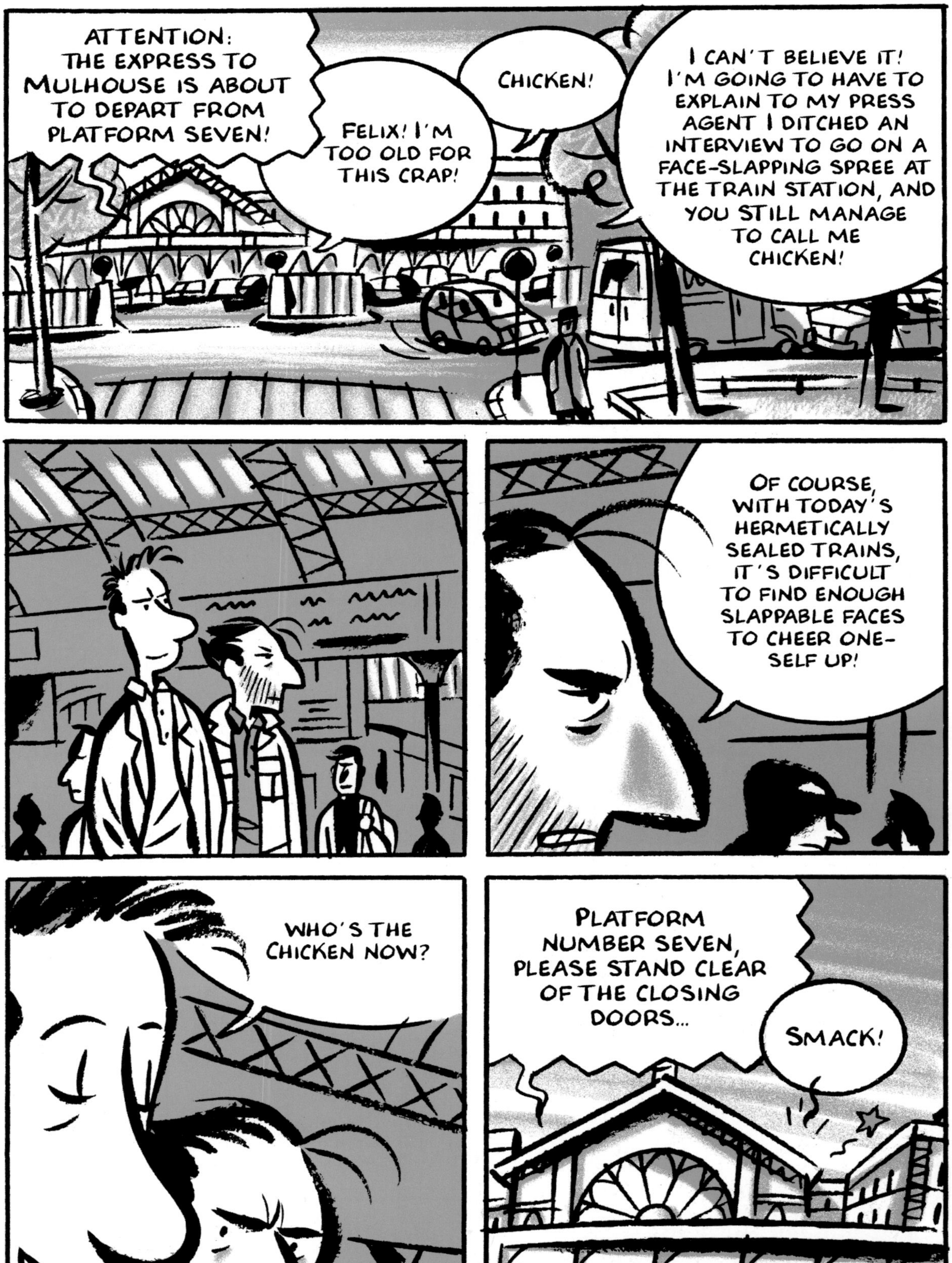
ATTENTION: THE EXPRESS TO MULHOUSE IS ABOUT TO DEPART FROM PLATFORM SEVEN!
FELIX! I'M TOO OLD FOR THIS CRAP!
CHICKEN!
I CAN'T BELIEVE IT! I'M GOING TO HAVE TO EXPLAIN TO MY PRESS AGENT I DITCHED AN INTERVIEW TO GO ON A FACE-SLAPPING SPREE AT THE TRAIN STATION, AND YOU STILL MANAGE TO CALL ME CHICKEN!
OF COURSE, WITH TODAY'S HERMETICALLY SEALED TRAINS, IT'S DIFFICULT TO FIND ENOUGH SLAPPABLE FACES TO CHEER ONE-SELF UP!
WHO'S THE CHICKEN NOW?
PLATFORM NUMBER SEVEN, PLEASE STAND CLEAR OF THE CLOSING DOORS...
SMACK!
11

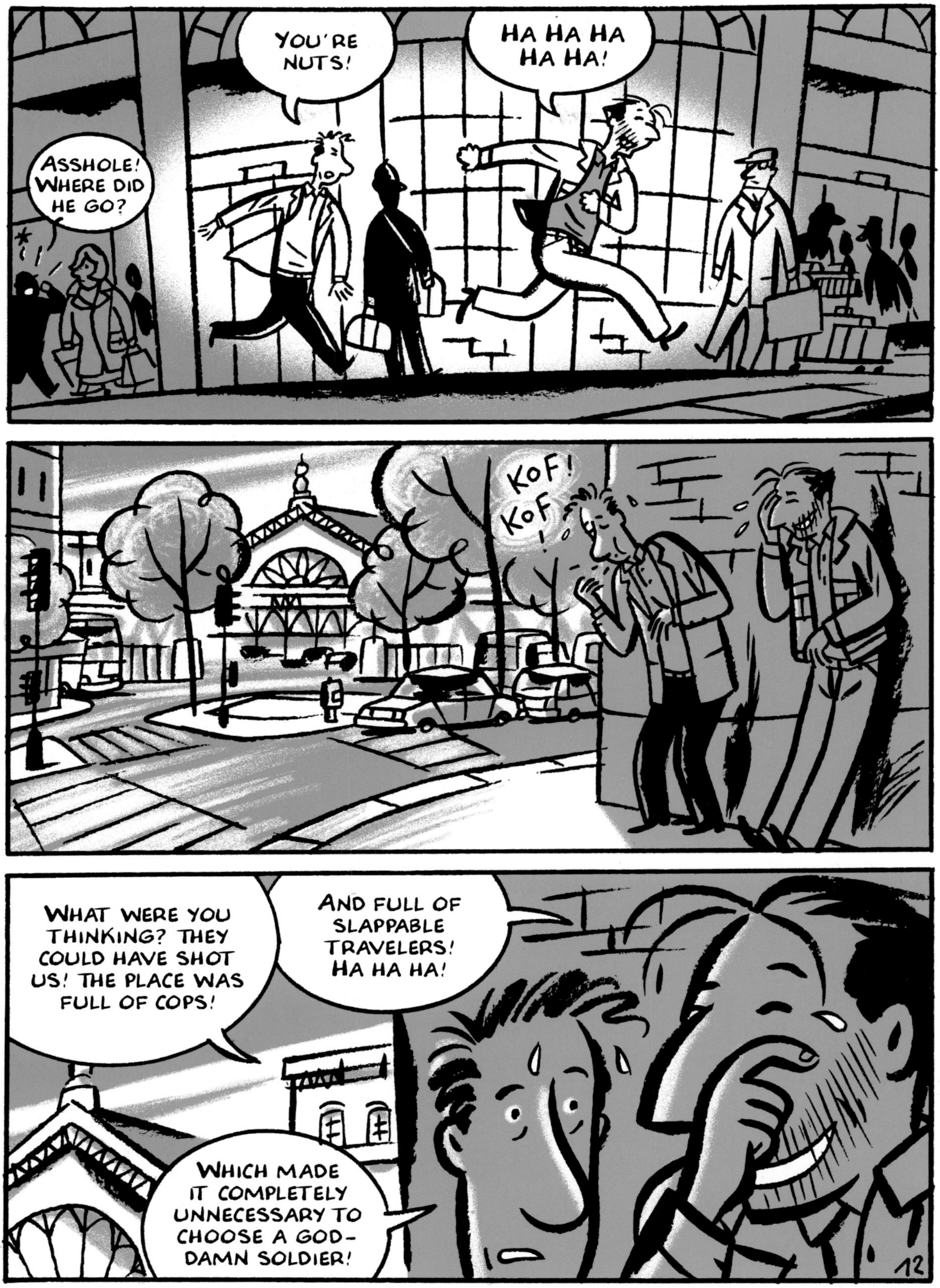
ASSHOLE! WHERE DID HE GO?
YOU'RE NUTS!
HA HA HA HA HA!
KOF! KOF!
WHAT WERE YOU THINKING? THEY COULD HAVE SHOT US! THE PLACE WAS FULL OF COPS!
AND FULL OF SLAPPABLE TRAVELERS! HA HA HA!
WHICH MADE IT COMPLETELY UNNECESSARY TO CHOOSE A GOD-DAMN SOLDIER!
12

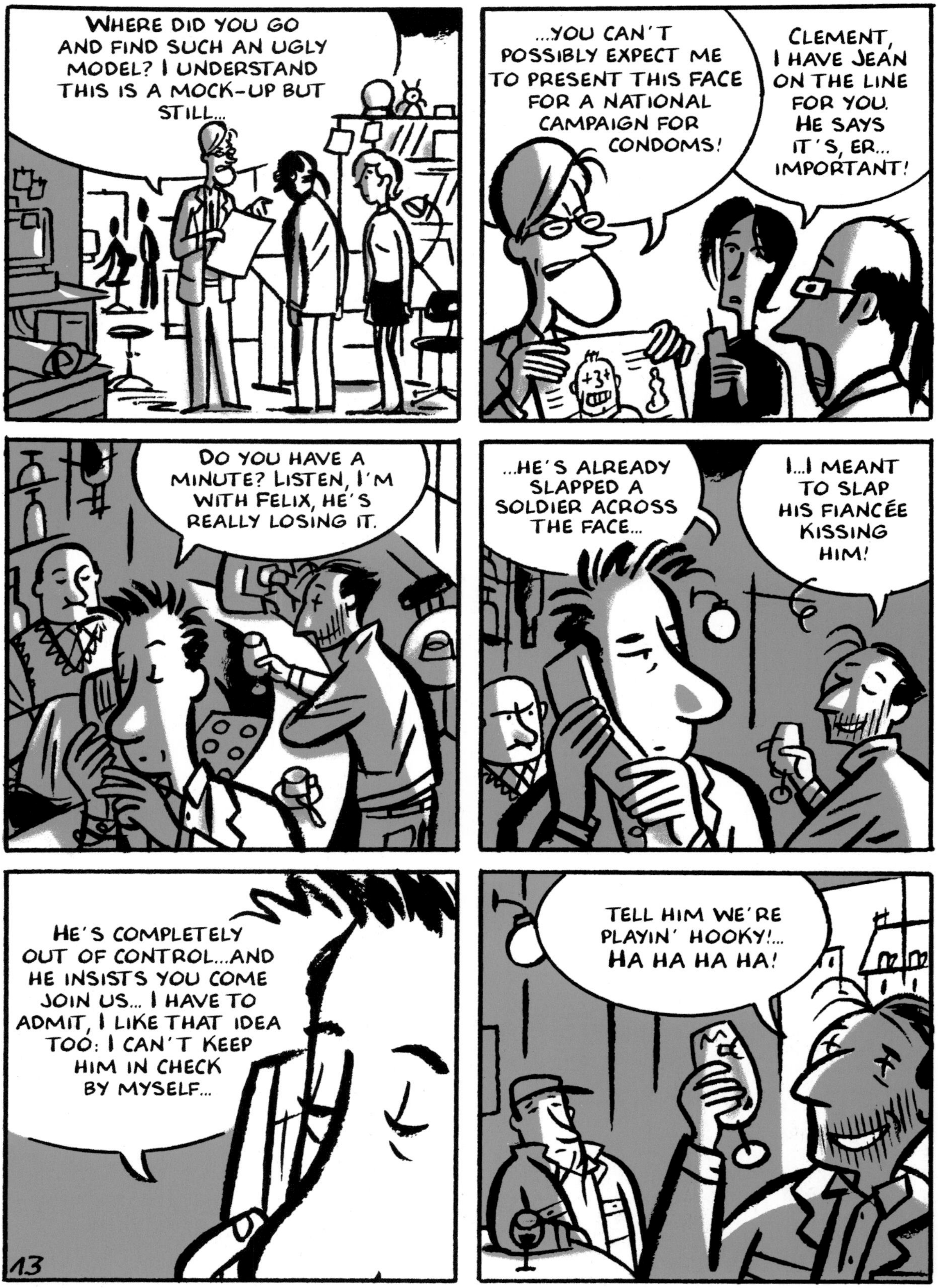
WHERE DID YOU GO AND FIND SUCH AN UGLY MODEL? I UNDERSTAND THIS IS A MOCK-UP BUT STILL...
...YOU CAN'T POSSIBLY EXPECT ME TO PRESENT THIS FACE FOR A NATIONAL CAMPAIGN FOR CONDOMS!
CLEMENT, I HAVE JEAN ON THE LINE FOR YOU. HE SAYS IT'S, ER... IMPORTANT!
DO YOU HAVE A MINUTE? LISTEN, I'M WITH FELIX, HE'S REALLY LOSING IT.
...HE'S ALREADY SLAPPED A SOLDIER ACROSS THE FACE...
I...I MEANT TO SLAP HIS FIANCÉE KISSING HIM!
HE'S COMPLETELY OUT OF CONTROL...AND HE INSISTS YOU COME JOIN US... I HAVE TO ADMIT, I LIKE THAT IDEA TOO: I CAN'T KEEP HIM IN CHECK BY MYSELF...
13
TELL HIM WE'RE PLAYIN' HOOKY!... HA HA HA HA!

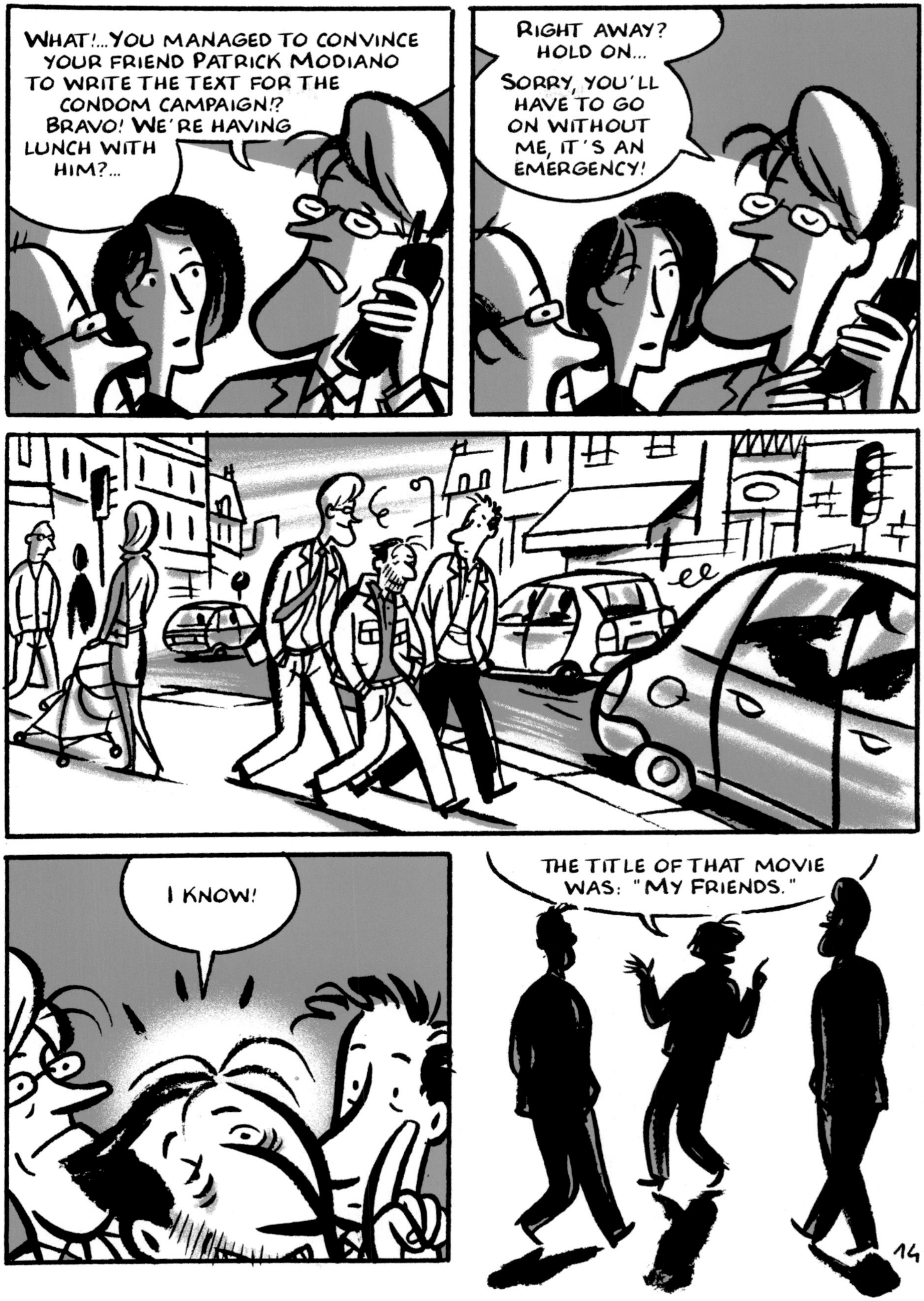
WHAT!...YOU MANAGED TO CONVINCE YOUR FRIEND PATRICK MODIANO TO WRITE THE TEXT FOR THE CONDOM CAMPAIGN!? BRAVO! WE'RE HAVING LUNCH WITH HIM?...
RIGHT AWAY? HOLD ON...
SORRY, YOU'LL HAVE TO GO ON WITHOUT ME, IT'S AN EMERGENCY!
I KNOW!
THE TITLE OF THAT MOVIE WAS: "MY FRIENDS."
14

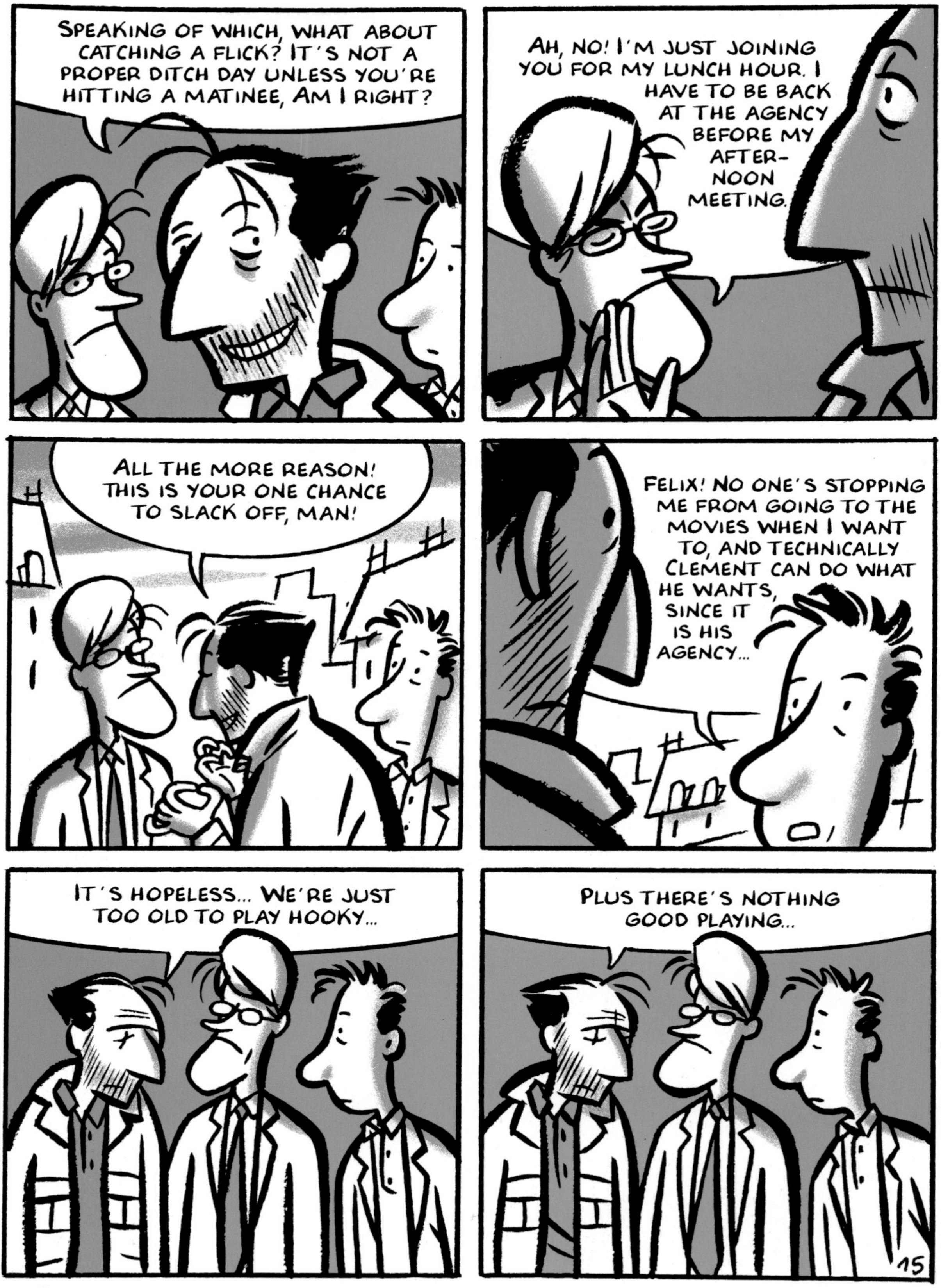
SPEAKING OF WHICH, WHAT ABOUT CATCHING A FLICK? IT'S NOT A PROPER DITCH DAY UNLESS YOU'RE HITTING A MATINEE, AM I RIGHT?
AH, NO! I'M JUST JOINING YOU FOR MY LUNCH HOUR. I HAVE TO BE BACK AT THE AGENCY BEFORE MY AFTER-NOON MEETING.
ALL THE MORE REASON! THIS IS YOUR ONE CHANCE TO SLACK OFF, MAN!
FELIX! NO ONE'S STOPPING ME FROM GOING TO THE MOVIES WHEN I WANT TO, AND TECHNICALLY CLEMENT CAN DO WHAT HE WANTS, SINCE IT IS HIS AGENCY...
IT'S HOPELESS... WE'RE JUST TOO OLD TO PLAY HOOKY...
PLUS THERE'S NOTHING GOOD PLAYING...
15

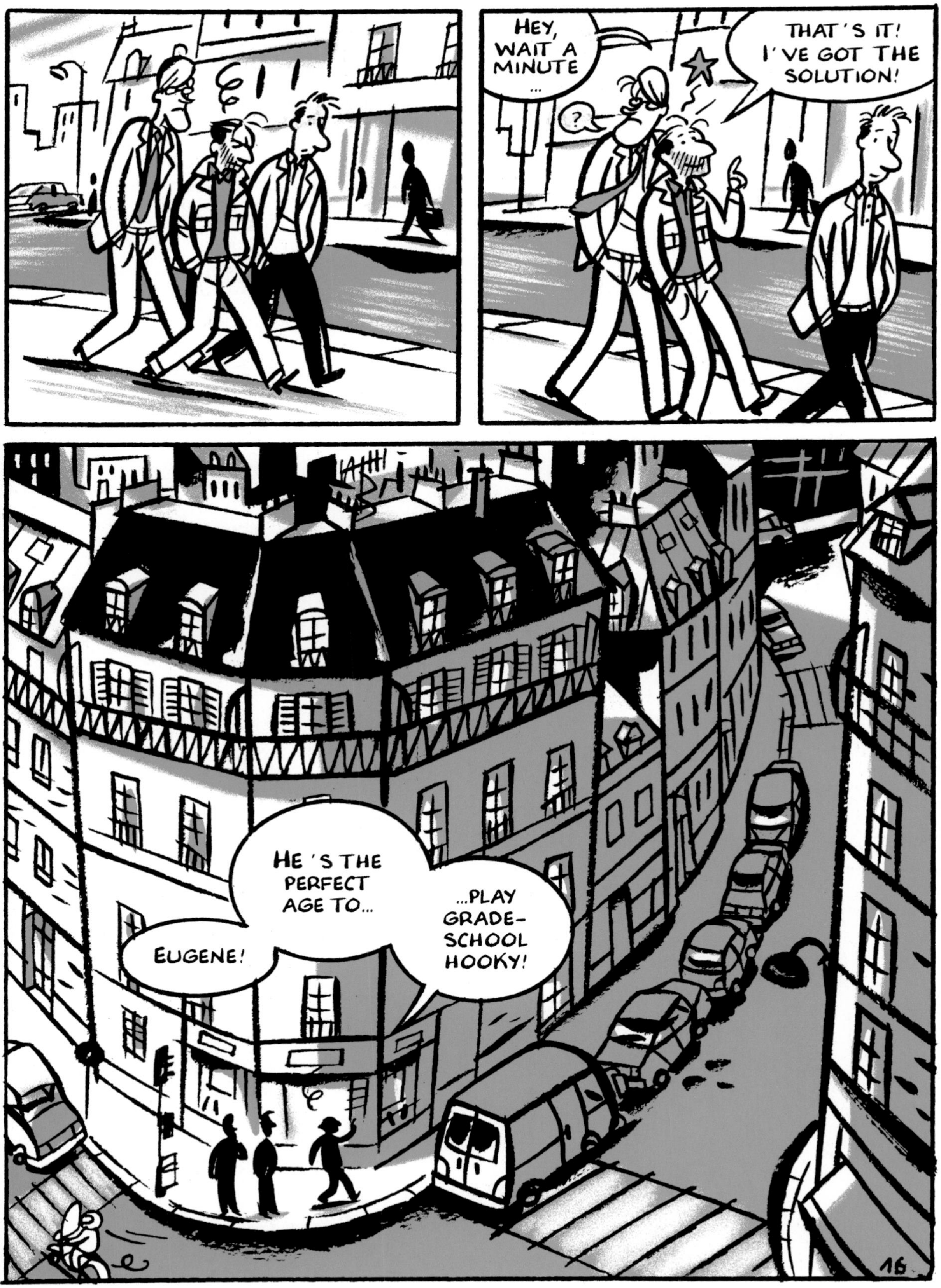
HEY, WAIT A MINUTE ...
?
THAT'S IT! I'VE GOT THE SOLUTION!
EUGENE!
HE'S THE PERFECT AGE TO...
...PLAY GRADE-SCHOOL HOOKY!
16

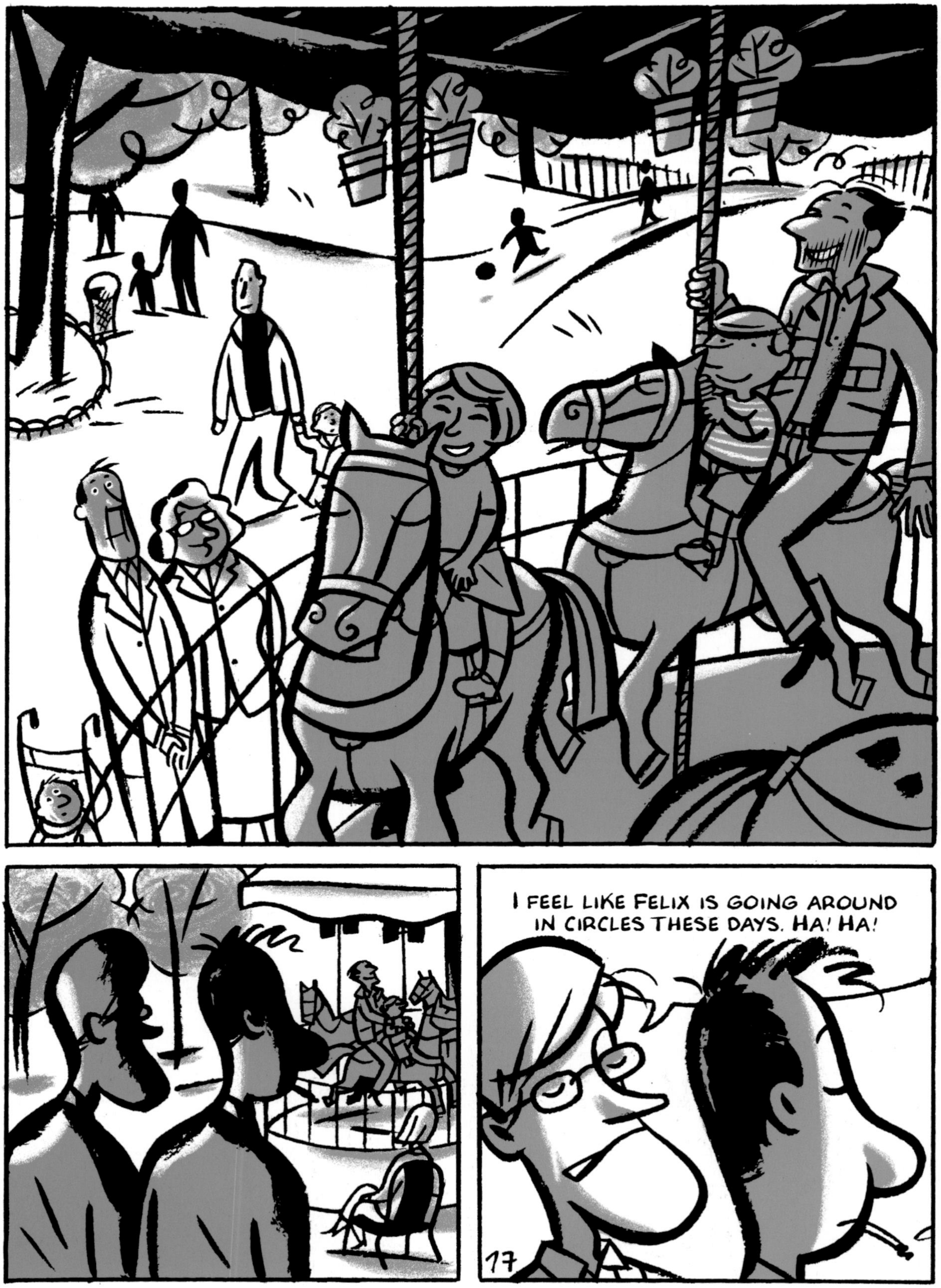
I FEEL LIKE FELIX IS GOING AROUND IN CIRCLES THESE DAYS. HA! HA!

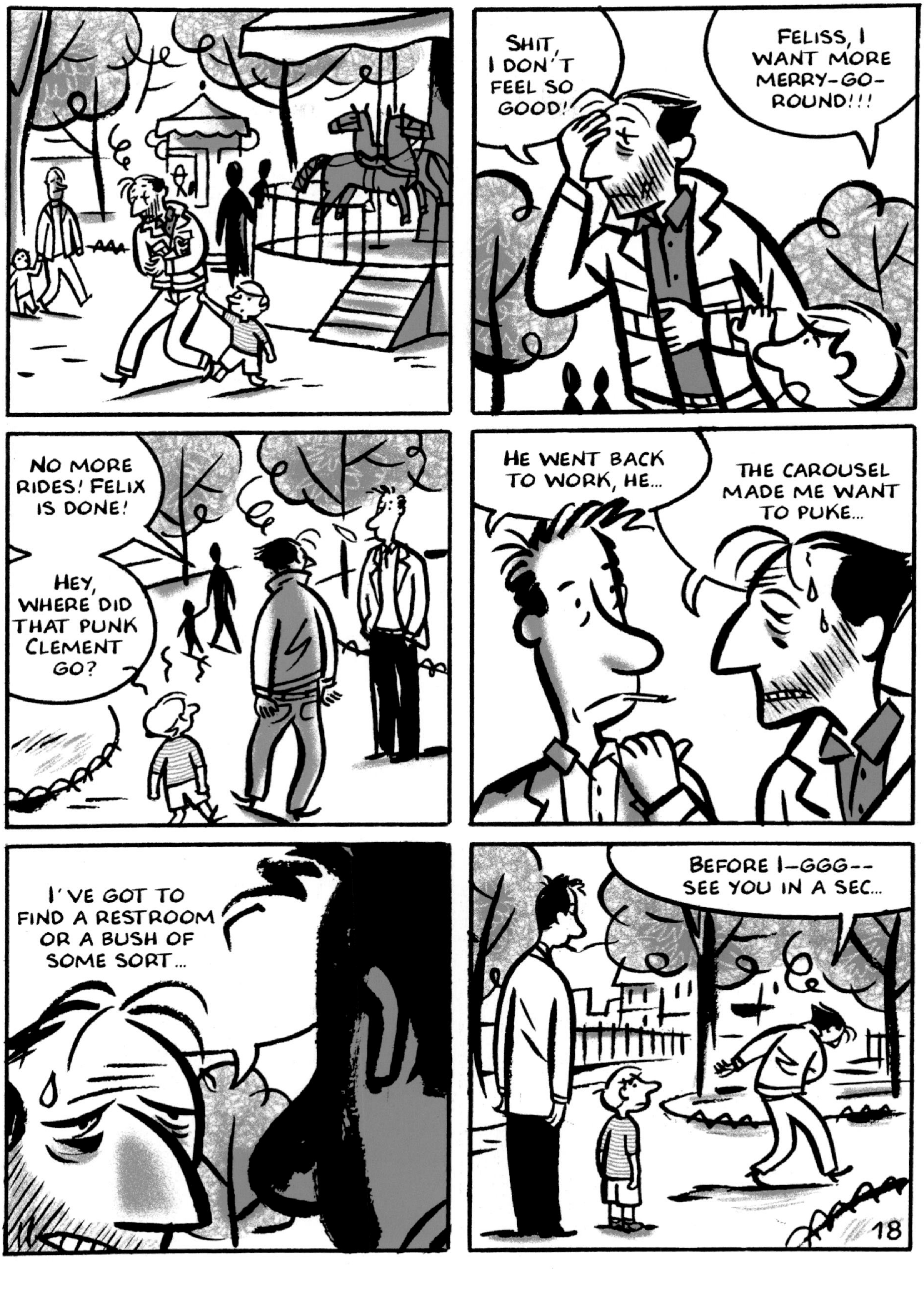
SHIT, I DON'T FEEL SO GOOD!
FELISS, I WANT MORE MERRY-GO-ROUND!!!
NO MORE RIDES! FELIX IS DONE!
HEY, WHERE DID THAT PUNK CLEMENT GO?
HE WENT BACK TO WORK, HE...
THE CAROUSEL MADE ME WANT TO PUKE...
I'VE GOT TO FIND A RESTROOM OR A BUSH OF SOME SORT...
BEFORE I-GGG-- SEE YOU IN A SEC...
18

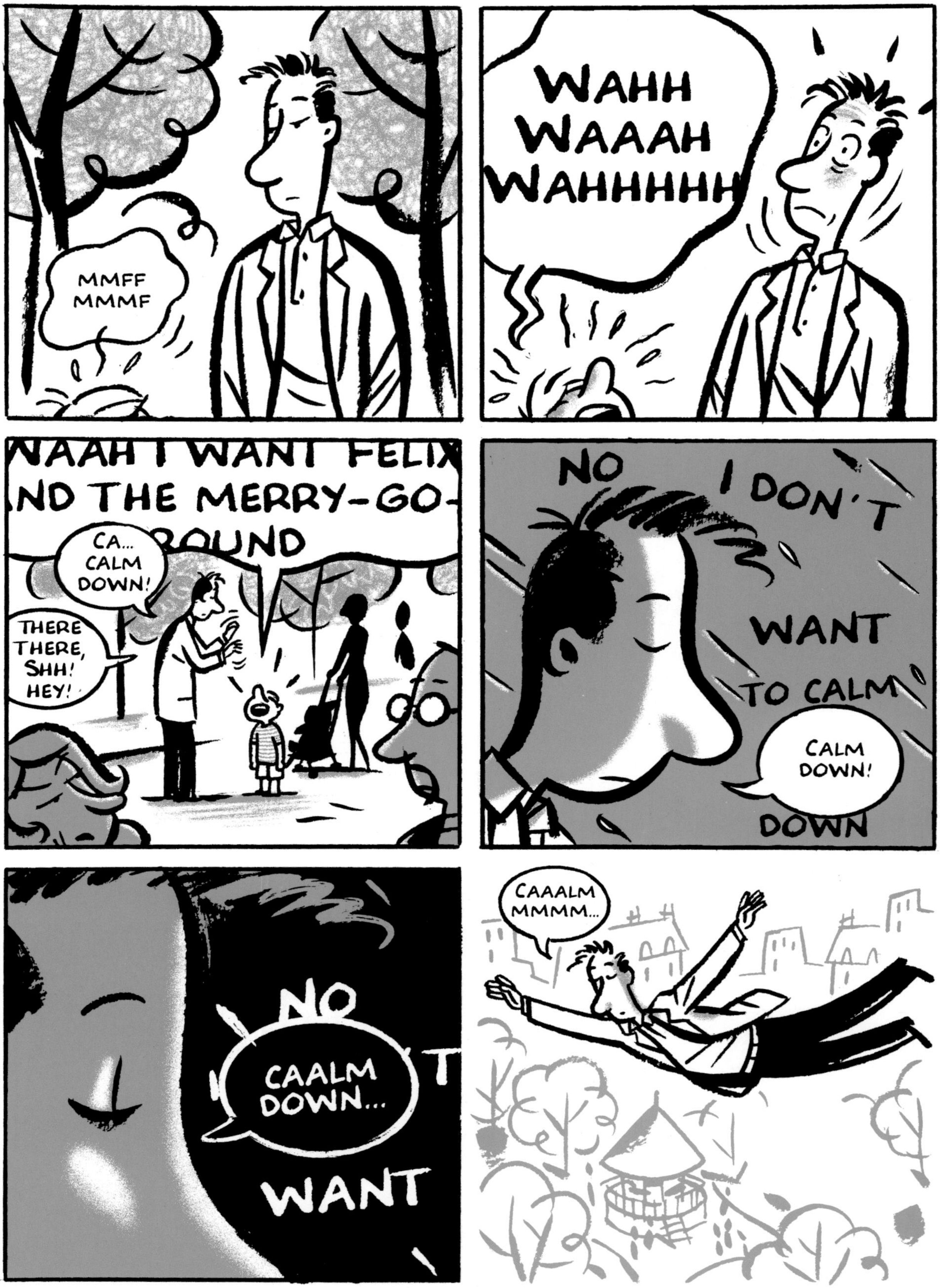
MMFF MMMF
WAHH WAAAH WAHHHHH
WAAH I WANT FELIX AND THE MERRY-GO-ROUND
CA... CALM DOWN!
THERE THERE, SHH! HEY!
NO I DON'T WANT TO CALM DOWN
CALM DOWN!
NO
CAALM DOWN...
WANT
CAAALM MMMM...

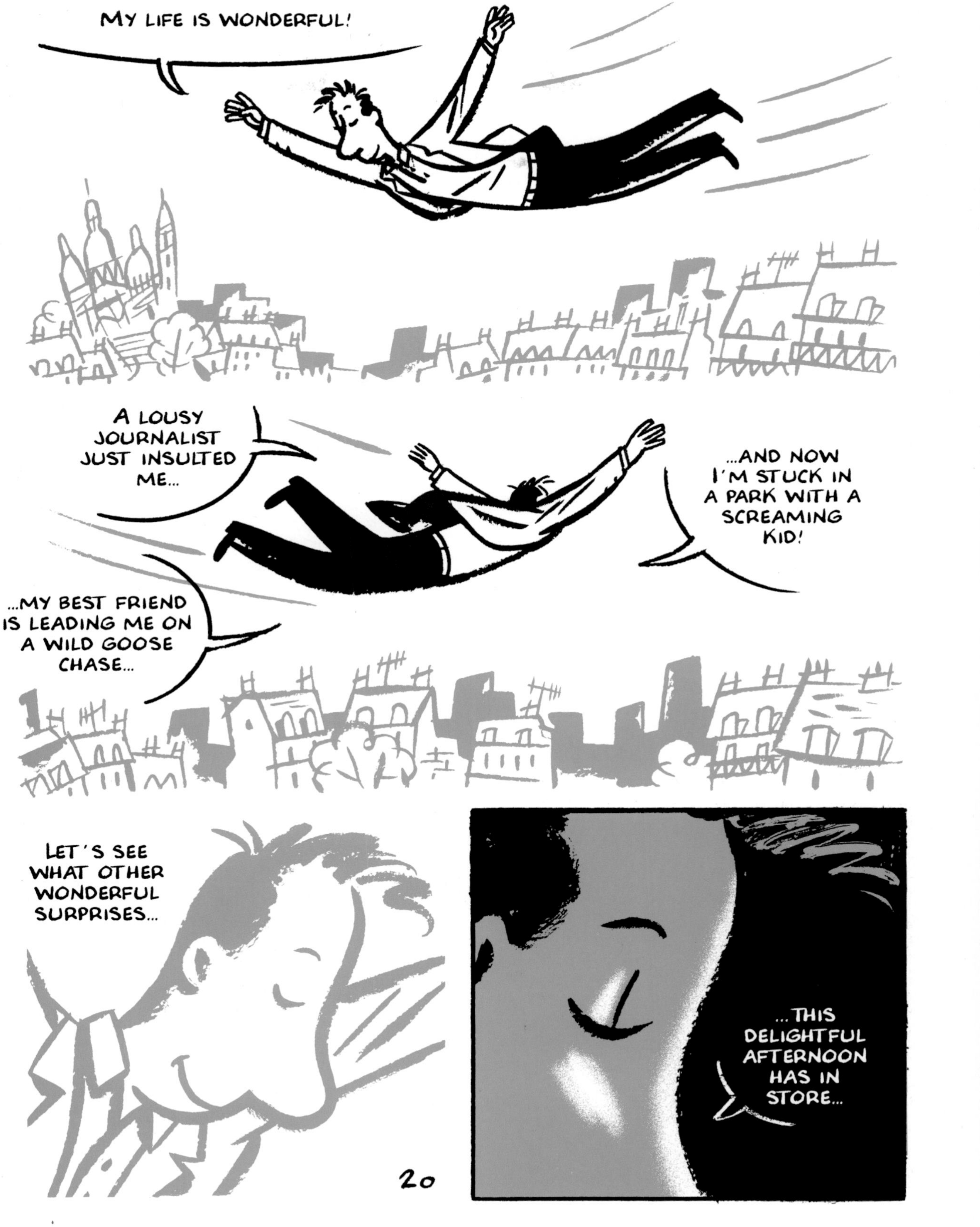
MY LIFE IS WONDERFUL!
A LOUSY JOURNALIST JUST INSULTED ME...
...AND NOW I'M STUCK IN A PARK WITH A SCREAMING KID!
...MY BEST FRIEND IS LEADING ME ON A WILD GOOSE CHASE...
LET'S SEE WHAT OTHER WONDERFUL SURPRISES...
...THIS DELIGHTFUL AFTERNOON HAS IN STORE...
20

EXCUSE ME, DO YOU NEED HELP?
WA AAAA AAAA HHHH HH
MAYBE...
WA A AAA
CAN YOU TELL ME WHAT BUTTON TO PUSH TO MAKE IT STOP?
WA AAAAAA AAHHHH
HEY, WHAT'S YOUR NAME?
EUGENE.
21
HI, EUGENE. I'M HILDE AND THIS IS CLEMENTINE...

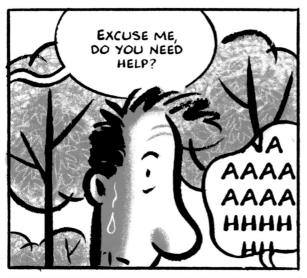

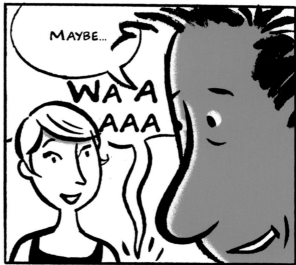

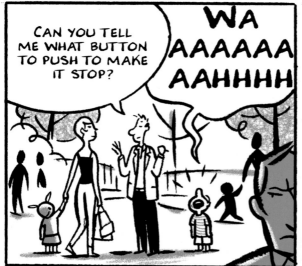

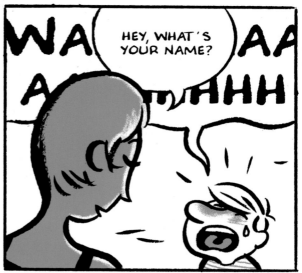

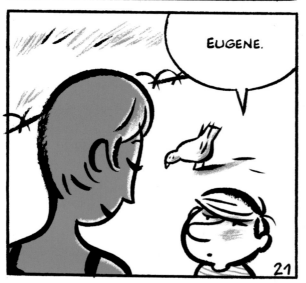

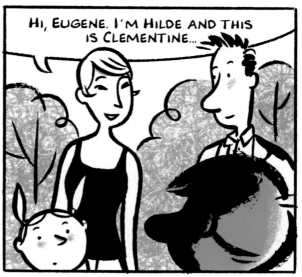

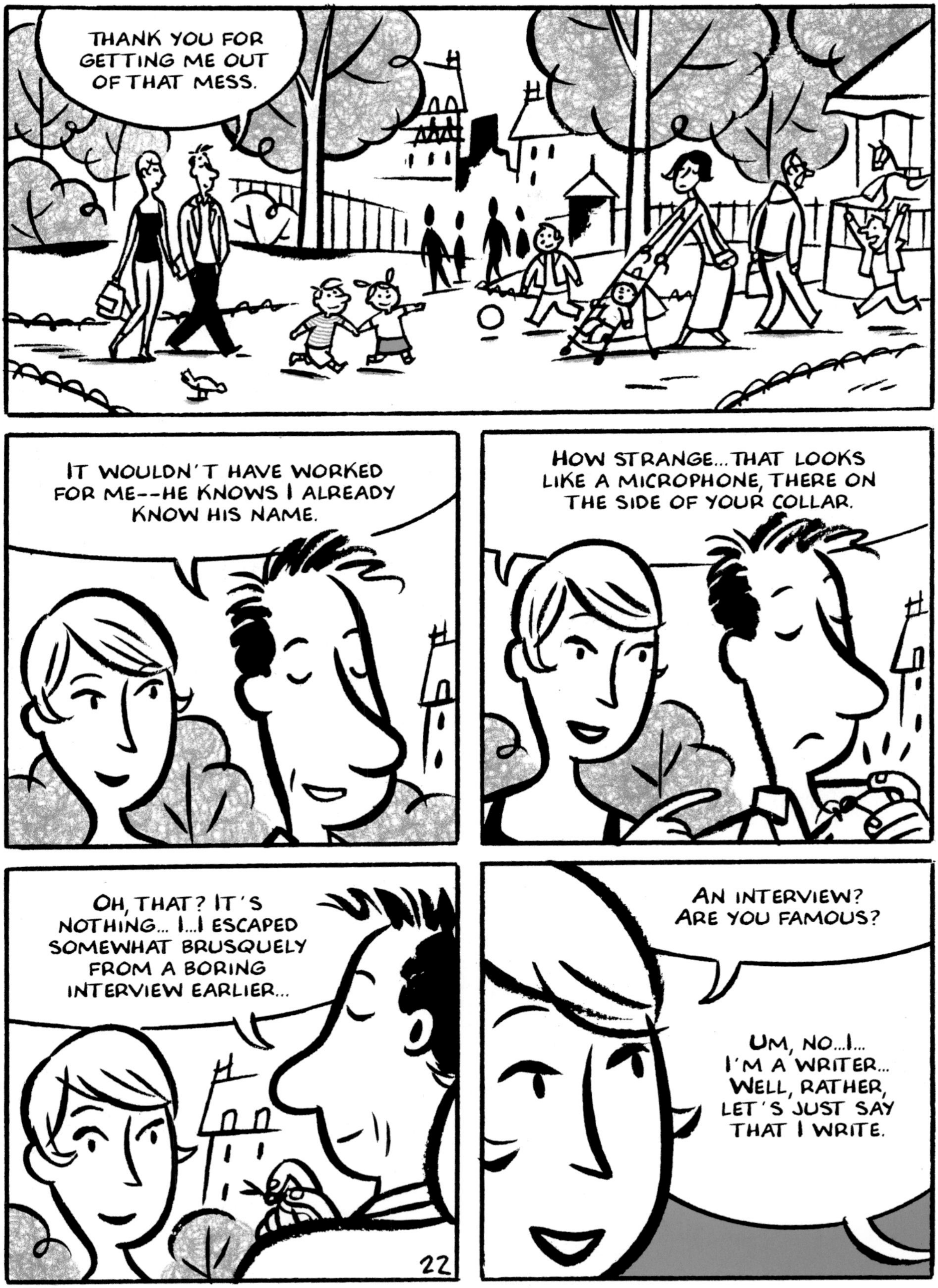
THANK YOU FOR GETTING ME OUT OF THAT MESS.
IT WOULDN'T HAVE WORKED FOR ME--HE KNOWS I ALREADY KNOW HIS NAME.
HOW STRANGE... THAT LOOKS LIKE A MICROPHONE, THERE ON THE SIDE OF YOUR COLLAR.
OH, THAT? IT'S NOTHING... I...I ESCAPED SOMEWHAT BRUSQUELY FROM A BORING INTERVIEW EARLIER...
22
AN INTERVIEW? ARE YOU FAMOUS?
UM, NO...I... I'M A WRITER... WELL, RATHER, LET'S JUST SAY THAT I WRITE.

AND YOU?

I'M AN ARCHITECTURE STUDENT, AND I'M IN PARIS FOR THREE MONTHS AS AN AU PAIR...

WHERE ARE YOU FROM?

BERLIN.

BUT YOUR FRENCH IS FLAWLESS.

MY MOTHER IS FRENCH.

BUT I DON'T KNOW PARIS AT ALL. I ONLY CAME HERE ONCE WHEN I WAS FIVE.

IF YOU WANT, I COULD BE YOUR TOUR GUIDE TO THE CITY... ARE YOU FAMILIAR WITH HECTOR GUIMARD'S ARCHITECTURE?

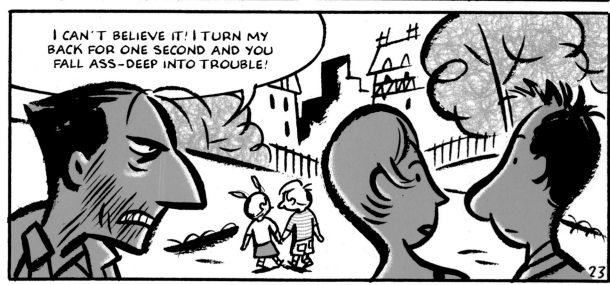

I CAN'T BELIEVE IT! I TURN MY BACK FOR ONE SECOND AND YOU FALL ASS-DEEP INTO TROUBLE!

23

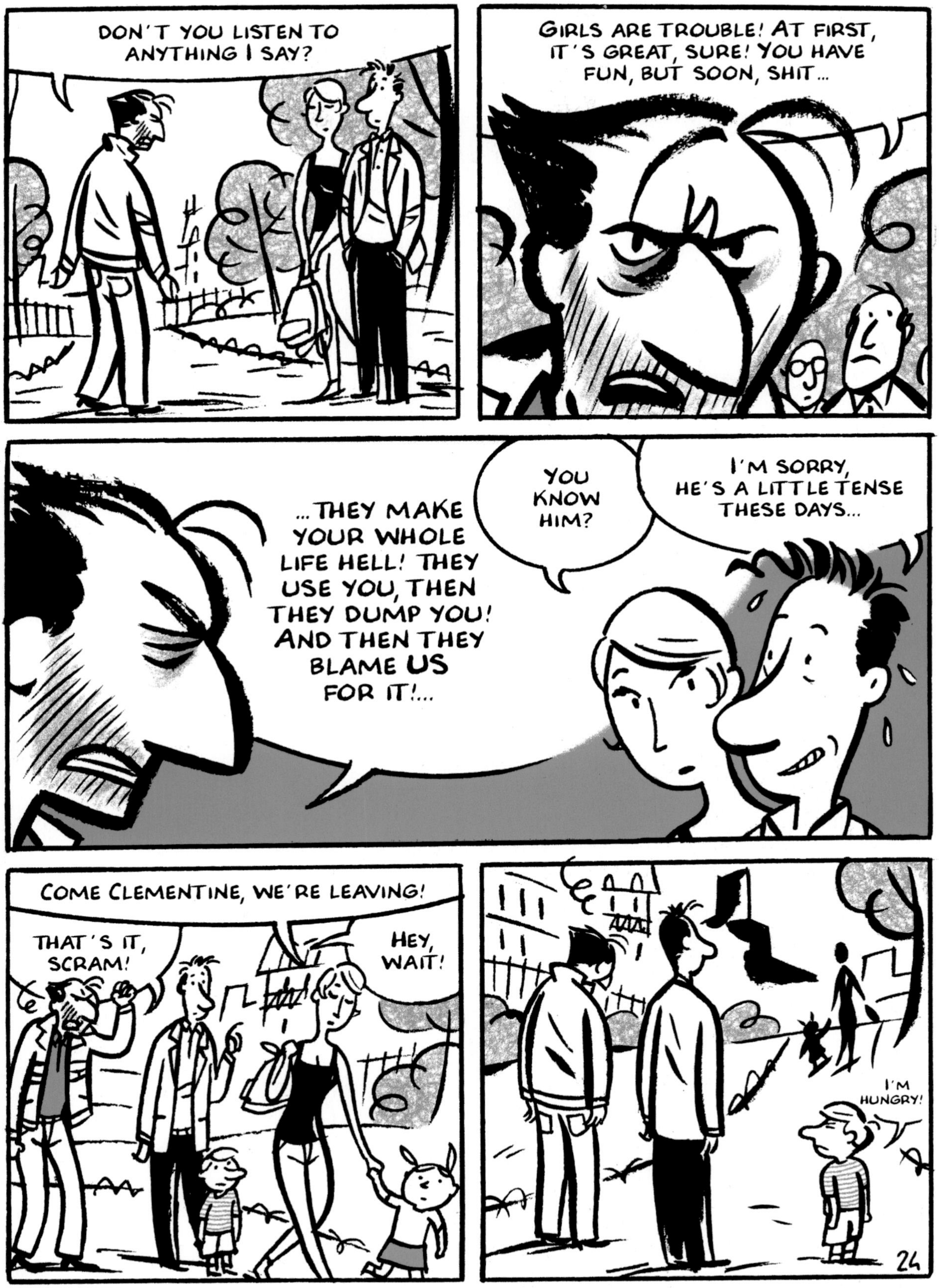
DON'T YOU LISTEN TO ANYTHING I SAY?
GIRLS ARE TROUBLE! AT FIRST, IT'S GREAT, SURE! YOU HAVE FUN, BUT SOON, SHIT...
...THEY MAKE YOUR WHOLE LIFE HELL! THEY USE YOU, THEN THEY DUMP YOU! AND THEN THEY BLAME US FOR IT!...
YOU KNOW HIM?
I'M SORRY, HE'S A LITTLE TENSE THESE DAYS...
COME CLEMENTINE, WE'RE LEAVING!
THAT'S IT, SCRAM!
HEY, WAIT!
I'M HUNGRY!
24

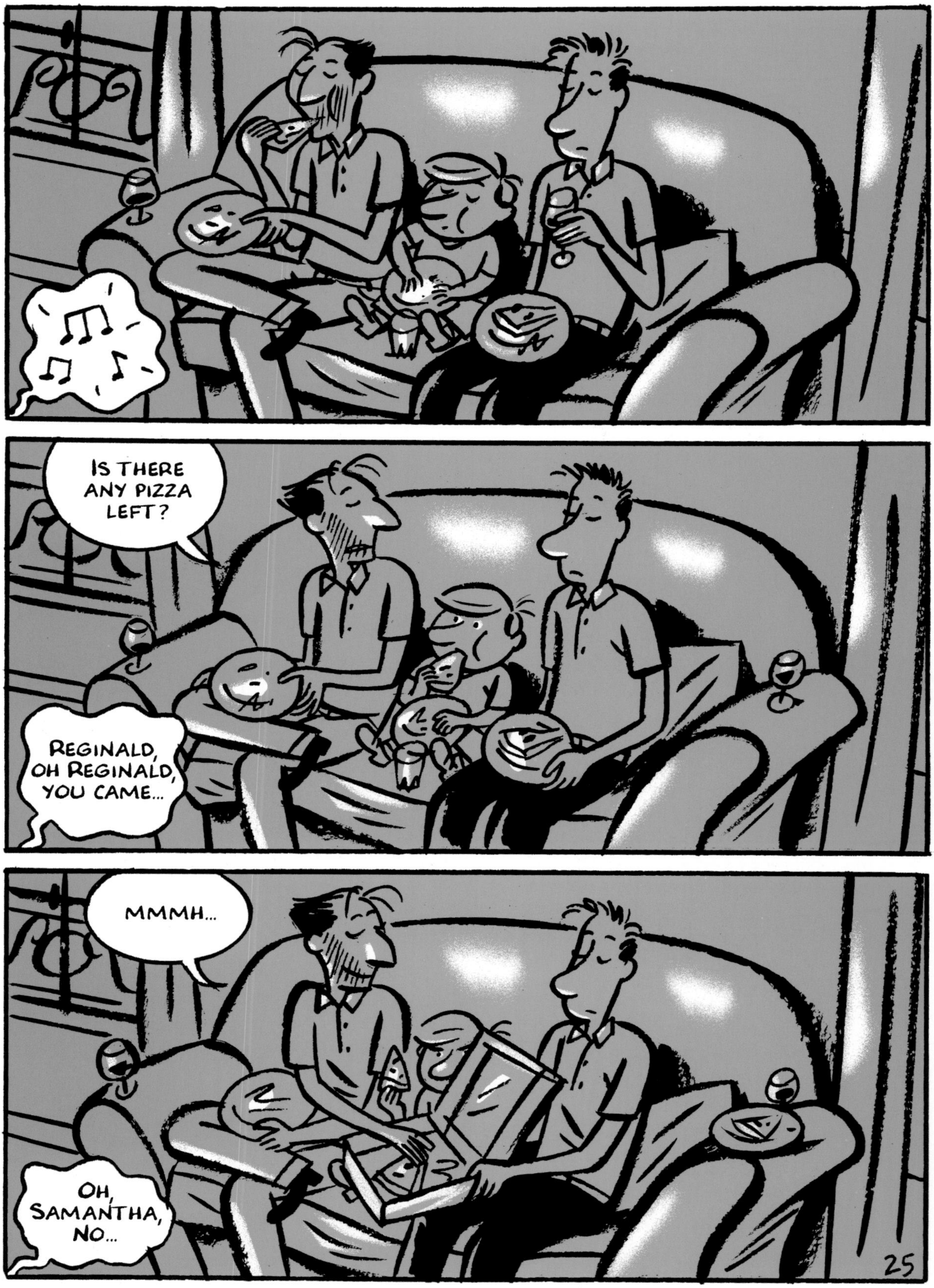
IS THERE ANY PIZZA LEFT?
REGINALD, OH REGINALD, YOU CAME...
MMMH...
OH, SAMANTHA, NO...
25

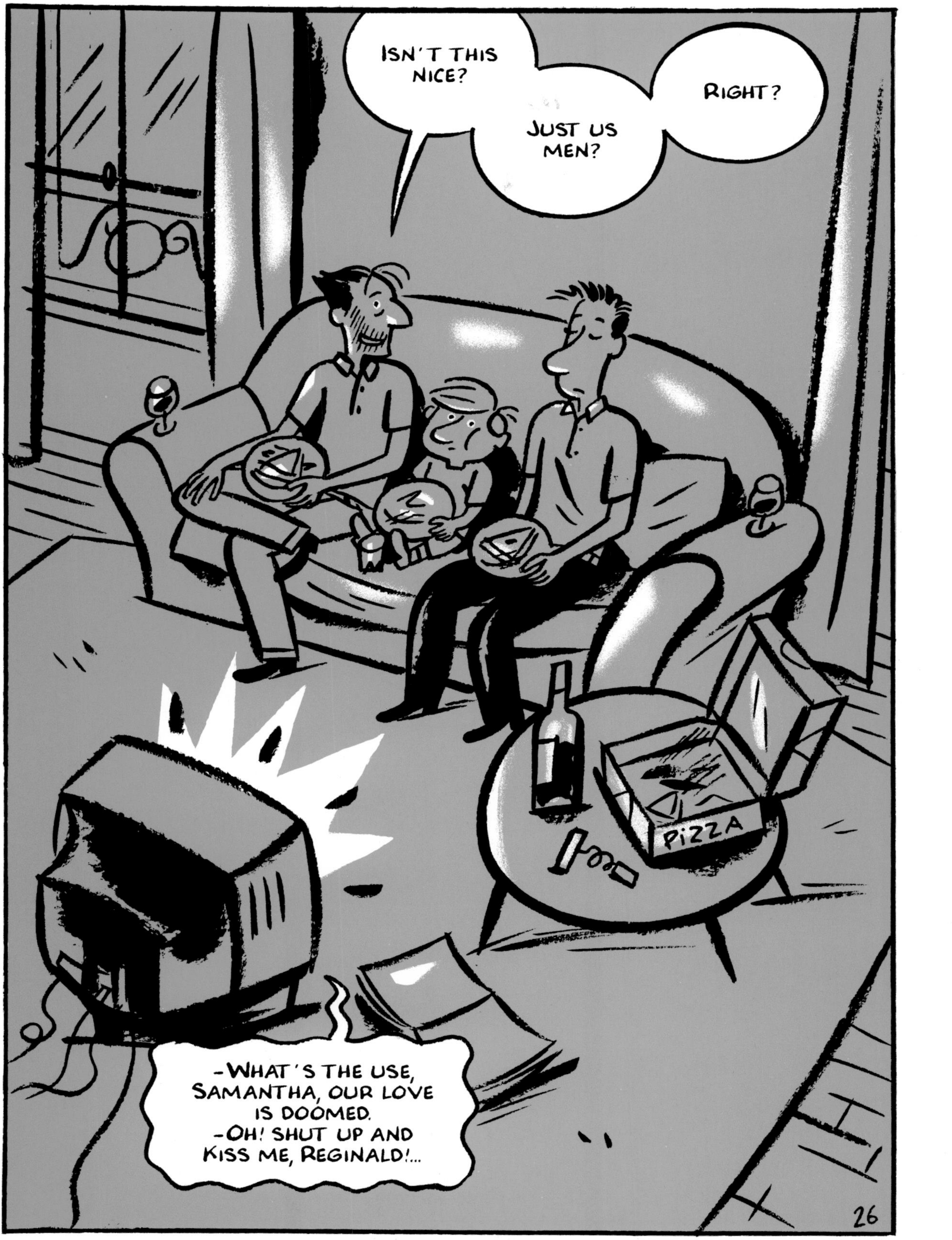
ISN'T THIS NICE?
JUST US MEN?
RIGHT?
PIZZA
-WHAT'S THE USE, SAMANTHA, OUR LOVE IS DOOMED.
-OH! SHUT UP AND KISS ME, REGINALD!...
26

Felix's Elevator Ride

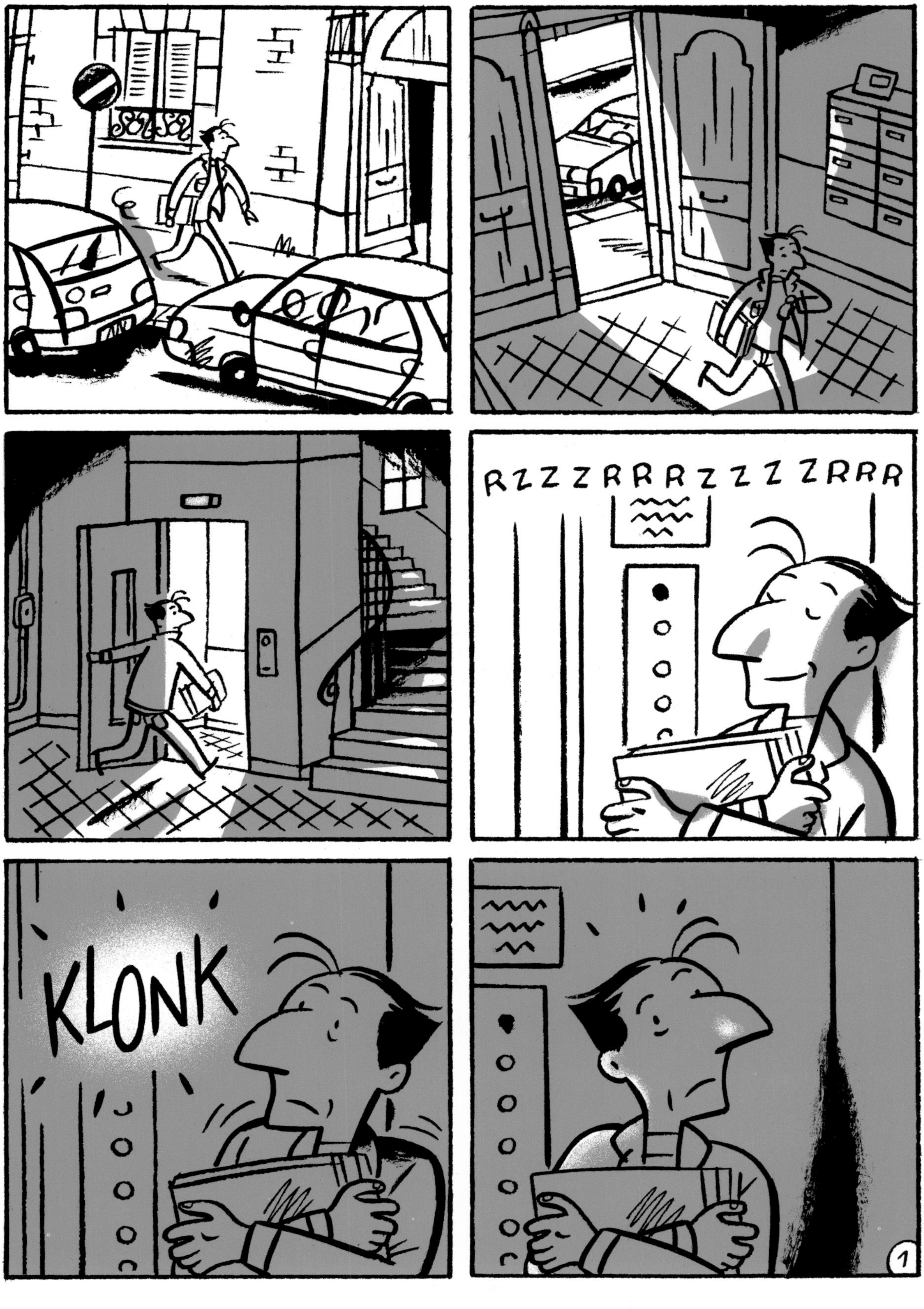
RZZZRRRZZZZRRR
KLONK
1

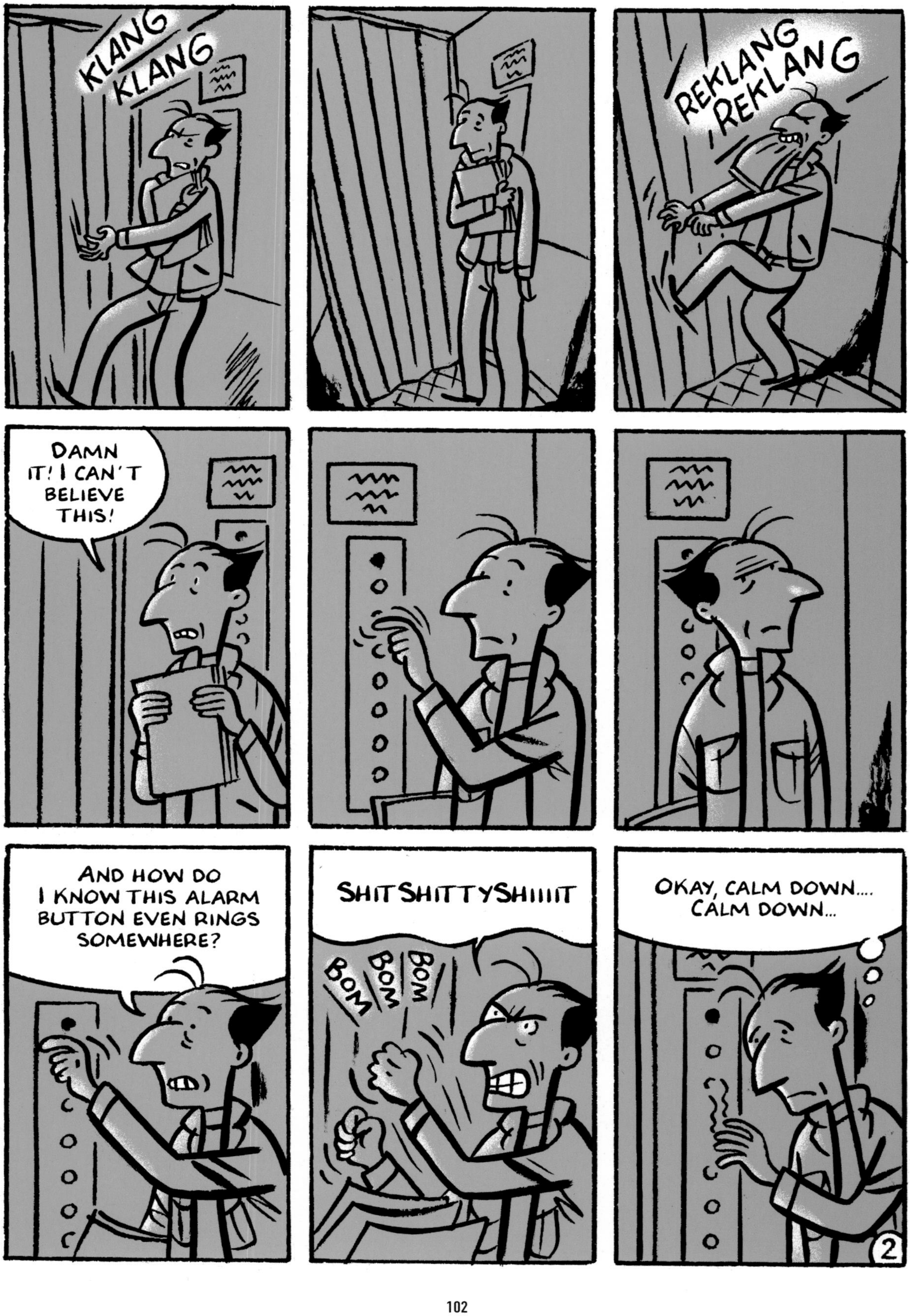
KLANG
KLANG
REKLANG
REKLANG
DAMN IT! I CAN'T BELIEVE THIS!
AND HOW DO I KNOW THIS ALARM BUTTON EVEN RINGS SOMEWHERE?
SHITSHITTYSHIIIIIT
BOM
BOM
BOM
OKAY, CALM DOWN.... CALM DOWN...
2

HELLO, HELLO, THE ELEVATOR IS STUCK...
AND I'M INSIDE IT...
INSIDE
INSIDE
THE ELEVATOR IS STUCK AND I...
YES
HI! THE...THE ELEVATOR IS STUCK AND I AM STUCK IN IT... C..COULD YOU PLEASE...
YES...YES OF COURSE...DON'T GO ANYWHERE.
LET ME JUST SLIP ON A LITTLE SOMETHING AND I'LL BE RIGHT THERE!
MAXIMUM WEIGHT OF 300 LBS
WHAT A VOICE...
WHAT A SULTRY VOICE!
3

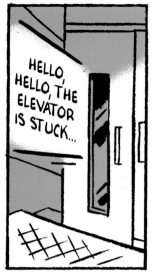

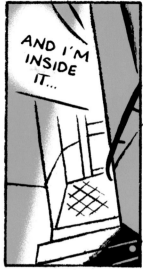

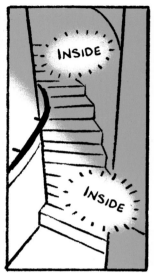

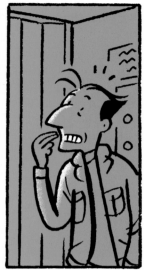

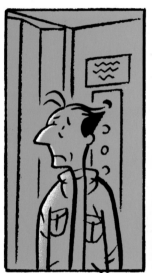

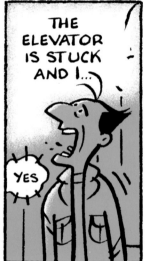

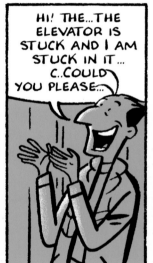

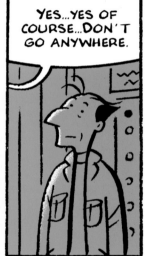

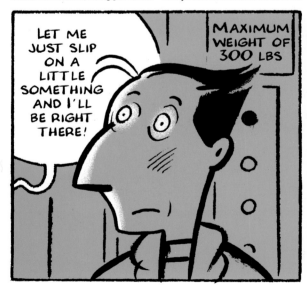

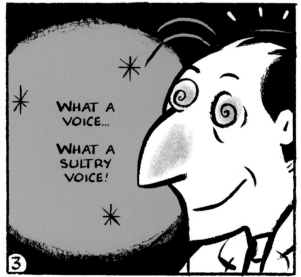

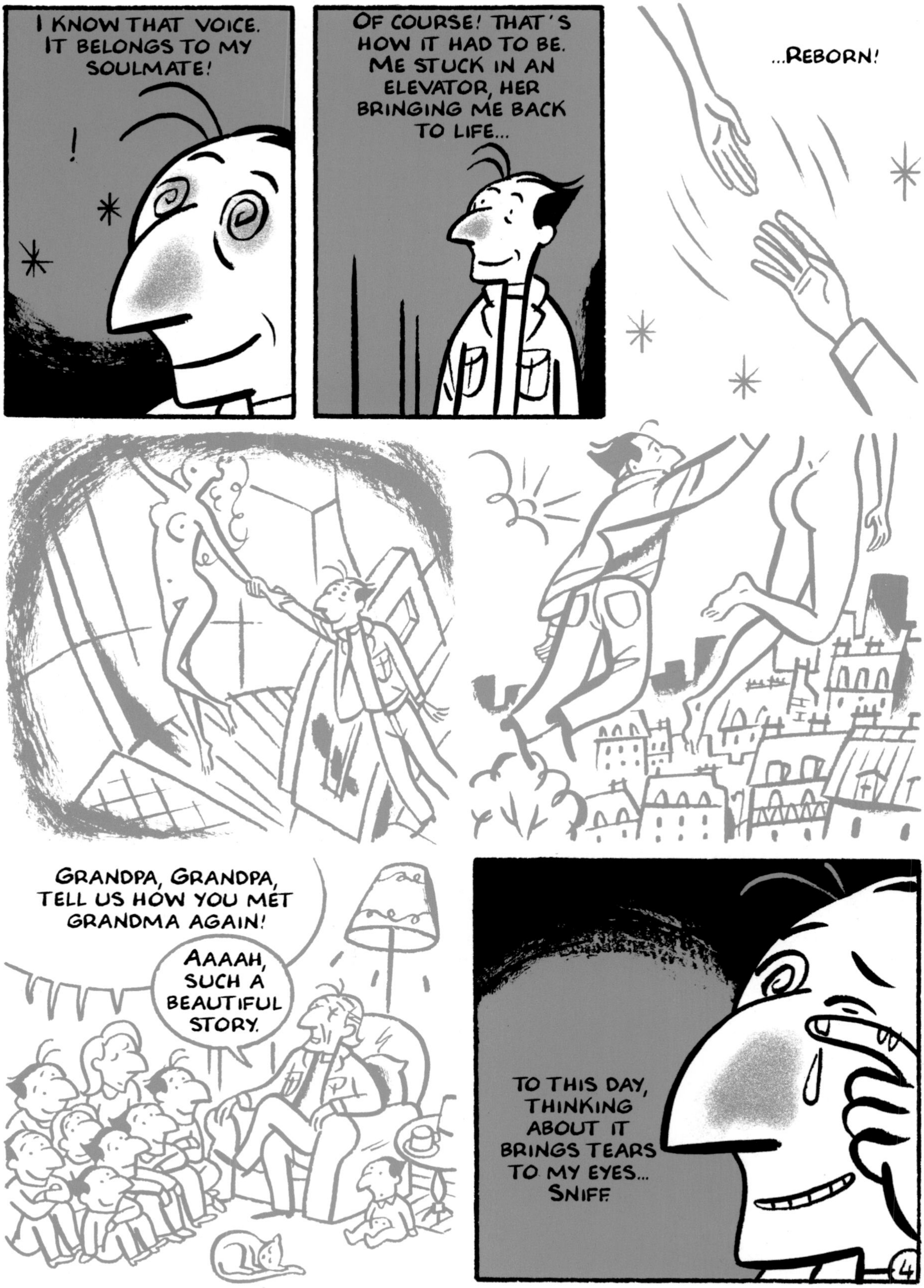
I KNOW THAT VOICE. IT BELONGS TO MY SOULMATE!
!
OF COURSE! THAT'S HOW IT HAD TO BE. ME STUCK IN AN ELEVATOR, HER BRINGING ME BACK TO LIFE...
...REBORN!
GRANDPA, GRANDPA, TELL US HOW YOU MET GRANDMA AGAIN!
AAAAH, SUCH A BEAUTIFUL STORY.
TO THIS DAY, THINKING ABOUT IT BRINGS TEARS TO MY EYES... SNIFF.
4

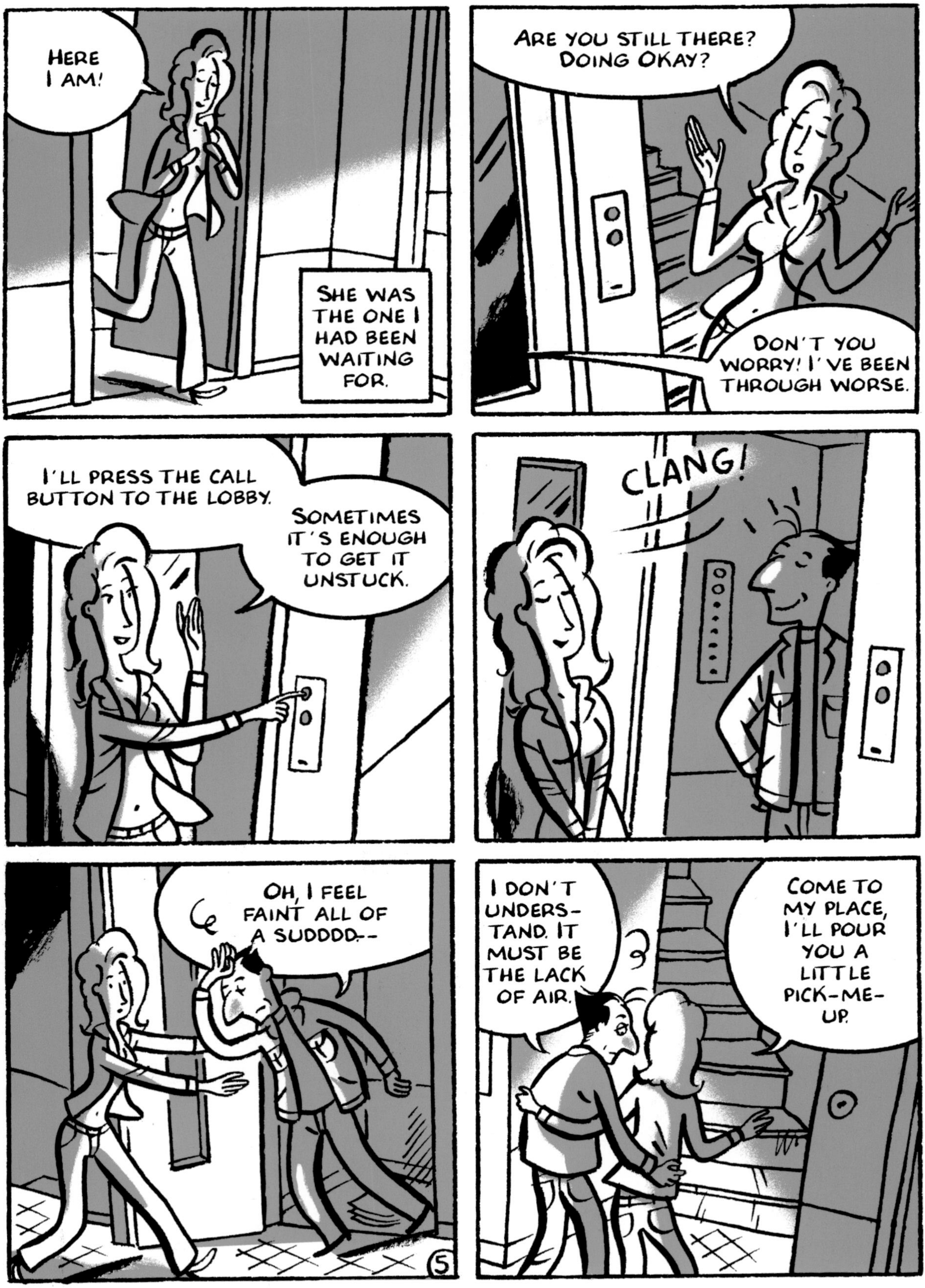
HERE I AM!
SHE WAS THE ONE I HAD BEEN WAITING FOR.
ARE YOU STILL THERE? DOING OKAY?
DON'T YOU WORRY! I'VE BEEN THROUGH WORSE.
I'LL PRESS THE CALL BUTTON TO THE LOBBY.
SOMETIMES IT'S ENOUGH TO GET IT UNSTUCK.
CLANG!
OH, I FEEL FAINT ALL OF A SUDDDD--
5
I DON'T UNDERS-TAND. IT MUST BE THE LACK OF AIR.
COME TO MY PLACE, I'LL POUR YOU A LITTLE PICK-ME-UP.

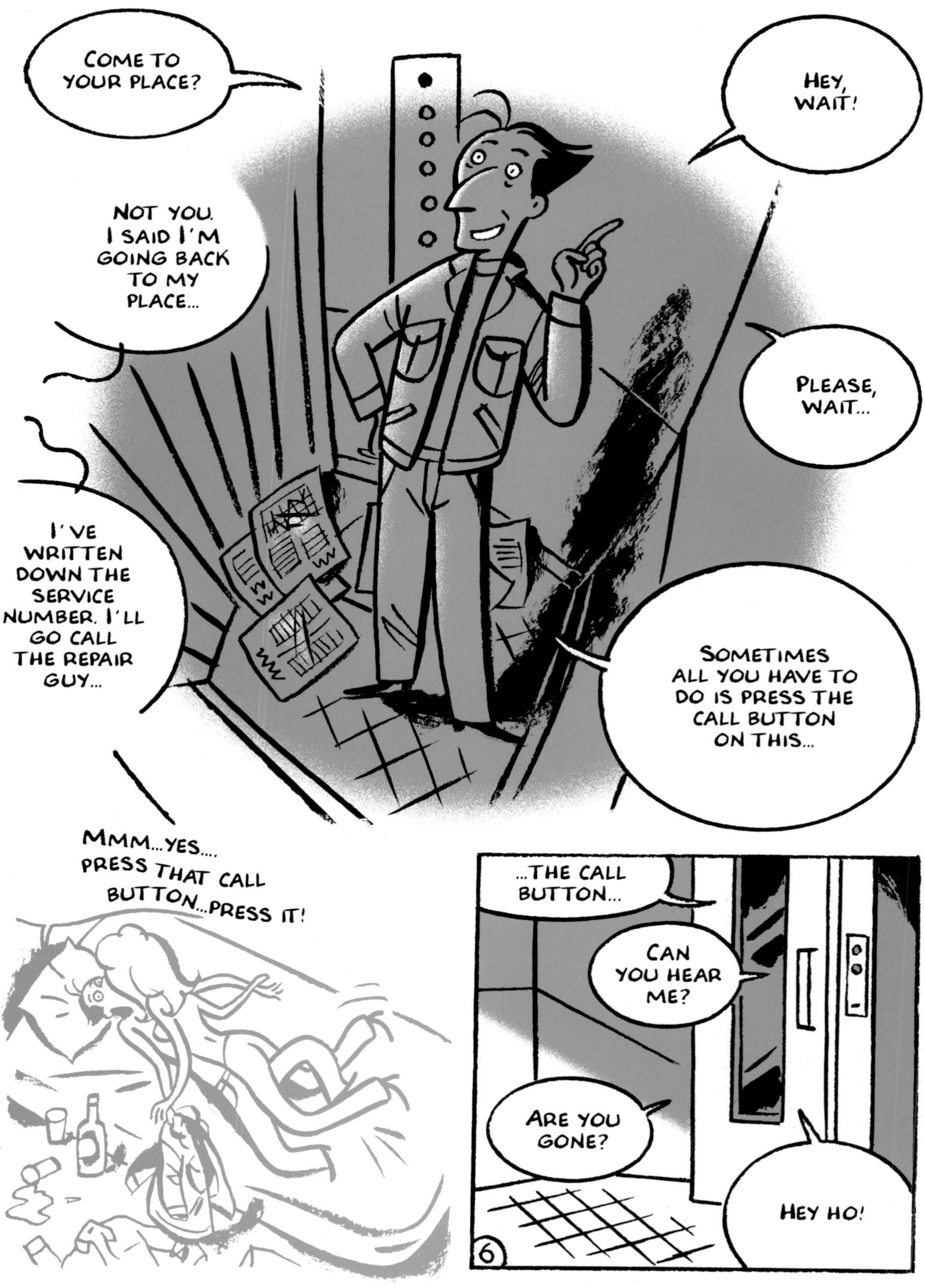
COME TO YOUR PLACE?
HEY, WAIT!
NOT YOU. I SAID I'M GOING BACK TO MY PLACE...
PLEASE, WAIT...
I'VE WRITTEN DOWN THE SERVICE NUMBER. I'LL GO CALL THE REPAIR GUY...
SOMETIMES ALL YOU HAVE TO DO IS PRESS THE CALL BUTTON ON THIS...
MMM...YES.... PRESS THAT CALL BUTTON...PRESS IT!
...THE CALL BUTTON...
CAN YOU HEAR ME?
ARE YOU GONE?
HEY HO!
6

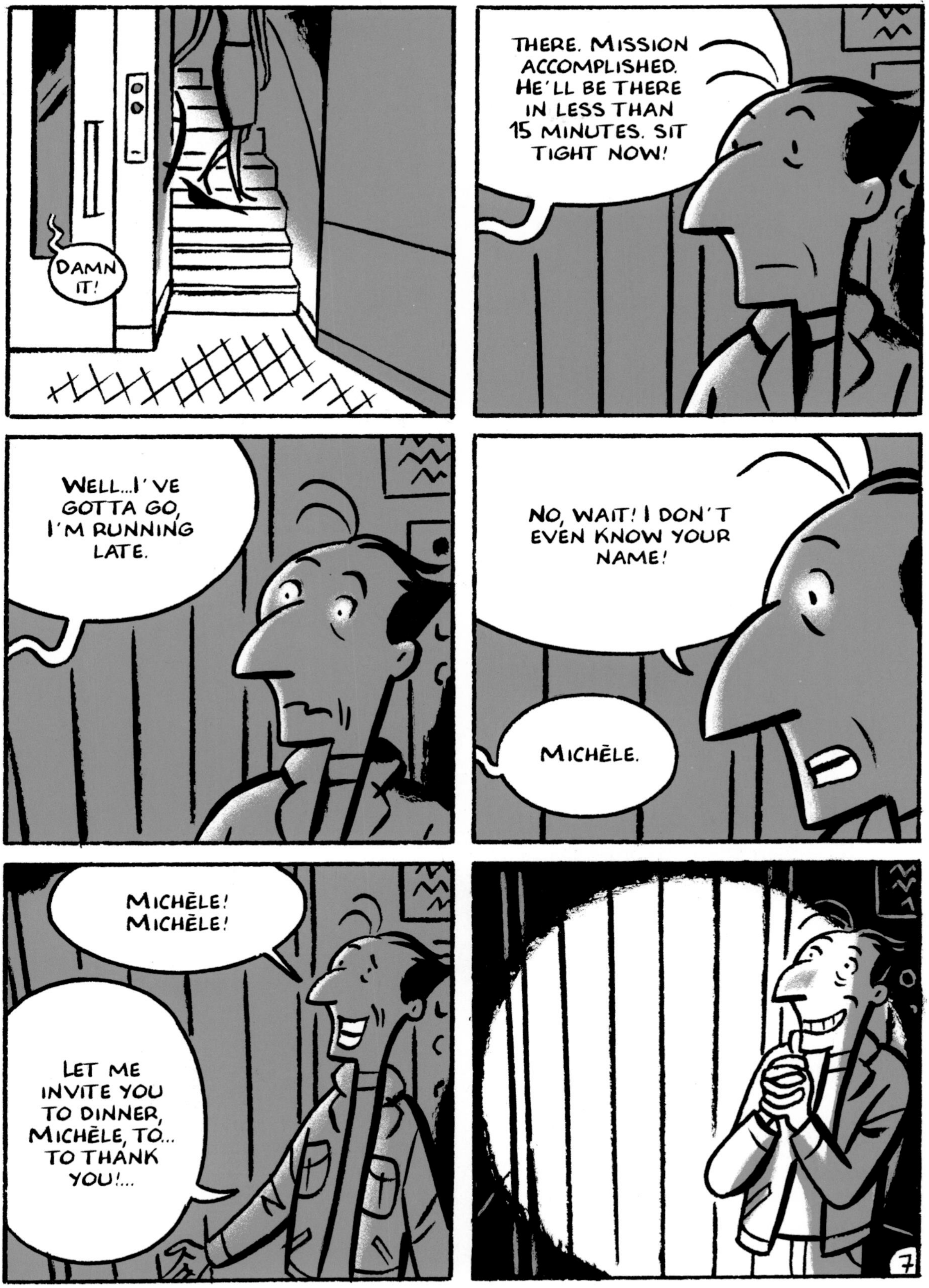
DAMN IT!
THERE. MISSION ACCOMPLISHED. HE'LL BE THERE IN LESS THAN 15 MINUTES. SIT TIGHT NOW!
WELL...I'VE GOTTA GO, I'M RUNNING LATE.
NO, WAIT! I DON'T EVEN KNOW YOUR NAME!
MICHÈLE.
MICHÈLE! MICHÈLE!
LET ME INVITE YOU TO DINNER, MICHÈLE, TO... TO THANK YOU!...
7

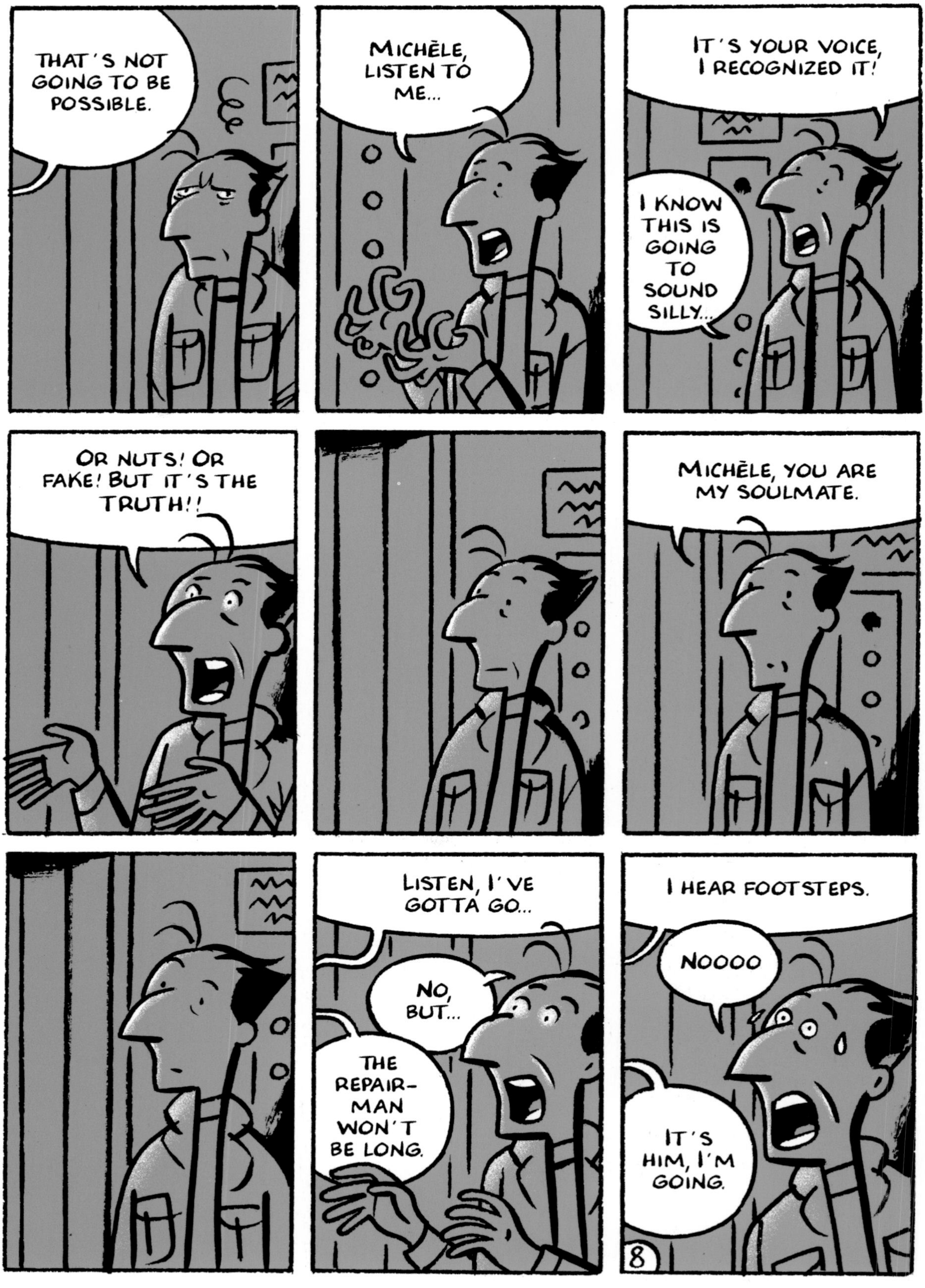

THAT'S NOT GOING TO BE POSSIBLE.
MICHÈLE, LISTEN TO ME...
IT'S YOUR VOICE, I RECOGNIZED IT!
I KNOW THIS IS GOING TO SOUND SILLY...
OR NUTS! OR FAKE! BUT IT'S THE TRUTH!!
MICHÈLE, YOU ARE MY SOULMATE.
LISTEN, I'VE GOTTA GO...
NO, BUT...
THE REPAIR-MAN WON'T BE LONG.
I HEAR FOOTSTEPS.
NOOOO
IT'S HIM, I'M GOING.
8

DAMN IT, HURRY!

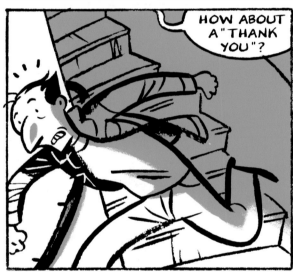

HOW ABOUT A "THANK YOU"?

⑨

SHIT SHIT AND SHIT

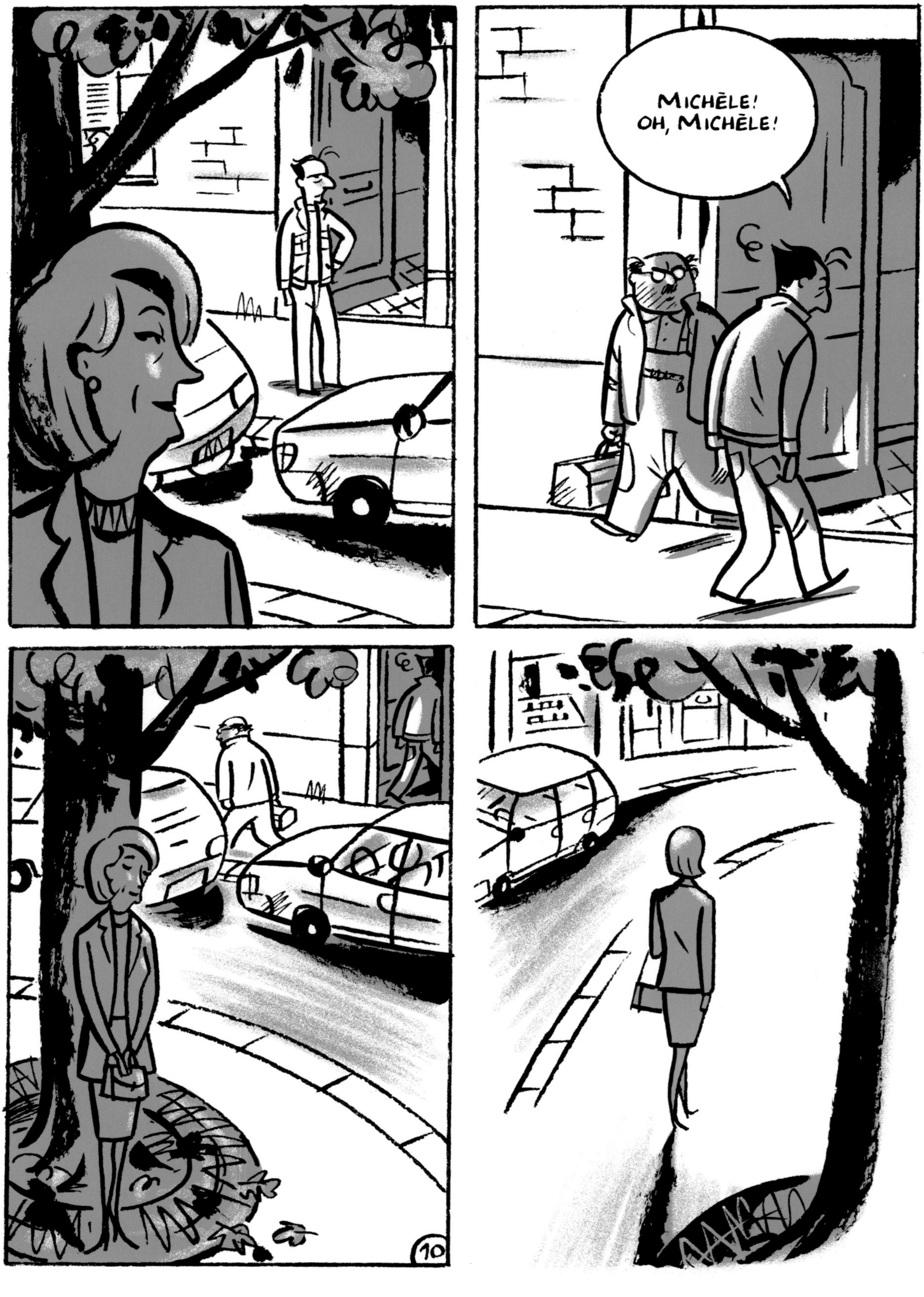
MICHÈLE!
OH, MICHÈLE!

Jean Gets Some Fresh Air

Still having those silly dreams, pal?
zzzzzzzzzzzzzzzzzzz
Ever say to yourself, "I'm wasting my time here, and I don't have that much time to begin with..."
"...What's more, my hairline's receding..."
No kidding...
Why don't you put on a hairpiece?
Shatner wears a hairpiece, ya know.
No kidding?

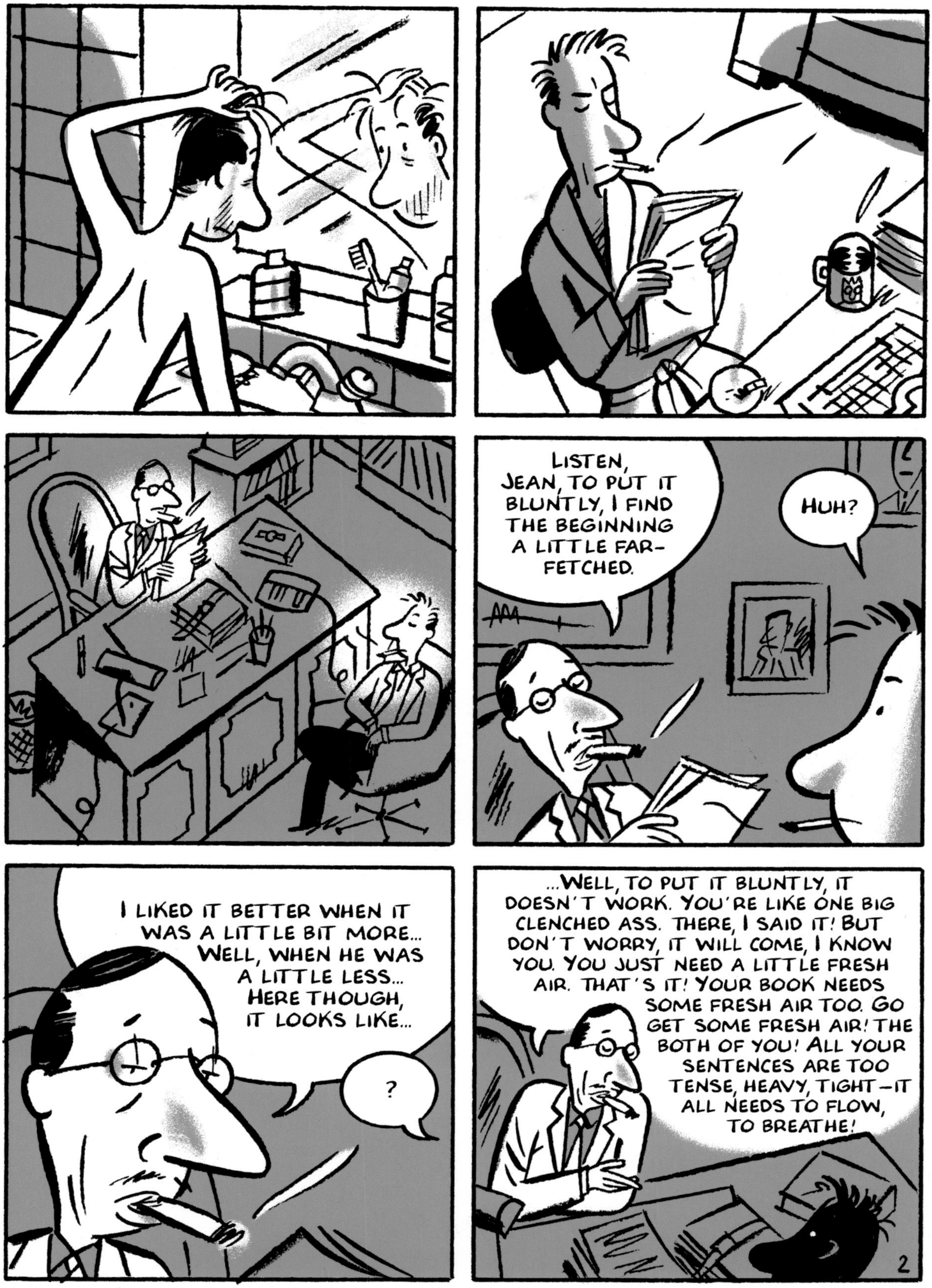
LISTEN, JEAN, TO PUT IT BLUNTLY, I FIND THE BEGINNING A LITTLE FAR-FETCHED.
HUH?
I LIKED IT BETTER WHEN IT WAS A LITTLE BIT MORE... WELL, WHEN HE WAS A LITTLE LESS... HERE THOUGH, IT LOOKS LIKE...
?
...WELL, TO PUT IT BLUNTLY, IT DOESN'T WORK. YOU'RE LIKE ONE BIG CLENCHED ASS. THERE, I SAID IT! BUT DON'T WORRY, IT WILL COME, I KNOW YOU. YOU JUST NEED A LITTLE FRESH AIR. THAT'S IT! YOUR BOOK NEEDS SOME FRESH AIR TOO. GO GET SOME FRESH AIR! THE BOTH OF YOU! ALL YOUR SENTENCES ARE TOO TENSE, HEAVY, TIGHT—IT ALL NEEDS TO FLOW, TO BREATHE!
2

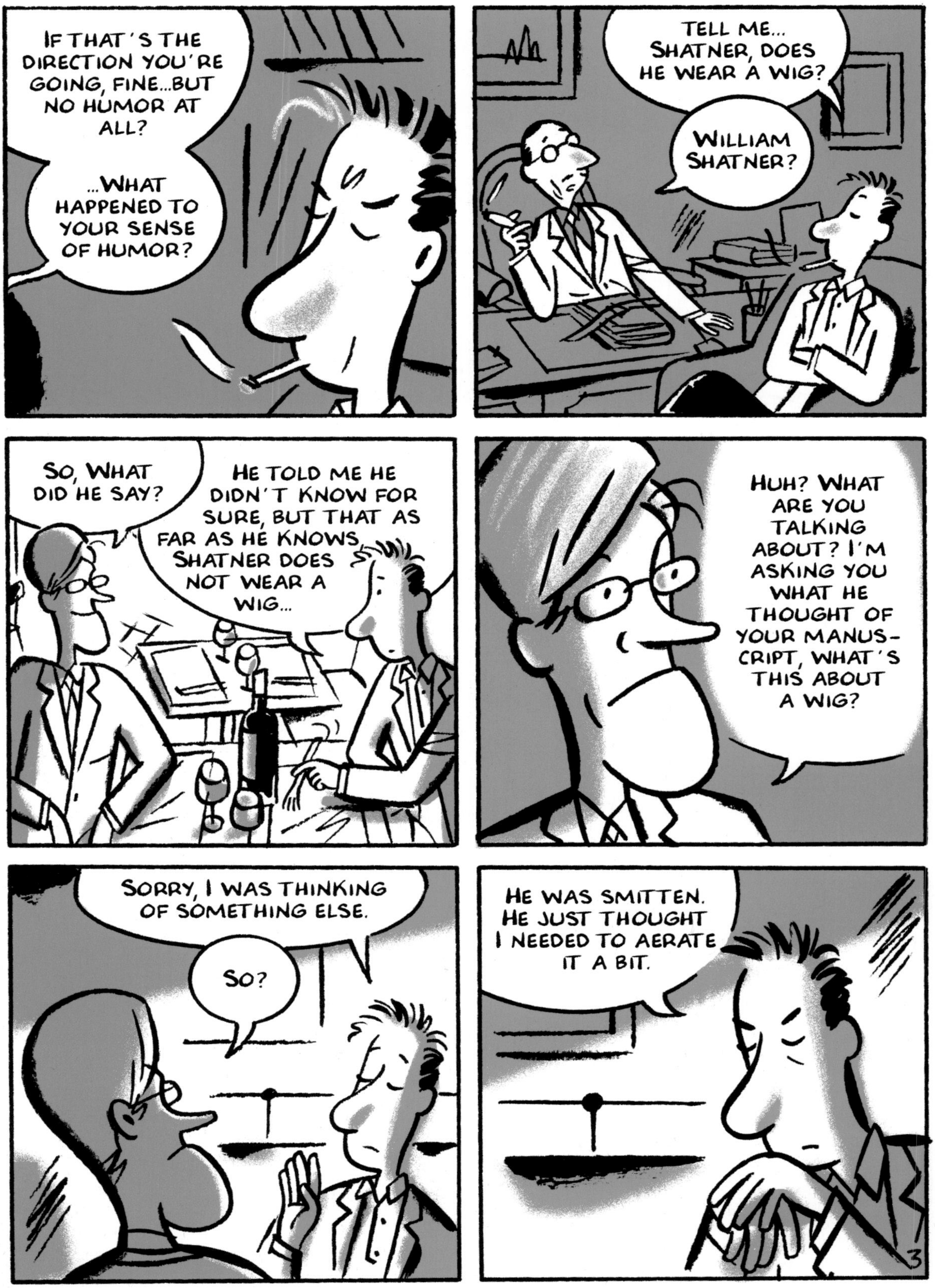
IF THAT'S THE DIRECTION YOU'RE GOING, FINE...BUT NO HUMOR AT ALL?
...WHAT HAPPENED TO YOUR SENSE OF HUMOR?
TELL ME... SHATNER, DOES HE WEAR A WIG?
WILLIAM SHATNER?
SO, WHAT DID HE SAY?
HE TOLD ME HE DIDN'T KNOW FOR SURE, BUT THAT AS FAR AS HE KNOWS, SHATNER DOES NOT WEAR A WIG...
HUH? WHAT ARE YOU TALKING ABOUT? I'M ASKING YOU WHAT HE THOUGHT OF YOUR MANUS-CRIPT, WHAT'S THIS ABOUT A WIG?
SORRY, I WAS THINKING OF SOMETHING ELSE.
SO?
HE WAS SMITTEN. HE JUST THOUGHT I NEEDED TO AERATE IT A BIT.
3

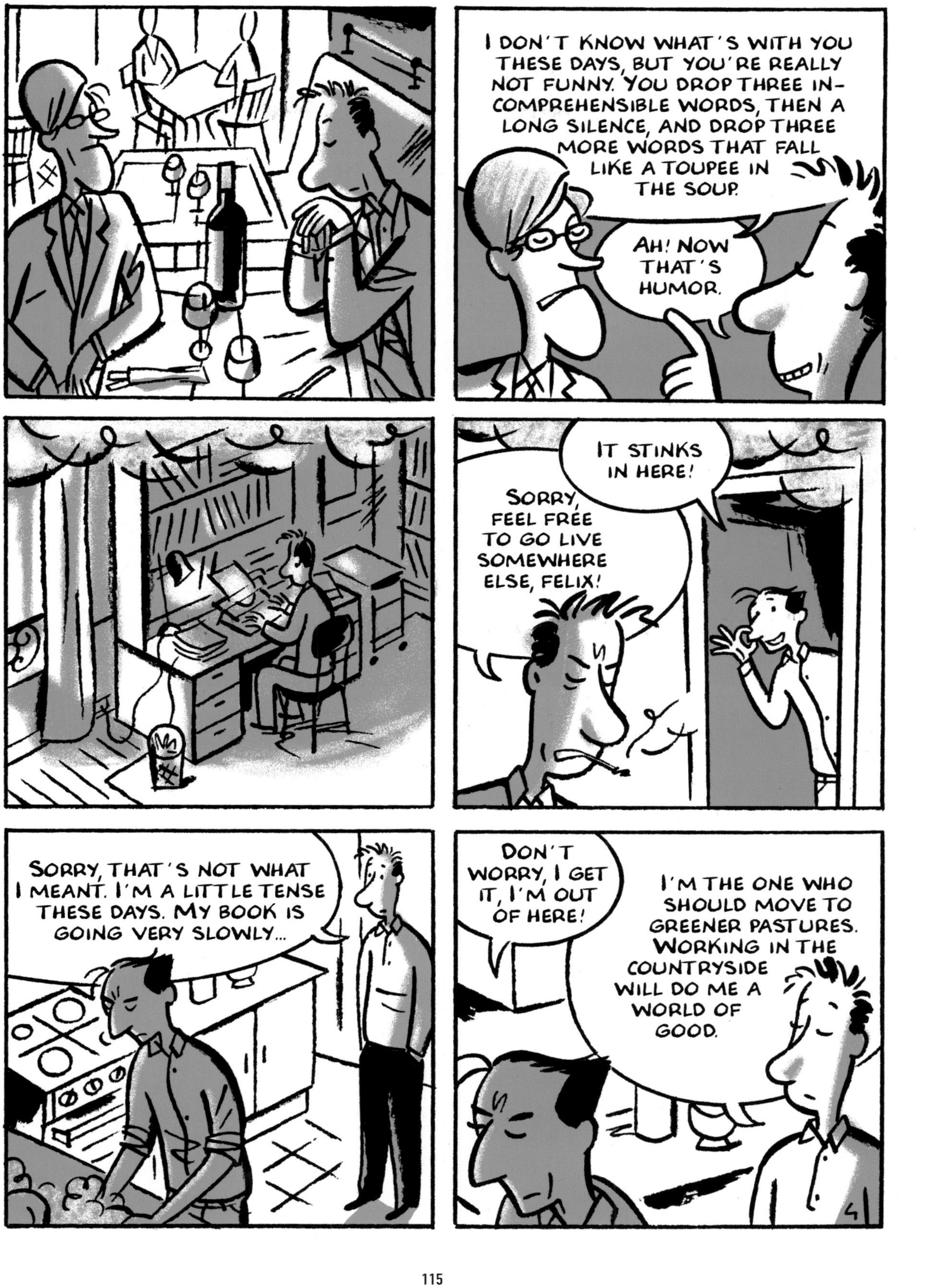
I DON'T KNOW WHAT'S WITH YOU THESE DAYS, BUT YOU'RE REALLY NOT FUNNY. YOU DROP THREE INCOMPREHENSIBLE WORDS, THEN A LONG SILENCE, AND DROP THREE MORE WORDS THAT FALL LIKE A TOUPEE IN THE SOUP.
AH! NOW THAT'S HUMOR.
IT STINKS IN HERE!
SORRY, FEEL FREE TO GO LIVE SOMEWHERE ELSE, FELIX!
SORRY, THAT'S NOT WHAT I MEANT. I'M A LITTLE TENSE THESE DAYS. MY BOOK IS GOING VERY SLOWLY...
DON'T WORRY, I GET IT, I'M OUT OF HERE!
I'M THE ONE WHO SHOULD MOVE TO GREENER PASTURES. WORKING IN THE COUNTRYSIDE WILL DO ME A WORLD OF GOOD.

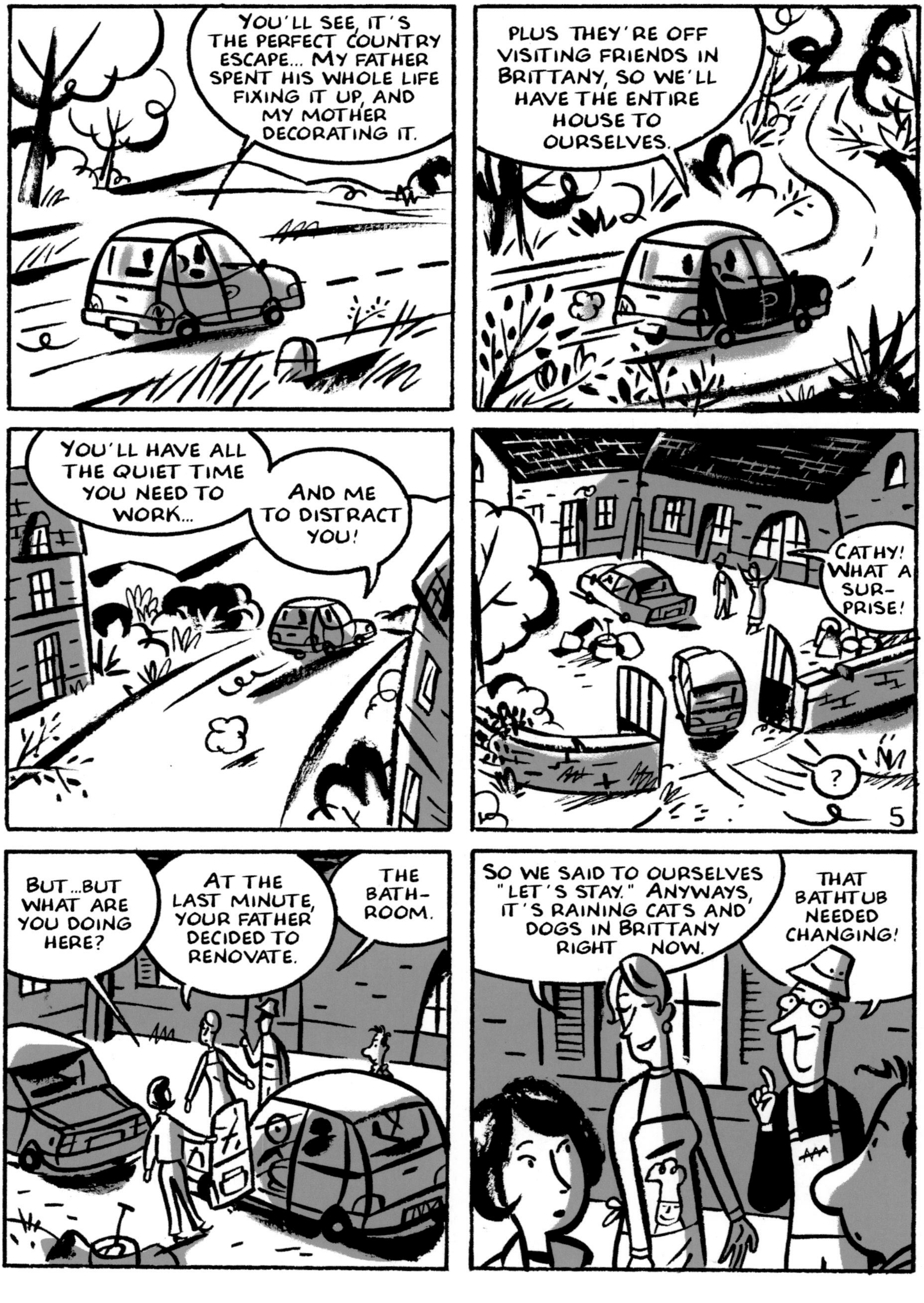
YOU'LL SEE, IT'S THE PERFECT COUNTRY ESCAPE... MY FATHER SPENT HIS WHOLE LIFE FIXING IT UP, AND MY MOTHER DECORATING IT.
PLUS THEY'RE OFF VISITING FRIENDS IN BRITTANY, SO WE'LL HAVE THE ENTIRE HOUSE TO OURSELVES.
YOU'LL HAVE ALL THE QUIET TIME YOU NEED TO WORK...
AND ME TO DISTRACT YOU!
CATHY! WHAT A SUR-PRISE!
?
5
BUT...BUT WHAT ARE YOU DOING HERE?
AT THE LAST MINUTE, YOUR FATHER DECIDED TO RENOVATE.
THE BATH-ROOM.
SO WE SAID TO OURSELVES "LET'S STAY." ANYWAYS, IT'S RAINING CATS AND DOGS IN BRITTANY RIGHT NOW.
THAT BATHTUB NEEDED CHANGING!

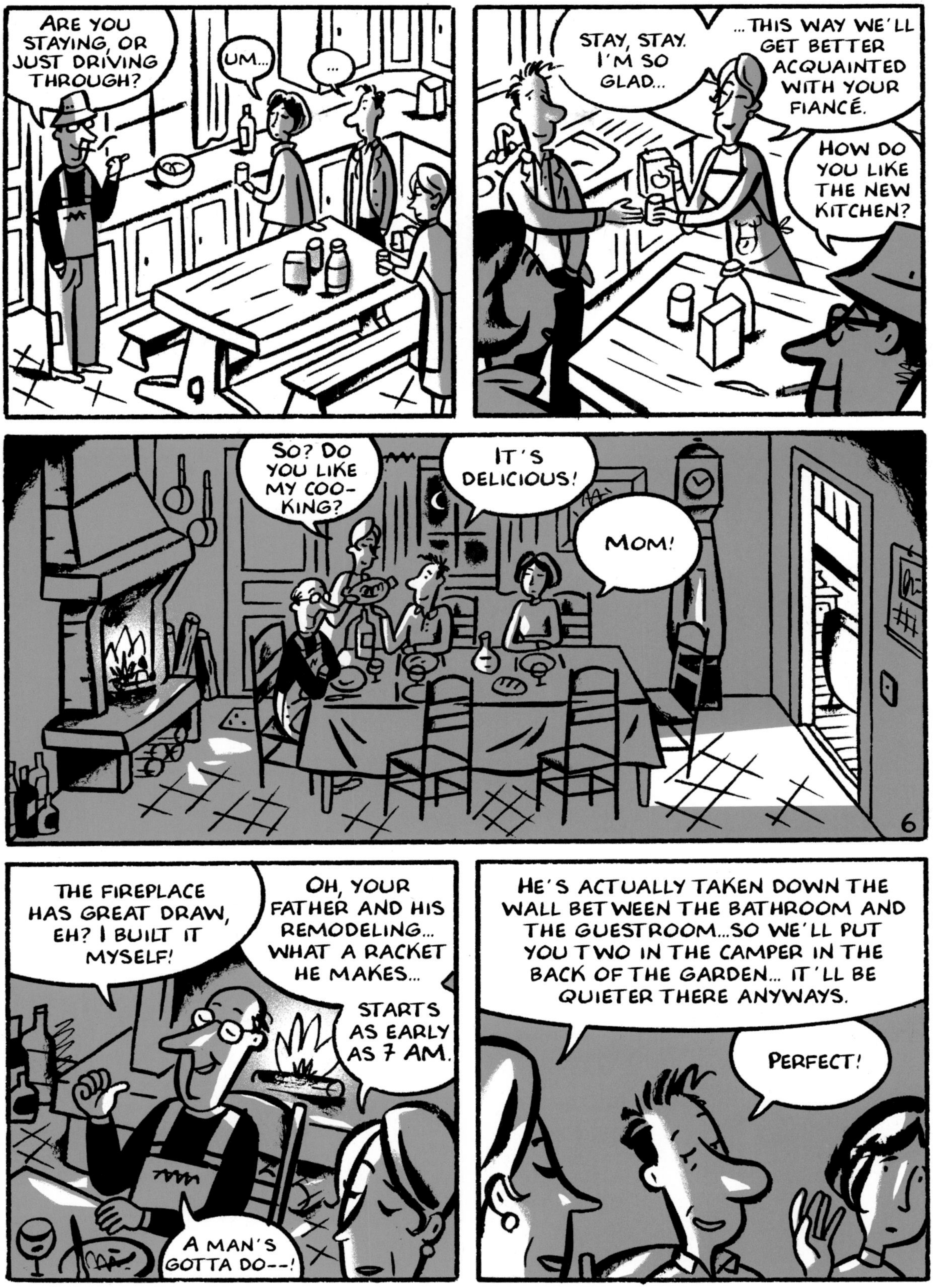

ARE YOU STAYING, OR JUST DRIVING THROUGH?
UM...
...
STAY, STAY. I'M SO GLAD...
...THIS WAY WE'LL GET BETTER ACQUAINTED WITH YOUR FIANCÉ.
HOW DO YOU LIKE THE NEW KITCHEN?
SO? DO YOU LIKE MY COO-KING?
IT'S DELICIOUS!
MOM!
6
THE FIREPLACE HAS GREAT DRAW, EH? I BUILT IT MYSELF!
OH, YOUR FATHER AND HIS REMODELING... WHAT A RACKET HE MAKES...
STARTS AS EARLY AS 7 AM.
A MAN'S GOTTA DO--!
HE'S ACTUALLY TAKEN DOWN THE WALL BETWEEN THE BATHROOM AND THE GUESTROOM...SO WE'LL PUT YOU TWO IN THE CAMPER IN THE BACK OF THE GARDEN... IT'LL BE QUIETER THERE ANYWAYS.
PERFECT!

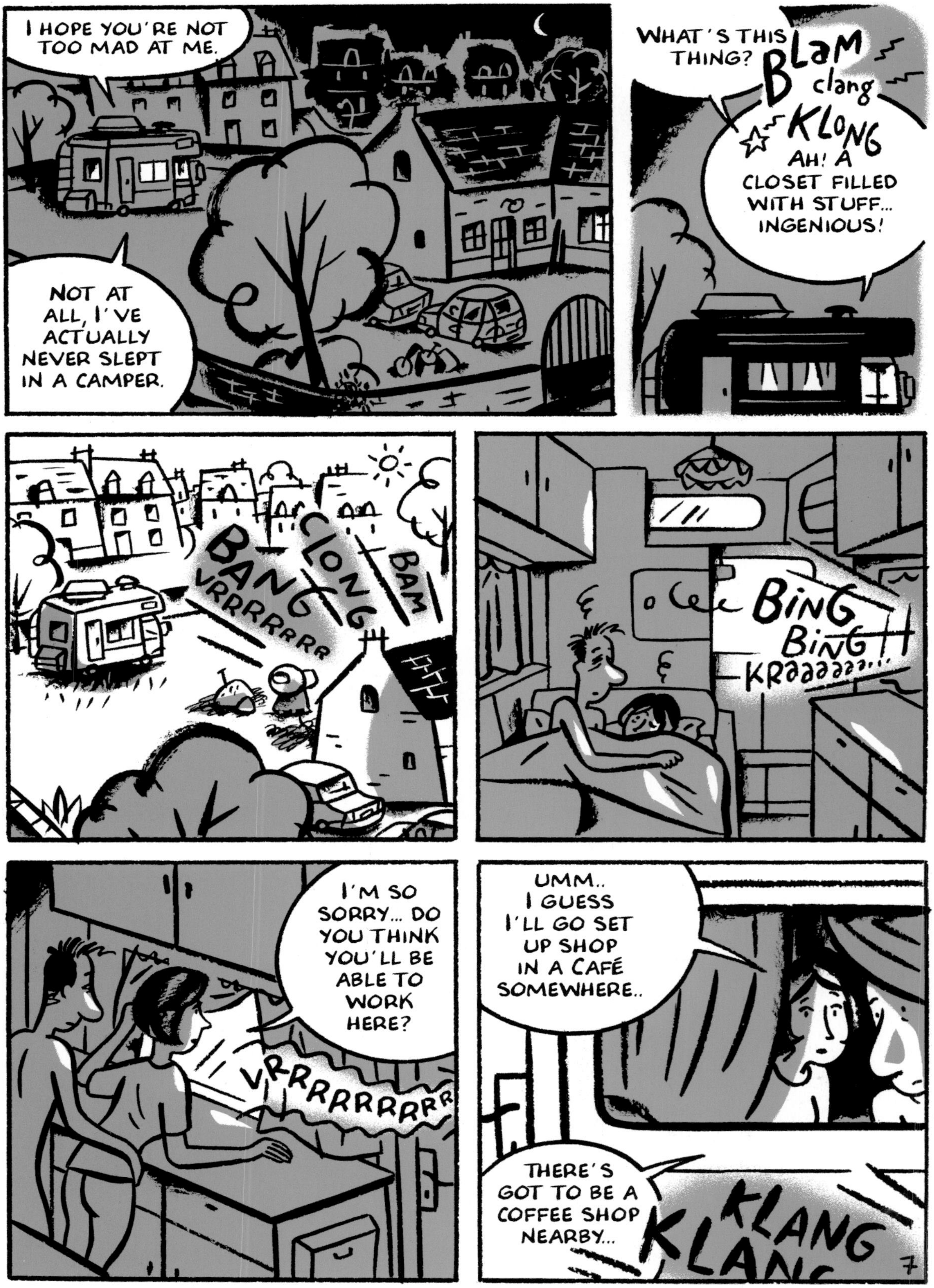
I HOPE YOU'RE NOT TOO MAD AT ME.
NOT AT ALL, I'VE ACTUALLY NEVER SLEPT IN A CAMPER.
WHAT'S THIS THING?
BLAM clang KLONG
AH! A CLOSET FILLED WITH STUFF... INGENIOUS!
BANG
CLONG
BAM
VRRRRRRRR
BING BING KRaaaaaa...
I'M SO SORRY... DO YOU THINK YOU'LL BE ABLE TO WORK HERE?
VRRRRRRRRRR
UMM.. I GUESS I'LL GO SET UP SHOP IN A CAFÉ SOMEWHERE..
THERE'S GOT TO BE A COFFEE SHOP NEARBY...
KLANG KLANG

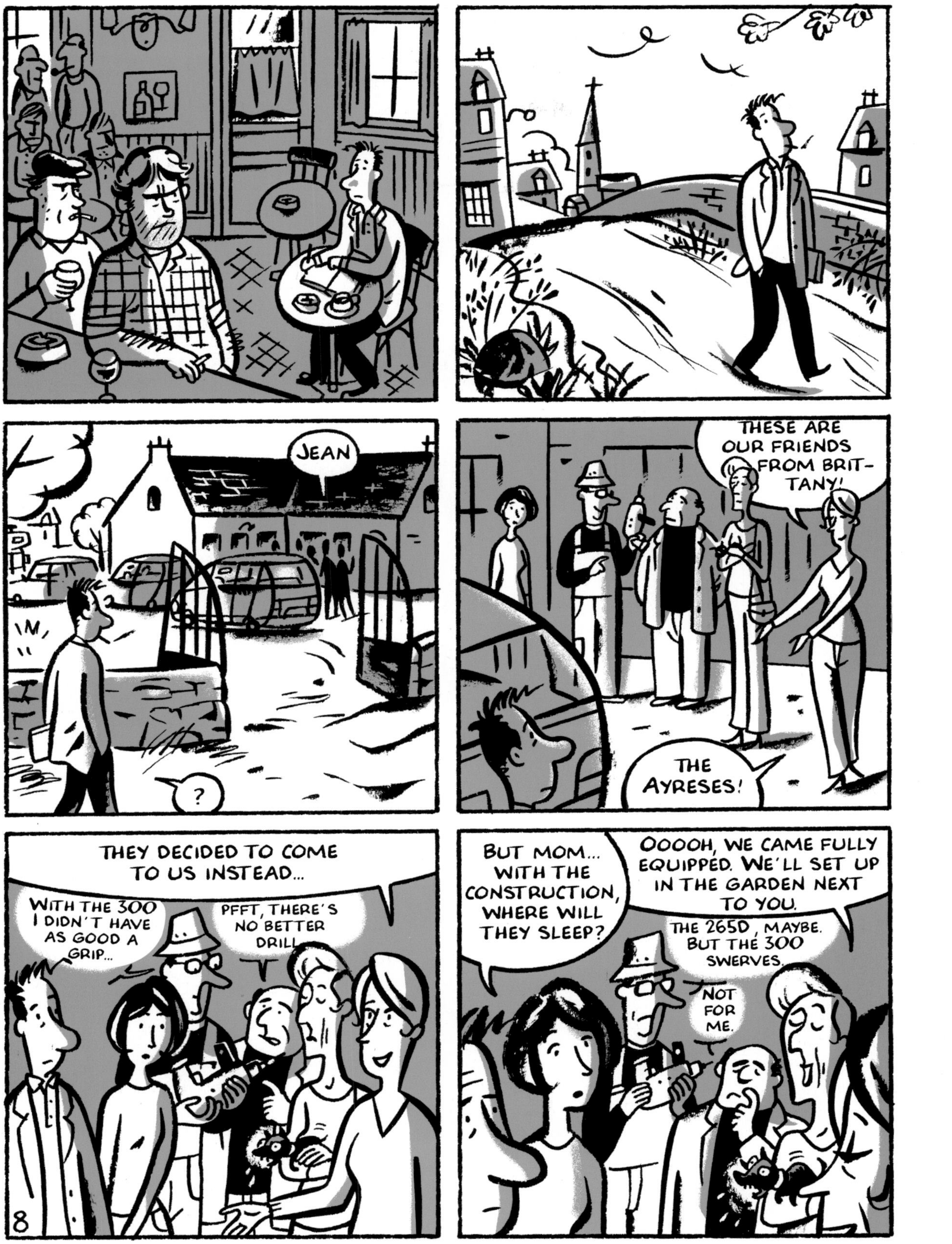

JEAN
?
THESE ARE OUR FRIENDS FROM BRITTANY!
THE AYRESES!
THEY DECIDED TO COME TO US INSTEAD...
WITH THE 300 I DIDN'T HAVE AS GOOD A GRIP...
PFFT, THERE'S NO BETTER DRILL
8
BUT MOM... WITH THE CONSTRUCTION, WHERE WILL THEY SLEEP?
OOOOH, WE CAME FULLY EQUIPPED. WE'LL SET UP IN THE GARDEN NEXT TO YOU.
THE 265D, MAYBE. BUT THE 300 SWERVES.
NOT FOR ME.

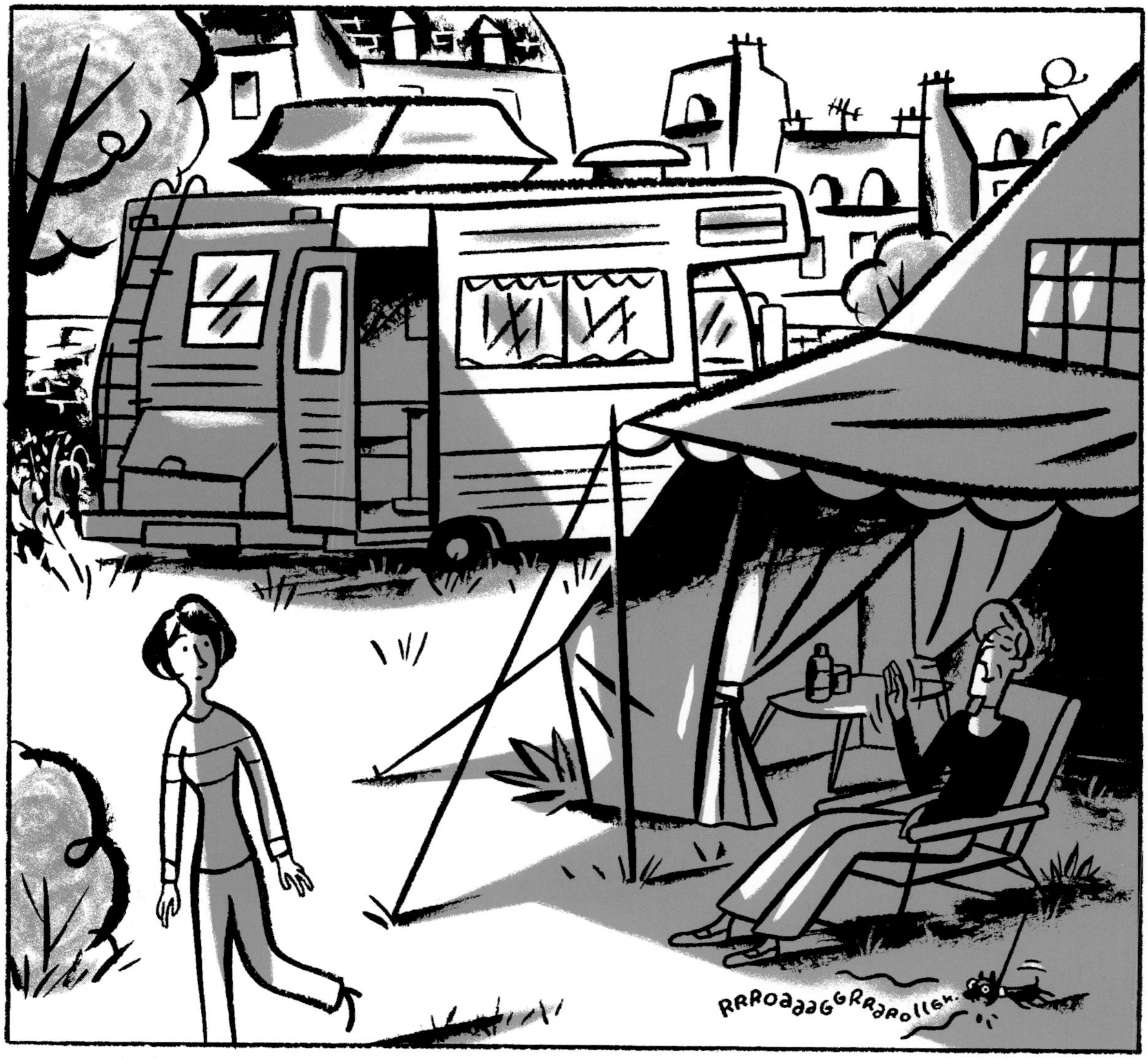
RRROaaaGGRRaRollGk.

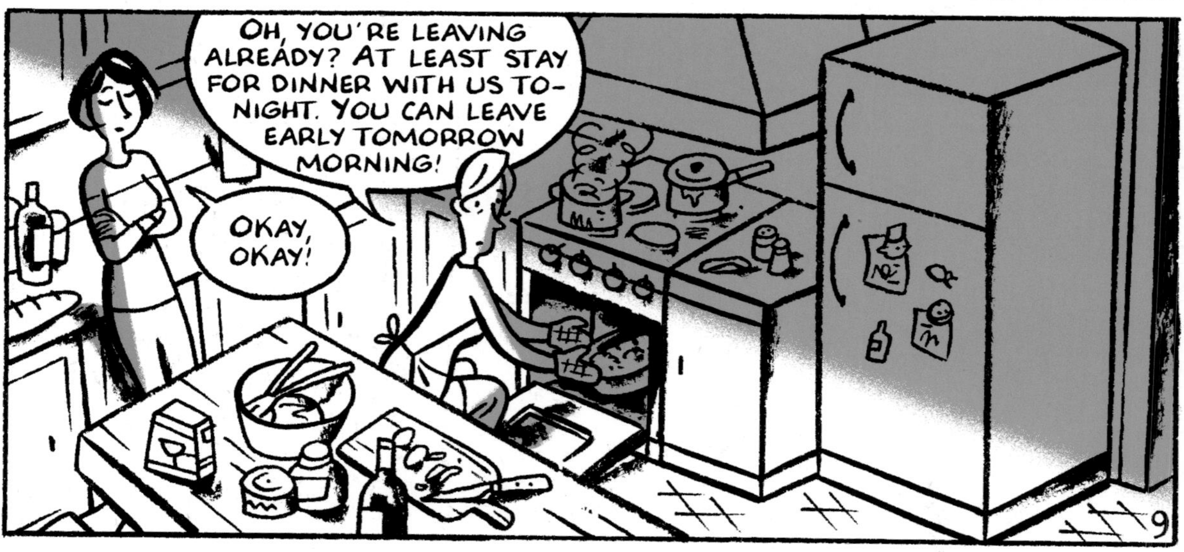
OH, YOU'RE LEAVING ALREADY? AT LEAST STAY FOR DINNER WITH US TO-NIGHT. YOU CAN LEAVE EARLY TOMORROW MORNING!
OKAY, OKAY!
9

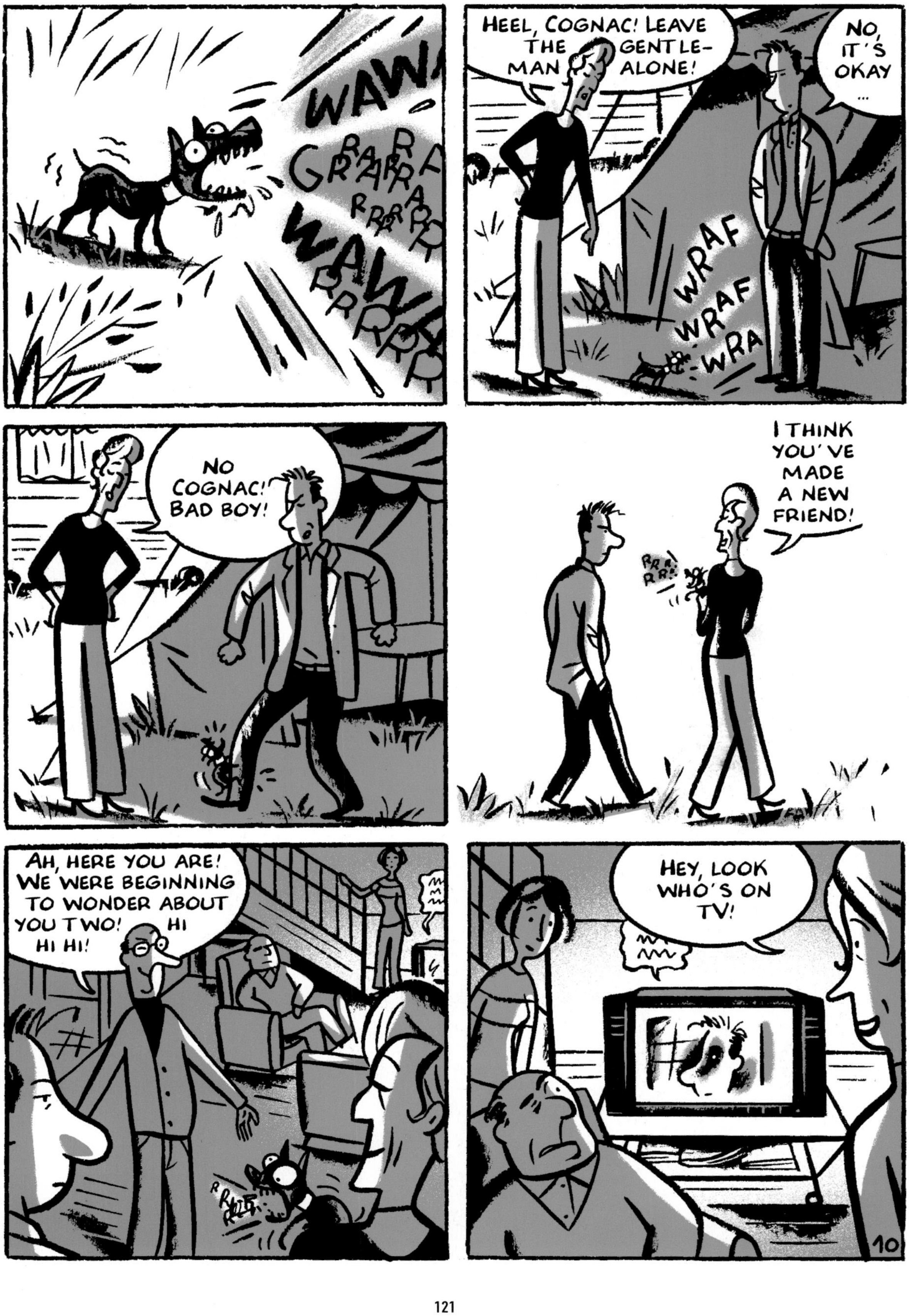
WAWA
GRARRARRARRRRRR
WAWA RRRRRR
HEEL, COGNAC! LEAVE THE GENTLE-MAN ALONE!
NO, IT'S OKAY ...
WRAF
WRAF
WRA
NO COGNAC! BAD BOY!
I THINK YOU'VE MADE A NEW FRIEND!
AH, HERE YOU ARE! WE WERE BEGINNING TO WONDER ABOUT YOU TWO! HI HI HI!
HEY, LOOK WHO'S ON TV!
10

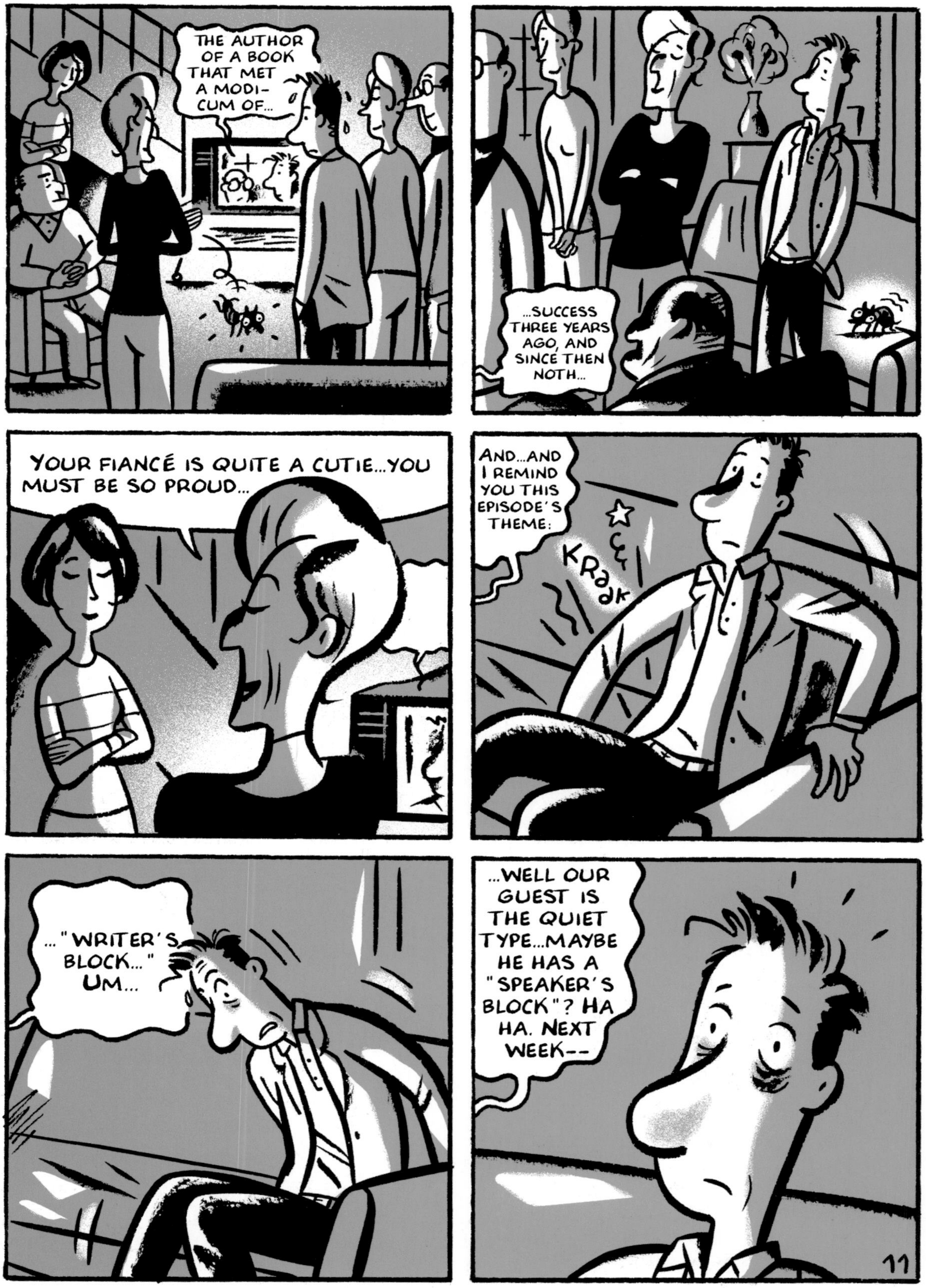
THE AUTHOR OF A BOOK THAT MET A MODICUM OF...
...SUCCESS THREE YEARS AGO, AND SINCE THEN NOTH...
YOUR FIANCÉ IS QUITE A CUTIE...YOU MUST BE SO PROUD...
AND...AND I REMIND YOU THIS EPISODE'S THEME:
KRAAK
..."WRITER'S BLOCK..." UM...
...WELL OUR GUEST IS THE QUIET TYPE...MAYBE HE HAS A "SPEAKER'S BLOCK"? HA HA. NEXT WEEK--
11

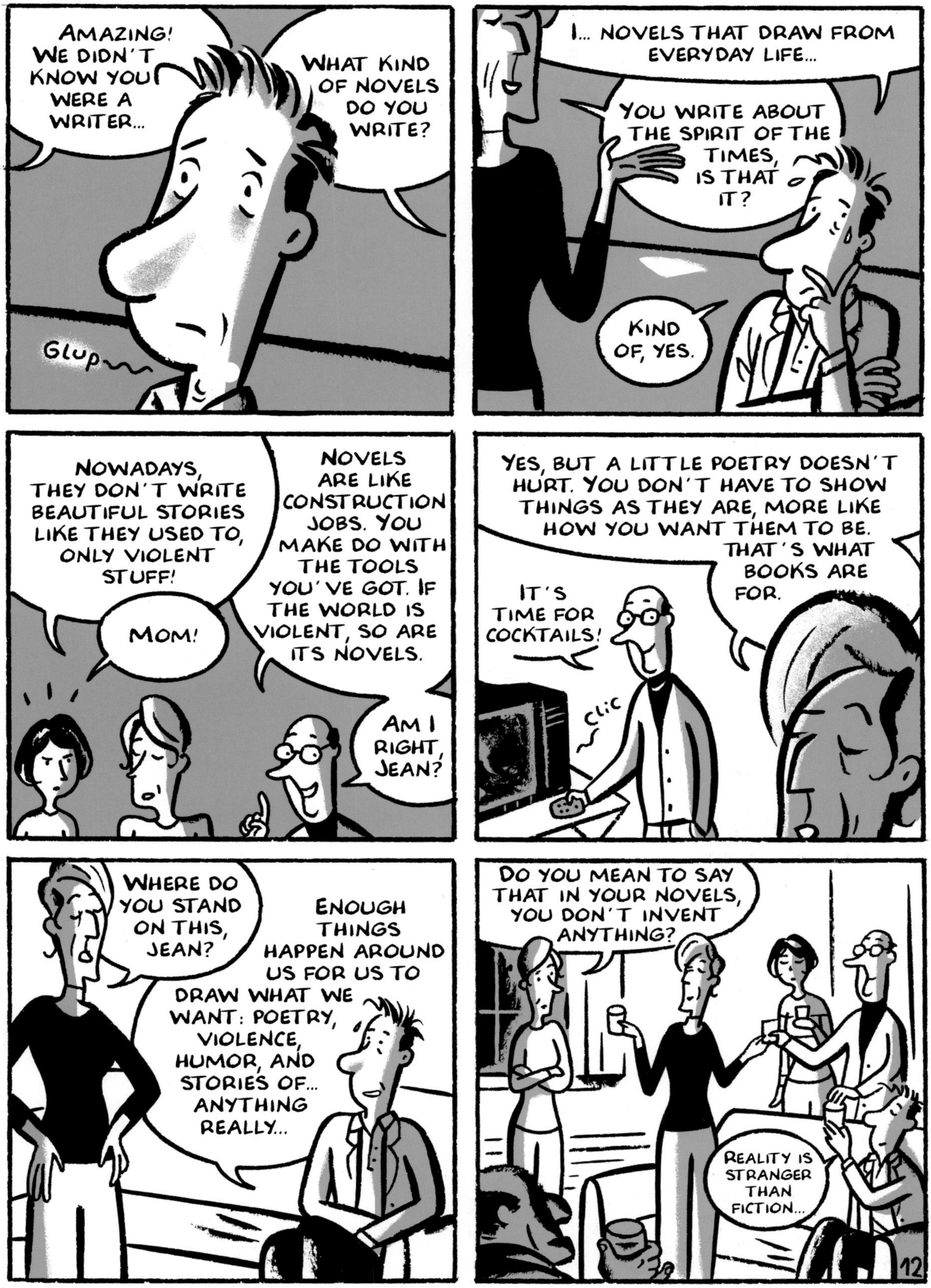
AMAZING! WE DIDN'T KNOW YOU WERE A WRITER...
WHAT KIND OF NOVELS DO YOU WRITE?
GLUP
I... NOVELS THAT DRAW FROM EVERYDAY LIFE...
YOU WRITE ABOUT THE SPIRIT OF THE TIMES, IS THAT IT?
KIND OF, YES.
NOWADAYS, THEY DON'T WRITE BEAUTIFUL STORIES LIKE THEY USED TO, ONLY VIOLENT STUFF!
NOVELS ARE LIKE CONSTRUCTION JOBS. YOU MAKE DO WITH THE TOOLS YOU'VE GOT. IF THE WORLD IS VIOLENT, SO ARE ITS NOVELS.
MOM!
AM I RIGHT, JEAN?
YES, BUT A LITTLE POETRY DOESN'T HURT. YOU DON'T HAVE TO SHOW THINGS AS THEY ARE, MORE LIKE HOW YOU WANT THEM TO BE. THAT'S WHAT BOOKS ARE FOR.
IT'S TIME FOR COCKTAILS!
CLIC
WHERE DO YOU STAND ON THIS, JEAN?
ENOUGH THINGS HAPPEN AROUND US FOR US TO DRAW WHAT WE WANT: POETRY, VIOLENCE, HUMOR, AND STORIES OF... ANYTHING REALLY...
DO YOU MEAN TO SAY THAT IN YOUR NOVELS, YOU DON'T INVENT ANYTHING?
REALITY IS STRANGER THAN FICTION...
12

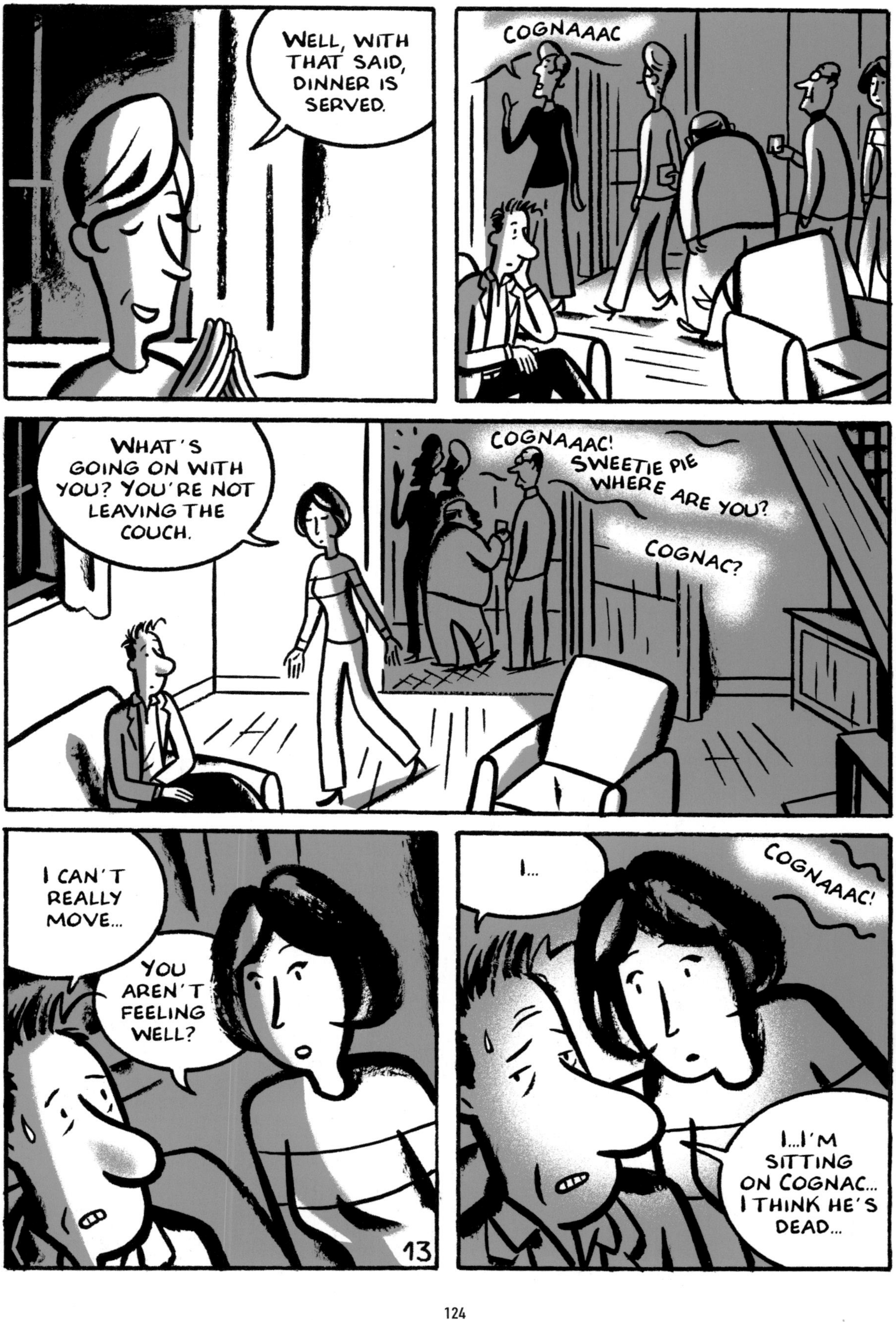

WELL, WITH THAT SAID, DINNER IS SERVED.
COGNAAAC
WHAT'S GOING ON WITH YOU? YOU'RE NOT LEAVING THE COUCH.
COGNAAAC!
SWEETIE PIE WHERE ARE YOU?
COGNAC?
I CAN'T REALLY MOVE...
YOU AREN'T FEELING WELL?
13
I...
COGNAAAC!
I...I'M SITTING ON COGNAC... I THINK HE'S DEAD...

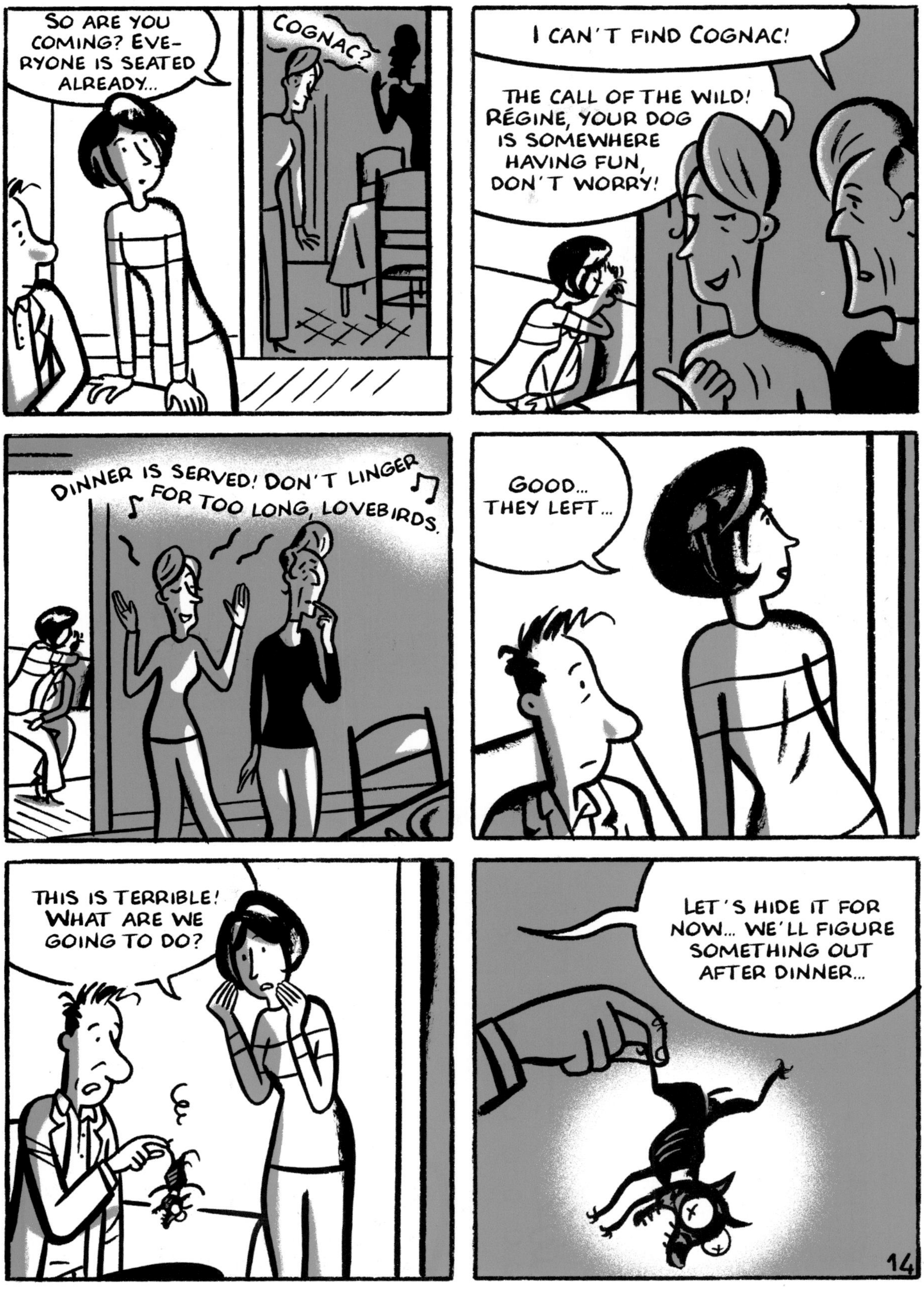
SO ARE YOU COMING? EVE-RYONE IS SEATED ALREADY...
COGNAC
COGNAC?
I CAN'T FIND COGNAC!
THE CALL OF THE WILD! RÉGINE, YOUR DOG IS SOMEWHERE HAVING FUN, DON'T WORRY!
DINNER IS SERVED! DON'T LINGER FOR TOO LONG, LOVEBIRDS.
GOOD... THEY LEFT...
THIS IS TERRIBLE! WHAT ARE WE GOING TO DO?
LET'S HIDE IT FOR NOW... WE'LL FIGURE SOMETHING OUT AFTER DINNER...
14

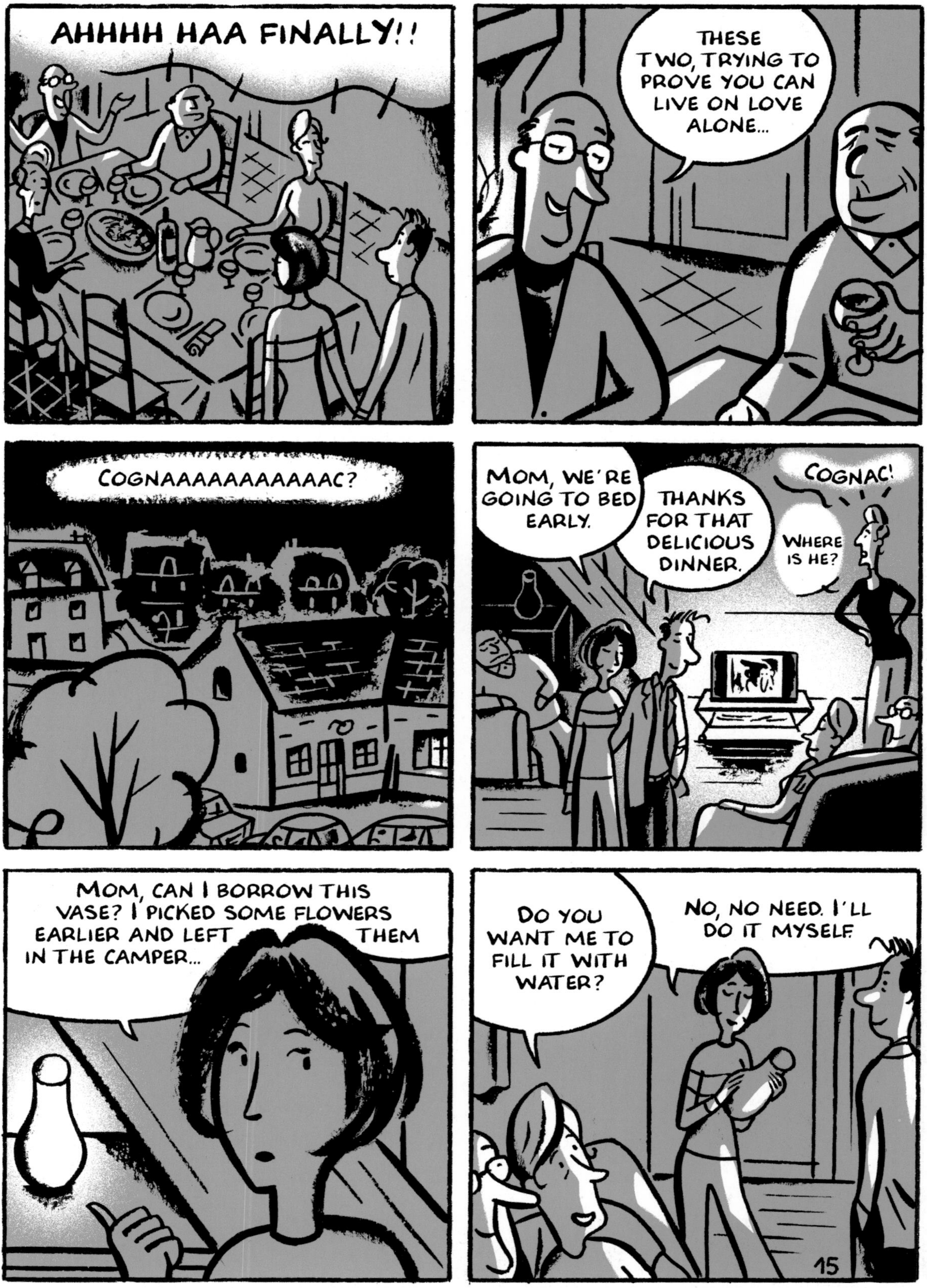
AHHHH HAA FINALLY!!
THESE TWO, TRYING TO PROVE YOU CAN LIVE ON LOVE ALONE...
COGNAAAAAAAAAAAC?
MOM, WE'RE GOING TO BED EARLY.
THANKS FOR THAT DELICIOUS DINNER.
COGNAC!
WHERE IS HE?
MOM, CAN I BORROW THIS VASE? I PICKED SOME FLOWERS EARLIER AND LEFT THEM IN THE CAMPER...
DO YOU WANT ME TO FILL IT WITH WATER?
NO, NO NEED. I'LL DO IT MYSELF.
15

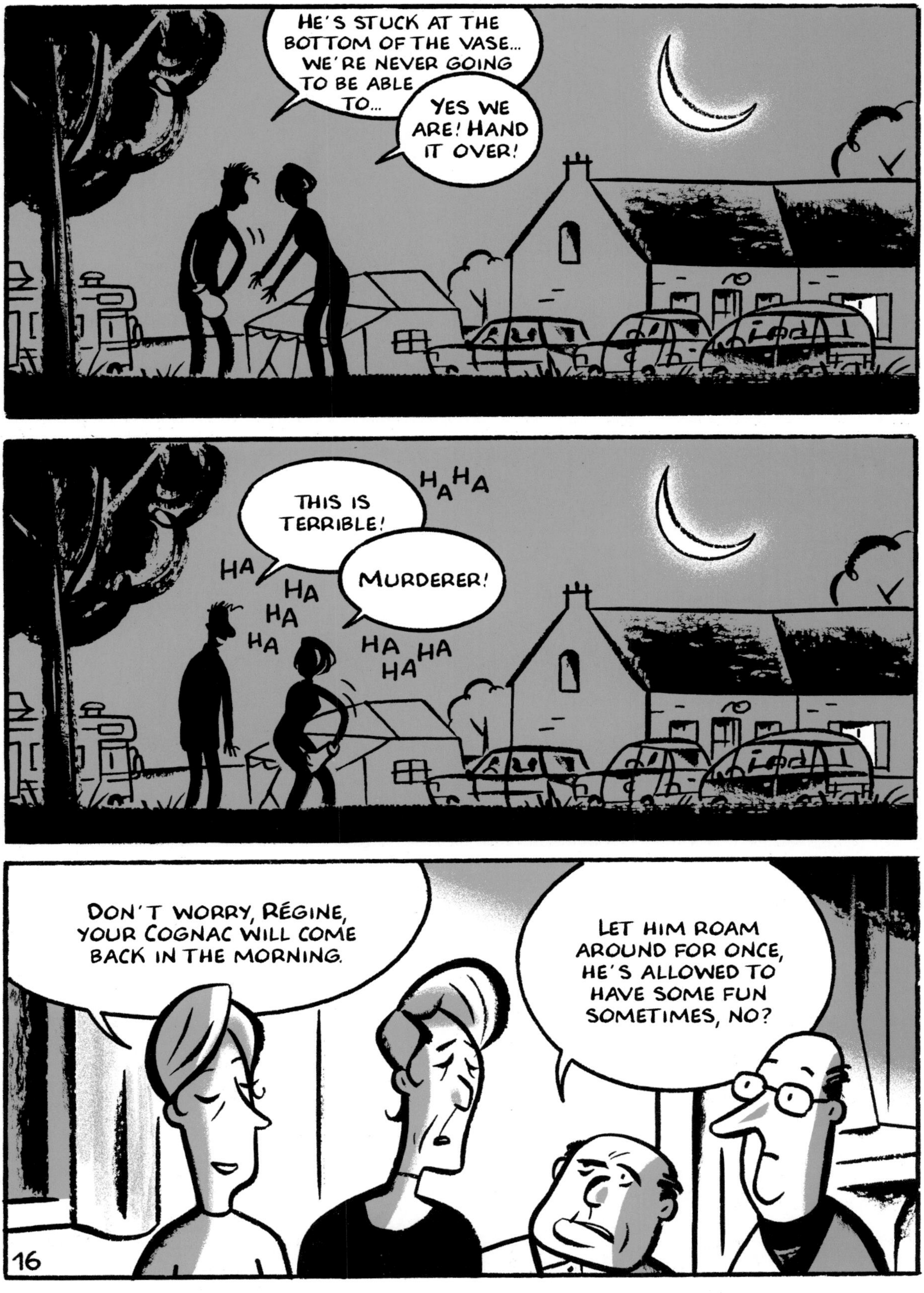
HE'S STUCK AT THE BOTTOM OF THE VASE... WE'RE NEVER GOING TO BE ABLE TO...
YES WE ARE! HAND IT OVER!
HAHA
THIS IS TERRIBLE!
HA
HA
HA
HA
MURDERER!
HA HA HA
DON'T WORRY, RÉGINE, YOUR COGNAC WILL COME BACK IN THE MORNING.
LET HIM ROAM AROUND FOR ONCE, HE'S ALLOWED TO HAVE SOME FUN SOMETIMES, NO?
16

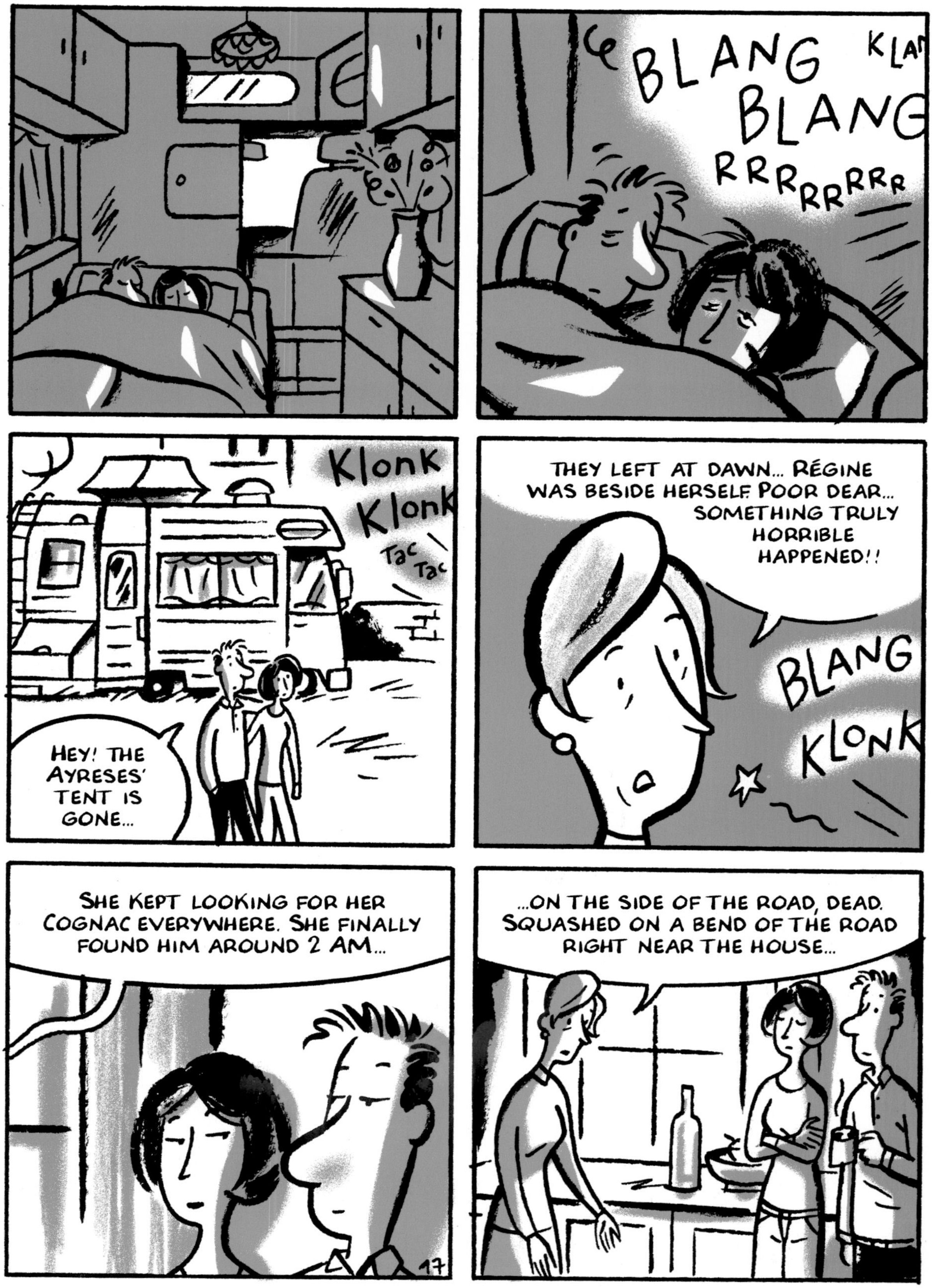
BLANG
BLANG
RRRRRRRR
Klonk
Klonk
Tac
Tac
HEY! THE AYRESES' TENT IS GONE...
THEY LEFT AT DAWN... RÉGINE WAS BESIDE HERSELF. POOR DEAR... SOMETHING TRULY HORRIBLE HAPPENED!!
BLANG
KLONK
SHE KEPT LOOKING FOR HER COGNAC EVERYWHERE. SHE FINALLY FOUND HIM AROUND 2 AM...
...ON THE SIDE OF THE ROAD, DEAD. SQUASHED ON A BEND OF THE ROAD RIGHT NEAR THE HOUSE...

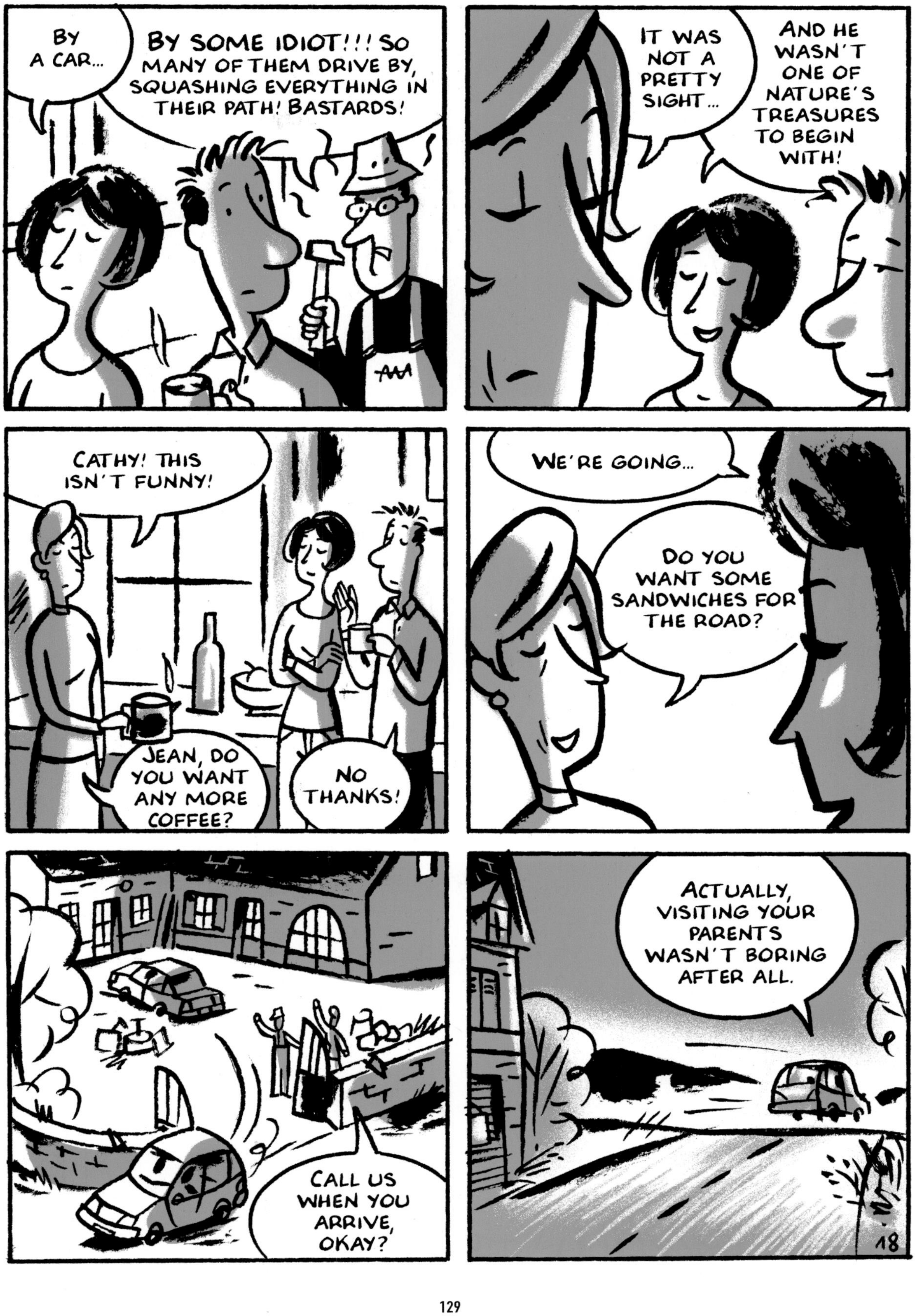

BY A CAR...
BY SOME IDIOT!!! SO MANY OF THEM DRIVE BY, SQUASHING EVERYTHING IN THEIR PATH! BASTARDS!
IT WAS NOT A PRETTY SIGHT...
AND HE WASN'T ONE OF NATURE'S TREASURES TO BEGIN WITH!
CATHY! THIS ISN'T FUNNY!
JEAN, DO YOU WANT ANY MORE COFFEE?
NO THANKS!
WE'RE GOING...
DO YOU WANT SOME SANDWICHES FOR THE ROAD?
CALL US WHEN YOU ARRIVE, OKAY?
ACTUALLY, VISITING YOUR PARENTS WASN'T BORING AFTER ALL.
18

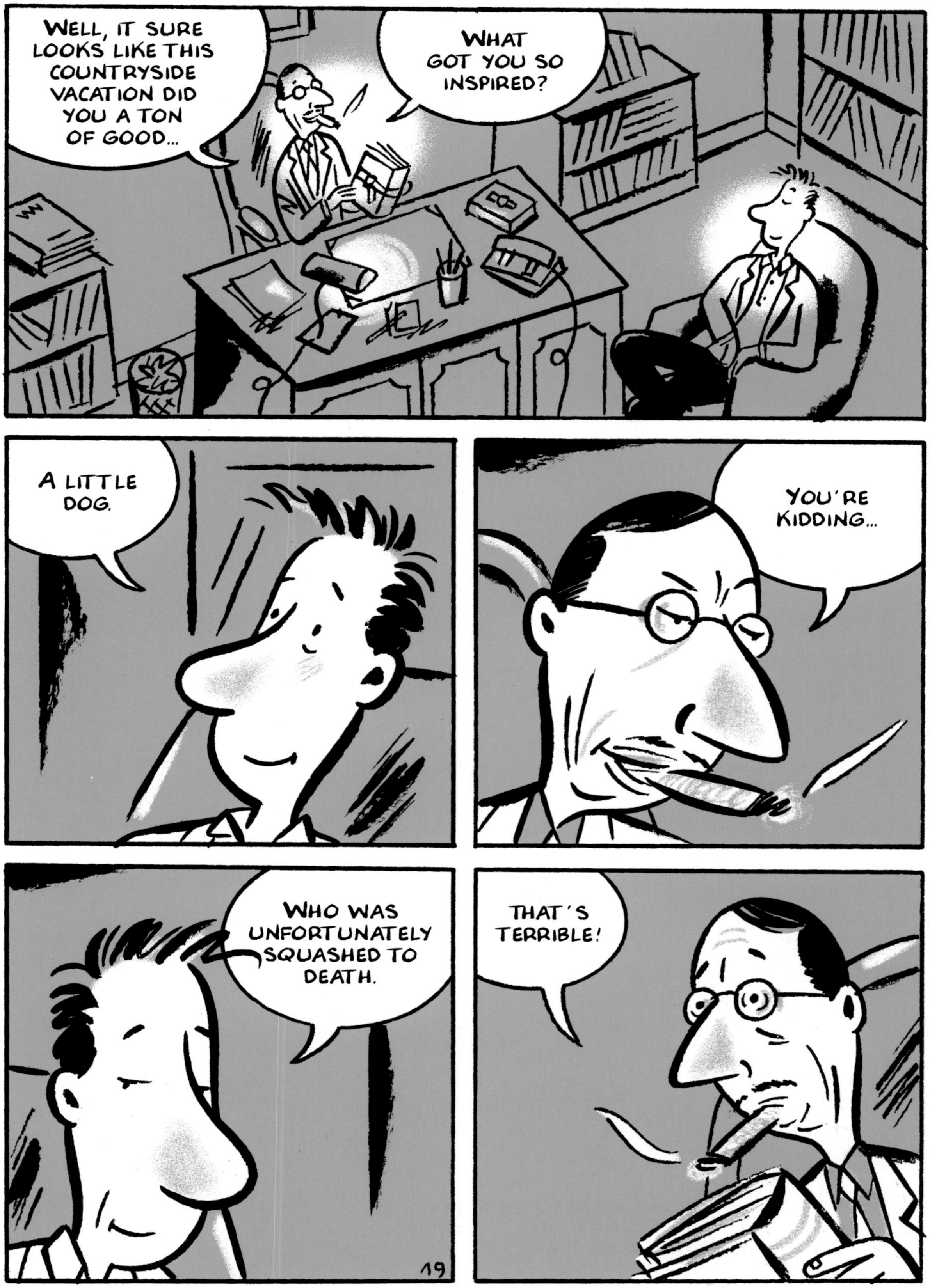
WELL, IT SURE LOOKS LIKE THIS COUNTRYSIDE VACATION DID YOU A TON OF GOOD...
WHAT GOT YOU SO INSPIRED?
A LITTLE DOG.
YOU'RE KIDDING...
WHO WAS UNFORTUNATELY SQUASHED TO DEATH.
THAT'S TERRIBLE!
19

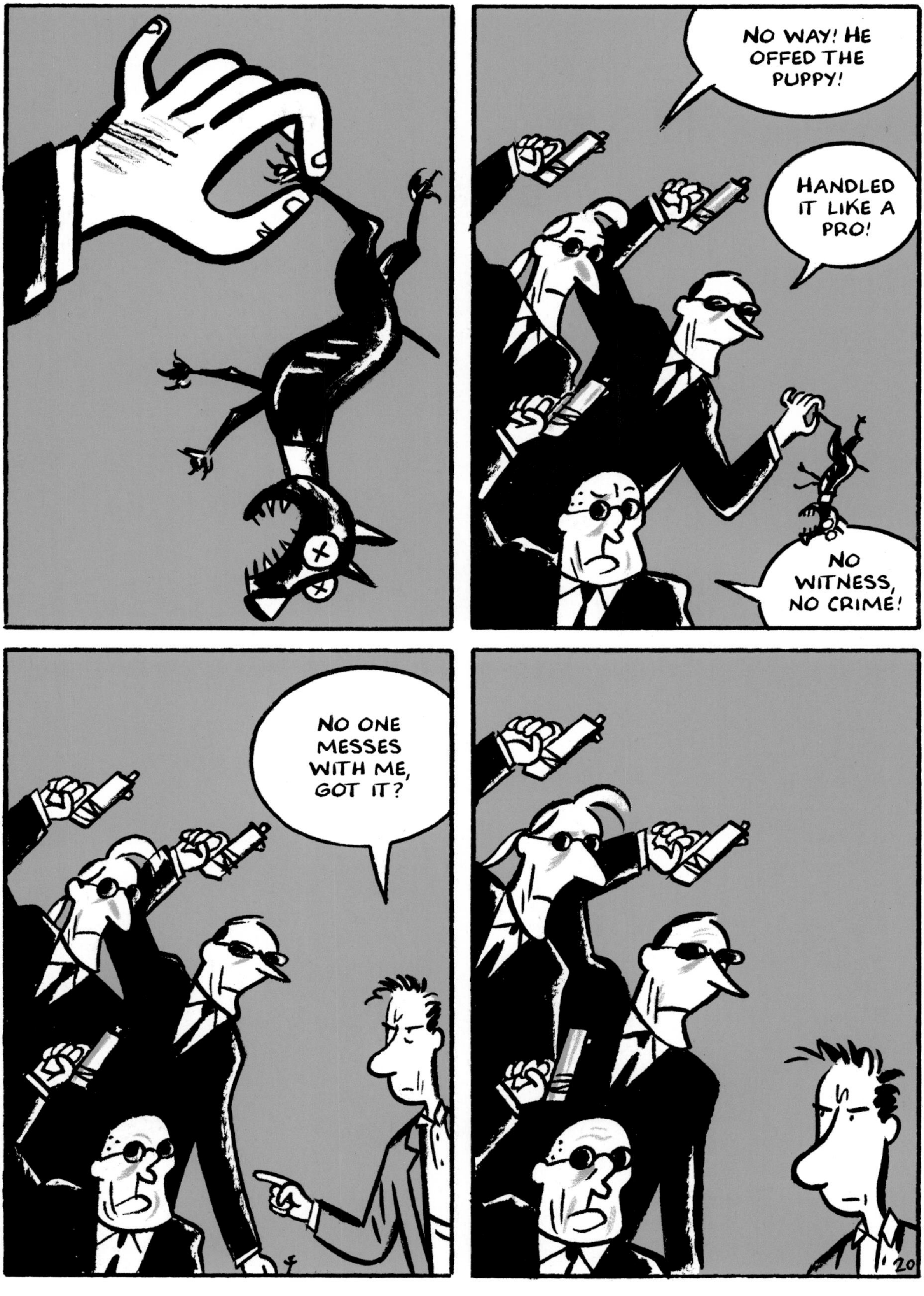
NO WAY! HE OFFED THE PUPPY!
HANDLED IT LIKE A PRO!
NO WITNESS, NO CRIME!
NO ONE MESSES WITH ME, GOT IT?
20

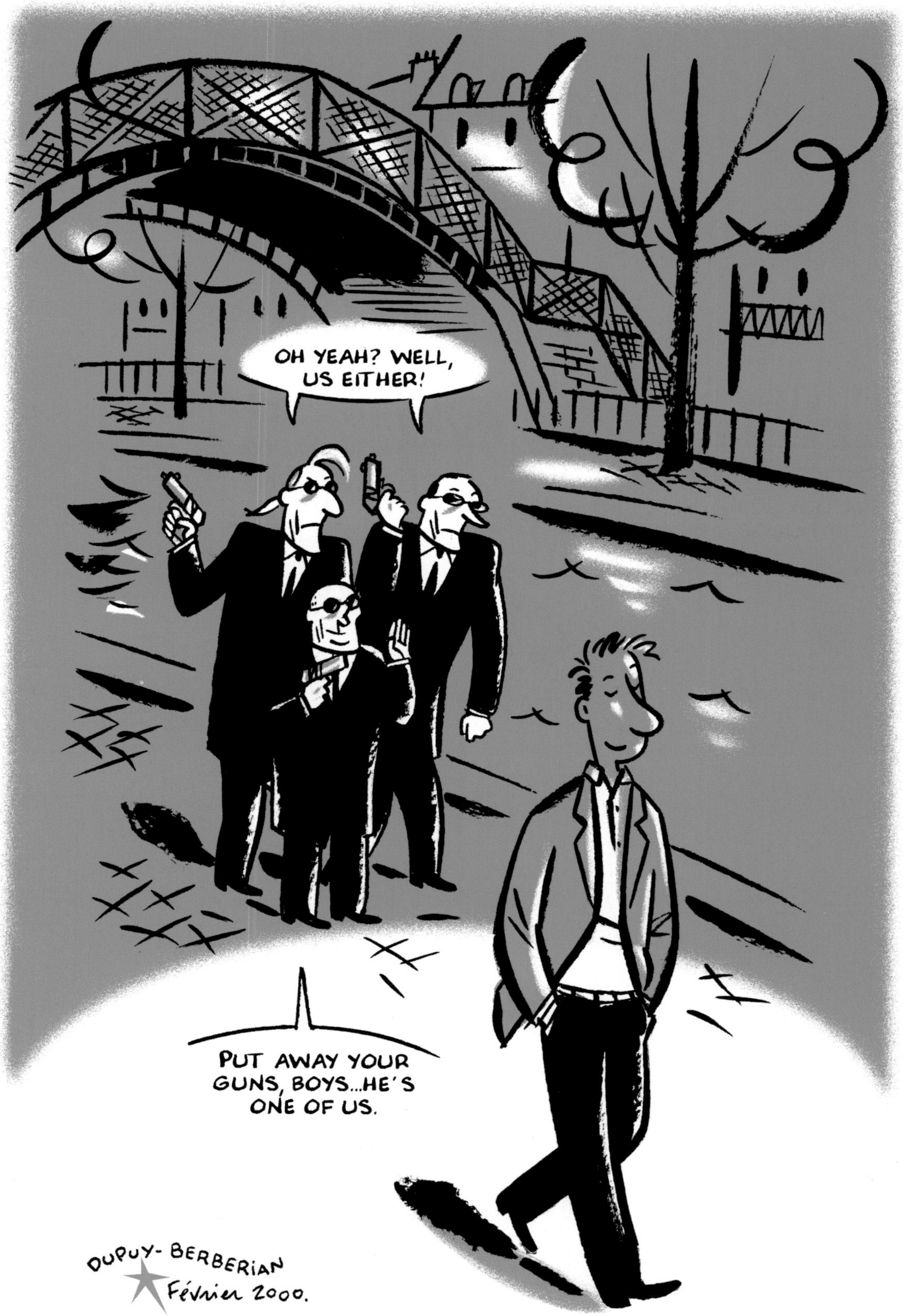
OH YEAH? WELL, US EITHER!
PUT AWAY YOUR GUNS, BOYS...HE'S ONE OF US.
DUPUY-BERBERIAN Février 2000.

END.

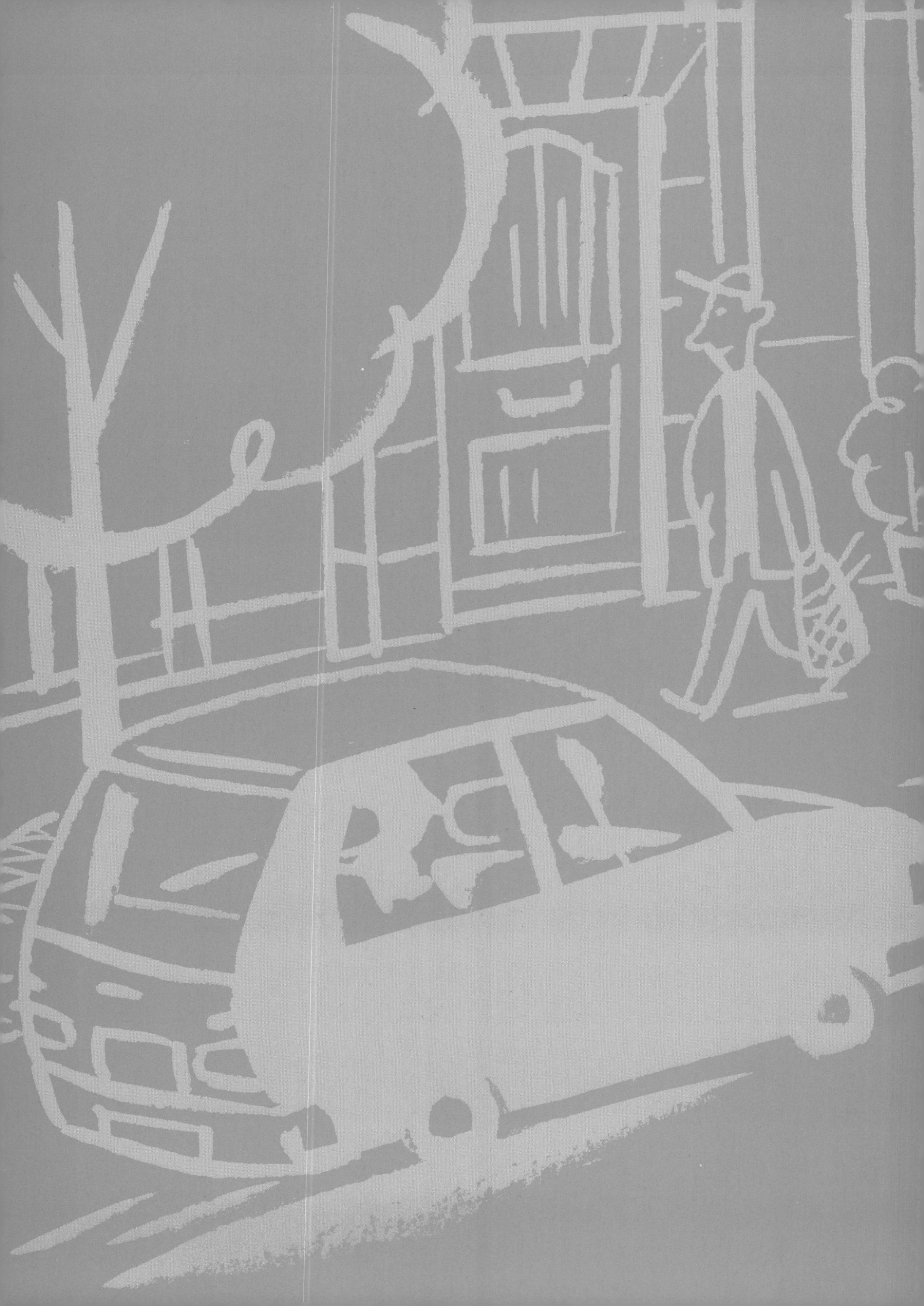

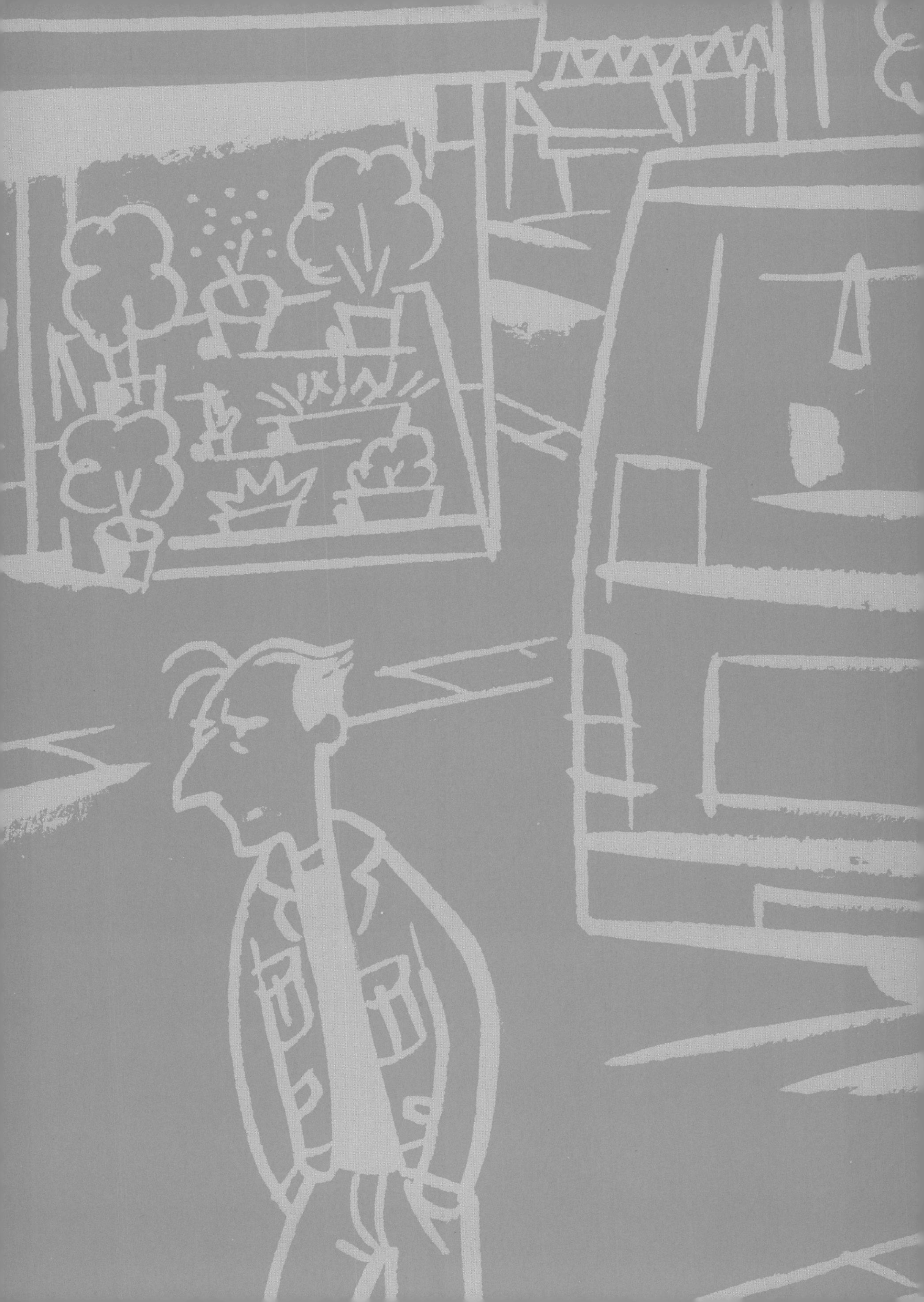

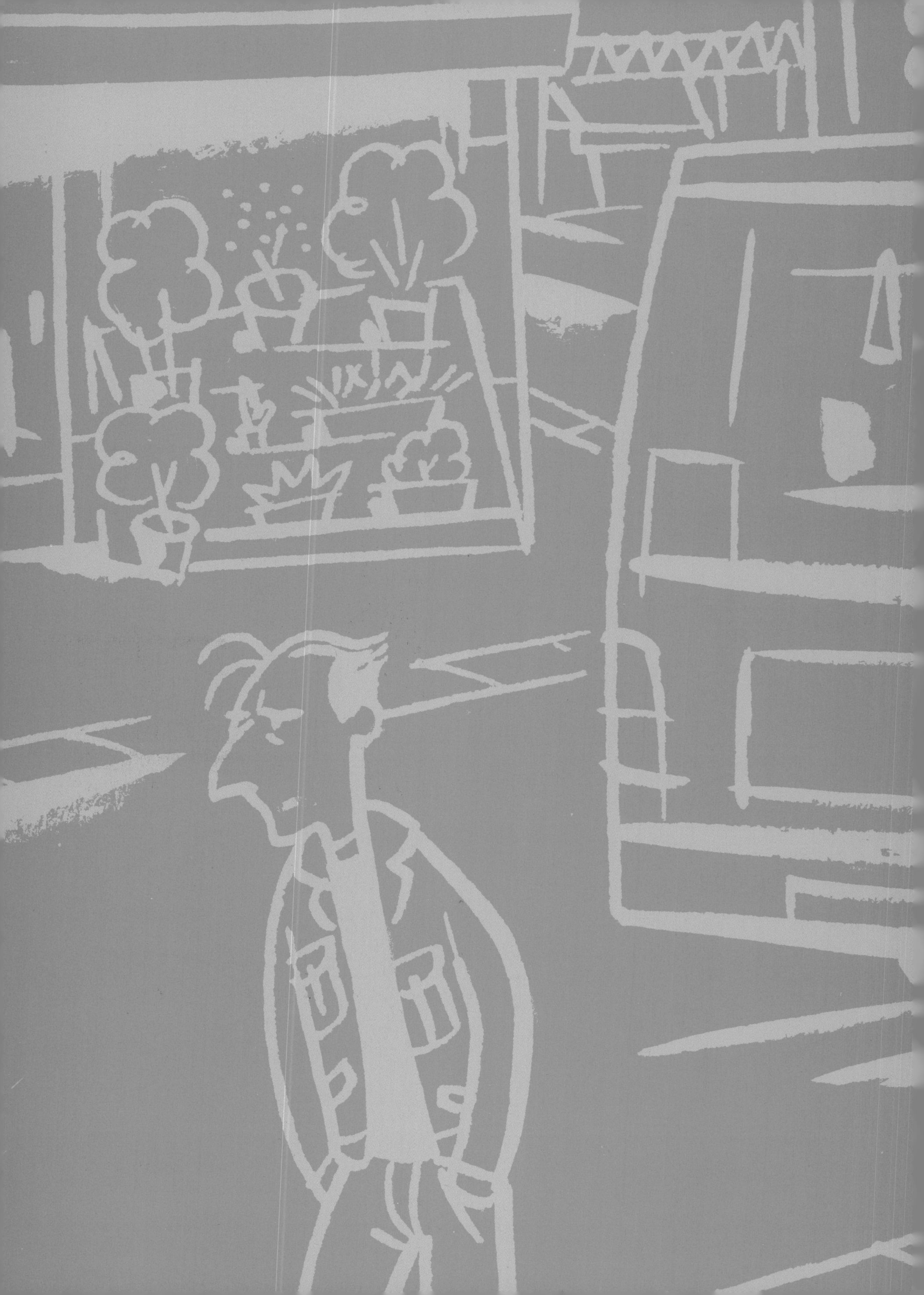